Melabeth

The

Vampire

To the Patrons of the Ashville Library! My beautiful wife Betsy grew up reading at your wonderful library. So proud to have my work in her home town.

E. B. Hood

By

E. B. Hood

This book is dedicated to my brother Nick Hood. Wish you were here bro. R.I.P 4-12-1978 to 11-18-2009.

Melabeth The Vampire (Melabeth Series, Book 1)
(www.melabeth.com)

Copyright © 2012 by Eric B Hood.
(melabeththevampire@gmail.com)

Alley Cat Publishing
alleycatpublishing@gmail.com

ISBN 978-0-9884100-1-5
Paperback V.3
Editing by: Bill Stanton

Cover: photography by Wendy Hood.

Cover Art By: Mirella Santana
Digital artist and genius, Thanks for all your hard work!
You can find Mirella Santana at
https://www.facebook.com/mirellasantana.digitalartist

Table of Contents

Bio & Acknowledgments

I was born on the West Coast, in Loma Linda, California, in 1975, and raised in Beaumont, CA – where some of my book takes place. I grew up with two brothers and one adopted sister. My parents were strong Christians and wonderful parents. They never fought, drank, or cursed; I had to visit my friend's houses to see that. I was an Eagle Scout and loved to go camping with my family. We spent a lot of time off roading through the desert on ATC and dune buggies. I picked up my love of target shooting from Boy Scout camps. I still love to shoot, and, instead of riding the desert on my ATC, now I ride the waves on my wave runner.

I got married when I was 18, had two boys – Tyler in 1993, and Cory in 1996 – as a young father, I worked at Pizza Hut, until 1997; the same year my first wife and I were divorced.

I had the opportunity to help start a satellite plant in North Carolina for a micro connectors company, so I moved across the country to Salisbury. A year later I was offered a chance to become a tool and die apprentice, and worked as a tool and die maker for nearly nine years.

During these transitions I met the love of my life, Betsy, who is a school teacher. We were married 2003. We welcomed a baby girl, Sonja in 2007. I was unexpectedly laid off while my wife was pregnant. I then began working at a plastic company as a CNC programmer. Once again, after another lay-off in 2009, I decided to be a stay-at-home dad, and also started a computer repair business from home.

Another reason I didn't return to work when I was laid off in 2009, was to help my parents with my brother, Nick, who was dying of a brain tumor. Nick was my baby brother, three years younger, and my best friend. It was always Nick's dream to become a writer. I came up with a book idea for my brother to write years ago, but he became too sick, and the story was never written.

There have been a lot of changes in my life in the past five years – jobs, the loss of my brother, the birth of my daughter, and watching my sons grow up so, here I am trying to live out my brother's dream, and it is to Nick whom I dedicate my first book. Nick was the model for one of my main characters. I do not consider myself to be a writer. I am, and always will be, a story teller. I have always made up stories in my head, and this is my first one that I wish to share with the world.

I am new to writing, but so far I love it and it has captured my attention completely. I love to read and never really thought that I would like writing as much as I do. Everything I write is from my head. I think out parts of the stories and make many revisions inside my head, so when I sit and write the story, it just comes out. The largest challenge for me has been the grammar, speed reading and emailing coworkers has not helped. Still, even with my challenges, I plan to finish writing three books. I hope you enjoy reading them as much as I have enjoyed writing them. I have finished my first novel in under a year. I have to give thanks to all my family and friends for all their ongoing support and encouragement.

Special Thanks, to my wife for putting up with another woman (Melabeth) who has become a big part of our daily lives. Also very special thanks to my test subjects –who have read every chapter after I had written it, and before they had been edited - they gave input and the motivation to keep writing. So, thank you Mom, Dad, Joyce and Bridget.

First to my oldest son Tyler, who will not read this "thank you." He is in boot camp right now. He joined the Army, and I am so proud, it's beyond words of expression. I drove him crazy through his senior year with the telling of Melabeth, and to think, he only has two more years. I should be done with the series by then, maybe. So, thank you for all your support son.

To my second son Cory, who happens to be my biggest fan. Not only does he read his dad's writing, but he has been my sounding board; he has allowed me to speak my story out loud for hours, refining the details of the story. I started writing this story Thanksgiving 2011, but I have been working on the characters' outlines and overall ideas for much longer. Cory has been a great inspiration for me to write this story down on paper; I am thankful for such great boys.

To Bill Stanton, who put countless hours editing my book. Very special thanks, and if anyone finds any grammar errors; let be known that it was a full time job to find them all. Bill's expert advice has been extremely educational, and as I begin the task of writing the next two books, I will be better prepared. Bill is my father-in-law, and a professor of English for Clemson University.

And to my sister in-law Wendy, and my brother Donny, who own and operate their photography studio; Wendy photographed the model, and edited all of the book art. She is very talented in her skills and it is eye opening to see her work, from beginning to end. Wendy and my brother have brought a very personal touch, and face to my book, so thank you, for all your help.

Chapter 1
Awake

I'm awake...

My eyes open only to find more darkness. Something is not right. My hand temperature is cold, but I'm not cold. In front of me there is material that feels like silk.

I push my hands all around me. I am feeling for a way out. Pushing... shoving; like I am in a box. I'm looking for a way out.

I can't find anything. I realize that I'm in a coffin. Why am I in a coffin? I must have forgotten something. What is it that I am forgetting? And how did I get here? I must think.

My head feels like its splitting open, and I can hardly believe this is happening. I take a deep breath. The air tastes dirty and smells like earth. Then I freak out; I am not breathing. How the hell?

I am a vampire; I don't need to breathe. Need to get a grip. Think back to the beginning, and try to remember how I got here.

*　　　*　　　*

First thing I remember is my name, Melanie Elizabeth Dare.

I guess this really starts with my lousy no good for nothing parents. Alright, maybe they were not always lousy and good for nothing; at one time they were sweet and fun. And what can I say? They were hippies.

My grandparents, Frank and Barbara Dare had a son they named Jack Dare, also known as my dad; he was born in 1944. In that same year, James Bergman and Norma Bergman had a daughter, Julian Bergman. Both my parents lived in the same city, Buffalo, NY. They went to the same schools and grew up together.

By the time they were 16, Julian was pregnant. Back in those days to be pregnant at 16 was a big thing. And so Jack and Julie were married. In 1960 a bouncing little girl was born. They named her Melanie Elizabeth Dare.

They say time goes by fast when you're happy; that must be true. The first 10 years of my life I flew by; I was extremely happy. I remember very little. You see my parents were good parents for two very good reasons: one, they loved me, and two they loved each other. They never had any other children. They were very happily married.

Now I grew up in the 60s, and my parents were living the hippie lifestyle. After being forced to be married at such a young age, they both took off right around 1963. Their parents put a lot of pressure on them to get jobs, stay married, and conform to society, especially since both my grandfathers were successful businessmen who ran factories during World War II, and they continued on with their tradition of making supplies for the military throughout the Vietnam conflict.

My life with my parents was pretty wild. We ran around inside colorful Volkswagen minivans, and it just seems like all we did was party and hang out, and talk about love, peace and how bad the war was. My mom did not send me to school, but I was home educated by her.

The rest of the time my mother felt like I needed to know important things like how evil the Vietnam conflict was and social issues of the time. And she taught me other important things such as: women's rights, how to pack a bong, and how to roll a joint. Yes, it was a good time for me, and I definitely got a lot of attention from adults, doing fun things, but fun things don't last. My parents' recreational drug use was becoming a serious concern according to my grandparents.

Well I guess you can say it all started going downhill in the 70s; my parents were forced to actually get jobs. We lived in a small apartment south of Buffalo. We lived with snow or the threat of snow for 11.9 months of the year.

My parents started partying real bad, and there were always these characters around. Men and women hung around the house getting high. I woke up in the morning to find persons I've never met sleeping on the couch, the floor or even in my own bedroom.

I guess, if I thought about it, I can remember a lot of small terrible things that happened to me through those years, although they seemed insignificant to what happened to me in 1972.

By this time my mother was shooting heroin. I remember her making a noise in her room; she was getting high, or whatever. Something was wrong; at first, it was the sounds coming out of her room, but then it was the quiet. It was too quiet.

I went in to check on my mother. I will never forget the image that was burned into my retinas. She lay there with no movement. Her skin was as white as a ghost with a needle sticking out of her arm. She lay next to her bed, the comforter of the bed underneath her. I knew without a word that she was dead.

I can't remember exactly what I did first, call 911 or ran to her yelling mommy, mommy. I don't remember. It's like somebody took a light switch in my brain and just turned it all off. And after that it's like a slideshow of images. My grandparents took me to their house to stay with them.

*   *   *

Having these memories while in a coffin is completely unsettling. I wish it was not so dark in here. My memories coming back to me is like being stuck in a theater tied to a seat, eyes forced open, and watching a really bad movie like Gone with the Wind which was my mother's favorite movie, one she forced me to go to one too many times. I think it became too many times for me the second time.

*   *   *

I lived with both of my grandparents back and forth for the next six months. They were both trying to keep me away from my father who was a complete wreck from my mother's death. Some people might learn from the experience, get off the drugs and the alcohol, but noooo, not my father. It sent him further down the rabbit hole.

My father came one day to pick me up for the weekend from his parents' house. If my grandmother would've stood up to her son, if she would have told him that until he got his act together he could not have me on my own, I would be alive today. As they say, a mother's love is blind. Then so was hers; she let me go with him, and he never brought me back.

Instead, we ran off to California. At first it was no big deal. To me I was with my dad. I was used to his drug abuse. Growing up in this situation really twists your mind. I really believed it was my job to take care of my father. So I cleaned up behind him, and whatever else I needed to do.

Also at this time I was still not in school. So, lucky me; I didn't have any friends. Instead I got to hang around with my father's buddies, and whores. And a few times his friends tried to touch me and do things to me. Now that I look back on the situation, it was the first sign of things to come. I was pretty good at fending them off. I had learned that if I cannot protect myself that no one else would.

My dad stayed too high or too drunk to keep a job. So, to pay for his habit he started dealing. I will never forget the night it all came to an end. It was a warm night; I just turned 15. The year was 1975; nobody even knew it was my birthday; it came and went just like any other day. My birthday, what day was that on? I can't remember. Oh yeah; March 6th, I remember now.

We lived in one of those apartment duplexes; in the backyard the renters before us had left an old swing set. It was all rusted and only one swing actually worked. I was sitting alone drawing and quietly singing to myself; I love to sing.

Not only do I love to sing, but also I'm a good singer; I remember that now. I always sang for everyone, and everyone thought it was so cute when I was little. I learned how to sing from my mom's friend in the 60s. Her name was Star; I doubt that was her real name, but that's what I knew her as.

Swinging back and forth, singing and humming, I heard a fight break out, men yelling, and my father yelling back.

You know fear does crazy things to people, like make you freeze, run away, or fight. I wish I had the runaway reaction, but not me; I got mad. How dare they yell at my father in our house? I ran this house. I was the lady of the house; time to kick some jerks out.

I came into the house and said, "WHAT THE HELL IS GOING ON? IF YOU GUYS..." A man came up behind me and grabbed my hair, pulling it back hard; next thing I knew I was staring at the ceiling.

"Shut up bitch before I hurt you" a man said.

From this view I could see my father sitting in a chair with one of the bikers standing over him; the look on his face was scared.

My father and I looked a lot the same. We both had fair skin with blonde hair that was yellow as the sun and deep blue eyes that were the color of the sky. Dad's hair hung loose and straight down to his neck; my hair was blonde and straight as well. It was so long, it ran all the way down to my butt. My dad was not a large man, 5 foot 10, and about 180 pounds. My mom was only about 110 pounds and 5 foot four. So somehow I got some extra height from somewhere. I was 5 foot seven. I am thin and have a hard time putting on any weight; I'm just too skinny.

"Please... just let my daughter go" my father cried out.

At this point I figured out my mistake; there were four really rough bikers standing in my apartment, and I knew who they were. They were the Blue Dogs, a biker gang. My dad had been selling drugs for them, and, unlike his drug head buddies, these guys were scary as hell.

The leader standing in front of my Father was Alex; he was six foot tall, and full of tattoos. He had the Santa beard, only more gray thin white; his hair was kept up in a black dew rag with a red hat. All the bikers dressed the same: blue jeans with leather chaps and boots. They wore black T shirts with some beer commercial on them, and all of them were wearing black leather jackets. On the back of their jackets was a logo for Blue Dogs.

The big biker was Jason Black; he was a big man. He didn't talk a lot, but he always scared me. He had long straight blonde hair that looked like mine only darker.

The other two men, Brandon and Randy, the Smith brothers. These two were screwed up at birth and were the fighters of the group; they both looked very similar in appearance black greasy brown hair that was shaggy; they both had black eyes. Both of them stood 5'10" and were overall, ugly.

"Well, Jack you do have one pretty little girl." Randy said. He let out a hollow laugh. He and the other bikers were looking at me with a look of hunger in their eyes.

With tears sliding down my cheek, I said, "Let me and my Dad go." Randy stared down at me with anger filling his eyes; I quickly added "please" with a weak scared voice. Randy responded with a swift kick to my side. All the air rushed out of my lungs, my side shot with pain. I let out a small noise followed by me gasping for air.

"Listen Jack" Alex bellowed "let us get right down to it. You owe us a shitload of money, you little shit, and I am guessing you don't have any of it."

"I was robbed… it wasn't my fault. I am trying to get your money" my Dad said. I could see the fear in my father's eyes. I could also tell he was high, and, worst of all, I don't think he had any of the money.

"Well I have info that you were not robbed." Alex retorted. "You have been smoking up all the drugs yourself with some help from your friends and whores."

"That's bullshit, dude…"Dad tried to reply, but then Alex put his hand up in front of my father's face. With his pointer finger up, he added the shhhh noise to shut him up.

"It does not matter to me how. Or why you don't have our money. I just want my cash… and I am not leaving without it" Alex said, with a low menacing voice.

"I don't have any money." My father replied, almost in tears.

"Well, breaking your legs and killing you will have the same results… no money." Alex replied, while he slowly shook his head back and forth.

Randy was standing over me looking down at me with a strange look on his face. "Hey I have a way we could get our money back. This little blonde is cute; we could take her to Devon."

Brandon added in his two cents. "Yeah, she is one pretty girl." He was definitely the stupid brother.

And then Jason who had said nothing up to this point added. "Yeah, think what Devon would pay us for her to star in one of his movies."

Randy standing over me, said. "What a waste; we should keep her for ourselves."

Brandon piped in. "Think we could star in that movie with her?"

"I like that idea!" Jason said, as a cruel smile spread across his face.

Thank god my dad spoke up. "What do you mean? That is my daughter you're talking about. I am not going to let you hurt her."

Alex said, "Well hold on there a minute, Jack. What else do you have to pay us with?"

My Dad said. "But… I can't give you my daughter…" his voice cracking from the stress.

Alex ignored him. He started to pace back in forth in front of my dad like he was a great thinker and not a thug. "It's not just your debt that's the problem, but your future."

"What do you mean by that?" Dad said.

Alex continued on, "Well you'll need fresh supplies of product in order to sell and make some money. Then you will be able to buy your daughter back. It's not like we will hurt her."

Dad replied in a low and slow voice, "So, no debt, and some startup supplies?"

I started to say something, but Randy stood above me and said. "Say one word... I dare you." I couldn't believe what was happening.

*   *   *

As I lay in the coffin, anger was rolling through my body at the fresh memories. Tears started sliding down my cheek. Well, that answers one question; vampires can cry.

The rest of the memory was of the bikers taking me away and throwing me into the back of a van. I was crying, and I started to scream, so the brothers tied and gagged me inside the van.

My hatred burned like a fresh cut, and I knew why I was a vampire... to kill those men and my father.

I was now weeping out loud. Suddenly the inside of the coffin lit up. I went as still as a board and did not make a noise. The sudden light had me freaked out, but soon as I stopped moving, the lights went off. Then it was blacker than night. What was that?

I said. "That was weird" and the inside of the coffin lit up again.

Well it wasn't really light; it was like l was viewing a black and white TV, and on the screen was the inside of the coffin. The really strange part was that I could see all sides of me, and, soon as I went quiet, it was dark again. The picture was fuzzy, but I could tell the shape of myself and the inside of the coffin.

Well now, that is just strange. Not like this whole situation isn't strange, but I wasn't expecting that. Then again, what was I expecting?

So I tried something. I started to whistle; the whole coffin lit up again. So I tapped my hand against the side of the coffin. It lit up again, but this time I noticed that the picture was really bright around my hand and in the mid part of my body. So it does not take a genius to figure out that I am seeing sound; it's a form of sonar. Oh man does this mean I am part bat?

So being in a dark small place was bringing back the next set of memories.

*   *   *

After the bikers took me out of the van, they took me into some house and threw me into a closet, slammed the door shut and left me in the dark. I was tied up and gagged and had no idea what was going to happen next.

After an incalculable amount of time, someone opened the door. Then someone removed my blindfold. I was now looking at a middle age white guy. He had brown hair, with balding in the middle. He wore glasses with large rims; he dressed and looked like a high school teacher. He wore slacks with a dress shirt with one of those sleeveless sweaters, bowtie and all.

"Hi I am Devon Wright, and I am the director of the film you're about to star in." he said with a vile grin.

I would have screamed or yelled, something, but all I could do was make some noise. I still had on my gag.

He stepped back, and let the big biker Jason haul me out of the closet. He threw me over his shoulder and carried me. He brought me into what I believe was the living room of the house. All the windows were covered up by big draperies of mixed colors and design. There was a couch, and in the middle of the room a bed. Around the bed, cameras were set up, and there were lights on poles. I may be a blonde, but I hung around enough drug head guys to tell you where this was going.

I was sure I understood the story; I just didn't understand the ending. Thinking of this event in my life is like watching a horror movie. The images pass through my mind with ever increasing pain. Every one of the bikers had a turn with me and not one at a time.

I push the memories away, but the last one is the clearest. My mind and heart is breaking just thinking about it.

The leader Alex was on me; I was looking up at his face. He was already having his way with me.

"Alright, it is time for the last scene." Devon said, with a sickness I had never heard before.

Brandon, half dressed, sitting on the couch, resting with a beer in his hand, said. "Do we have to kill her? I think it's kind of a waste... she is smoking hot and hell of fun in the bed."

Devon eyed him. "Well the difference is what it will make this film worth. I have a rich client that will pay $150,000 for snuff film, or, if you want to keep the girl alive, he will pay $5000.00."

Jason, still naked, with tattoos all over him, his long, dirty, blonde hair, hung off to one side of his head, got off his chair and strolled over to the cooler and grabbed a beer out. "Her Dad owed us $15,000 as if that really matters. I would do this regardless. Does anyone else need a beer?"

"Sure." Brandon called out; Jason threw him a beer.

"Let's ask little Melanie what she thinks." Alex said, sitting on his knees right between my legs. I stared at him and knew the truth. He was waiting for this part. He wanted my fear.

"I am ready to die. Kill me now, for I never want to think about this again." I said, with an eerie calm. I don't know where my mind was; maybe it was in shock. I don't know.

Pain, anger, revenge, were locked away, and, in that moment of my certain death, all was calm.

As I looked up, I heard Devon say. "Final scene... action!"

Alex got on top of me; my body was numb. I could no longer feel him, as he had his way with me. Then he started to choke me.

I freaked out. I fought back, but it did me no good.

His face started to dim away. Then it all went black.

Free at last.

*   *   *

I screamed at the top of my lungs. Slamming the coffin door with all my might, it moves up but only a few inches. As the door lifts up, the dirt comes spilling in around the edges. This would not have mattered, except I was screaming, when the dirt went into my mouth.

That calms me down. I close my eyes. I have to spit the dirt out. I am sure I could dig, and push my way out, but I need a little down time. My emotions are running amok.

I know that I am a vampire. As I lay there, I come to realize that I don't need to breathe, and I have no heartbeat to speak of. Vampire or not, I am dead. As my mind calms a little, a fuzzy memory surfaces to the top of my mind. It's like a dream, not clear, but I remember now what happened.

*   *   *

I was in the arms of a man, being carried from where to where I did not know. I could tell things were passing by, so I knew that we were moving quickly. Yet it didn't feel like he was walking, more like floating... so smooth, with no motion. The air was cold, and it was dark outside. A tree, building and other objects of uncertain origin passed by, as we moved to some unknown destination.

The man was cradling me; my legs draped over one arm while he held me to his chest with his other arm. I looked up at him. He had long wavy hair that parted down the middle. In the light I could not determine what color his hair was. It looked black; it could have been blonde, who knew? His face was young and beautiful with a long mustache that wrapped around his mouth and down his chin hanging down into braids. I believe that I trusted this face; his eyes had red smoldering light shining through them letting me know this man was not natural.

"You're awake." The strange man said, with a small smile. Strange how it seemed he was staring at me and nothing else, but yet we were still moving at what felt like an incredible pace.

"Who are you?" I squeaked out.

The strange angel of death said, "It really does not matter, but you may call me Nicks. And let me start by telling you that I found you in a dumpster, dead. I have sought to save your life, but I have failed and die you will. You were too dead for any human to have saved you, but I thought that vampire blood may restore you."

Did he say vampire? I was thinking, with those eyes, angel of death was closer. "Nick..." I started to say.

"No... I said Nicks" he replied curtly.

"Oh sorry.... I... what do you mean I am going to die? I feel fine right now, not like I am dying." I said with anger building up within me.

"I know this is a lot to take in, and I have no time to explain it. One answer will lead to another question and so on; this is knowledge that would take years to pass on." Nicks replied with a thoughtful look on his face.

"I am scared. I have been through hell, and I need to understand what is happening... PLEASE" It came out all at once; I felt the mental break coming on. I was so confused, and this guy was between the scariest person of all time or my long lost brother. How does one meet someone and see a monster, and a father, all in the same person?

"You're right; you need a little bit more information, just in case." He mused.

"In case of what?" I replied nervously.

"Alright, I have decided to give you some information, but you can not interrupt me or ask any questions. This is all the time I have to tell you." After Nicks made this comment, he lifted his head up with a strange look. I noticed that we had stopped moving, and then he continued. "We are here. I really would like to tell you more, because I really wish I could do more for you, but, alas... I cannot. You would not believe me, when I say you are like my child, but it is true. From the moment I saw you, I fell in love with you as if you were my daughter."

I was moved by his words; it was strange. Right after I thought he was like meeting my father for the first time, I had noticed that we had arrived. "Why are we at a graveyard?"

"No questions." Nicks responded, with a remorseful look on his face looking back down at me.

"Sorry, please continue. I wish to know when you have time, and am willing to share with me before I die. It's just because I am so confused. I already thought I had died, but I am being held by my vampire father in a graveyard. I will try my hardest to listen." That's the longest thing I have said to anyone in the longest time. Things still felt like a dream and are still hazy around the corners of my eyes. Well maybe it is a dream?

"Well let's see how I can sum this up so it makes sense. Vampire blood can heal man; make him stronger, and even slow down aging. It is also a drug. No, better yet, it is a poison, and as long as you do not take too much of it, it will not kill you but make you stronger. The longer you drink from the dead, the more your body requires it, and after a time, depending on certain factors, such as the power of the vampire, the addiction is irreversible. If you die with vampire blood in your system, you will rise in three to seven days from the grave. Now there is no guarantee that you will rise. Only in the movies and books does it work all the time. Certain factors can contribute to the reason for not rising, such as the health of the human and how long they were a Ren. Ren is what we call humans addicted to our blood, a little play on Renfeild from Dracula." He chuckled at this and then found a headstone and took a seat.

Still holding me in his arms he started to continue. Before he could speak, I said. "Do you know Dracula?" I couldn't help myself; it just came out.

He gave me a heated look "Do you wish me to continue or talk about things that have no bearing on your immediate need?"

"Sorry, please continue." I said this like a little girl that had just got scolded for talking out of place. It has always been hard for me to hold my tongue. And normally I find no reason to apologize, but I had a feeling that whatever he had to say was more important than my need to smart off.

"Very well," Nicks said while he readjusted me, so now I was sitting up looking at him. "Let me see, where was I... Oh yeah it is always a good thing to be a Ren for at least a year before changing. And see there is your first problem. You have been a Ren for a whole hour. Even if that was not the case, I regret to inform you that I am infertile. See, I have been unable to make any new children in thousands of years, and trust me I have tried. So I have tried to change many persons, and I have had many failures, so I gave up. When I found you, I had to put so much blood in to you to revive you that you have already begun to start the change. Now it is not all hopeless. There are always miracles and other things that I don't believe in." He chuckled at his dumb joke. "So I have brought you to this graveyard, to bury you, so that no one will find your body and do something stupid to it, like cremate you, or embalm you, which would stop the process of the change. A couple of my friends, Jeffery and Liz will be here shortly to prepare you for the burial."

With a voice that I even I could hear the sadness in, I said, "So you don't think there is much of a chance that I will rise from the grave?" I formed it like a question, but I said it more like a statement. He gave me one of those understanding looks, the one that said, yep and that's why I am trying not to get all worked up about you, because you're going to die. Anger ran through me, and I said with some hurt in my voice. "Damn there is no justice. I would have loved to rise from the grave to revenge myself. Do you think you could kill those men who did this to me?"

He gave me a sad look, and said. "Do you even recall who did this to you?"

Having a fuzzy memory, for some reason I could not recall all of what had happened to me. Nicks held me quietly while I tried to remember.

"No," I replied to Nicks and then added, "Why can't I remember what happened to me?"

Nicks said, with a sad look on his face, "Sorry, part of the change and speaking about change, my friends are here, and not a moment too late; you don't have a lot of time left."

Nicks' friends arrived carrying a coffin with them. And this is when I noticed that there was a dug grave, just under a tree not far from where we sat. I looked down and noticed that I was wearing a white dress. It had short sleeves, and the dress hung down to my knees. It was plain and made out of soft cotton. I guess this was a funeral dress.

Nicks looked over at me and said. "We have taken the liberties of preparing your body. Once you die, that is how you will always be. Your hair will not get any longer or shorter; you will always be the same as you are now."

"Once you rise as a vampire, even if your arm got cut off, it would grow back exactly the same, and the old one would turn to dust."

The friend named Liz was a tall slender girl dressed like a cowgirl. The other friend Jeffery was an average middle age guy, who was well built but had a little bit of a belly going on. They laid the coffin before me and then Jeffery lifted the lid, and the inside was lined with white fabric. Jeffery grabbed a pillow out, which I thought was kind of strange, seeing as there was still a little white pillow in the coffin.

Jeffery looked at Nicks. "All is ready Master."

Liz looked at me and said with some pride in a southern accent. "You're already to go sweetheart and you don't worry about a thing. It's all going to work out fine. Now sweetie I have made sure you were completely shaved, I didn't miss a spot, and, hell maybe even got more than you wanted." She laughed out loud like a banshee. "Now, don't get upset. Look at the bright side. If you ever become a vampire, you will never have to shave again."

I was about to tell this little southern bell the way to hell. Before I could tell her off, a pain in my gut hit me like someone had stabbed me.

"Enough." Nicks said rising to his feet. "The time is among us; to wait any longer will just make her suffer through the worse pains imaginable. I am sorry, but it is time to die. Know this… I love you, and if you rise, you will remember who did this to you, and then you'll have your justice."

With that he laid me down into the coffin. Jeffery handed him the extra pillow. "What's the pillow for?" I asked Nicks. I was just now finding my voice, for the pain was still there but had backed off.

"Sorry... my sweet Melanie; the only way to kill you without messing up your beautiful body." Nicks said looking down at me in the coffin.

"Wait NO..." and before I could get out a word, I was suffocated again.

*   *   *

Well the memory was fuzzy. So at least this time was not as bad as the first time. I was not mad at Nicks for doing it. I knew the pain in my gut was the beginning, and he was just trying to save me from suffering. Nicks was not making a movie of my death for others to enjoy.

That's funny. In the movies the vampire is the bad guy.

During this time, thinking through these thoughts, I had started digging my way out. And, before I knew it, my head popped out of the ground into the night. Snow lay all around as I pulled myself out of the earth.

I took my first look with my vampire eyes.

Chapter 2
Hunger

I had just finished crawling out of my grave.

It was amazing to look around with my new eyes. There was snow everywhere; I looked up into the sky and could see it was night time. It was overcast, yet it was as bright as a cloudy day. I was standing in the same cemetery that Nicks buried me in. I noticed that it sat high on the hill, and down below a small town nuzzled in the valley floor.

Well looking at the leafless trees and evergreens I was not in California anymore as far as I could tell. I could be anywhere.

The world was bright, but at second glance it was black and white. I was marveling at the lack of color, when the clouds opened up. The sliver of a moon came into view and when it did so did the world. Everything had color and depth now that there was a small amount of light.

I realized that when the clouds covered the moon and stars, it should have been so dark, that I would have had trouble seeing my hand in front of my face. Even in darkness so complete the world was only black and white. The smallest amount of light brought the color back. I don't know if I can go outside during the day, but something tells me even if I could the sun would blind me.

Standing in my muddy, dirty, used to be white dress I came to another fact; I needed a bath. Then yet another thing came to mind; I had no shoes on and I am standing in snow! Yep, check, not cold, it is harder and harder trying to talk myself out of being a mystical creature of the night. Funny thing is I could feel that it was very cold, but I was not cold. I would have to describe it as walking out of my home on a cold day. The first few seconds you're outside the cold bites at your skin, but it is not uncomfortable; after a few minutes that feeling changes. Now I am standing outside, barefoot in a thin cotton dress and even though I know that it is freezing outside, it is only knowledge and nothing more.

Still standing over the hole I just crawled out of, I have no real direction, but I think it is time to go. I am not sure where these legs will take me but away from this cemetery is a good start. I started off walking toward the edge of the cemetery where I could see an old stone wall; I moved like the wind; I have to say it was the coolest thing ever; my feet didn't sink into the snow, and I made no noise to speak of.

Suddenly a noise off my left shoulder, then several things happened all at once. First I jumped really high, spun to my left; at the same time I was in a back flip, landing graceful like a cat, and as quiet as a mouse. I landed on top of a gravestone. I released a growling hissing sound; also I could see in my head an outline of the object that made the noise sitting in some branches.

It all came together in my mind. The noise was a hoot; the image that created the noise was an owl, and my ninja moves were completely unnecessary. Well I could tell getting used to the overwhelming senses was going to be tricky.

Tricky maybe… fun definitely. The next few minutes I was playing a fun game of jumping from gravestone to gravestone. Flipping, cart wheeling and spinning through the air, I landed on the old stone wall on the edge of the graveyard. I was dancing on the top of the wall when I let out a squeal of pain and bent over with stomach spasms.

I will tell you being hungry is nothing new to me; I may have been homeschooled, but I have read a few books in my time, along with missing a few meals. Being a child of hippies had its ups and downs. Sometimes my parents would run out of money, and we had to beg for food.

The Donner party comes to mind and so does Flight 571 that crashed in the Andes. Only 16 people survived that flight, and they were not living off of pudding; that just occurred a couple of years ago. That happened in 1972, the same year my mom died. And I remember listening to the story while sitting at my grandma's house waiting to go to the funeral. The 16 survived by eating the other dead passengers on the plane, and at the time I was thinking that I would have died of starvation before I would have eaten anyone.

I guess I am about to find out if that's true. I don't really believe animal blood will work. I have read vampire books and other fantasy, plus watched a bunch of vampire movies, and all of them always go on and on about the blood lust. I guess Americans have not missed a meal in such a long time that we need to believe that the hunger to take another life must be supernatural.

Well that's not true; when people are truly starving, we will eat anything. My problem is that, one thing about all the legends of vampires agreed upon is that vampires need human blood, and only blood. Crap, not good. So I guess eating pudding is out, and the pain in my stomach is only worsening with every passing second.

I am not sure what I should do, but one thing is clear; I am starving. I don't know how long I have been in the ground; I feel thin and empty. My teeth ache and my abnormally long fingers have long razor sharp claws. I stare at my own hands in disbelief. I can feel my long sharp teeth with my tongue. Maybe after I eat, I will look more human; at least that is what I am hoping. There are other problems going on in my head; where do I stay during the day? I need a place to wash, some new clothes, I look homeless, and where is all that vampire wealth? I am dead broke, no pun intended.

I headed toward the town, first walking, and then running. At first all I could think of was the pain in my stomach, but the sudden sensation of running through the forest at such speeds took my mind off of the pain.

I was heading down the side of the mountain, dodging branches, trees and bushes. I could feel the wind whipping my long hair behind me. My mind was keeping up with this speed; it felt as if time had slowed down.

I let out a laugh, and of course, when I did, the black and white details of the terrain came into view in my mind. That gave me an idea, so I started to whistle as I ran, and the world lit up as I flew down the ever-decreasing mountainside.

As I flew through the trees, I noticed with my second sight that there was a cliff coming up. I don't know how far the bottom was, but I was wondering if I could fly. I thought it would be a good idea just to go for it. I figured I would have a gay time flying through the air.

By the time I got to the edge, I changed my mind, but I couldn't stop in time. I fell onto my back sliding toward the edge. The ground was too steep for me to slow down. The ground was covered with a thick layer of pine needles; I couldn't get a grip. I slid right off the top of the cliff. And, of course, to go with my luck, it wasn't a little way down.

It was more like three hundred feet judging by the treetops. I was falling for the ground faster than I had been running.

I flew toward the ground, falling like a sky diver flat on my belly. I still had plenty of time to think about what an ass I was, but my fast mind wasn't going to help me with a fast stop.

My luck held solid; I didn't fly, and I was unable to grab hold of a branch of a tree. It was like I aimed for the only opening in the forest floor.

I tried to use my hands in front of me to break the fall, but all that I accomplished was breaking my arms. Slamming face first into the ground, the darkness swallowed me up.

When I came to, I had no idea how much time had passed, but it felt like maybe only a few minutes, which was amazing considering I should be dead. I could feel pain throughout my body which was not surprising in the least.

Most of my body felt like a bag full of glass that someone smashed against the ground, only the glass was my bones. As these thoughts went through my head I could feel my body knitting itself back together again. It was so strange and honestly it didn't really hurt as badly as it should, and truth be said, I think my hunger was now worse than breaking my bones.

Pain had been like the cold air, just information, but the hunger felt like more. I had to find food soon, or I am afraid that I will be unable to move and burn to death in the sun.

Maybe I don't deserve to live, but I needed to exist to revenge myself to kill the bikers who brought these horrors into my life. Finally I was able to get to my feet, but I could tell I was too weak after healing myself for anymore stupid stunts. In fact it seems I will be walking normal speed the rest of the way to town.

The rest of the trip was uneventful, and not that far from the base of the cliff, that I had just fallen off of, I came to an empty road. I crossed over the road, walked through some more woods and finally arrived at a little square of homes. Half a dozen houses of modest means sat in a semicircle. Beyond was the rest of the town, but it was still about a mile off; it was real quiet; I have no idea what time it is, but I am guessing it is early in the morning.

I sneaked up to the first house which sat at a further distance away from the rest of the homes. I walked up to the back door; I hated myself for what I must do.

At the back door, I listened to what was going on inside. All was quiet, but, as I listened closer, noise begun to filter through the door of the house. I came to realize it was the noise of a TV from the front of the house. I couldn't tell if anyone was home. They could have just left the TV on. So I just decided to go for it. I was hungry and had no idea how much time I had before sunrise.

I tried the doorknob to see if it was unlocked. I guess they didn't lock up at night; good for me, bad for them. I snuck in to find myself standing in the kitchen with only a small light on over the sink, but I could see everything crystal clear. Treading carefully, I moved to the other side of the kitchen and looked into the living room.

Closing my eyes, the sound from the TV allowed me to see the entire living room in my head. I could see a man sitting in front of the TV, taking swigs out of his bottle. The image in my head was black and white, and I noticed it lacked detail as well. I knew he had a bottle, but I could not see the label, and I could not make out the finer details of his face. Regardless, I could see what he was doing, and that he was alone.

With that knowledge, I went into the room and snuck up right behind him for the couch was positioned in the middle of the living room. I was too hungry to worry about much, and, with that, I attacked. I grabbed his mouth to keep him from yelling, pulled his head to one side and sank my fangs into his neck.

The blood, oh the blood, it was everything I ever wanted and more. I didn't know because I have never had consensual sex, but this felt great.

My body shook with desire; never had I ever been more at peace in my entire life.

At first I took the man by surprise; he pulled me over the couch, and we slammed into the coffee table, but, even with all this, I was too busy sucking and lost in the pleasure to even care. The weaker he got, the stronger I got. This didn't happen quickly like the movies, but it was over quick enough, maybe 10 or 15 minutes.

He lay dead. I was laying there on the floor with his body still on top of me, his face still skyward. I pushed his body off by rolling it to one side. I jumped up off of the ground. I felt like a million dollars; I was completely healed and feeling so good when I heard another noise down the hallway.

I could make out a heavyset woman coming down the hallway from one of the other rooms of the small house. I was standing over a dead man in the middle of her living room, wearing nothing but a filthy piece of cloth over me, covered in mud with blood around my mouth. I was hoping just to kill this man and leave, but it appeared I was out of time, and so was this woman who approached me.

"Roger what the hell is your drunken ass doing? Are you trying to wake the children...?" The woman stopped in midsentence after she flipped on the light switch.

The sudden light blinded me; it took a few seconds for my eyes to adjust. I could see the woman clearly; we were five feet apart with a couch between us. We just stared at each other in utter disbelief. I didn't know what I should do. She said there were children down the hall. I hadn't even thought about that, and, at the same time, this was probably her dead husband I was standing over.

Then she surprised me and started to speak.

"I...I...I don't know who.... Or what you are, but I have children. Please don't hurt me!"

I put my hands out in front of me like I was surrendering. "I won't hurt your children lady. I am sorry I was so hungry." I paused looking down at the dead man and back at her, then finished with a "sorry."

The lady calmed a little. Then I realized I could hear, feel the beat of her heart. I could see the pulse of her veins; this was a little disheartening. She then, looking at the dead man said, "Well Roger wasn't worth a whole lot alive, drunk most of the time, and a lousy husband and father. I always figured the booze would get him. Then I would get the life insurance; look, if you leave without hurting me, or my children, I won't say a word to no one." Then she half said to herself. "It's not like anyone will believe me anyhow."

She looked back up at me with a plea in her eyes. Her face changed quickly to surprise. I rushed her, leaping over the couch and slammed into the woman. She hit the wall behind her.

The woman was my height; she had me by twice the mass not just in weight, also in build. Still her 250 lb husband didn't stand a chance and neither did she; shoving her up against the wall was too easy.

The sound of a picture frame hitting the ground, and her air rushing out of her lungs is all I heard. As if she was a weak child, I twisted her head to the side and bit down on her neck. All I had to do was bite and then pull my fangs out and the blood rushed into my mouth, and it was so wonderful.

The woman trying to catch her breath, cried out. "Please... my children; don't kill ME."

I licked the wounds on her neck and the saliva in my mouth healed them up. I thought this would work, because, when I was looking down at her dead husband, his neck had no marks. After he had died, I had licked the yummy blood on his neck. The wound had healed even though he was dead. This would be good to know so I didn't leave a trail that someone could follow.

Being that there are, in fact, vampires, I would guess that there would in fact be vampire hunters. And something else to note, there wasn't blood everywhere just around my lips, I had licked the evidence off of poor old Roger's neck. Heck I hadn't even drained the man dry, but I am thinking I am stealing life not just blood.

If the body is a car engine, then it is built to make energy for the soul. My engine died so I am just stealing the life energy from someone else. I don't know if this is true, but I feel like it is close to the truth.

Looking right into her eyes, I said as cold as possible. "I am leaving now. You will not see me again... if you tell no one."

The woman with fear in her eyes said. "I will tell no one... I swear to God. Thank you, for sparing me... and my children." She had no backbone; that made me want to finish her.

As I rushed out the front door into the night, a thought came to me; did someone just thank me for not killing them? Wow that is funny, to be thanked for not doing something as vile as killing children in their sleep. What a strange world we live in and now for something completely different to think about.

Where am I going to sleep tonight? And where the hell am I? Maybe I should have asked a few more questions to that lady? Second thought, I don't think she could handle anymore, especially after donating blood and watching her husband be murdered, begging for her life and the life of her own children. She can have the rest of the night off.

After I left, I found my power had returned. No longer did I feel any pain; all the damages from the earlier fall had healed. I ran at ridiculous speeds toward town. When I got to town, I jumped from tree to rooftop and back again. In fact, I found that I was more than just rejuvenated. I was twice as powerful with more speed and grace. My sight was even sharper; my second sight was there when I heard or made noise. My sense of smell and hearing were keen, beyond my reckoning.

When I landed on rooftops and stayed still for a minute, I could put my head to the roof and hear people sleeping. I think my hearing was sharp enough to count how many people were in the house.

I landed on a roof of a large two story home. Feeling confident this house was empty, I checked the upper stories' windows; I found one unlocked. I guess the owner had not pictured a vampire girl hanging from her toes that were attached to the gutters. Checking that particular window and finding it unlocked, with catlike grace I opened the window and jumped through it.

Twisting through the air landing on my feet I was safe and sound inside. It appeared to be a boy's room. The door was open so I stood there listening to make sure I was alone. Also I made a high pitch whistle, so, with my second sight, I could see down the hallway.

I had noticed when I was jumping around town that, when I whistled, dogs barked or howled; I had used it to make my second sight come to life. I think but don't know that maybe I was making the sound at such a high pitch that humans may not be able to hear it. If that were true, that would be handy and prove once and for all, that I was Bat Girl.

I relaxed; the house was empty. I was wondering if I could stay all day without being discovered; I guess I would find out. As I looked around this boy's room I started to take in some of the details, and something was very wrong. First, there was this huge box with a TV on top of it. In front of the box was what appeared to be a typewriter or maybe just the keyboard of a typewriter? The box said IBM. Ok I have no idea what that means.

That wasn't the strangest thing in this boy's room. His bed cover was really crazy. On the cover there was the same picture over and over again; on the top of this picture were the words STAR WARS, in gold letters. Below was a picture of a man in a white bathrobe holding up what I guessed to be a flash light surrounded by robots and a giant robot with a black face in the background. Okay, maybe his mom and dad were really creative or something, but then there were shelves of strange toys; where the hell do you buy this stuff? I have been in toy stores, and never have I laid eyes on any of this stuff. Then there was a creepy doll robot guy. His face was the same as the picture on the bed, and he was holding what appeared to be a red stick. Maybe it was supposed to be a sword.

Then I noticed the light outside. I was sidetracked by something really crazy. It was a clock; I have no idea how to describe what I am seeing, giant red numbers displaying the time 6:45 AM. Then the numbers switched with no moving parts to 6:46 AM... wow, no way. I need to get a hold of myself.

The sun is rising; time to put a plan into action. I closed the window and quickly walked the whole upstairs trying my hardest not to get too distracted with all the stuff these people had that I have never laid eyes on before. I found the entrance to the attic, pulled the handle and up I went. Just as I thought, from the dust on the boxes, they only come up in the attic twice a year, one time to bring down the Christmas decorations and then a second time to put them away.

Collecting some sheets, blankets and a pillow from what I deemed to be guest locations, I made me a little hidden bed, in the corner of the attic. Before the sun came up completely I had noticed that one of the rooms upstairs was an office. I bet a dollar that I could figure out where I was and what the date was. Some basic info would be nice.

So I walked into the office and noticed, on the corner of the desk, some mail. Perfect, I picked it up; to James Richa, 304 High St, Collbran, CO 81624. Well one mystery put to rest. I am somewhere in Colorado; I camped a couple of times in Colorado with my folks. I was eight or nine, and I stayed almost a year with Star. She is the one who taught me how to sing. I miss her and wonder if I could look her up, or should I look her up. Maybe, on second thought, I will look her up some other time.

What, no way, what the... that can't be right. On the desk lay one of those calendars that took up most of where you worked. According to the calendar it was February 2, Friday 1990. 1990, only it is 1975. Nicks said five to seven days, not fifteen years; NOT FIFTEEN YEARS... WHAT THE HELL. That can't be right. It's not right, stomping my foot against the floor.

I am tired and the sun is coming up. Noticing the room was filling up with the light of day, I will have to figure all this out tomorrow.

I ran up to my hiding place. Pulling up the ladder, I slunk off to my corner curled up in my blankets and pillow. Then I did what any, strong, self reliant, independent, woman or man would do in my situation. I quietly cried myself to sleep.

I sleep like the dead. It was kind of strange; I didn't move an inch and had no dreams whatsoever. I simply fell asleep, then woke up with no real idea how much time had passed away. The attic was dark but not dark enough for night time.

I move into the middle of the attic and listen to make sure no one is home. After listening for a little while, I was sure the house was empty. Plus

I saw a notice on the calendar that it was marked for a weekend trip to Grand Junction, to visit mom for the weekend.

So I kicked the ladder down and went down to the second level again, but this time, when I stood in the hallway, I could see all the sun streaming in from the adjacent rooms except for one. I had closed the blinds to the boy's room with all the strange toys. I am glad that I did; I walked back into the room and looked at the strange clock. It stated it was 4:15 PM, so much for sleeping all day long.

I am thinking my first idea of burying myself would have sucked. I would have been stuck underground for hours wide awake. Well I am not a person to sit around and feel sorry for myself. I need to go forth, though I have no idea how. Sometimes you have to start with what you know. And what I know right this moment wouldn't get you a cup of coffee, but I am dirty and dressed in what's left of a fifteen year old cotton white dress that isn't white anymore.

Down the hallway there are three rooms. The first room is the boys' room; the second across from his room is an office; the third is full of exercise equipment, with filing cabinets and random stuff everywhere, and one more door at the end of the hall, a beautiful baby blue bathroom, which happened to have an outside window.

I could see the light shining out of the bathroom. The sunlight was not as blinding as I believed it would be. I found these really groovy sunglasses in the boy's room called Oakley's, they are really strange looking. They're just one big lens, and they are really dark. With them on I am enjoying life just a little bit better.

Now here comes the hard part; do I really burst into flames just because a little sunlight hits me? Well there's one way to find out for sure, and find out I must, or I have to wait till tonight to get a bath.

I walked up to the edge of the doorway. Why could I have not covered all the windows up last night? In my defense the whole 15 years missing had me a little preoccupied. Enough stalling, I stuck my hand out into the light. My whole body tensed as I got ready for the pain.

Then nothing happened. I could feel the heat of the sun, but my hand was not on fire; whoopee, so I stepped out of the hall into the bathroom. It was annoyingly bright and now that the sunlight from the window was on my entire body, it was quite bothersome.

I really couldn't complain because I wasn't bursting into flames. So, with that, I covered the window with the boy's comforter with the strange Star Wars symbols on it, and now it was very groovy in the bathroom. So I started the water. I ripped off the soiled cotton dress and did what I've been dreaming about since I woke up in that grave. I had a long hot bath.

Bath, shower, bath, shower, and then a bath; I was white again. Well maybe even more white than I remember. I never had a tan living in California; I was still as white as a snowflake, but now I was taking white to a new level.

I watch my claws come out of my hand like a cat. It was so weird; even my fingers became longer. I found that my teeth moved like a new muscle that extended and retracted at will; they never went completely away. If I lifted my top lip, the teeth lay right in front of my old teeth. I guess you can say that my teeth didn't change; rather, new ones grew in. It was the same with my nails; the new nails were thick and hard, pointier and sharp around the edges. If I looked under the nails, I could kind of see my old nails.

And now that I did find my claws and teeth, I couldn't help but play with them like a new toy. I moved them in and out. I did something I remember Nicks telling me about; I cut my hair off rather than cleaning it. Throwing it over onto the bathroom floor watching it turn to mud as it mixed, with the water on the floor, I kept cutting it off until all of my hair was brand new. It was the cleanest I could ever recall it being.

I was playing with my claws in the bath. I looked up into the mirror that sat above the sink. I stood up and looked at myself. I lifted my hands up and made my claws go long; at the same time I elongated my teeth and opened my mouth. Then I made a growling sound; I scared myself; I wanted to run away.

I put my teeth and claws away. I looked almost human. The things that gave it away were my skin tone and my eyes. It took me a second to really understand what was wrong with them. My eyes were huge. I stepped out of the tub and walked closer to the mirror.

My eyes were twice the size than they originally were. It was like I had owl eyes, and man, did I look like a freak. My eye color didn't change; they were still blue as the sky, just more to look at. If I kept my teeth up, and my claws away, the only thing that keeps me from passing for human are these eyes. I will need to keep my sunglasses on.

After that, I went downstairs and found my way to the master bedroom. Wearing nothing but a pair of sunglasses, I ransacked the room for anything of use. I found several items, first a good-sized gym bag with a strap. That would hold clothes I found in the closet that semi-fit me.

Second, I found a 45 1911 pistol, with one clip of ammo that might be handy even though I have never shot a gun before, I shoved it inside the gym bag. After digging around a little bit more, in the same drawer that I found the pistol, I also found $200 in cash, now that I needed.

I've always worn dresses and skirts, not pants, so it was good for me this lady had some dresses, but most of her clothes were pants. I wonder why? I guess in 1990 a lot of things are different; nonetheless I found black tights which I put on.

I slipped a dark blue dress on that hung to my knees. A big bulky jacket with a big hood finished my outfit. I settled for the pink snow boots. This lady's feet must be huge, or mine small; all her other shoes won't fit. They just fell off. Walking barefoot was what I wanted to do, but that would bring way too much attention to me, especially since there was snow on the ground, with the temperature hanging around freezing; I couldn't go without footwear. With my sunglasses on, and the hood over my head, I put my gym bag over my shoulder.

I was ready to hit the road, but I was hungry again. Now this wasn't the starving of last night, but I was still ready for some breakfast. Since no one was around to help me out in my new life, I was not sure what to do.

I was finding out that most of the legends were bullshit, like inviting me in, and sunlight burning me. I had an image in the mirror. So maybe I could eat food too?

*   *   *

It is so unfair; I made French toast, scrambled eggs and bacon, and here I am puking my guts out in the sink for 15 minutes.

Damn, where is someone to hold my head? It would've been one thing if the food was nasty or smelled bad, but no it smelled delicious, and it tasted fantastic. Where's the justice? This means I'll have to go through my existence, smelling food that I once loved and be unable to eat it.

*   *   *

It was around 7:00 PM when I got out the door and headed down the street. I was heading for uptown, with a simple plan to catch a bus back to LA and then eat bikers.

As I walked I couldn't help thinking of those poor people's house that I just left. First they were robbed of a gun, clothes, and cash. Then the perpetrator destroyed their bathroom with mud, leaving a ring around the tub that will never come out. Then someone threw up in their kitchen sink, vandalizing the entire kitchen and living room.

It was like a giant tornado, or a 15-year-old vampire throwing the biggest fit you've ever seen. Apparently I was strong enough to toss the refrigerator into the next room landing on the TV. The walls shattered like paper when I punched and kicked them; even the two by fours, shattered like toothpicks. I couldn't help but laugh, as I imagined how the insurance agent looked as he wrote the claim.

I was now walking down High St at 8:30 at night. Apparently this town was in the middle of nowhere. When I reached the uptown area, they didn't even have a bus station. After walking up the main drag, there were only four little shops, and an old country hardware store.

In front of the hardware store is where I ran into a nice helpful middle aged woman. She directed me to Grand Junction City. She told me that's where the big city was and the nearest bus station. The confrontation was strange, and she was glad to see me walk away. Apparently I did not put out a good vibe.

So now I am hitchhiking down highway 330 to I-70 to Grand Junction. At least that is the plan. Now it is awful strange that no one has stopped for me. When I was a child, me and my parents hitched around the country, and it was never more than a few minutes before someone stopped. My dad used to say it helped to travel with girls, because, if it was just him, it could take almost fifteen minutes before someone would pick him up.

I think, but I am not sure, that I have been walking for a half an hour. A dozen cars went by, and I hardly got a brake light. Now I guess I could just run there, but that seemed like a bad idea because I was already hungry again. And it is not rocket science that motion takes energy. Finally a big, old looking Chevy Impala pulled over in front of me, so I ran up to the passenger side and jumped in the backseat; there were two men sitting in the front.

"Thanks for stopping," I said to the men in the front of the car. I threw my bag in the empty seat next to me, and had barely got the door shut when the man took off.

Both of these men looked to be about forty; it was hard to tell. The men were both sporting beards of gray and brown hair. One had long messed up hair that he kept in a ball cap. The driver just looked like he missed his haircut by a week or so with a much neater and shorter beard to match. They were both heavily dressed for the cold with flannel jackets and jeans. The Old Spice one of them was wearing didn't even start to cover up the smoke smell or the scent of their blood for that matter.

The passenger turned to face me and had a friendly face. "Where you going on this God forsaken night?"

"It's not the only thing God has forsaken." I replied with a little laugh; then I went on to say. "Need to get to Grand Junction bus station."

The passenger gave a little chuckle at my remark. The driver turned around and gave me a quick go over. He then went back to driving before saying in a nice soft voice. "What a strange thing to say." And, after a short pause, he continued. "You're not running away from home or anything like that?"

"No sir; I am heading back home." I said to the driver. There was something off about these two guys as they gave each other a quick look. Some unsaid understanding passed between them. The driver went back to looking at the road, while the passenger went back to looking at me.

"My name's Dave" said the passenger "and this right over here is my coz Jim... what's you go by?"

I paused; what is my name? I don't think I should tell him my name is Melanie Elizabeth Dare. I was caught off guard; and I said the first think that came to mind "Melabeth"

"That's a real pretty name you have" offered up Dave.

"I have never heard the name Melabeth before. Are your parents from around these parts?" asked Jim. He was definitely trying to find out a little background info.

"No sir." I was not going to offer up too much info.

"Well it don't matter none, Jim" Dave said as he spun himself forward in his seat. "And don't forget my stuff at the hunting lodge; we need to get it."

Jim gave a look at Dave, but then he looked forward to the road again. "Oh, ya, I almost forgot. No problem Dave. Little girl..."

Dave cut him off. "It's Melabeth, Jim."

Jim said smoothly with his soft voice. "I am sorry; meant no disrespect Melabeth; I was just sayin; it will only take a few minutes to grab Dave's stuff. Then we will be able to drive you all the way to the bus station."

Before I could respond, Dave added. "And you wouldn't have to stand outside hitching."

"Maybe never again." Jim said with no real emotion in that soft voice.

I wasn't meant to hear that, but my hearing is amazing, so I just answered. "Yep, no problem. Do what you need to; if you guys don't mind, I am going to grab a little shut eye." Not that I had to sleep. Far from it, I was wide awake. I just didn't want to talk anymore with these men, and, if their intentions were not pure, well I guess I wouldn't have to go hungry all night after all.

As I lay there pretending to be asleep, memories of my past came to my mind as I thought back to the first time I was called Melabeth. My father wished for my name to be Melanie, something about being the music to his heart. That was the story he gave me, but it was probably the name of his ex-girlfriend. My mother wanted to name me Elizabeth, after her grandmother who had already passed away.

I guess it's better than being named after my grandmother Norma. After my mother passed away and my dad was out on his drinking binge, I lived with my grandparents James and Norma Bergman, who were the closest things I ever had to real parents. My grandfather James used to sit me on his lap and tell me all kinds of stories; after my mother died I was a little too big to put on his lap. Too big for the lap maybe, but never too big for the stories, he used to tell me the stories every night sitting on my bed, until I fell asleep.

For a 12-year-old girl dealing with the death of her mother, it was the only thing that kept me sane. Every time my grandfather looked at me, you could see that I reminded him of my mother, his only daughter, and there was a deep sadness in his eyes that I feared would never leave him. One night my grandfather was sitting on the end of my bed, telling me a story about my mother and father. He had a great way of telling stories.

*   *   *

My grandfather started his story one night. "Well you see honey for years I believed you had a sister. I know I never saw her, but your father always called you Mel. And your mother always called you Beth. So see every time you came to visit, you liked to play hide and seek. And who were you hiding from? I don't know, but then I could hear your parents calling for you... MEL WHERE ARE YOU? BETH COME DOWN TO EAT. And when you did not answer, they would call for your sister. MEL BETH, MEL BETH; and so that's when I begun to understand that your sister, Melabeth, was better at hide and seek than you were."

As my grandfather told this ridiculous story, we were busting up with tears in our eyes. After that story, for the few short months I lived with him, he would come up to me when I was sad and say. "Hey Melabeth, everything going okay?" And then he gave me a big old wink.

No matter how many times he did that, it brought a little smile to my face. The story made me forget about my mother for a minute or two and wonder where my sister was hiding.

My father's parents were good people but a little on the flaky side. It was on a weekend visiting them that my father picked me up and took me to California.

*   *   *

So here I am sitting in the back of an old Chevy Impala that was probably brand-new when they shoved me in the ground in 1975, and in the front seat are either a couple of weird rednecks or perverts. Of course pervert is also spelled lunch for vampires, and I was kind of hungry.

After a long ride down back roads, the two men in the front smoking cigarettes and chitchatting about hunting, we finally pulled onto a dirt road. Jim looked back at me, and said something along the lines. "If you're awake, we're almost there."

Pretending to be asleep is no longer an option. As the car rocked back and forth down the old dirt road, between the ruts and poor suspension, I had to hold on for dear life. It was hard not to be thrown across the car.

Finally the car pulled up in front of an old wooden cabin. From the outside it didn't look to be much more than a shed with windows. It was square with four windows in the front and a small porch with antlers over the door. Boy, I didn't see that one coming; antlers, who would have guessed?

Jim shut off the car, got out and headed towards the cabin. Dave opened his door, then turned around and looked at me and said. "Come inside; it's nice and warm. This may take a few... and I don't want you to shiver."

Oh sure just need to grab some stuff. Of course I didn't mind going along with this. I think in another life it would have been scary, but this was exciting. So I responded, and tried my hardest to sound hesitant and a little fearful. "Okay... I guess... you guys are not going to take too long are you? I mean I need to get to the bus stop. I am kind of in a hurry." And then I couldn't help myself and added. "And no one knows where I am."

I guess I sounded hesitant and scared enough to Dave, because he was already to reassure me. "We'll hurry lickety-split. I just don't want you to get cold, and you'll be nice and warm if you come on in."

"Alright," I agreed. Wow, they must think I'm stupid.

As I got out of the warm car and followed Dave up to the cabin, I could see smoke starting to puff out of the chimney. Probably a human wouldn't be able to see the smoke. It was a moonless night, but you have to be an idiot to believe that a cabin in the forest was already warmer before we got there.

I followed Dave into the cabin. When I came in through the door, he shut it behind me, and I could hear him locking the door. It was cold in the cabin. Jim was standing over a fresh fire that he just started. Not only that, but I could tell from the smell and the look of things, that no one had been here for days.

Dave ushered me over to a gross looking little loveseat. I sat down, and then Jim came over and sat right next to me. At this point, it was really, really hard to keep the smile off of my face.

They may not be bikers, but for tonight they will do.

Chapter 3
All My Friends Are In
Dead Places

I love running through the forest at night with my hair flying behind me and wearing nothing as the cold air wraps around my naked body.

I was in a hurry; Jim was getting away. I really screwed up.

All this power and I don't know how to fight. Slipping through the trees at high speed I could feel myself losing it. I couldn't stop worrying about Jim escaping me. I was running to fast, I jumped up onto a low lying branch.

I had my legs bent so that my butt was on my heels, my arms straight over my chest with my hands holding onto the branch. I took a calming breath and then another one. Smelling the air, I could taste the smell of Jim's Old Spice and cigarettes. I looked into the direction of the smell; I understood what direction he went in.

Now I could tell where there was a path. Now that I have calmed a little, I can track him. I can't make mistakes, not like at the cabin. I started to run toward the smell.

As I ran, my mind wandered back to what happened at the cabin.

*   *   *

Jim was sitting next to me on the loveseat, and Dave took residency across from us in an old recliner. I guess Dave had forgotten that we were here to grab a couple of items because he was all relaxed in his chair.

Dave and Jim both cracked open a couple of beers, lit up cigarettes, and started bullshitting back and forth. The next thing that I knew they were trying to strike up a conversation with me.

It didn't take long before the conversation became real creepy. They wanted to know if I was a virgin. I played stupid and nervous. Then they started to offer money for me to take off my clothes. Of course, I refused. And then they threatened me, so I pretended to be scared. Then I did what they asked, and walked across the room to take off my clothes.

Now I wasn't scared; I was excited because I felt the way these men felt about hunting animals in the wild. I knew I was stronger and faster, but I was also inexperienced.

I was about to find out how much.

The cabin was basically one big room with a fireplace on one wall. There was a loft in the roof of the cabin; the staircase came down almost in the middle of the room. The bottom of the staircase came to a landing that leads to the rear of the cabin. The staircase acted like a wall that separated the cabin and made it feel like more than one space. On the other side of the staircase were a washing basin, refrigerator, stove and a few cabinets. That made it kind of a makeshift kitchen.

The bathroom appeared to be outside where an old outhouse was. This was serious rustic living. I'd never taken into account that all my speed would be hard to use against them in such a small area.

I had never been in a fight in my life. I just had to take these two guys out fast. I'd never been around men that knew how to hunt and kill. I started off on the right foot; I wanted them off guard; that's why I stood there taking off my clothes, throwing them into the corner of the room. My nakedness would distract them, and I wouldn't mess up my dress.

After I was naked, Jim walked up to me and put his arms around me. He kept talking about how he wasn't going to hurt me or make me do anything I didn't want to do; he just wanted me to be warm.

When he started trying to kiss me, I knew that the game was up. I wasn't going to be able to take one of them off into another room, so I decided to take them both on at the same time.

So I spun Jim around and tried to bite the back of his neck. I was a little surprised; I was pushed back by Dave, and then all hell broke loose.

I clawed at Dave first, but he stepped back. I swung into the air. Then I took a punch to the face from Jim.

I was able to take the damage, but it still hurt. It was a full on brawl: punching, clawing, kicking, and throwing each other around the room.

It didn't help that they still were wearing all their clothes. They were wearing thick winter jackets. Every time I clawed them, I just ripped up their clothes; my punches and kicks where softened against their heavy outfits. Even though they had the extra protection, I was still beating the hell out of them.

At the same time, I was taking a beating too. The room was too small to maneuver, and all my extra strength was offset by their weight. When I grabbed hold of one, the other one would pull me off, and throw me into the wall or the floor.

The few pieces of furniture were tossed all over the room. I picked up the recliner and threw it at one of the men smashing a large hole in the wall.

I would have kicked their asses if I knew how to fight; just watching them beat me up was a learning experience. I was seeing all kinds of things I didn't know: the way you swing to punch, how to use a person's weight against them, and how to avoid a punch or kick.

I couldn't recall how long this went on, but, at one point, I got on Jim's back and bit his neck. He ripped me off; my fangs where still attached to his throat, causing it to tear his skin open. Blood sprayed everywhere.

He turned around and shoved me into the wall. I pushed myself off the wall to attack again when a loud noise, followed by what felt like the hand of God punching me.

The right side of my chest was hit hard. I slammed against the wall and fell down into a slump.

It took me a second to realize that Dave was standing over me with a shotgun. I lay perfectly still, while I felt my body stop the bleeding. Then it started to put itself back together again.

I knew I could get up in only a few seconds after being shot, but I thought I should play dead or take a chance of getting shot into pieces. I didn't know how much damage I could take before I would finish dying and wasn't ready to test it.

This fight was not going so well. I needed a minute to revise my plan of attack.

*   *   *

As I was thinking of my giant screw up. I was running toward Jim's scent. Hopefully I would catch up to him before he made it to a house or car.

I stopped running at the bottom of a tree; the forest appeared to be black and white which meant it was real dark where I was standing. It also meant that humans couldn't see me; directly ahead of me I could see Jim hiding in what appeared to be a hideaway for hunting.

He was doing something, behind the camouflage, but I planned on being careful and not making a mistake. I can't underestimate this man like I did earlier.

*   *   *

Remembering back to being shot, I was playing dead.

Dave checked to make sure I was dead, and then he went to check on Jim. I came up with a new plan to end this.

Jim had grabbed a rag and pressed it to Jim's neck while he muttered loud curses. Dave had turned his back to me, and was holding the shotgun by the barrel; the stock rested on the floor. Dave used his free hand to help Jim, while Jim was sitting on the edge of the overturned loveseat.

Dave hovered over him saying. "Just let me take a look at it; she got you good."

Jim replied with pain in his voice. "You fool; I can't believe you shot her… she was gorgeous. We could have handled her."

Dave looked at him, and said. "She was unnatural, Jim." Then, in a whisper. "She had the devil in her."

I had enough of talk. Time to show Jim that Dave is right and I have the devil in me. I stood up and went toward Dave.

My body had repaired everything but my right tit. It was still missing; thank goodness that everything grows back. I hate to be uneven.

I was only a few feet behind Dave when I let out a loud hissing scream. Dave spun around in surprise; so far so good.

I could tell which leg he was putting most of his weight on. I dropped onto one knee, and with all the strength I had, my arm swung out in a large arc. It made contact with the side of his knee; the sound of breaking bones filled my ear.

He fell to the floor.

In the same moment, I grabbed his shotgun from his other arm. Once I had the rifle, I stood up. Then I swung it like a bat, right on top of Dave's head, only I kind of missed and hit his back.

Nonetheless he went to the ground.

I swung the rifle around in my arms until it was pointing where Jim was. Jim was gone. He had dashed out the front door as I took out his buddy. I ran out the door after him; this is the part where I underestimated him again.

As soon as I stepped out the door, he slammed me in the chest with this huge hunting knife. I dropped the shotgun while I was falling backwards from the blow of the blade. He had stuck the knife right through my last good tit, right where my heart is. I landed on my back unable to breathe.

Lucky for me that's not a requirement.

Jim wasted no time. He was already bending over to get hold of the shotgun. Using my arms I pushed up from the ground-staying vertical, and then kicked Jim in the side as I flew through the air. I heard him let out a loud yelp as he flew off the front porch, and landed on the ground.

After that maneuver; I had landed back on my back. I sat up immediately to see Jim getting back up off the ground.

Staring at me with eyes of bewilderment, he searched his pockets for something and then ran off into the woods; I figured he probably was looking for his car keys. I needed to catch him and keep him from getting away; this whole situation was so out of hand.

At that point I stood up and yanked the knife out of my chest. I heard a noise from behind me. Dave was getting back up, but this time was the last time. I ran over, jumped on his back and sank my fangs into his neck.

I fed on him until he was dead. It took me 10 minutes to finish Dave off. I didn't get to enjoy him as much as I would have liked knowing that every second gave Jim more time to get away.

So now here I am standing across the clearing as Jim readies himself.

I must be careful; if that would've been a wooden stake, I'd be dead. At least I believe I would be dead. I don't know which legends about vampires are true and not true; but, just like the blood, stakes seem to always kill vampires.

I am hoping Jim hasn't figured out what I am, but I wouldn't be surprised if he's guessed. At any rate he's liable to try a wooden stake or dynamite, anything that might finish me off. And I don't know what he has in that hideaway. It took me 10 minutes to finish off Dave and at least that long to track Jim down.

I could smell the blood from his neck but not as strong as before. So I figured he must have used some of that time to bandage himself up. The remaining time he could have been up to anything.

So I quietly moved around in the shadows, circling his little hunting hut. It's awful quiet and he's not making a lot of noise. Now that I have eaten, the healing went even faster, and I could breathe without labor. All my cuts where gone; my right tit grew back. My breasts were not big, but I would have missed one.

So, I whistled and let the images fill my mind. Also I was still hoping that human ears could not pick up the frequency. So far there was no stir from inside the hut. I'm guessing he could not hear me. My second sight could not see through the hut walls; it gave me a great 360° panorama of what was around me, but it did not allow me to see through objects. Finally I heard some movement.

In one giant leap, Jim burst out of the hut with a hatchet in one hand and a wooden stake in the other. Well I guess that answers several questions. First, he had bandaged his wound. Second, he had been spending his time whittling, because, he had guessed what I was.

Letting out a wild cry, Jim yelled out into the woods. "Bring it on devil… I'll send you back to hell, whore… I ain't afraid of no hell bitch!"

I was off to Jim's right side. Still standing in the darker shadows, I replied in a low purr. "Now, now there Jim; that doesn't sound like a man, that's not afraid."

Jim spun to his right. Now he was facing me, but I could tell by the way he was straining his eyes, that he still couldn't see me. He said with a loud mean voice, "Bring it on HELL BITCH; AND I WILL SHOW YOU FEAR!"

I giggled, and then said. "I thought we were going to have sex? Take off your clothes, and we'll make love not war; that's what my parents always said."

Jim, still trying to see into the dark, spit out his reply. "You come on out of there. I will send you straight to hell where all those hippies are waiting for you. Come on whore. What are you waiting for?"

He was trying to chide me into coming out to make the first move. I had the advantage in the dark shadows. He could not see and I could. No, I couldn't go into the field and face him. Now that I knew that I don't know how to fight, he'll hold nothing back. I have to figure out how to get him to attack me in the dark.

I do have some time to figure this out; it's only about midnight. I shouldn't rush this and get myself killed. My mother used to tell me. "Beth, remember this; never make a decision faster than you have to. Take all the time that's allotted to you."

Yes, I will take my time; sometimes you make fast decisions because you have to. Sometimes we make fast decisions because we choose to; those are the same decisions that we come to regret. There'll be no regret tonight.

Jim was rattling off a string of insults and curses at me. I could see that he was standing in a clearing with only the light of the stars. All around him were black shadows; some of them were too dark for me to see into. My second sight allowed me to see even clearer, even in the darkest areas of the woods.

I made a simple plan, harass him until he makes a run into the woods. And there I can attack him in the dark where I have all the advantages. I looked at a spot behind him. That's a good place to start; all I had to do was get over there.

Where am I?

I was now standing in a different location; Jim's yelling let me know he was behind me. I spun around, and there he was. He was yelling into the forest at where I had been, and now I am behind him. What happened; did I teleport or something?

All I did was concentrate on where I wanted to be and, bam, here I am. That's cool; Jim was still yelling, but I didn't even care. I had to try this again. I concentrated on the spot I was at a minute ago; it didn't look like it was working.

Okay, I will concentrate on that place, and then I will try to move there.

Wait, where am I? Okay that is official; this is a little disorienting. I am now standing where I started from. I was paying more attention this time. So, when it happened, I noticed there was blurring as I traveled, so I don't think I was teleporting. It was more like moving so fast that my eyes couldn't catch the image. It reminded me of a card trick. The hand is faster than the eye.

I will have fun playing with this new power of mine; a new plan popped into my head, how to deal with Jim.

I turned to face Jim who was saying. "Bring it on, whore; come on, give me your best shot!"

I let out a giggle and said, "Ready or not here I come"

With that, I moved behind him with what I am now calling my flash power; I let out a giggle, and said. "I am going to get you."

Jim spun around, and I could see the confusion in his face. With a loss of confidence, he said. "What the hell? YOU ARE THE DEVIL… Dave was right… DEVIL WHORE."

I flashed to a new location, and said. "We're both monsters, Jim, and one of us is going to die."

Jim spun around to my new location, but before he could reply, I had flashed again to a spot behind him, and said. "Guess? Guess who is going to die?"

Jim spun around to face me again, but this time he wasn't talking to me; instead he was praying. "Dear God; please save me from this… Devil whore… help me. I swear… I will repent for all the evil I have done. Jesus, don't let this happen."

I flashed to a new spot, and this time I just laughed as evil as I could; every time I flashed to a new location, I would laugh, and Jim would spin around trying to keep me in front of him.

It only took a few minutes before Jim was out of breath. He stopped spinning and started to pray to God. God had no intention of helping him. God didn't save me from bad men, and God wasn't going to save a bad man from me.

I guess I am not good at multi tasking because, when I was thinking about how God wasn't going to help this man, it brought up thoughts of my death, and now I am lying on my back. I was heading to a new point to laugh at Jim. I wasn't paying enough attention to where I was going. I slammed right into a low lying branch; it clothes-lined me right at my neck.

I was moving so fast I didn't even have time to register what happened. The branch broke right off from the tree making a loud noise; at the same time it scared Jim enough that he jumped back a few steps.

It hurt, but only for a minute; the pain in this body was like that. At first it hurt, but even before the wounds went away, the pain did. Like the cold, pain was just info and nothing more.

I picked up the branch and threw it at Jim. I couldn't believe how far and hard I threw that branch. It caught Jim right in the chest; he fell onto his back. Letting out a string of curses, he grabbed his stake that he dropped when he hit the ground. He was able to keep hold of the hatchet in his other hand; he quickly jumped to his feet.

It would have been a good time to have charged him, but I hadn't planned that out. Throwing things at Jim gave me a new idea. I picked up a nice size rock off of the ground.

It was a game to me, a sick and twisted game throwing a rock at Jim, then flashing to a new location and doing it again. I felt like a little girl playing a mean trick. I did know better, but I was still enjoying myself.

I don't know if this dark side of me was because I was a vampire, raped and killed or just a part about myself that I never had the power to act upon before. Nonetheless, here I was, flashing from one spot to another, stoning Jim to death.

Jim screamed or yelped every time a rock hit him. He was down on his knees after half dozen rocks hit him. I threw one that caught him in the side of the head. It didn't knock him out, but it dazed him enough that he dropped his weapons. Blood was now gushing out of his head.

It was time to stop playing with Jim. I moved in behind him with blinding speed; grabbing his arms to his side, I held him around his chest. Then, without any more hesitation, I bit into the side of his neck.

The blood was filling my mind once more; it was truly bliss. My mind was full of pleasure drinking the blood. It was over before I wanted it to be.

I lifted Jim's body off the ground; and headed back to the cabin. It was amazing how light Jim's body was, minus the blood, I enjoyed the walk back even though I was carrying a dead man over my shoulder.

The woods were not lost to me. I enjoyed the forest. With my new senses I could hear and see all the little animals; it was amazing. I returned to the cabin in no time at all.

Running through the forest chasing Jim had felt like a great distance. I guess I was afraid that Jim would escape. It made time slow down; now that I was relaxed, I realized that Jim didn't get very far at all. As I came into what was left of the cabin, I dropped Jim's dead body on the floor, not too far from Dave's. I looked around wishing these rednecks would have put in a nice shower with hot water. I don't need hot water; I just like hot water.

"Thank you."

Did I just hear thank you? I spun around and didn't see anything. It had sounded like a woman, no, a girl. It had sounded like, thank you. Well, that's official; I was losing it. Wait, make that lost it, or maybe I never had it to begin with.

Just as I was thinking I had an overactive imagination, I caught movement up in the loft. I couldn't see up there. I listened; I couldn't hear anyone.

I used my second sight and whistle, but I could not make out the shape of a body.

There were a couple of beds up there. There were also two dressers and two end tables; one of the tables had a lamp on it. The other table had an assortment of stuff scattered across the top of it. The only way that I couldn't see someone up there is if they were hiding under one of the beds.

Well, I guess I will have to check; ok I am a vampire; why is it that I am all spooked? I need a moment; if someone is up there, they will have to wait.

I went over and picked up my dress that I had tossed into the corner of the room. Thank goodness that none of the blood spray got on it. I went to the little makeshift kitchen. I placed my dress on a little round dining table.

There was a big stainless steel sink, big enough for my entire body, probably used for cleaning their kills. Oh well, I jumped in and washed all the blood off with the little spray hose. Pleasant surprise, they have hot water. I hopped out, dried off and got dressed, turned and looked at the bottom of the staircase. Ok coward, time to investigate.

I was three quarters up the staircase, and just high enough that my eyes were level with the floor of the loft. I could now see under both beds. There was nothing but dust under them. Wow, I need a friend; I am going crazy; there is no one up here. I walked all the way up to the top of the stairs… empty beds. I turned to go back down the stairs.

Who is that? Right down in the room, a girl was standing. She was looking down and staring at the two dead bodies.

She looked to be about my height and build. She had on jeans, cowgirl boots, and western style shirt. She was pretty with brown hair that hung just past her shoulders with just a little bit of curl; unlike mine, straight as a ruler. The only thing that was missing was a big old cowgirl hat and a giant buckle for her belt.

Well how did she come into this cabin without me hearing her, and that's not all. I have been practicing like crazy with my second sight. I am always letting out a little whistle to look around me.

I whistled again, and there was no one there. How can that be? Sound bounces off of the body and comes back to my ears… whoa, hold the phone. Now that I have been watching her for a minute, I can see through her.

Of course, my luck is unbreakable. Of course, there is a ghost in this cabin. If my luck stays true, she will want to haunt me for killing redneck perverts.

I didn't know what to say. I just decided to see if she could speak to me and find out what she wanted. "I just want you to know that I am not afraid of no ghosts."

The girl looked up at me in surprise but then started laughing.

"What's so funny?" I said.

She stopped laughing, and said. "That's the line from Ghostbusters; you're pretty funny aren't you?"

"What?" I replied, what on earth is a Ghostbuster?

"Oh, I am sorry, how rude. Like my mom didn't teach me no manners or anything. My name is Carrie; I am just so happy you can see and hear me. How is that anyway?" The ghost just keeps on talking while she asked questions "And thank you for killing these guys; maybe I will be at rest soon. Don't you think? Or do you think I have to wait until daytime or something? Oh, wait you probably don't know that I disappear during the day, do you? Every time they bring a girl up here I hide up in the loft. Boy, I wish I could leave this shithole; can you leave? I thought they were going to kill you; boy did it surprise me when you started fighting them. Where did you learn to fight like that? I have seen my brothers fight but not like that. Boy, Oh boy, can you hold your own. Have you been in a lot of fights? Just listen to me prattle on and on and not let you add a word in edgewise, didn't I? My mother said I could talk a rooster into not crowing. What you think she meant by that? She was always sayin stuff that didn't make a lick of sense. Don't take this the wrong way or anything; what are you? I reckon it ain't any of my business or anything…"

I couldn't take it. I held my hand palm forward and said "I am a vampire, and my name is Melabeth. I know the dead have no need to breath, but I fear for you, that you might suffocate; one question at a time please."

The girl looked a little ashamed and said, "I am sorry; just ever since these guys killed me, I haven't had anyone… Sorry I don't mean to be a bother."

"No that's okay," I said, feeling a little like an ass now, but I went on by saying, "I haven't had anyone to talk to for a long time either; sorry, please don't get upset; I would love to talk to you."

The ghost gave me a big smile, "I wasn't going anywhere. Well, technically, I can't anyway. I can never go more than a few hundred feet from the cabin, and I disappear during the day. I don't even know where I go; as soon as the sun comes up, BAM, it is night again."

"I have never heard of a daytime haunting." I said to Carrie. "I wonder what the significance of night for the dead is?"

Carrie said. "Not sure. Haven't met any other ghosts; hell, you're the first person I have been able to speak to for the last year, not to say that I have had a lot of opportunity to try. The only folks that come around here are Dave, and Jeff and their victims. And I never can seem to warn them. Not that it would help; by the time they got them in this cabin, they ain't escapin."

Her deep southern accent made me think she wasn't from around here. So it seems these men hunted more than deer. I had to ask. "Did they rape you before killing you?"

The ghost image went out of focus as rage crossed her face. "Why the hell would that be any of your business?" She looked down at the floor and I could see the rage melt away to pain. "I just don't want to talk about that; you wouldn't understand. I didn't let them and we all can't fight like you. I didn't reckon it would be so dangerous to hitchhike without my boyfriend. We wanted to see a concert in Washington. We live in Georgia. See, it was my fault I got mad at Rick. Rick is my boyfriend, or he was. Probably goin with someone new, I got so mad at Rick when we reached Colorado; I stormed off and thought I could hitch to the concert by myself. Then, when he finally caught up to me at the show, he would be sorry. Only now I am the only one that is sorry."

I quickly clarified. "Oh… well the only reason I asked is that is the way I died, only a few nights ago. Well, technically it was fifteen years ago, but I was asleep in the ground. This is only my second night as a vampire, and I haven't had anyone to talk to about what happened to me."

The pain melted off of Carrie's face, and then she looked at me with understanding and said. "Well doesn't that make us two peas in a pod."

I realized that I was still standing at the top of the stairs, and neither of us had moved this entire time, so I asked. "Would you like to sit and talk? You don't have to."

Carrie smiled, and said. "I would like nothing better. Not that I ever need to sit."

I laughed. "Me too; I could stand forever, or it feels that way. It is all most impossible for me to describe."

Carrie walked around to the bottom of the staircase, and then started up to where I was standing. The closer she got to me the more solid she became. I moved into the loft area as she followed behind me. I took a seat on the edge of one of the beds. That's when I noticed Carrie looking at her hands with this strange look on her face.

"What on earth. I feel like I am alive, almost like I could touch something." Carrie said.

She looked solid enough to me, so I encouraged her. "Well, try to pick something up."

"Okay." Carrie responded.

She walked over to one of the end tables. She reached down and picked up an old pocketknife. She rolled it around in her hands and opened and then closed the blade. She looked over at me and said. "I have never been able to pick stuff up; with all my concentration the best I ever been able to do is move something." Then she got all excited and started with high-speed questions. "Do you think I will be able to wear new clothes? I have been wearing this outfit for a year, not that I stink or sweat. Do you think maybe I could leave this cabin with you? Would you let me come if I could? Do you think I will disappear during the day?"

I cleared my throat loudly; then she stopped and I said. "I am not sure if I have any answers for you, Carrie, but maybe we can figure out something together. And if you can come with me, you're welcome to."

"Thank you, Melabeth." Carrie said. Then she jumped over to me and gave me a hug, which was the strangest hug I have ever had. She felt solid, but at the same time she had no life to her. She pulled away and gave me a sheepish grin. I knew then that I had made my first friend.

On the way over to the cabin, Jim and Dave were playing some music in the car. I have never heard of any of the songs. Most of them were country, which I didn't care for much. The DJ on the radio said. And now for a new song, from Garth Brooks, Friends in Low Places.

I guess you can say that all my friends are in dead places.

Carrie and I stayed up all night talking about everything; also, we did some experiments to see what she could, and could not do. Then, as soon as the sun crested, she disappeared, right in front of me. I laid down on one of the beds in the loft; I was tired. As I rested my head against the pillow, I thought about all the things that me and Carrie did and talked about.

We both shared our experience of being murdered. After that wonderful conversation, we lightened the mood and talked about movies and music. I guess I have missed a ton of stuff. Go to find out the picture on that boy's blanket was from a movie called Star Wars. Carrie said, it was a must see; also, I guess when I said that I wasn't afraid of no ghost Carrie had started laughing, because I was quoting a movie called Ghostbusters. The president of the United States was George Bush, and he just took office from Ronald Reagan, the actor? That's hard to believe; I will have to check up on Carrie's information; she might be unreliable.

We spent a lot of time discovering her abilities. She was still unable to go more than 100 yards away from the cabin. The further she got away from me, the less solid she became; the strongest she got was in the back of the cabin. It only took a minute for Carrie to realize she was the strongest when we stood over the spot where the men had buried her body.

At first, I thought maybe this was why there were no more ghosts at the cabin, that the men had buried the rest of their victims further away. Carrie informed me that all the victims were buried behind the cabin because these men were sooo lazy. So it didn't make a lot of sense to me why she was the only victim haunting the men, and why she was not at peace now.

I promised Carrie that I would sleep here and see if she returned the next night. I don't know why I promised, seeing as I need to get back to California, but she is my only friend. I hope she doesn't come back. I hate to leave her at this cabin all alone, and it was obvious that my vampire power somehow gives her power to feel and touch again. How can I take that from her? Well, I need to get sleep; with rest, I will be able to think clearer. Hopefully, I will be able to work all this out tomorrow night.

I woke up around three in the afternoon. The clothes I had on seemed fine. Now that I don't sweat, and my skin has no oil; changing clothes seemed optional. I woke up with an idea on how to deal with the mess downstairs. So I zipped down the staircase. I looked down at the two dead bodies. I didn't want to leave a trail. I had to make this seem to be an easily solved case for the police. If cops were half as lazy as my father used to tell me they were, I have an idea.

I picked up the shotgun and I shot Jim's dead body on the floor, then I laid the shotgun next to Dave's body. I went over to my bag and took out the gun that I had stolen. I stood next to Jim's body and fired four rounds into Dave's body. Then I stuck the gun into Jim's dead hand. Now this probably would not work if I left this cabin the way it was.

My thinking is that, first, they will link that gun to the house I broke into. Second, I will dig up some of their victims behind the cabin. My hope is that the cops will realize that these men were kidnapping girls, then raping and killing them. Also they will think they have been robbing houses in the area. This insures that they will pin every unsolved crime on these guys.

If I am right, the cops will not really care to solve their murders. After all, these are the bad guys. So they will come to the conclusion that they got into a fight over moving the dead girls' bodies and killed each other. Case closed.

Part two of my plan; I really didn't look forward to. I found a shovel behind the cabin in a little storage locker. Soon I was digging in the spot that Carrie pointed out the night before. It didn't take long to find her bones around her mud-stained rags. Her feet still had her cowboy boots on; also I could see shredded pieces of her jeans.

If it wasn't for my sunglasses, I wouldn't be able to see anything, it was a bright sunny day with few clouds and no wind; it was also very cold. As I looked across the ground, it didn't take me long to find three more graves. One of the graves was real obvious, I think, because it was dug recently. I would have never found these graves if the snow hadn't melted here.

Here I am now standing over four dug up graves; the bodies were at different stages of decomposing. Carrie and another girl were nothing but bones; one of the other girls still had flesh around her bones. The girl that was buried in the newest grave had just started to decompose. I could still clearly see her face and her red hair; none of the girls were more than three feet deep.

I don't think these guys worried too much about anyone coming around and finding them, and, most likely, because this was a hunting cabin, it wouldn't have raised any alarms to smell rotting flesh.

I shoved the end of the shovel into one of the mounds of dirt and dusted off my hands. I looked at Carrie's remains one more time, and a thought came to mind. What if I picked up Carrie's bones and put them in a bag? Then maybe she could come with me.

As I bent over to collect Carrie bones, something caught my eye as the afternoon sun shone down on Carrie's remains; I could see something shimmering from her neck. I got down on my knees to get a closer look; it was a necklace. I reached down to grab it.

When I touched the necklace, it shocked the tip of my fingers. "Ouch" I said out loud. It was more of a knee jerk reaction, because it really didn't hurt. It felt like static shock but somehow different.

I reached down again, this time ready for the shock. It shocked me again, but this time I didn't pull back. It really wasn't shocking me as much has tinkling the tip of my fingers. It almost felt like a low voltage of electric current was going through the necklace.

It took me a minute to work the chain around to undo the clasp, and then I was able to slide the chain out without disturbing Carrie's bones. Once I got the necklace off of Carrie's neck, I stood up and walked into the cabin to wash off the dirt, so I could get a better look at it.

After washing the necklace off, I went up the stairs to the loft where I took off my sunglasses, there were no windows up in the loft. I could see a lot better without all the blinding light. The necklace was silver, and the chain had thick links. The pendant was silver and shaped like a half gallon glass milk bottle. On each side were carved markings. The markings looked as if they were glowing green.

It was really a striking necklace, and from human eyes they may see it as a pretty piece of jewelry with strange green symbols on it. With my eyes, I could see or maybe feel the power coming out of this piece of jewelry.

In fact, it would surprise me if this were not the reason for Carrie's predicament. A cursed necklace comes to mind. When she reappears, which I am sure she will, I will have to ask where she got this from.

I put the necklace around my neck and grabbed my bag. It was only a few hours before dark. If I am right, I don't need to wait for Carrie; as soon as the sun goes down, she will reappear right next to me. If she is attached to this necklace, then I am giving this necklace power; all I have to do is wear it. I will have me a friend to keep me company.

I headed back down the dirt road where the men had taken me to the cabin. I traveled at least five miles through the forest before I came to a small country road. On one side of the road ran an old barbed wire fence bordering a field. I have to say this was beautiful country; the sun was starting to set so everything had a red tint.

I laid my bag on the ground and sat down on a fallen tree; I figured I would wait here for Carrie. Hopefully, I am right about this necklace; otherwise, I will have to walk back up to the cabin. I will find out in a few minutes.

As soon as the sun went behind the trees, Carrie faded into existence right in front of me. She looked, at me then spun around confused; then I said. "Well goodnight to you, Carrie, looks like you will be following me around for awhile."

Carrie looked at me, and then said. "Well I'll be a monkey's uncle, or aunt. You figured out how to free me from the cabin. So how did you do that? And where are we going? And do you think I will ever pass over to the other side? Or do you think I am stuck here forever? Or maybe I still have unfinished work; do you think that's it?"

I laughed at her. "I don't know about unfinished work, more like unfinished questions. I think it will be nice to have you with me, I think, to answer just a few of your ongoing questions. You will need to tell me what you know about this." I pulled the necklace out of my shirt and showed it to her.

This also was the first time I realized something else. When she reappeared as a ghost, she was dressed and looked just the way she did when she had died. Only one thing was different, no necklace.

Carrie's eyes opened wide. "Well, I wondered where that was; that's my necklace. Where did you find it? I thought those guys stole it and hocked it or something. Was it in the cabin? Or did you find it in one of the men's pockets? Oh, wait, I bet it was in a drawer I couldn't open. Wasn't it?"

Boy, she was going to be hard to get used to. I stuck my hand out in front of me holding one finger up and said, "And, if you stop asking the same question in different ways, I would be able to tell you. I found it on your dead bones, which I dug up. Before you go off into a parade of questions, I would like to start walking. To answer one of your early questions, we are going to California for a little R and R which stands for Revenge and Retaliation."

Carrie jumped up and down in excitement, and then she squealed out, "California, I have always wanted to go there! Do you think we will see movie stars?"

This is going to be fun, I thought sarcastically, and then I looked at an overexcited Carrie and said, "Let us start walking; grab my bag and carry, it Carrie. Then you can live up to your name."

She gave me a look, then crossed her arms over her chest and said. "Why should I?"

I gave her an evil smile, and said, "Figures, another question, Carrie you're attached to this necklace. Wherever this necklace is, you are. If it is near me, then I give you power to become solid. Or I could toss this into the woods, and you could haunt the forest for the next thousand years, unable to touch anything, with no one to talk to. Or you could pick that bag up, choices, choices."

Carrie dropped her arms from her chest in defeat, and said, "Wow, you're mean." She then went over and picked up my bag. As she tossed it around her shoulder, she continued by saying, "Better to be a slave than alone; okay, Melabeth, after you, but I have a few questions for you."

Well, don't that figure.

So we walked down the old country road talking. I will admit to myself only that I was really enjoying Carrie's company. After about 2 hours, or 4235 Carrie words, we finally walked to a major road, where I was sure we could hitch a ride to Grand Junction. From there, I should have enough money to get both of us a bus ticket to LA. If I go during the day, I wouldn't have to buy Carrie's ticket.

The only concern I had was that I was already hungry again. I will have to try to feed on someone without killing them. I guess, if I think about it. I had to eat three or four times a day when I was alive. I shouldn't be shocked that I have to eat every night. Too bad there was no drive through Blood Banks. I did get to hear the story on how Carrie came to own this necklace, and boy did it make me think.

According to Carrie, she had taken this necklace from her dead Grandma who had forbidden her from ever having it in the first place. It all started when she was little and visiting her Grandma. She was sneaking through her Grandma's stuff when she found it in a wooden box; she fell in love with it immediately. She put it around her neck and was looking at herself in the mirror when her Grandma came into the room.

I guess Carrie's Grandma was always sweet and nice. So she never understood why other members of the family would call her a witch. When her Grandma saw her wearing the necklace, she had a fit. She told Carrie she could never wear or play with this necklace again. When Carrie asked why, Grandma said it was because it was cursed.

A few years later, her Grandma was killed in a car accident; Carrie had never stopped thinking about that necklace. So, as soon as her and her mother went over to Grandma's house, she found the necklace and shoved it into her pocket. She never told her mother, even though her mom later was looking for the necklace. Knowing her mom was on the hunt for it, she always wore it under her shirt when she was at home.

Her Grandma was a witch, and this necklace was cursed. I told Carrie the best thing we could do is try to find a witch and see if we could free her. Of course this was secondary to my R and R.

I stuck my thumb out and a big car pulled off of to the side of the road. Carrie had laid my bag on the ground; I didn't wait for her; I picked it up. I ran up to the car, opened the back door and tossed in my bag. Carrie jumped in and I followed.

There was an old man with white hair in the front seat; he was turned around facing me. His glasses were huge and thick; boy I hope we make it.

The old man said with a kind old voice, "A young girl should not be hitchhiking all by herself. Now I am not trying to tell you what to do or anything; it's just dangerous. So where are you heading?"

Carrie looked over at me and said, "Well I may be solid, but unless his glasses aren't thick enough. I am still invisible."

Carrie was always a loud person, and this was no exception; the old man gave me a strange look and said. "What was that, sweetheart? I couldn't make out what you said. You going to have to speak up; these old ears don't work as well as they used to."

I gave the old man a smile, and said, "Sorry, I talk softly sometimes; I am going to Grand Junction bus station. How far can you take me?"

The old man turned around and started to pull back onto the road, and said, "I will take you straight up to the front door of the bus station, honey. I couldn't sleep at night if I didn't know you were safe. By the way my name is John. What's yours?"

"Melabeth, and thank you very much for your kindness." I replied. Well, I knew two things. One, I would have to wait for the bus station to get something to eat. And two, I will not be able to have Carrie carry my bag for me. Now she is completely useless. Well, I would never tell Carrie this, but it is nice she does all the talking.

I don't want to be alone.

Chapter 4
David

David Drye Journal February 4, 1990

    I haven't bothered to write anything down for awhile now. I have been too angry with the world, and my Dad. Or should I be calling him Peter, for disowning me for nothing. It has always been a mystery to me that Peter always freaked out every time something strange happened.

    My Dad is great, fun, funny and kind. He manages the apartment building that we live in and everyone loves him. Yet it seems like the older I have been getting the weirder he acts whenever I say that something out of the ordinary has happened.

    I used to go visit my mother in California often when I was little. Now strange stuff was always going on there and that's why I stopped visiting my mother by the time I turned 12. I would tell my father about what happened at Mom's and then my father fought with my Mom and I haven't visited her for two years now. I am just one month from my 16th birthday and now I am being forced to go live with her.

    I guess that's why my father had a problem with me being strange. I must have reminded him too much of my mother. I really did miss Mom and it would be kind of cool to see my half sister and step sister. It's kind of messed up that the only reason I get to see mom, is because of events out of my control.

    I should journal what happened to me in the first place. That way in the future I could read this again and still not understand why this is all my fault. According to Peter, this was time for my mother to deal with me and that he wasn't equipped to deal with me. What on earth does he mean by that? I asked him what he meant and he never really answered me. He just said something along the lines of, your mother will explain everything to you, I can't, and you wouldn't understand if it came from me blah blah blah… Well of course I can't understand when you will not talk straight to your only son; how can I understand anything? And now it will all be made sense to me by my crazy mother, when I only talk to her on the phone once a month.

    I can't see how three black kids jumping me outside of our building could be grounds for removal. And that is one of those times a strange thing happened. The three gangbangers had caught me trying to take a short cut through the park. I know it was stupid, and I knew better than to go that way. I didn't even see them until it was too late. I tried to run but one of the kids caught me and shoved me to the ground; I jumped back up to my feet only to find that I was surrounded. They shoved and kicked me calling me names. I was so scared but then I closed my eyes. I got mad, that's all; I just wished I could make them feel my fear. I opened my eyes and was ready to fight them. That's when I made the strange thing happen.

They all started screaming, like a bunch of girls. I was amazed, as they ran away screaming like hellhounds were after them. I went home kind of laughing to myself. That evening after my father got back in he had a date with Sue, their second evening out. I think he may be going for a record. I was just finishing my homework and was about to watch some TV, when the doorbell rang.

My father answered it. I looked up the hallway to see my Dad letting in some police officers. It wasn't the first time the cops had come by. Sometimes there were problems around the building and the police would want to talk to the building manager. I even remembered when there was a murder in one of the apartments.

This time the cops were not here for the building, but to talk to me. In short the gangbangers had ran to their homes and hid in their closets. All three kids did the same thing and they didn't live together or anything. After about an hour of telling the cops over and over again, I didn't do shit to those guys. The police finally left.

After that is when my Dad lost it. And the very next day he announced that I was going back to my mother's. She lives in Beaumont CA, or also know has blowmont. The wind blows 360 days of the year. At least I will never have to comb my hair again.

*   *   *

After the old man had dropped me and Carrie off at the bus station, I went over and bought a ticket to San Bernardino, California. The bus didn't leave until nine o'clock the next day. It was kind of nice when the sun came up; I was ready for a Carrie break. I slipped onto the bus and there was only one seat open. I sat down without making a noise.

Here I am reading over the boy's shoulder, and apparently he doesn't know I am here. Some might think it is bad manners to read someone else's journal; then again, I don't need to listen to some other people's rules. Ok I am definitely making excuses to snoop into somebody else's journal; a.k.a. a boy's diary.
Well now that I am snooping, what he is going on about is really weird. Ok maybe I should try not to judge, but then again, judge and jury is my specialty. I can't help but notice the boy is my age, taller than me and cute. He has sandy blonde hair that was shaggy and hung almost to his neck. He has a good build, but I can't see his eyes, because they are concentrating on what he is writing. His pen stops moving and he looks out the window, lost in thought. He starts to write again:

*   *   *

Well I have had some suspicions of late concerning my mother and sisters; I think they know something about me. How else would I explain their strange behavior when I visited? It would not explain why my mother did not tell me.

I have done things that many would consider magic; whether or not that makes it magic is yet to be explored. I need to be careful of what I write down, it could be tragic to me if anyone else were to read it, for they are sure to believe me to be crazy.

*   *   *

As he finished writing his last sentence, it was hard to keep from laughing, for apparently I was making this tragic for him.

He turned and looked right at me. He froze, just staring at me with his pretty green eyes. At first, I thought he was staring at me like someone he just caught reading his journal. That was probably just a guilty conscience speaking, but then I noticed something else in his face.

He looked confused, then surprised and finally a little bit scared. I was still wearing my hoodie; I turned my head forward. The hoodie hung over enough so that now we had no eye contact. We only had stared at each other for a few seconds, but it was enough to make me feel uncomfortable. I wondered how I looked to people. Most people just seemed to be uncomfortable with me.

When he looked at me, it was like he could see me for what I was, and there was no question to it. The bus made a lot of noise as it began to move; at the same time, with my second sight, I could see David putting away his journal into his backpack. He then began to pull out something I had never seen before; it was hard not to turn my head to see it with my own eyes because my second sight just showed me shapes.

It looked like he was putting a small record into a walkman. I could make out the earphones he put over his head. Then, with my amazing hearing, when he started the music, it was like I was wearing those headphones myself. And the music was like nothing I had ever heard before. I loved it.

About a half hour later, David was still listening to music, looking out the bus window. He turned off the music; I really hated that he did that; I was really enjoying it. Then he looked over at me.

"No one sits that still," he said with a kind but careful voice. I didn't answer him; I didn't know what to say.

"My name is David… sorry for being rude earlier. You kind of surprised me; I am not used to people sneaking up on me." David said, still looking right at me. I wasn't sure if I should talk to him or not. After a minute, he turned his head back toward the bus window; he started to put his earphones back on.

"My name is Melabeth," I said quickly, before he had a chance to start up his music.

David turned his head toward me and said, "That's a cool name; I have never heard that name before."

"Well, I made it up" I said, still not looking at him.

David let out a laugh, it was wonderful. It made me turn and look at him. This time I didn't turn away from him. Wow, he was good looking; I could look at that all day long. On the other hand, the look on his face was a cross between scared and intrigued.

Then David said, "Those are the most amazing eyes that I have ever witnessed. They're the color of lightning, and I could swear that they belonged to an owl before you had them; they're huge… and pretty."

If I could have, I would have blushed. I had forgotten that I had taken off my sunglasses; I knew from looking in the mirror how strange my eyes were. The way he said it made me feel like giggling.

I kept the giggles in, and said, "thank you, your eyes are really pretty too." Well, I may not have giggled, but he is going to think I am retarded by my response. Big eyes, small brain.

He smiled at me, and I was captivated by him; then he said, "So where are you going?"

"California, and what did you mean by no one sits that still," I said a little worried that he might think me weird.

"Well… for the last half hour or so, you haven't moved one little inch. In fact I could swear you weren't even breathing." David said, trying to keep eye contact with me. I could see he was nervous just saying it.

Well, I had to wonder if he knew or guessed what I was. So I said, "How could you know; you have been staring out that window the entire time; you haven't looked my way even once." Well, there, I got him now, let's see him answer that.

"I could see you perfectly… from the reflection of the window." David said defensively, then added "wait, you never moved your head…how did… never mind."

He was now visibly nervous and unable to make eye contact with me. He turned his head and faced out the window.

"What's wrong? Did I say something to upset you?" Even though he was the one saying I was acting weird. And, yes, he was right; I was weird, but I am not sure he knows that I am not human.

He let out a breath, then turned and looked at me. "It's not you, it's me. I always do this. I meet someone, then I think something strange about them and next they don't want to hang with me. I have an overactive imagination. That's what my father says."

"You didn't upset me." I smiled and said, "Relax, and trust me when I say, there are things out there that defy belief. You may just be seeing things that everyone else is turning a blind eye to."

David looked at me and gave me a smirk, then said, "I see… so you were reading over my shoulder."

I laughed a little bit and said, "Now why would you think a thing like that? I do believe your dad may be right about that overactive imagination."

David said, "That wasn't a denial. If you didn't read it, then I think I should let you know that strange things happen to me. And sometimes I see things. It's really hard to explain, but I look at people and sometimes, it's like I can see their soul under their skin. When I look at you... well" he started to blush. "It's like your soul is on the outside; you seem like you're magical or something. See, I told you I don't make a lot of sense." I could see his embarrassment.

I reached over and gently laid my hand on his hand. David froze; I then said, "you make sense, you make sense to me." David turned his head back toward me and looked at me with a look that I couldn't figure out. "You seemed like you were going to say something else when you said, "when, I look at you.""

David, with that strange look in his eyes, said, "I was going to say that you were beautiful beyond compare." He looked down at our hands touching, and then looked back into my eyes "what are you?"

I let go of his hand. That had been a mistake; I let him know something, but I am not sure how or what. So I figured the best answer for someone as special as David, would be "just a girl" I lied.

David gave me a little smile, "Okay. I can deal with that."

I don't know if I can trust this guy, but I wanted to. He was so pretty, and I just wanted to touch and bite him. Well, I better keep my hands to myself. I need to do something normal, even though that feels like a hundred years ago. Less than one week ago it was 1975, and I was a girl, a girl swinging on an old swing set, dreaming of meeting prince charming, becoming a doctor and having a family.

Before the sadness could swallow me alive, I said, "What were you listening to on your walkman?"

David gave me a look. The look of what planet did you come from, and then he said, "That was Michael Jackson. Where have you been? And this isn't a walkman it's a compact CD player. My dad got it for me at Christmas. Isn't it the coolest thing? I bet he paid close to 300 dollars for it. Sorry, I don't mean to sound braggish or something. I just get real excited with new technology. I am kind of hoping I can save up for a computer."

Carrie's nonstop talking was starting to pay off. I knew that a lot of people had computers in their homes. And she had mentioned that there was a CD player, kind of like a record, only instead of a needle, it uses a laser. It was hard to believe her when she told me, but there it is in that boy's lap.

I gave the boy a smile; I will tell the boy the truth. So I said, "That is really cool. I haven't kept up with technology because I was buried in the ground in 1975. I have only been out of the ground for a few days."

David's beautiful laugh filled the air. Then he said, "So you had strict parents. I had a friend, Will. His parents were like that; he wasn't allowed to watch certain movies, or listen to a lot of music. So he just snuck around watching movies, and listening to music with his friends."

I smiled at him; the truth was too hard to believe. I knew that when I said that, but it was easier than making up stories. This way he made the story up himself, like overprotective parents. Boy, if he knew how much he missed the mark on that one.

I said, "Well it's hard to sneak out with 4 feet of dirt on you. Do you mind if I see what albums you have?"

David laughed again, "Yah that would be fun. Let me get out my collection. I don't have a lot of CD's. I do have a lot of cassettes, and I have a walkman in my bag."

So, for the next hour or so, me and David went through his music collection. We laughed and talked as he pulled out his favorite songs from different artists. It didn't take us long to figure out we had a lot in common and enjoyed the same music. After a couple of hours I felt how tired I was.

David picked up on this and said, "Go to sleep; I will watch over you, I promise… rest."

It was weird on how he knew exactly what to say to me. How did he know I needed him to watch over me? I was afraid to sleep on this bus. I wasn't even sure if I would wake up if I needed to. I must have been tired.

I woke up lying on David's shoulder. I jumped up "sorry… I didn't mean to fall asleep on you."

David looked at me then said, "It is okay, I didn't mind. Of course all the snoring is probably going to leave some permanent ear damage."

I gasped in horror. "I am so sorry! I didn't even know I snored."

David burst into laughter. I was really falling in love with the sound of his laugh. He looked at me as if trying to read me. "It was a joke. You don't snore when you sleep. You don't even move; you have been asleep for 8 hours, and, in 8 hours, you didn't take one breath. So I checked your pulse. And as you probably know, you don't have one. So I did the next logical thing; I listened for a heartbeat. Nope, no heartbeat, so I did the next logical step, I leaned your dead body against mine so it didn't fall into the aisle of the bus. And before you ask, yes you did almost fall into the aisle of the bus. That's how I came to notice all of this."

I was speechless. Well, that answered a few questions. I don't wake, well not easily. And I did sleep like a corpse. I guess I should have not fallen asleep on the bus, I really screwed up. What am I going to tell him, or should I tell him anything? Maybe I should kill him? No, I like him, bad thought.

Before I could answer him, David said, "Don't get upset, please. You have been lying on my shoulder for 8 hours now. You don't see me freaking out or anything. See, I know what you are."

"You do?" I responded in surprise.

David shook his head up and down in a yes motion. Then he said, "Yes, I have met your kind before, well not normally during the day. I have only met one of you during the day."

"Really?"

"Really" David smiled.

Well, that made sense; my kind wouldn't be out in the day much. He must know stuff that I don't. I had to ask, "So you met one of my kind during the day, where?"

David smiled at me and then said, "Well, the first time was in high school. It was my freshman year. I met her in the library, and we hit it off right away. We would talk for hours, about everything. I didn't understand why other kids would walk by and laugh at us. I am a little nerdy for sure, but this girl was hot."

"Prettier than me?" it came out of my mouth before I could stop it.

"She was nowhere close as pretty as you," David said, with a little bit of blushing. Then he continued his story, "well you could probably guess why people were laughing. They couldn't see her, being like you. So everyone thought I was talking to myself; I was picked on a lot after that."

"Wait, she was a ghost?" I thought this story was about vampires.

"Well, I don't know for sure." David said.

"I think I am a little confused, what do you mean you don't know what she was?"

David put a finger up for a minute. I could tell he was looking for the words to answer my question. "I know there are different kinds of spirits, some you can only see at night; I guess those are ghosts. Then there are more powerful spirits that you can see during the day. Of course I have only seen the day spirits inside buildings. They can speak to you, and sometimes they can touch you. You might call them poltergeists."

"And vampires?" I asked a little impatient.

"Vampires?" David said.

"Yes, vampires David." I could really care less about the ghost stories; I was too excited about finding out more about me. Plus it would be dark soon, and that meant Carrie was about to pop into the picture. And now I am thinking David would see her, and then I wouldn't be able to talk until morning. Maybe I could get David to pretend he couldn't see her.

"I don't know anything about vampires. All I have ever seen were ghosts, like you." David said...

David had never met a vampire, and knew nothing about them. He saw ghosts, so that's why he acted so strange when I sat next to him. He thought I was a ghost. Quickly I made the decision that I would rather David think that I was a ghost. He is comfortable with ghosts; I'd probably just scare him, if he knew what I really was.

I said, "I am just wondering if you had ever uncovered a vampire?"

"No... no vampires or ghouls, just different kinds of spirits like you." David said.

I think I better let him know about Carrie, so I said, "David, one thing you should know."

"Yes"

I continued on, "Well you know how girls don't travel alone... I kind have a friend with me. Her name is Carrie; she should pop in soon. She's one of those kinds of ghosts that only come out at night, and its already sunset."

"Really," David said with a lot of surprise in his voice. He continued on by saying, "normally ghosts haunt places, and don't travel. I kind of figured you were a poltergeist that was haunting this bus, two spirits in the same bus. I don't think I understand you at all. Are you haunting this bus?"

"No" I said.

Then I reached over and grabbed the back of his head, and pull his face towards mine. I have never kissed a boy before. My emotions were everywhere, but, in the state that I was in I must take what I want. I am free, tortured and only have revenge to keep me company.

I want this boy, and I plan on taking him. I stop, inches from our lips touching, and say, "Sorry, I am very impulsive. No more questions about what I am. Just know that I like you, and mean you no harm. I can travel where I choose, and right now I am choosing to travel with you."

David was quiet for a minute. Then he whispered, "Wow, what a way to change the subject. Just let me know before you disappear, ok?"

"Ok." I say. I pull my face away from his. I don't think I am ready for kissing him. Not yet, soon though. I would like to know what it's like to kiss a boy.

If anyone listened to the rest of our conversion, they would have thought I started the rumor about blondes. David was explaining a lot of things that I had missed in the last fifteen years.

He didn't ask anymore about me; I don't think he thought I was a ghost anymore. Even if he didn't believe I was a ghost, he was still willing to hang out with me, and I do think he actually likes me. Of course, night came, and, with night, came Carrie.

She reappeared right in front of me. Well, actually inside the chair in front of me. Carrie jumped out into the aisle. The lady she reappeared inside of started to complain to her friend that there was cold air all around her.

Carrie looked at me and said, "Great, a bus." Then she looked around and said, "A full bus, I guess I am standing all night watching everyone sleep. At least I have some new faces to look at. Melabeth, I see you got lucky. That boy you are sitting with is hot."

David chuckled and then said, "thank you."

Carrie got all excited and started to jump up and down, saying over and over again, "he can hear me, he can hear me." She then floated through the air and landed right between me and David. Of course she could pass through objects, well except for me.

"Stop pushing Carrie," I complained.

Carrie started to say, "Sorry, touchy v…"

"Shhh… don't say that. It's just Melabeth, Carrie." I said venomously.

The next few hours went better than I had imagined. Carrie, I and David got along great. We laughed and talked into the early hours of the morning. Then, after a few yawns, David curled up against the window and fell asleep.

I figured I better get something to eat while David was sleeping. I don't believe he thinks that I am a vampire. So I explained to Carrie that I did not want David to know what I was. She thought I could trust the boy, but I don't even trust her.

Most everyone on the bus was asleep, so I snuck down the aisle of the bus on all fours. I moved like a cat; it was no problem to hold my weight on the tips of my toes. I went to the back of the bus and got lucky. All the people in the back rows were sound asleep.

There was a big man snoring, with his arm dangling over the arm of his seat, and into the aisle of the bus. So I snuck up and bit his wrist. He didn't wake, which did not surprise me. My teeth were sharp, I bit fast and the blood flowed into my mouth. It took a lot of willpower to stop before the man died. I licked the wound and it healed up; he would probably feel a little crappy tomorrow, but he would live.

Sitting right across the aisle from the man was a large woman. I had to pull her arm out to bite her, but she did not wake either. So, after successfully feeding on two adults, I snuck back to my seat.

I felt great, and it was good to know that I didn't have to kill someone every night just to keep myself fed. Of course, I noticed if I didn't kill, I needed two humans instead of one. In the future that could be tricky; I will have to deal with that in the future. Tonight I had a full belly, and probably will spend the rest of the night talking to Carrie, and dreaming of David.

Just before sunrise, the bus stopped. It woke up David; we both thought this would be a good time for a walk. So all three of us took a walk around the bus stop; I wasn't even sure where we were. The morning was almost here, so Carrie was complaining about missing the daytime.

"You guys don't understand," Carrie was saying with her hands as much as her mouth. "Yes it is better to be with you all, but I miss all kinds of stuff during the day. Everyone is sleeping and there isn't a good conversation to be found. Not trying to be mean or anything Melabeth, but you ain't exactly talkative. You never say more than three words, and one of them is usually shut up or some other putdown."

"Shut up is two words Carrie," I said dryly.

"So she is mean to you. Is that what you're sayin'?" David said, with a smile. He was humored by Carrie's complaining. Of course this just made Carrie more irritated.

"Not you too," Carrie said, throwing her hands up in defeat. "You know what she likes to call me don't you?"

"No."

"Slinky," Carrie said with a sad face.

David laughed; every time he did I wanted to jump his bones. Then he asked "and what on earth do you mean by that Melabeth?"

"Well," I start off saying, "see a slinky is completely useless, but still fun to push down a staircase."

"SEE," Carrie yelled.

David burst into laughter, the kind where tears came to his eyes. "You are so mean, Melabeth." He said in between fits of laughter.

"Great horny toads, you are as bad as her. Great, I must have been some kind of bad to deserve the both of you," Carrie moaned.

I looked at her, and with the most sincere voice said, "You are my only friend; I will try to be nicer. See, you have to understand; it was my time of the month when I died. So now and forever will I be on the rag; so, in short, get over it. And also I love you."

Carrie and David both laughed. Then Carrie said, "Now girl I love you too, but you can't be sayin' shit like it's your time of the month when we both know you're a special kind of mean."

I smiled my deviant smile; she knew me pretty good already. Of course she witnessed me killing two men, and we shared some of our history. It was kind of weird, but I was really comfortable with Carrie.

We all got back onto the bus; a few minutes later we were heading back down the road. The sun finished coming up, and Carrie disappeared. It took a little bit of convincing by David, but finally he talked me into going to sleep. He promised me on his life that he would take care of me, and I would be safe as I rested. So, for the first time since I started this second life, I decided to trust someone.

It was a big step for me; I still had power over Carrie, and to give David power over me was kind of hard. Also he was a boy, and I was still having a little trouble with the male species right now. Nonetheless, I lay into his arms and fell asleep, to the rhythm of his heart.

When I awoke, David was putting away his journal. I wanted to read it. I looked up at David's face, and he was smiling down at me like I was someone special. If I had a working heart, it would have sped up. Then David said, "Good morning sleeping beauty. Rest well?"

"Yes, did my snoring bother you?" I teased.

"No, but something else kind of did…" Great, now what weird stuff did I do in my sleep? David looked at me trying to gauge my reaction. Then David went on, "a lady passed down the aisle of the bus and told me that we made a cute couple."

"And that bothered you? In what way did it bother you, that they think that we are cute or that we are a couple?" I was kind of teasing him, but I was a little concerned about why that would bother him.

"No, not the cute or the couple." David said, "The fact they can see you. I know I am not allowed to ask you questions, but you can't be a ghost. And I don't understand how another ghost follows you around?"

Crap, well it was only a matter of time before David noticed that I was not invisible to other people. I wasn't sure what to say, but I wasn't willing to tell him the truth. So I said, "Sorry David, I am not ready to tell you. People can hear me and see me, but they don't treat me normally. They don't know why I am strange to them, but they just lie to themselves rather than believe that I am different. I am not a ghost as you have already figured out for yourself. Just forget about it for now, please."

David looked at me with a frustrated look. Then he got a little mad and said, "Maybe I don't want to forget about it. Maybe I would just like you to trust me a little."

That pissed me off. I sat up straight and said, irritated, "I already trusted you, when I allowed myself to rest in your arms. Don't you even try to force me to share with you; when or if I decide to share with you…you will be the first to know."

David looked like he was about to pee himself. Okay, I know I could be a little scary, but he was really affected by my anger. He shakily said, "Sorry… Mela… beth I didn't mean… you're right."

Touching his hand and in a soft voice, I said, "relax, I am not going to hurt you." My anger had melted away, I felt bad for scaring him.

He visibly relaxed, took a deep breath and said, "Please don't do that. When you get angry, I can feel your energy. I know you can kill me so fast; I don't know how I know; I just do."

I gave his hand a little squeeze, "I will not bring any harm to you, I promise. I really like you."

"Ok" David said with a little smile.

The rest of the time on the bus was fun after that little fight, if that is what you would call it. We talked about music, movies, and shopping. He promised me that when we got to my stop that he would take me shopping at a mall he knew of. I still had a little money left; also I planned on using my super powers to rob some of these passengers of their cash. Now, not only were they blood donors but they were ATM's too.

David had not slept much last night and had decided to take a nap. I told him, worry about nothing I would watch over him. And then a few minutes later he was sleeping. This of course means there is only one thing for me to do on this bus while he sleeps, and that is to read his journal.

*   *   *

I always feel the presence of people around me. I even know when there is a ghost in the next room. I never even knew when this girl set down next to me. She could have been there for a half an hour I don't even know, and that really bothered me.

When I finally got enough nerve to try to talk to her I wasn't really ready for what I discovered. Soon as she faced me she was completely unreal. Her face was like marble, perfect from flaws. Her eyes are what really give it away, they're too big, like two blue orbs of power. I noticed she keeps her sunglasses on around everyone else; I think she screwed up, she really did not mean for me to see those eyes.

It would not have mattered; I still would have known that she is not human. I also know she is no ghost, even though I told her that's what I believe she is. I was half hoping she would tell me, but at last she does not want me to know. At first I was thinking maybe an alien or something. I can always feel someone's spirit, but not hers.

After I started talking to her, I finally felt her spirit. It only shows itself when she has an emotion. And then it's like a freight train, when I play songs that make her happy, I can feel it. If they make her sad it's like someone kicked me between the legs. At one point she tried to kiss me. The lust came off of her in waves; I wanted to rip her clothes off, and could hardly control myself. When she stopped that emotion, I felt like I needed a cold shower, and she never even touched me.

I have to keep reminding myself, this girl is dangerous. I knew soon as I realized she was sitting next to me. I felt the fear pass through my system, warning me of danger. Somehow this girl is keeping a ghost tied to her; how? I don't know.

The ghost's name is Carrie. She is real friendly, and, as far as ghosts go, not anything to fear.

She spent the whole night trying to warn me about Melabeth. She at first made little jokes about how dangerous her friend was, nothing too obvious. Later that morning I feel asleep. I was awakened by Carrie. I am not sure where Melabeth went, but Carrie was in a hurry to tell me something. So in short she warned me that Melabeth was dangerous and I should not hang out with her for too long. Then she told me to pretend I was asleep before Melabeth got back.

Not long after Melabeth had returned, she and Carrie fell into a conversion that sent me back to sleep. I know deep in my heart that she is dangerous, but there is something else too.

She is funny, smart, witty, strong, and hot as hell. Did I also mention the curves on this girl? There's something more than good looks. Something terrible has happened to her, I just know it. She is strong in spirit; she got angry at me, and it shook me to my core.

Her power, yes, but most of all the pain, pain like I have never known. It overwhelmed me; she thought I was scared of her hurting me. Maybe I was, but mostly I was reacting to emotion; it just confirms to me that something truly awful has happened to this girl. I am completely intrigued with this girl. I am still trying to make a decision on if I should follow the white rabbit. She's starting to wake; I will finish this later.

*   *   *

Why that little shit. I can't believe that Carrie was warning him. Well, I am not sure how I feel about that. On one hand, she is probably right to watch out for David's well being; on the other hand, she has no right to warn people about me. I shall let this go; what choice do I have? If I give Carrie a hard time, David will find out about it. Then David will know I have been sneaking into his journal, and I don't want to get caught; how else can I find out what he is really thinking? No, I guess as long as Carrie does not tell David that I am a vampire, and then I will not have to punish her.

I woke David up shaking him, "sleepy head, we're here. Let's move; there is important shopping that needs to be done."

"Ok, ok, just ten more minutes." David said, then stretched, yawned then stood up. "Alright let's get a move on. If I don't start to walk, my legs will shrivel up and fall off from lack of use."

*   *   *

I was having the time of my life dragging David through the mall, and he was enjoying himself too. Of course that's probably a lot to do with the fact that I was flirting so much.

I was trying on a lot of outfits. "David, what do you think of this skirt? You don't think it's too short, do you?"

"Well it looks great, but it is a little short," David said as his eyes were locked onto my ass. "I don't think it fits."

"Oh," I was having too much fun; there would have been little difference if I just gave him a lap dance. "What about this outfit? My underwear isn't showing, is it?"

"No, I like that one. And I loved the dresses from earlier." David said trying to be helpful.

He was picking the ones I was going to buy, which was a good thing because I was modeling a bunch of outfits that made me look like a whore. I would hate to think that's the way he would like his woman to dress.

I was trying on a red dress that I loved. I found black tights and tall boots to go with it. The boots went up to my knees and had high heels. I could have never worn heels before I was a vampire. Now I could balance on stilts. I was looking at myself in the mirror, singing and dancing in my new outfit.

"You're amazing" David said from behind me, "I have never heard a voice like yours. And you dance like nothing I have ever witnessed." Then he took my hand and dragged me over to him. "I could watch you dance and listen to you sing all day, but you should probably stop for now."

"Why" I said with a little pout, "if you like it?"

"I do like it" David said reassuringly, "I love it, it's just that. Well..." then David lowered his voice and whispered into my ear. "It makes your special side stand out. If you could see and hear yourself, well you might not believe you're human."

I looked around and noticed some other shoppers were staring at me. This one girl was grabbing her friend and pulling her around the corner to where we were. I could hear her saying to her friend, "you have to see this girl; she is amazing; I think she's totally unreal."

"Oh, I see, let's buy this stuff and get out of here," I said with a sense of urgency.

"Good idea," David said gathering my stuff and heading off to the cash register.

I spent all of my money. Well, I guess you could say I spent all of the other people's money. I had four really good outfits, plus boots and a pair of shoes. I was wearing my new outfit; it was a dark blue skirt that went to my knees. And I had a great baby blue blouse to go with it.

I put the rest of my new clothes into my gym bag; I threw away the stolen clothes; they didn't fit anyway. After that I went with David to the food court so he could eat.

David sat across from me with two slices of pizza and garlic bread. He also had bought two Pepsis, one for each of us. I was sipping on my

Pepsi as he took his first bite. I loved the taste of Cola, and dying had not changed that. Furthermore I was learning that I had to pee, so liquids did not bother me. Food, on the other hand, never stayed down for long. So even though I would love some of that pizza, especially since it was my favorite food, I was not going to eat any, not unless I wanted to go to the girl's room and throw it up, Yuk.

David finished swallowing and then took a drink of his soda and said, "Do you ever have to eat?"

"Nope."

"Can you eat?" David said as he took another bite of his pizza.

"Yep, but I always throw it up; so yours truly is on a liquid diet." I don't know if I am being too honest so I added, "Plus, I thought I said no more questions?"

"Is that not a question that you just asked me?" David said between bites.

"You're right, it was. I meant no more questions about me, smartass," I said smiling.

I was really enjoying hanging with David. I know that eventually I will have to tell him. Once I do, I fear that this will end, that he will fear and hate me. I will try to enjoy this as long as possible, so I will have to stop the questions for a little while. "Ok, I will amend my rule about questions. You can ask questions, just not about my special side."

David laughed; every laugh was so wonderful to me. Then he said, "Well, that's okay, I have some less inquisitive questions, such as, where are you planning on staying in California? Do you have a place, or are you staying with someone?"

"Ok, never mind; let's go back to no questions about me," I said with a frown. "So where are you staying?" Then putting an oversized smile on my face, and holding my head at a slight angle.

David almost spit his drink out. Then he said, "Oh come on, I should be able to ask where you are staying."

I shook my head back and forth in a no motion, and crossed my arms over my chest.

"You don't scare me," David said. "I am staying with my mother. She lives in Beaumont; it's about a twenty minute drive from here." He looked at me for a minute. Then he reached a decision. "So you don't have any place to go, do you?"

"The world is my oyster," I said defensively.

"Stay with me," David said with a serious face.

"Don't know about that," I responded. I really wanted to stick with him. I don't even know where the bikers lived. And those kinds of guys don't stay at the same address for fifteen years. I was lonely and with David everything felt better. Then again, if he knew, what I was? "I will think about it. That's not a yes."

David's face lit up like a Christmas tree. "I will talk you into it, and don't worry about my mom. Trust me, she will let you stay. And if not, I will help you find a place; I am your friend, and I need to know that you are not sleeping outside."

Wow, David's a pretty amazing guy, willing to step up for a homeless girl. Of course I bet it helps that he thought I was hot. Still you have to work with the tools God gives you. "Thank you, really. You are the first person to worry about me in a long time."

After that, we decide to go back to the bus station to catch a ride to Beaumont. David had to call his mom to tell her why he was late. He wasn't supposed to get off in San Bernardino. The next bus wasn't going to leave until later in the evening. So, with time to kill, David and I put our stuff in a locker at the bus station. Then we decided to take a walk to where all the uptown stores were.

More shopping!

After checking out some local shops, we grabbed a coffee and talked for awhile. Time slipped away from us, and the next thing you know we are hurrying back to the bus station. David reached over and took my hand; he gave me a tug as he pulled me down an alley.

David said, "This is a short cut; otherwise we will have to make a run for it."

"Okay, fine by me," I replied. Then I headed down the alley still holding David's hand.

I really enjoyed his warm hand, and the warm fuzzies I felt when holding his hand. All my attention was on David. He was taller than I had realized on the bus. He was at least six foot; his build was muscular, yet he was not finished growing. His arms and legs were a little on the dangly side. I think he is hot; still this relationship is doomed, I need to be careful about how I let myself feel about him.

My head is full of thoughts and my eyes were on David, I was not using my second sight, so I was a little surprised when we came to an intersection where another alley connected; there were three men standing there. They looked like they were waiting for something. From the look on their faces, and the fact they went from relaxed to ready, they had been waiting for us.

Chapter 5
David and Goliath

Two of the three men stepped into the intersection of the alleys. We had walked right up on them, and they only stood five feet away. The two guys closest to us both wore black suits, with really thin ties; one was red and the other was blue. That's where the similarities ended.

The one with the red tie stood to my right; he was my height and thin. He was a white guy with a pair of cheap sunglasses on; his hair was a mess, and he seemed kind of tense. He also looked like he was smelling the air; what a weirdo.

The man to my left with the blue tie was a black man, and he stood at least six-five. He looked as if we just killed his kitten; what did we do to piss him off?

The man behind them didn't fit at all. He was standing about fifteen feet further down the alley; he was tall with black jeans, black tee shirt and a black trench coat. He also had big black boots, and had greasy, long wavy black hair. He had a bored look on his face and was busy playing with the silver jewelry on his hands.

The black man boomed, "Who do you think you are coming into our territories? You must think you're some kind of badass to walk around in broad daylight. I am going to crush your ass, you little mother..."

"Sorry, sorry, we didn't know this was your alley; we will go around." David said holding his hands out in front of him. That's when I noticed they weren't looking at me; they were all staring at David.

The black man threw his arms up in anger, "Oh, you think you're funny, do you? I'll show your punk ass funny." And with that he reached around to the back of his jacket.

I could tell David didn't understand what was about to happen, but I did. Time to kick ass! This time, no messing around; I am not going to worry about eating. New goal, kill these guys, fast as I can.

I knew that black man was about to pull out a weapon: a gun, knife maybe a ray gun. This is the future.

I tried to flash the distance between us. Oh boy, another thing I didn't know; during the day my flash power didn't work, or maybe it was because I was standing outside in the sun. No matter what the reason, I will have to close the distance by foot.

I ran at the black man and was in front of him before he could register that I even moved. I couldn't flash, but I still was fast, and he was too busy paying attention to David.

I caught his right hand as it rose up from his back. In his hand he had a 1911 45 auto, chrome with pearl handles.

I did two things almost at the same time. First, now that I had caught his wrist that held the gun, I squeezed it as hard as I could, then twisted at the same time. Second, with my right hand, I grabbed his blue tie and pulled down on it hard.

With my second sight, I could see the second man had started to run over to help this guy but was intercepted by David. The black man dropped his gun with a yelp, but he also swung his free arm at my head.

I ducked below the swing; it was powerful but slow. I let go of his tie, jumped straight up into the air, spun around and kicked the black man in the head. I kicked him hard; there was a cracking sound as my foot connected with the side of his head.

I landed softly on my feet, and the black man landed with a thud on his head. At almost that same moment, I saw with my second sight David taking a punch in the side of the head, by the small guy. He hit David hard, and then David sank to the ground.

I spun around in anger; I was so mad; he hurt my DAVID. My claws and teeth came out, and I hissed at him.

The small man looked at me with surprise, but I was a little surprised when I noticed he was not human. He had yellow eyes and sharp black claws; his teeth were sharp. He let out what sounded like a dog growling.

Then the man said, "One slash," he held his hand up showing me his black claws, "and you're a dead vampire."

He knew what I was. Still, he needed to die for what he did to David.

I attacked; I think this surprised him. I guess he thought his little threat was enough to stop me. I ran straight at him; he swung at me, and I dove under his swing. I landed on my right knee; holding my hand flat, I struck up at his side.

Then something happened I didn't plan for. My hand cut through his side under his rib cage; my hand was moving at an upward angle. I put so much force in the punch, my arm slid up into his body where my hand came to rest around his heart.

Grabbing onto his heart like a baseball, I pulled my arm back down toward me. I could already see his claws swing down after me, so I jumped back and rolled across the ground.

His claws had missed me by inches. I stood up, and he was holding his side with a strange look in his eyes.

Then I said, "missing something, asshole,"

I held his heart up in my right hand; there was blood all the way past my elbow. Then I tossed it behind me like it was an old apple core. The small man looked at me like he wanted to say something, then fell to the ground, dead.

I was suddenly knocked back by an explosion.

There was now a wall of fire burning across the alley. The third man was standing there straight as a board with his arms out. His eyes were wide open as he chanted something I didn't understand. Then a ring of light lit up around his feet.

Great, a wizard, I didn't know what he was trying to cast, but I bet I won't like it. The wall of fire was there just to stop me from touching him while he worked his magic; that's probably why he was standing so far away in the first place.

If he likes distance, I better get close, and fast. So I did the stupidest thing yet. I ran straight for the wall of fire.

I could feel the heat before I even got there; this was going to hurt, or worse. I ran through the fire as fast as I could run. The pain was so intense; I would have screamed except I feared to open my mouth in the flames.

I came out the other side on fire; my clothes were melting to my skin. The wizard froze in mid sentence as I jumped through the air at him. I bet he didn't see this stupidity coming.

I slammed into the wizard, and grabbed hold of him; when we hit the ground together, I began to roll us down the alley to put out the flames. When the last of the flames went out and I stopped rolling, I was face to face with the freaked out wizard.

He lay on top of me; before he could do anything else, I pushed him into the air. He was falling back down on top of me; I brought my legs over my chest. The wizard landed on my feet with a thump. Before he could catch his own balance, I kicked him towards the wall of the alley with all my force. He slammed into the wall hard, and it knocked all of the air out of him.

The wizard was now on his knees, dazed and trying to catch his breath. I jumped to my feet and ran over to him. I grabbed the back of his head with my left hand and grabbed his face with my right hand. I twisted his head until I heard this horrible cracking noise.

Then I pulled up with all my strength; I had to put my knee onto his shoulder to keep his body from lifting into the air. Then, with another terrible sound, I ripped his head right off.

Blood was everywhere, and that made me all excited. I tossed his head, and it bounced down the alley with a strange hollow sound.

My burns were already healing, and I tore what was left of my new clothes off. Damn, I really liked that outfit.

My second sight warned me to a new threat. The large black man had stood back up; he was looking at both of his dead friends. I better finish him off, I thought; when the man doubled over like he was in some kind of pain, he let out a yell and his clothes started to stretch.

He was expanding, and his clothes ripped and tore, as he got bigger and bigger. His skin stretched, and his shirt was all but gone, then he stood up. There stood a giant; instead of a black six foot man, now there stood a ten foot monster. The guy just Hulked out on me; he didn't turn green but still, his muscles were swollen, and the only clothes that managed to stay on were his jockey underwear, and his blue tie.

Welcome to the world of… what the hell is that?

It charged me with amazing speed, but I was faster. I moved between its large arms and feet. It swung at me, but it missed.

I clawed it on its arms, legs and back, but it did no good. Every time I clawed the monster, it cut right through the flesh, but the flesh was thick and spongy. My claws were not long enough to really hurt this thing.

I decided to go for the monster's head, so I jumped on its arm, bounced off its arm into a flip and landed on its shoulders. I grabbed its head and tried to twist it around; I wasn't ready when the monster smashed his head into the wall of the alley.

I smashed into the wall face first; it only stunned me for a second, but that was long enough for the monster to grab me by the throat.

It had me by its right arm; I tried to pull free, but it was too strong. It slammed me up against the wall, and it was squeezing my throat. Lucky for me I didn't need to breathe. The monster grabbed the top of my head with its free hand; it began pulling. It was starting to rip my head off.

Gee, I wonder where it got that idea from?

I was trying to get free to no avail, and I could feel my neck starting to rip apart. I guess my luck finally has run out.

"LET HER GO NOW," I heard David yell.

I looked down to the right and could see David was standing four feet away, with some blood trickling down the side of his head. He had a look on his face of rage, and his green eyes had power.

The monster stopped trying to pull my head off. It let go with his left hand so that it could turn its body towards David. It was still holding me around the neck, as it pushed up against the wall.

Then the monster spoke in a low deep voice. "Ready to die little man?"

David shook with anger, and then his face went black with shadows. His eyes burned a green color; his face looked like a skull with green eyes; before my mind could really process what was happing, a green light burst from David, it covered me and the monster. I felt the monster drop me and my body fall…

*   *   *

I woke, and all was white… white sky, no buildings, no monster, no David, just nothing but white as far as the eye could see. "Hello," I said. No echo, my voice sounded flat.

Go figure, David killed me! I sat down on the white ground. I felt like I should be afraid, but I wasn't. Then, as my eyes adjusted to the surrounding light, I could see figures moving about. I got up and went toward them, but, as I did, they ran away from me. They were afraid of me in death too.

"Melabeth, Melabeth are you okay?" It was David's voice, but it sounded far away. "Please wake up; how can I even tell if she is dead? Wake up damn it, wake up."

I could hear the desperate pleas of David through the air. I closed my eyes, and then it felt like I was falling again. This time I opened my eyes to find David holding me in his lap.

"You alright? I thought I hurt you. You scared the shit out of me. Are you ok? You look badly burned," David said with deep concern.

"I am fine; the burns will heal soon enough." I noticed him gently pulling his fingers through what was left of my hair. Most of it was burned off, not that I was worried about that.

The blood on the side of David's head now had my attention. I just realized it had been a while since I had a chance to feed, and that fight had taken a lot out of me.

I felt my teeth in my mouth become longer, and my ever increasing hunger was kicking in.

"Are you sure you're ok, Melabeth?" David said, "You look like something's wrong."

Don't bite him; get control over yourself. I sat up; David was still holding onto me just in case I fell back down. What he didn't realize is that falling back down wasn't the issue, and I needed some space.

"A little space, please," I said tight lipped; I didn't want him to see my fangs.

"Oh, ok sorry… just trying to help" David said, as he moved away.

Then I heard crying, I looked over, and there was the black man curled up in a ball crying. He was no longer a giant; he lay on the ground in his jockey underwear and his blue tie.

David will figure out soon enough what I am. Why try to hide it? Why pass up a meal? Still sitting on the ground, I slid over to the man and helped him sit up.

"What are you doing, Melabeth?" David said, sounding a little worried.

Not answering David, I said to the big man, "Shh… it's ok; everything will be alright."

I leaned him back and opened my mouth… the pleasure, the peace, I loved to feed.

After a little while, I felt the man die. I dropped his body on the ground and stood up. During the feeding, all my burns had healed, and my hair grew back down to my waist.

I looked down at David, who had never stood up and was still sitting on the ground. He had a look on his face of horror, fear, and disgust.

I smiled at him and said, "I knew it. By the look on your face, this is the first time you have ever seen a naked girl." I laughed at my own joke, but David still just stared at me.

"Come on, Goliath is dead. Stand up, David," I said as I helped him to his feet. "We need to get out of here."

"Yeah, you're right. Ok let's go." David said with a really shaky voice. "You're naked."

"Yeah, I mentioned that; I will need some clothes." I looked around. The only option was the bloody trench coat the wizard had been wearing.

David said, "Let's try breaking into one of these buildings. Maybe we'll be able to find something for you to wear, before someone sees us. How would we explain…?" David looked around in dismay. There were three dead men: one of them without a heart, and one without a head, and there was blood everywhere, splattered against the walls and puddle up in the middle of the alley. "All of this?"

"Suicide" I said, as I headed for one of the doors in the alley.

With great strength, I broke the steel door open. "Follow the white rabbit, David, or the naked girl. Now that I think about it, it makes more sense than following a rabbit."

"You have been reading my Journal," David replied grumpily.

"Hurry, let's go" I said. I reached over, grabbed David's hand and pulled him through the doorway.

David was still in shock; he had this dazed look, like he wasn't sure which way was up. We had entered a warehouse. It looked like it was full of furniture; I was hoping for clothes.

At least it didn't seem like anyone was around. We hurried through the warehouse until we came upon some office doors. I went into the first office, but found nothing to wear. The second door ended up being a broom closet full of cleaning supplies. It's in the broom closet that I got lucky; there, hanging on a hook was a dark blue work suit.

I pulled it off the hook; it was dirty and smelled, but I couldn't run down the street naked. Holding the work suit in my hand, I looked over at David. He was staring at me; no, he was staring at my body. If he was looking higher than my chest, he would have noticed I was looking back at him; if his tongue fell out of his mouth, I wouldn't have been surprised.

"Do you like?"

David jumped as if I just caught him sneaking cookies. "Yeah, everything is ok." He looked away and his face turned the color of a tomato. "Sorry, Melabeth."

"It's ok." I said. "You didn't answer my question. Do you like? Do you like what you see?"

"Yes," he said quietly.

"Then I don't mind you staring, but I think it's only fair if I get to see you naked. So take off your clothes, please," I said teasing.

"What… Now?" David looked really nervous all of a sudden. I liked that; it made me more comfortable to be around a man that wasn't experienced.

"Just kidding, we need to get out of here." I slipped on the work suit.

It took us at least five minutes to work our way to the front of the warehouse without being seen. The warehouse was open, and there were people working. We slipped out the front, and, then we walked really fast to the bus station.

About the time we were going in the bus station door, we could hear the sirens in the distance. With no time to waste, we grabbed our bags from the lockers. I rushed into the girl's room, tossed the work outfit in the trash and put on one of my new outfits. I took out the only pair of jeans that I bought and a white top. All I had left were my knee high boots; they would have to do until I got another pair of shoes.

We ran to get on the bus; the bus driver gave us an irritated look, as we found our seats. We both let a gasp of air out as the bus started driving out of town.

I sat next to the window looking out. I could hear David's heart beating over the noise of the bus. We were quiet for a little while.

I was not sure what David was thinking; finally he looked over at me and said, "You killed three men."

"Yep" I said. What does he mean by that?

David looked at me with a pained look on his face. Then he said, "Yep. That's your answer for murdering a man?"

"Murder? I didn't murder them; I killed them!" I said. That hurt; how could he be thinking badly of me? "I did it to save us."

"I don't know everything that happened," David said. "I was knocked out; when I awoke, you were ripping a man's head off. Then, before my eyes, the other man turned into a giant. You both started fighting, and then the giant got a hold of you. I was afraid he was going to kill you. I felt the fear in me, and, at the same time, I knew I could stop him. I got his attention, I felt fear for myself. I pushed all my fear into him, and it also went into you."

"Is that what that was... fear?"

I wasn't sure how I felt right now. Was he calling me a murderer or not? He said he was afraid for me; I will let him finish before I lose my temper.

"Yes," David responded. Then, with a little hesitation, he went on to say. "Remember I told you I can feel what you feel?" I nodded my head yes. "Well I felt you dismiss the fear. And when you awoke, I felt your hunger. Then you killed that man in the alley. You didn't have to; he wasn't going to attack us again. So my question to you is, do you have to kill a person to eat?"

"No," I felt tears building up in my eyes.

"Then that's murder." David said bluntly.

One of my tears betrayed me and jumped down my cheek; I turned my head back toward the window, I didn't wish for him to see my tears. How could he make me cry? I saved his life, the ingrate. "You don't know shit David."

"When you killed those men, you almost felt nothing, and if you did feel something, it was excitement; I know that," David said with a soft voice. "I now know what you are, and after seeing you do what you did, should I fear you?"

Tears fell down my face as I responded to his assessment of me. "If you had something to fear, you would be dead. Those men were not out to get me; they were out to kill you. And yes you're welcome,"

"Well, if I didn't say thank you..." David started.

"And another thing, what do you believe I am anyway," I said; my pain was turning into anger.

"Please don't get mad at me. I don't mean to be ungrateful to you. I am sorry for hurting your feelings, because I am scared of you." David held his head down. "I am having a hard time putting it into words; I know I am not making a lot of sense. Let me try to explain this to you... please don't get mad."

"I'll try," the way he kind of begged helped me calm down, but I still felt like crying. I didn't move my face away from the window to look at David. I still didn't want him to see me cry.

David started to talk. "Where do I start? I guess first I should say that I know you're a vampire. I think I have always known."

I couldn't help myself; I turned to look at him; the tears were still threatening to show themselves. David went on by saying, "I know you saved my life today, and I will always be thankful for that. I can feel a great darkness in you, but, at the same time, I can feel a great… love. You need to be careful, or else that darkness will swallow you up. You can't just kill people."

"Do you trust me?" I asked.

"Yes and no. I trust you wouldn't hurt me. I trust you as far as I am concerned personally. I don't trust that temper of yours." David said. "I can feel your pain, and it's greater than I have ever encountered."

I think he still likes me as a friend, and that made me feel better; I was still afraid he didn't want anything to do with me. I don't know why, but I needed him.

So I said, "David trust me when I say that killing bothers me. I think you are misreading me with your powers. In the moment, like in the alley, I always feel nothing, or sometimes I feel excited to fight and kill. You need to understand that it bothers me; I don't want to be what I am. I have only been like this for a few days. I have no friends or family. I don't know where to go, or where I have been. I don't know who to trust, and, in four days time, five men have tried to kill me. I know I am a vampire, but I don't know shit about vampires. My master left me by myself to find my own way. The weird guy I fought in the alley, his hands were claws that I have never seen before. He told me with one swipe that I would die. Why would I have died? What the hell was he? And will more come after me for killing him? I have questions, no answers. And I am alone." Now I was crying; tears ran down my face freely, and I felt ashamed.

David quickly wrapped his arms around me and pulled me tight. I cried into his shoulder as he held me. For the first time, in a long time, I didn't feel alone.

After I cried some more, David whispered in my ear, "sorry for not understanding. You would think, out of all people, I would understand. I don't even know what I am… or how to control my powers; I could have killed that man myself. Hell, I could of killed you."

I held him tight, and then said, "It's ok. You are my only friend, and I need you. Also you are right; I murdered that man. I did it without even thinking about it. I need someone to tell me that; I don't want to become any more of a monster than I am already."

David pulled back from the hug, and then he looked me in the eyes and said, "You are not a monster. Trust me when I say, I have seen monsters. I can see people's souls, or something like that. I understand their emotions; I have felt terrible things from men and women. They were monsters, monsters in human clothes."

"Really?"

David wiped my tears from my face. "Do I look brave enough to lie to you?"

I laughed, then David smiled brightly and said, "I love the sound of your laugh, and the way you sing; makes me feel like my soul is on fire with passion. I had no idea you were new to this... life. I will help you make your way, I promise."

"Thank you; you don't know what you already mean to me." As I said this, I looked at David's hands. That's when I noticed he had blood on them. Confused, I said, "Did you cut yourself?"

"No" David said, and then gave me a small smile, "your tears."

"Oh, my tears." I wiped my hand across my face. When I pulled my hand back, I noticed that my tears had blood in them. "Crap, I am making a mess."

"Don't worry about it." David said, as he started to pull a shirt out of his bag.

He pulled off the shirt he was wearing, because there were bloodstains on his shoulder. Wow, he had a lot more muscles with his shirt off, nice abs with a very tight chest; it took willpower not to reach up and rub my hands all over his body.

Unfortunately, he put on his clean shirt. Then he used the dirty one to clean me and him up. Finally I have a friend; deep down I know I need him. Lucky for me he needs me too. Someone is after him, and he doesn't know why. He has powers that he does not understand, and they are most likely the reason those men came after him. He and I are kind of in the same boat.

We both are something more than human, yet we don't know the rules of what we are. I have a feeling that we both need to figure out what we are, and how it all works. We need to find out as fast as possible. At least I don't have to figure it all out on my own.

"So," David started to say after putting away his soiled shirt. "What's it like to be a vampire?"

I answered him by saying, "I am not sure I can explain it."

"Well do crosses burn you? I already know the daytime thing is bullshit." David said.

I answered him by saying, "I don't know about crosses. I kind of hope that is bullshit; I hate to think that I am an evil creature from hell. I would like to think that I could be forgiven for my sins." I had been too scared to try out the cross and the churches in town. "Your right, the sun does not bother me. And I can go into houses without being invited."

"I wonder if that's true." David replied with a look of deep thought.

"If what's true?" I responded; I was a little confused.

"The part of being able to go into homes without being invited." David answered me.

Not sure where David was going with this, I said, "I have gone into two different homes. I was not invited into either of them."

David, still looking at me, said, "I don't know this for a fact, but I think that some homes are protected. Let me try to explain what I have witnessed."

"Ok, go on."

David leaned back into the bus seat as he started to explain this information to me. "Well you know I can see spirits. And I can also see other things that are hard to explain.

I can see people's spirits or souls when they are still alive. I have also witnessed magic walls; I don't know how I can describe what I have seen. The walls are like someone took Reynolds wrap, and wrapped it around the building, or house. Now, when people go through these walls, I notice it pushes on their spirit. Their body just drags their spirit through, and I don't think anyone even notices the wall.

When I see spirits try to come in or out, the wall stretches, and then shoves them back, and the spirits cannot get in or out of the wall. See, I have noticed, when I look at you, it's like your spirit is on the outside of your body, animating it, whereas with people alive, the spirits are inside of them.

Not all of the buildings have this wall around them. I have noticed this wall on older houses, churches, and some new houses."

"You think someone put this wall there?" I asked.

"Yes, I do, maybe like wizards or witches or something along those lines." David said. Then he went on by saying, "I also witnessed something in my apartment complex that kind of ties this all together."

"What was that?" I inquired.

David said, "It happened about four years ago, in my apartment building. There were two different apartments with this wall around them. In one of them, an old lady died, and, about six months later, the woman who lived in the other apartment with the wall was murdered by her lover. Now their deaths had nothing to do with each other. The only thing they had in common was that they both happened to be in apartments that had a wall. And the other thing that they had in common was, afterward they both were ghosts. I know because I could see their spirits. My dad was the apartment manager, so I helped him out from time to time. When I went into the apartments, I could see both ghosts. Now, it is important to know that the mean ghost was not the murdered woman. She was nice, and I talked to her almost every day. I used to wait for my friend Tom to walk to school with; I waited out in the hallway, and there I talked to her through the door."

"Why did you do that?" I wondered.

David gave me a sheepish grin, "I could tell you that I did that because she was lonely and very nice. I also could tell you that I felt sorry for her trapped inside that apartment without any furniture and no place to go. The real reason was I could talk to her about all this strange shit in my life. Who was she going to tell? No one would move into the apartment because of the murder, and the wall started to disappear. One day the wall was gone, and so was the ghost."

I asked, "Why did the wall disappear?"

David stretched, then said, "not sure, but I think it is because no one lived there. All things that do something take energy. So, what I think, and am not sure about is the wall is powered by the souls of the living inside of whatever building it is surrounding. See, the old lady was a mean old bag, and she had died six months earlier. Even so, no one had a problem renting an apartment from an old dead lady that wasn't murdered, so she haunted everyone that moved in. One day this couple moved in, and a few days later they had a lady come over and do a séance. I was told she asked the spirit to leave, and the apartment was fine after that. See, the way I saw it, was that she invited the spirit out. So if the living invite the spirit, it should be able to come and go at will. The old lady could leave, and then she went to where old grumpy ladies go."

"And where is that?"

"To hell, to bitch and nag at men." David said with a laugh. I laughed too, and then David added, "Just kidding; I have no idea where the dead go when they find peace."

"So you think when I come to a house with this wall, I won't be able to enter, at least without an invite." I said. Wow, if he is right there is so much stuff I still have no idea about.

"I guess we will find out soon." David answered, and then he asked. "When you bite people, do they turn into vampires?"

"No, thank goodness" I responded, with a gasp. "That would be horrible. My master didn't tell me much, but, lucky for me, he did explain how that all worked. You have to drink my blood, and what I understand is you have to get addicted. Then you need to die, and, if you're lucky, you rise again. Or maybe you're lucky if you stay dead. I don't know; the verdict is still out."

"Wood stakes?"

"Not about to test that one." I laughed.

"Mind powers?"

"Obviously not, or I could control you, and then I would make you carry my bags and shut up." I said with a smile.

David laughed, "I would carry your bags anyway; getting me to shut up, now that's going to require some serious mind powers. You're so new to this I wouldn't rule it out. You may need time to learn how to use your different powers, or it may just take time, before you become strong enough."

"Maybe" I said, "it would sure be nice to have those mind powers."

"Can you fly?" David asked.

"No, and before you ask, yes I have tried and it didn't go so well. Of course I could have picked a smaller cliff to try on." I said with a pouty face.

David burst into laughter. I could listen to him laugh all day. When he laughed, something moved in me… passion… I could feel it. I wanted to reach up and kiss him. I was ready to try; no not yet. David stopped laughing and then said with concern, "what's wrong?"

I smiled at him, "nothing, I enjoy your laugh, that's all."

"Good, I enjoy your company too." David said, with a look that made me feel like my heart should be beating against my chest. He reached up and touched the side of my face.

I need to cool this down, "Stop that please. I know you can feel my emotion."

"Sorry." David said with a hurt look on his face. He pulled his hand away from my face.

"No, don't take me wrong. I like it, I like it a lot. Just, I think we need to be careful; I have some control issues. If I ever hurt you… well I don't even want think about that right now. Not only that, but I am a vampire. Don't you want to… well you know, date humans?"

David turned to look at me with that smoldering look again. His face was serious, but full of passion. "Melabeth, I am not human. You and I are friends, maybe one day more than friends. If we are not more than friends, it will not be because of the fact you are a vampire."

I think he is full of crap. I don't want to argue with him; I just want to grab him and… "Thank you." I said, before I let my emotions get away from me again.

I turned my head toward the window of the bus and took a deep breath. David touched my arm, and was about to say something when the bus came to a stop. The bus driver announced our arrival. Saved by the bell; I needed some fresh air.

David told me we were only a few blocks from his mother's house. So we grabbed our bags, and started to walk. It was close to five now; David said he was starving, and that made two of us. Plus I was tired; I hadn't been able to sleep all day.

My body didn't feel tired, but my brain sure did. It was getting harder to think clearly; I will sleep when I get to David's.

"That's not good," David announced.

"What's, not good?" I said, looking harder in the same direction that David was looking in. I couldn't see anything wrong.

"That's my house," David said pointing at a single story ranch house.

It had stucco siding painted some awful yellow, gray roof with dark brown trim, complete with chain link fence around the property. The yard was full of all kinds of plants; it looked like a jungle of green. The only thing that was not green was the lawn. The driveway led up to a porch that had two swings under it, and plants in planters all over the place. "Can you see the wall around my home?"

"No... Oh great, it has one of those you can't enter unless I invite you walls." I said it a little on the grumpy side. I was tired.

"We're about to find out if you can come in, and, if not, I will try to invite you; I am sure that will work." David said, but not with a lot of confidence.

I guess I will probably be sleeping outside tonight. We went through the gate and headed up toward the door of the house. David reached up and grabbed the door handle, only to find it locked. He reached into one of the many planters that were sitting next to the door and retrieved a key.

He then went into the house saying, "Hello, is anyone home?" No one answered. "Well, I guess not. That may be a good thing no one is here; try coming in, Melabeth."

"How exciting," I said sarcastically. I stepped forward and was met with a wall. It felt like I was trying to shove myself through saranwrap; the more I pushed forward the tighter it became.

Finally like a rubber band, it threw me backwards. With my perfect balance I only slid a few feet away from where I started, and I was still standing. "You called that. I hope your inviting me works, or I will be sleeping outside."

David said in a loud and clear voice "Melabeth, you are invited into my home. Please come in." He stood to one side, and then gave a little bow as his arm made a sweeping motion.

I laughed at him as I entered the house, with my hand out in front of me looking for the wall. Sure enough, the wall was not there to stop me. "So the wall is gone then?"

"No" David said as he lead me into the living room. He fell down into the couch; I joined him even though I had no need to sit. David let out a yawn and then said, "It's still there. It will let you through now, now that someone invited you."

"Can anyone invite me?" I asked.

David said, "Not sure, but I think you need to live at the place that you are invited in. Then again, I don't know how this home would know that I live here. Maybe you just need to be a living person. I am sure we will figure it out."

Something was off. I normally figured things out pretty quickly, but I was tired. Something wasn't adding up, and I couldn't put it together. I was starting to worry about meeting David's mom.

So I asked, "So, when is your mom getting home?"

David responded with a worried look in his eyes. "I would think soon. You need some sleep. Come with me into my room, and I will set you up so you can get some rest. Don't worry about my mom; you'll see."

That remark only made me worry more. David was worried about something too; I wasn't sure what it was. I followed David into a little bedroom. There wasn't much in there except a bed, dresser, bookshelf and a closet. David carried both of our bags into the room.

Too tired to think straight, I laid down on his bed; David laid blankets over me and said, "Goodnight, sleep tight, don't let the bedbugs bite."

I looked up at David and said with a smile, "you have bugs?"

"Sleep," David whispered. I closed my eyes.

*   *   *

When I opened them, it was still pitch black. Then I realized that I was buried under blankets.

I heard Carrie's voice, "you awake yet? You might want to wake up, damn; it's hard to wake the dead."

"I am awake." I grumbled. "What time is it?"

"It's about time." Carrie said, as she pulled the blankets off of me. I was still in David's room, but it was dark. "It is about ten after nine, and I think you need to be awake." There was worry in Carrie's voice.

Carrie's worry woke me up; I shot up out of bed. I used my second sight; we were alone in the room. "What's going on, Carrie?"

Then she said, "Don't freak girl, but you need to be awake. Let me tell you what you missed."

I calmed down. I could hear some people talking quietly in the house but could not make out what they were saying. "What's been happening?"

Carrie sat on the edge of the bed and said, "Long version or short version?"

This being Carrie, I knew there was no short version to be heard, so I said, "short."

Carrie frowned and then started to fill me in. "When I reappeared in this room, you were out for the count, and it looked like David went through some effort to hide you. Just look at all the blankets he laid on you; he put his bag in front of your body. Then he laid clothes all over you; hell, it took me a solid minute to find you in this room. I was a little scared you had dropped your necklace." I could see the thought scared her, "I am glad that was not the case. I took a walk around the rest of the house. Ran into David getting something to eat; I was starting a conversation with him, when some women came through the front door, a middle age lady and two young gals. They yelled to see if David was here. David came out into the living room, and, bam, they were hugging and kissing. We missed you David and all that shit; it didn't take long for me to realize that they couldn't see me. I told David, ha, they can't see me, and he gave me a little head nod. Then he went on pretending I wasn't there. After all their hellos, it didn't take but a few hours before David was askin' questions about his powers. His mom started to tell him that he was a Warlock that he came from a family of witches. They all are in a coven called the Shadow of Hills or some such thing. I would call my coven, Dancing Ponies, but that's just me. Then David started to tell them about all the things he could do and all of the ghosts he could see. That's when the cow shit hit the side of the barn."

"Why, because he was a warlock?" I asked. Carrie was a little hard to follow with her country accent, and it didn't help when she got excited about something.

"No, not because he was a warlock." Carrie said while she tossed her hand in the air like whatever she was talking about was easily understood. "Aren't you listening? See witches ain't supposed to see no ghosts. And then they started asking all these questions. I didn't understand any of it really, but what I did understand is that David is a Necromancer."

She gave me a look as if a Necromancer explained everything. "What the hell is that, some sort of learning disorder?"

Carrie let out a breath, and started to explain. "Well I thought everyone knew that. A Necromancer is a magic user that uses death magic, kind of frowned upon, kind a like vampires; no one likes them very much."

"Well, thanks a lot," I said.

"I don't have no problem with vamps. Then again, you can't eat me" Carrie quickly added, "not that you would, if you could."

"Yes, yes I would. And I would have already eaten you. Talking about hungry, I could use a bite. So stop talking about eating; what did David say about me?"

Carrie looked at me with sorry eyes, "well… kinda nothin'. He hasn't really told them about you. Somewhere in that conversation they were having, one of the sisters made a remark along the lines of, damn, my own brother's a Necromancer. It could be worse; he could be a vampire. After that David said, what's wrong with vampires? His mom said, don't even get me started; we have enough to worry about you being a Necromancer. That's kind of why I thought you should be awake, just in case they did find out about you. These kinds of folks are the kind that would drive a stake through your heart while you were napping."

Well, so much for a place to stay. Plus I can't really do this to David; he has enough on his plate without worrying about taking care of me. I still need to figure out where I could stay so I could hunt down the bikers.

I looked over at Carrie; I was glad she was with me, "Thank you Carrie, for watching out for me."

"What are girlfriends for sweetie?" Carrie said with a big grin.

That reminds me, "I read David's journal. I can't believe you went behind my back and warned David about me."

"That's low, reading a boy's journal." Carrie said with fear in her eyes, "you mad?"

I wasn't mad anymore. "No, I understand why you did it. You were trying to be a good friend to David. Just don't forget what side you're on."

"Then you don't know why I did it," Carrie said defensively.

"Why did you do it?" I replied with wonder.

Carrie looked at me with the most serious face I have ever seen on her, "because silly, I saw how you looked at him, and I was a little afraid you were going to screw up and accidently hurt him. Then you would have had a hard time living with that. You need your revenge, not drama."

I was taken aback with what Carrie had said. "Thank you Carrie; I misjudged you."

"It's ok." Carrie smiled, and then she hugged me.

Me and Carrie talked a little bit longer, mostly about how I felt about David. Carrie was sure I was in love. I was sure I would like to wring her neck if she didn't leave me alone about how I felt.

I decided that I needed to eat. First things first, I would go out and meet David's family. I know this could go bad, but I have two reasons for doing it. First, I had to say goodbye to David; second maybe these witches would know something about vampires, or, better yet, maybe they would know where I could find some other vampires.

Chapter 6
The Report

At this rate, I will be here all night typing these reports.

And now the phone is ringing; will it ever end? "Hello, this is detective Alex McDonald speaking. How can I help you?"

"Alex, you have a minute?"

A very familiar voice, my old friend Tony Abbott, he was the leader of a local witch coven. "I can make a minute for you Tony. What's going on?"

Tony said, "Well you probably have heard of the three murders near the Inland Mall by now."

"Yep" all afternoon the guys in the department have been going on about them. "Not my case."

"Is now." Tony responded.

"Damn, are you telling me this was supernatural?" As if I weren't buried alive with enough cases caused by humans.

"That's what I am saying; I am guessing you haven't heard the details in this case. If you had, you would have been expecting this phone call."

"All I heard was the official version. Three men killed in an alley, most likely a gang fight." I worked in a local police station, and the local police were never told the truth about these cases, not that they would believe them anyhow.

Tony said with a small laugh, "They are not even original anymore with the cover stories. This gang fight went down like this. Three men went into the alley. One got his heart torn out of his rib cage. The other man looked like he took a beating, and then had his head ripped off. And the third man died from blood loss."

I let out a deep sigh. "Damn, the gang problems are out of control." Tony laughed on the other end of the phone. "Give me the whole story."

Tony said, with a note of apology in his voice. "Sorry to do this to you, but you know you're the best there is on these kinds of cases. The Order needs to get more detectives out there."

I couldn't stand The Order for the most part. "I will solve the case; The Order will hand out justice. I just hope that I don't make a mistake when it comes to these special cases."

Tony responded. "That's why I call on you so much. We both know how The Order deals out their justice with the supernatural community.

You are one of the few detectives that I know that makes sure you aren't just handing them a name, but the right name."

Tony meant well; he really did care about people. "Not to bring up old rants or anything, I just think that The Order needs a little bit more oversight, that's all. I give a name, and they are judge and jury. You know all this, and I have a lot of work to do. So I don't mean to rush you, but what's the story?"

Tony said, "No problem; you can rant at me anytime. And, for what it's worth, I agree with you. So, back to the matter at hand; there is only one witness that saw the suspects, but didn't give a good description."

Tony had a problem with getting off track, so I said, "Just start from the beginning. I will make my own judgments, okay?"

Tony responded, "Ok, Alex."

I got my pencil and paper ready while Tony started telling me the story. "Ready when you are."

Tony started, "The three men who were killed were agents for The Order."

"Maybe a hit on The Order?" I thought out loud.

Tony quickly said, "Don't think so. And this is why; the three men were volunteers. It's kind of a new program started by The Order. They're trying to build cooperation between some of the supers. The leader of the group was a sorcerer who went by the name Mr. Big. He was an earth specialist. He was a large man and was known for hand to hand. The second was some werewolf. I can't even remember the name of his pack, but, from what I understand, he was relatively unknown. Then there was a warlock in the group."

Now that surprises me: a werewolf, sorcerer and a warlock. This sounds like there should be bodies everywhere. "Did they kill any of the assailants?"

"No," Tony went on "it appears to be one sided. See, this group was formed to be called in only when there was a disturbance. My only witness is the one who called in the disturbance. She works at a clothing store in the mall. She saw one of the two suspects using magic in her store. She said that, when the young girl was trying on some dresses, she started to sing and dance."

"Sounds like a crime to me," I said sarcastically.

Tony laughed, "I don't think it was the singing and dancing, all by itself. The witness said that she was moving in an inhuman way, and it was bringing attention to her. The boy who was with her, stopped her, and then they both took off."

Ok, sounds like a young super who let her power get away from her. "I am still having trouble trying to figure out why the volunteers were called in."

Tony went on, "well, they are there to deal with disturbances. Now all they would normally do in a situation like that was talk to the young magic user that was involved. You know, give a warning, write their names down and make sure they are not repeat offenders."

"So what do you think went wrong? If all they wanted was to give them a friendly little warning, how did that turn into the OK Corral?"

Tony was ahead of me on this question. "This was my first question too. I called in a witch friend of mine, Susan. She specializes in object memory."

"I am human, remember... so what's object memory?" Tony always acted like I knew all the secrets of the magic world. I was sucked in a few years back because I was always figuring out cases that involved the supernatural. The Order figured I was better working for them, than against them. Ever since, I have been working as a detective for two groups, the state, and the shady group that calls themselves, The Order. At least The Order pays better than the state.

Tony answered my question with passion. "She can touch objects; even by touching the ground, she can tell you what happened to that object. See, objects all around us collect energy and store it. If you know how to read it, you can see the history of the object depending on what the object is made of and how much direct energy it was exposed to is how much history you can get back out of it. Simply said, I only had a short time before the energy in the alley displaced, and there was nothing left."

Wow, I should stop asking these questions. "So what you're saying if I understand you? This witch, Susan, saw the history of what happened in that alley, and you or she can give me a report on it?"

"Yes, you got it," Tony said as if he taught a child a new word. "And now I can tell you what she found out. It's not a complete story, but it will give you an idea what happened."

"I am all ears." I'm not sure how much of this story is going to be useful or accurate; in an investigation of a crime you need hard facts.

Tony said, "Well this story is one for the books. According to Susan, the volunteers were waiting in the alley. She said that they had no ill intent toward the two suspects. When the suspects arrived, something set off the volunteers into action. At the same time, one of the suspects attacked the volunteers. Here's the crazy part; the suspect who attacked was a vampire."

"This was at night? I thought this happened during the day."

Tony said, "Nope, middle of the day and it gets better. The other suspect was a Necromancer."

"The way you guys feel about them is most likely the reason the volunteers attacked first. Do you think this Necromancer was controlling the vampire? Of course, that would be crazy. I didn't know a lot about Necromancers except that none of the magic community liked them. Their death magic scares the hell out of them. Hell, it scares the hell out of me. Still, I heard that Necromancers could control some vampires but never did."

Tony added. "If you controlled a monster of such power, you could not afford to lose control for one second, and that's why Necromancers didn't practice that, because it was a sure way to get killed. And vampires don't like Necromancers, because they do have the power to sway their thinking, but why else would a vampire fight in daylight? You know their blood is like kerosene; once it starts burning, they go up pretty fast."

I said. "Sunlight and fire will light them up; all it would have taken is one little cut. Hard to believe the vampire was willing to risk that."

Tony went on. "One more thing, the witch said that she believes that the vampire jumped through a ring of fire to kill the warlock. They don't heal as fast during the day. If that fire would have burned through her skin, poof, no more vampire. So it seems to me, unless this vampire is crazy, this Necromancer is controlling her."

"If that's the case this might be a very short investigation. The Necromancer will one day lose control, and the vampire will eat him. Case closed." I said.

Tony laughed. "We could always hope. Look, I will fax you a full report tomorrow. I just thought you should know about this before it landed in your lap. I need to get home to the wife; her son is coming in from New York tonight."

I remember him talking about his stepchildren. The oldest daughter lives with him, along with the little girl he and his wife had together. His wife had two previous children, from two different fathers. Her second child lived in New York with his human father, and didn't even know that he was a warlock. "Well, say hi to Mab and your girls for me. And tell your stepson hi too, I can't wait to meet him. What's his name again?"

"David, he should already be at the house. This is going to be so much fun having a third young magic user in the house to deal with. They are a lot more work than human children." Tony said with dread in his voice.

I laughed at him "I believe you, my friend, but I don't have either right now, just a dog; and I have a hard enough time keeping up with him. I will be looking for that report tomorrow."

Tony answered, "yeah, later in the afternoon. You take it easy, Alex."

"You too, later Tony," and I hung up the phone.

Great, now I have more work to do. I better study up on vampires and Necromancers. I can't stand dealing with vampires; they scare the hell out of me. It always sounds so easy to kill one; all you have to do is light his or her blood on fire, and they will burn into a pile of ash in less than ten minutes, except if you meet one and realize that they are so strong that they can rip your arms off. They move faster than I can see; you can't sneak up on one. So, basically, if you don't catch one sleeping, you're dead; yeah, I really hate these kinds of cases.

I better stock up on some garlic spray; I don't want this vampire to get my scent.

Chapter 7
Mile High Rd

I was just working up my nerve to go out and meet David's mom and sisters when I heard the front door open. And then a man said, "I 'm home."

Then the girls said in stereo, "hi Daddy."

A woman said, "We have been waiting for you Tony." She must have been David's mother. "Come into the living room, and talk with me and David."

She sounded worried, and then Tony echoed her tone by saying, "What's wrong?"

David's mom said, "come and sit down and I will bring you dinner. We have a little problem, but I am sure you will be able to figure it out."

David had told me about his family on the bus before we arrived at the Mall. He told me he had a mother named Mab Abbott. Before his Dad hooked up with her, she had a daughter from a previous boyfriend. His older sister's name was Kelly Doyle, and she is four years older. That would make her twenty now; Kelly is working and going to a community college.

A few years after David was born, Mab left David's father, Peter, and then married a man named Tony Abbott, and she had another little girl with Tony. They named her Tabatha Abbott, but everyone calls her Lizzie. She is two years younger than David and just turned fourteen.

It's all kind of hard to follow; David's father is Peter Drye. David was named after his unwed mother, so his name is Doyle. Wow, I will be amazed if I can keep all of this straight.

I was about to go out and introduce myself, but I chickened out. Instead I told Carrie to be quiet so I could hear what they were talking about. At first it was just normal conversation like, good to see you, and I missed you. Then it was kind of quiet as Tony was eating; they let the man enjoy his meal, before they dropped the news that David was a Necromancer.

I was getting the feeling that being a Necromancer wasn't much more popular than being a vampire. Finally Tony finished, and Mab said. "Well, sweetheart, here is the problem. We think that David's a Necromancer."

There was a moment of silence when finally Tony said, "And why do you think this?"

"Well this is what we know…" Mab said. Then she went into the whole song and dance about everything David had told her about him seeing a ghost, using fear magic and even the fact he could see protection from spirits.

I think she was talking about that wall around her house; if so, that means David was right, and the walls were some kind of spell.

During the time Mab was telling the story, David and Tony said very little, every once in awhile asking David small questions. Then he said, "It sounds like you're right. David being a Necromancer is not going to be easy, but I promise you I will help you out. I know everything must be very confusing to you; hell you just found out that we were witches. And I am sure you have a million questions, but we will have to start small. If you are patient, you will learn everything you need in time."

David said with a lot of emotion in his voice, "I have two questions. First, everyone is freaking out over me being a Necromancer. Is it a bad thing? Can I stop being one? And why haven't you told me about what we are?"

One of his sisters said, "That's three questions."

David snapped back, "Shut up Lizzie, and mind your own business."

Mab raised her mom voice, "stop both of you. This is serious, Lizzie. And, David, don't tell your sister to shut up; everyone needs to stay calm."

Of course, she sounded as if any second, she was going to lose it.

Tony said calmly, "to answer your questions, first it is not a bad thing to be a Necromancer. It is just that it scares other magic users. Using spirits and death magic is powerful stuff, and when people fear something, sometimes they act out badly, and I am sorry, but to answer your second question; can you stop being a Necromancer, the answer is no. You will need to learn how to use your power, even if you do not want to. Knowing how to use your power will help you control it. And I think your mom should answer the last question."

"You know it is getting late and I am sure you are tired." David's mom said.

"Just tell me mom." David whined.

Mab let out a breath, and said. "I am tired. Let me explain later; it is a long story. You haven't known for sixteen years; what's one more night."

David must have been tired because he gave up and said, "Ok mom, but tomorrow you will tell me, right?"

"Yes, sweetie" his mother said reassuringly.

"Yep it's late." Tony announced. "Everyone to bed, and that's an order."

The girls moaned, and I could hear the legs of the chairs being scooted out as everyone got up, and then everyone headed toward their rooms. Just in case one of the sisters came in, I hid under the bed.

David came into the room, and then shut the door behind him. He let out a breath and then said to Carrie, "is she awake yet?"

Before Carrie could answer, I slid out from under the bed. I grabbed his ankles and said, "Rrrrr."

David jumped into the air letting out a little yelp. I started to laugh. David looked down at me, and started to curse under his breath. "Scared you." I teased.

"What the hell is wrong with you?" David growled.

"Oh where do we start." Carried chimed in, "Need to start a list."

"I didn't realize you knew how to write, hick." I shot back.

"I wouldn't talk, sugar; I was close to graduation. Hell, you never even stepped in a classroom." Carrie said sticking out her tongue at me.

David was tired and upset. He put his head between his hands, and then he fell into his bed saying. "Can you both please shut up? I have had all I can take for one night."

"Sorry" Carrie and I said in stereo.

David didn't reply; he just laid there looking up. I sat down next to him and gazed down at his face. I put one hand on his chest and gently rubbed; he dropped his arms down to his side, and visibly relaxed. "Sorry about the scare. You would think I would be more sensitive to what you were going through right now."

David chuckled darkly then said, "I know this is not half of what you have endured, but you know what they say. You need to walk in someone else's shoes or some shit like that."

I looked at my sad David, and then said. "It's not a contest if it's where I would win no matter what." David smiled at that remark. "We don't feel other people's pain; we only know our own. And all I can do for you is nothing."

"Nothing." David smiled.

I smiled back; looking in his eyes I said. "Yep, nothing; well I guess I could be here for you, if you want me to be."

"Wow, that's special." Carrie said from behind me. Damn, I forgot she was still here. She went on by saying, "should I haunt somewhere else while you two have a moment."

"That would be real nice." I said with a smile. Then added, "It must be hard being a third wheel on a bicycle."

"It's more like training wheels, because you have no idea what you're doing." Carrie smarted back. Then she quickly added to David before I could reply, "honey you're not alone."

"If you two don't stop your fighting, I'll wish I were alone." David said.

I could already see David calming down. I guess if you are broken, being around other broken people helps. I was about to say something to David when there was a knock at the door. I dropped to the ground and slid under the bed.

"David, may I come in." David's stepdad said from the other side of the door.

David setup in the bed and replied, "Come on in." Tony came through the door and shut it behind him. David asked, "What's up?"

Tony said with a quiet voice. "We need to talk."

"Tonight?"

"Yes, it's important you and I have a heart to heart." Tony went on by saying. "Do you know anything about The Order?"

David looked puzzled for a second, and then said. "The Order? I have never heard of that before. What is it?"

Tony let out a breath, and then said. "I don't have time for all the details right this second. So the easiest way I can explain it, is that The Order are police for the supernatural community. They help keep law and order, and protect all of us from humans or humans from us. If the humans started to believe in us again, they would go back to hunting us all down, so, to make it safer for the supernatural community, we formed The Order. They make laws and carry out justice. My coven works for The Order, and helps them with individuals that step out of line. To make a long story longer, three of The Order's agents were killed today. They were killed in an alley near the Inland Mall."

"Really." David said with a voice full of panic and fear.

Tony let out another breath, and then paced around the room a few times. Then he said real quiet, "was it you? We had a report it was a Necromancer and a vampire. Soon as your mother told me you were a Necromancer, I put it together. The bus station is only a few blocks from Inland Center Mall. Your mom called me early today saying you missed your bus in San Bernardino, and you wouldn't be in until this evening. So what did you do all day?"

David said really fast and loudly, "They attacked us without warning. They didn't say they were with anyone, or who they were."

"Shhh… I don't want your mother to hear about this. She would freak out; don't worry, I will help you out." Tony said with a calming voice. "Look, it's getting late; you and I need to go for a car ride tomorrow. I need the whole story. Then I am sure we can figure something out. Try to get some sleep."

David said on the edge of tears. "Ok… thank you."

Tony was quiet for a second then said. "Did you really control a vampire?"

"No, I didn't control her. She did it on her own." David said defensively.

"Oh, so she let you go without a problem?" Tony asked.

"Yep… she let me go." David answered. Thank goodness he didn't tell him I was hiding under the bed. "Are there vampires in Beaumont?"

Tony opened the door and started to leave, and then he said. "There is a family of them that live off Mile High Rd. Don't worry, they're not going to find out you live here. Get some sleep; it will all work out; you'll see."

"I will try; night Tony." David said as Tony left, shutting the door behind him.

Carrie started in at a million miles per hour. "What we do now? Do you think they will be after us for some kind of crime? Or do you think that we will have to go to a trial? Do you think that they punish ghosts? Even though this ghost had no choice in the matter; and, if so, how do you know how they might punish me? Do you reckon that your stepdad will help you escape justice?"

David said with a chuckle. "Is there an off switch?"

I crawled out from under the bed and sat next to David on the bed. Then I said, "Let me help. To answer all of Carrie's questions, yes, maybe and no." then looking over at David. "Sorry David, I think I might have got you into some trouble."

David looked at me and said. "No, no you didn't. You saved my life; those men were not going to arrest me. They were going to kick my ass, or worse. You see how my whole family acted when they found out I was a Necromancer. I think somehow the guys in the alley knew what I was. Didn't the big man say something along the lines of, what makes you think you can come into our territory?"

I thought about what David was saying. He was right; there was more to this. And somehow they did know what he was; how they knew is another question. I looked at David and said serenely. "Careful who you trust David. Our biggest problem is that we don't know enough information about this magic world. We don't know the rules or the players. I don't think they knew what I was until it was too late."

Carrie spoke up. "David's dad said there were vampires off of Mile High Road."

David gave her, are you dumb look. "So?"

I jumped to Carrie's defense. "No, wait; she is right."

David looked at me dumbfounded. "Right about what?"

"Well," I explained. "At the risk of sounding like Carrie, we need info, about a lot of stuff, like what vampires can and cannot do? Who The Order is? What kind of trouble are we in, and so on and so on. I doubt these vampires are looking for us, so I could go to them for answers."

Carrie giggled a little bit then said. "All I was saying is that there are vampires on Mile High Rd. I didn't know I was sayin' all that, but that sounds like fun to me; I'm in."

David shook his head back and forth. "I don't like it."

"Well what am I supposed to do?" I said with a little anger in my voice. "Should I hang out under your bed? Or should we put all our trust in your stepdad?"

"And what's wrong with trusting Tony?" David snapped back.

I needed to get out of this house; I really didn't believe I would have to explain this to David. "I don't think your stepdad had me in mind when he offered to help. I also think it would be a good idea if we split up for a little bit. This Order is looking for a vampire and a Necromancer. Your family will know how to hide you, but I doubt that they will hide me. If I go somewhere other vampires are, and I am not hanging out with a Necromancer, I am sure it will make it harder for The Order to find us. More time is what we need."

"What about me?" Carrie whined.

"What about you?" David asked.

I jumped in and said. "She's right. You can see her because you're a Necromancer. I can see her because I am a vampire; logic says the other vampires will see her too. The closer Carrie gets to our kind the more real she is; also I can hurt her. I can reach out and grab her, and, if I squeeze her, it hurts her. I don't know how other vampires will react to her presence."

David looked at me, then at Carrie, then back at me again. "So you can hurt her. Gee I wonder how you figured that out."

"Didn't take her long." Carrie said while making a sad face.

I took my necklace off. "Let's try a little experiment."

"I didn't mean anything by it, Melabeth." Carrie cried; she ran over to me and put her arms around me. "Don't throw me away; it really didn't hurt that bad."

It took real will power not to roll my eyes at her. "Carrie, honey, take a breath. Calmmmm… that's it. I would never get rid of my only friend. At the same time, I am not about to take you somewhere that my only friend could be hurt."

I then dropped the necklace onto the bed. Carrie was a ghost again and no longer could touch me.

"Whoa, I get it; she is also attached to the necklace." David said

I said, "Pick up the necklace David." Soon as he did, Carrie became solid again.

Carrie giggled with glee, and then said. "He can do it too. Hell I think he can do it better." A wicked grin popped on my face. Then Carrie quickly added. "Wait, I didn't mean it like that."

David was staring at the necklace in his hands. "This has power."

"I kind of thought it would work for you." I said "I bet this was some sort of Necromancer necklace or something; of course I am just guessing."

It took me another twenty minutes before I could convince both Carrie and David I needed to see these other vampires. It was close to midnight when I left. I felt better leaving Carrie with David.

Now they can watch over each other, hopefully not too closely; can Carrie even do that? Wait, am I jealous? Of Carrie? Well I can't think about that right this second. First thing's first. Find directions to this Mile High Rd. Second, bite someone, wait scratch that, bite someone first, and, lastly, make contact with other vampires and hope they don't kill me.

Well it sounds like a plan.

David had given me a big hug before I left. I think he almost kissed me. Not sure how I feel about that. I would have liked to kiss him, but I don't trust myself. Also just three days ago I was forced to… I am not ready. Just thinking about those men, almost brought me to my knees.

I had only walked about a block from David's house. There was a big oak tree next to the sidewalk; I leaned against the tree, closed my eyes and took big breaths. I felt like crying; my heart hurt even though it doesn't even work. I felt overwhelming pain through my whole body as I slid down the trunk of the tree onto my ass. I pressed my head between my legs. After a little bit, I calmed back down.

My pain turned to anger; I need to kill those bikers, rip them to pieces. Soon I will find them… soon.

I was still sitting under the oak tree. The wind blew cool air through my hair. I missed the east coast from my childhood; I missed all of the green. This area was high desert; the trees were spread far apart, and the air was dry. And, even though it was February, it wasn't that cold. Of course the wind blew off of the mountains, and, with it, cold air.

I had changed into my red dress; it hung to my knees, and, from there, my black boots took over. The dress was tight and there were thin straps that went over my shoulders. I probably looked like a hooker, but I didn't care because I loved how I looked in the mirror.

My favorite color was red; of course it might change soon. I loved blood; I hated blood. Maybe my new favorite color would be pink; on second thought no. I got up and started walking and soon was lost in thought.

I realized I was leaving where houses were, and now was walking down a road that boarded two large fields. I was in such a hurry to get away from David before he talked me out of going that I forgot to ask for some basic directions. He didn't know where Mile High Rd was, but I bet he knew the right way to the nearest gas station.

I could see the jack rabbits, owls and snakes. Nature did not notice me as I drifted quietly by. I missed my new friends, but I liked to be alone. I had mixed feelings about David, and I couldn't imagine not having Carrie around. Still it was nice to walk alone with the sound of nature, wind in my hair.

What the hell is that sound? I turned around to see headlights heading my way; I could hear the bass coming from the car. It was traveling at high speed and would be passing by in seconds; I could have flashed away, and they would have never seen me, but I needed directions.

The car passed by, only it wasn't a car; it was a truck, a little yellow truck with the word Nissan on the tail gate, I have never heard of a Nissan before, nor have I witnessed a truck so small. Not only was it small, but it was lying on the ground as if there were no tires.

The truck was going so fast it took a while for it to come to a stop; the loud music stopped and the white tail lights came on. The truck made a loud whining sound as the driver drove as fast as possible in reverse. Now I am thinking I should have hidden.

The truck screeched to a halt next to me. The passenger was hanging out his window.

With my vampire eyes I could see everything like it was daylight. The headlights had blinded me for a second, but now I could see the two men in the truck… correction, two boys, teenagers to be exact; the younger looking one of the two was the one hanging out of the side of the truck. He had long curly black hair that he kept in a black ball cap. He was wearing the ball cap backwards, how strange.

The driver was a larger boy with wild unkempt hair. Then again who could keep their hair combed in a city where the wind blew 360 days of the year?

The youngest one said. "You need a ride?"

"Yes" I replied. What the hell, if they were local boys they would know where Mile High Rd was, and both of them together would be a perfect meal.

The boy hopped out with a lot of energy. He held the door open and said. "Jump on in."

I got into the truck and slid into the middle of the bench seat. The thin boy jumped in and slammed the door shut; now all three of us were smashed together. I have never seen, or even imagined a truck this small; who would have guessed that in the future everything would shrink. The other boy took off as fast as the little truck would go, and they haven't even asked me where I was going.

The younger boy said. "My name is Eric." Then, motioning toward the driver. "And that's Donny; we're the Hood brothers."

"Umm, it's Melabeth." This kid was hyper, and spoke at thousand miles per hour.

Donny asked, "Where you headed?"

He might have spoken at normal speed, but he drove as if his house were on fire. The road was no longer straight as we headed up into the foothills.

If we hadn't been wedged together inside this cab, I would have been bouncing from side to side, for Donny flew around the corners so fast that the rear of the truck kept breaking loose and sliding, and, even though the truck was not staying on the road very well, he did not slow down.

They were both crazy.

"I need to go to Mile High Rd." I said a little bit nervous. His driving was starting to scare me. "Do you mind slowing down just a little?"

"Don't worry, my brother drives like this all the time; you're fine." Eric said matter of factly.

Donny barked over at his brother. "Where is Mile High Rd?"

Eric leaned forward and said, "Bro, that's where the Oak tree is at."

"No it's not," Donny respond.

Eric laughed, then poked fun at him, "wanta bet."

Donny went off the deep end. "You're always right about everything. When we go up to the Oak tree, and it's not on Mile High Rd. you WILL NEVER HEAR THE END OF IT."

"Ditto bro, drive, you'll see." Eric said laughing.

They bickered back and forth, and Donny never really slowed down. This truck is so small, that I had to spread my legs so the older brother could shift. Even though he was reaching between my legs he did not touch me in an inappropriate manner, and the same could be said about the younger brother; so they were out of their minds, but they were not crude men.

Of course about the time I was starting to like these guys, we made a turn and started heading up a small road. The brothers were telling jokes, and they were funny, but it was hard to laugh because they were starting to scare me. As they joked, the road got smaller, and windier than ever.

And I swear Donny sped up; we were rounding tight corners and switchbacks. We were going up a steep incline; to top it off there was now a cliff on one side of the road. At one point the truck slid, the back of the truck headed for the cliff. And if that wasn't unnerving enough, Eric said laughing. "Whee, we're all going to die."

Donny got the truck back onto the road and was still flying up the hill. He was laughing, and then he said to me. "Sorry if I scared you; we're just having fun; we're almost to the Oak tree." Then he slowed way down.

"What's wrong bro?" Eric asked his brother.

"Dude, look how white she is. I think I scared her a little too much; she is going into shock or some shit." Donny said, but he was laughing at the same time.

"Thank you" That's all I could get out; my body was frozen. I have never been so scared, and, to think, I am already dead. Yet these boys were trying to kill me again.

Eric interrupted my thought. "See, told you. This road turns to Mile High Rd. and right up ahead is the Oak tree. Looks like the shithead jocks are having a bonfire. Gee, I hope they don't fall in."

Donny asked. "You didn't say where you wanted to be dropped off at. Are you going to the party or somewhere else?"

"Yes, the party, that's where I am going. Just drop me off at the bonfire." I said; forget sucking these boys' blood. I just wanted out of this truck.

"No problem." Donny said, and then floored the truck. He passed by the dirt road that lead up to the Oak tree. He then pulled the E brake and slid the truck around in a 180 degree turn.

You know this guy could drive; he finally slid to a stop at the entrance of the dirt road.

"You sure you want to go hang out with these asses?" Eric asked. Then he went on. "Look it's not my business or anything, but you be careful. These guys take advantage of girls. Be careful what you drink; open your own beer. Do not take any pills these guys offer." With that he opened the door and slid out.

Both these guys were dressed in black and looked like a couple of thugs. Who would have guessed they were good guys? Then Donny added. "Be careful, and you can always come and hang out with me and my brother. We're meeting up with some of our friends, and they are a lot more fun."

I was taken back about their concern; I am glad I didn't eat them. If things weren't what they were, I would go with these guys. I need to find more of my kind, so I wasn't really going to this party. At least I knew where I was going to get a bite to eat.

So I said thanks to the brothers and watched them fly down the road. Well even though I let them go, it really didn't even matter, and because the way that guy drove they would never make to adulthood.

I was standing on the side of the road. There was a barbwire fence, on the other side of a field; there was an opening with a dirt road running through the field and straight up to a giant Oak tree. The grass was brown, knee high. Bordering the field, were giant bushes and a few scattered trees of different variety.

The oak tree didn't look natural, and, when I looked harder, I could tell there were remains of an old house under the oak's huge branches. Someone had planted that tree long ago, and now nothing remained of the old house except the walls. I traveled down the dirt road toward the tree, and then I moved quickly into the field.

I was moving around the tree, so I could get a full view of the tree. I found an outcropping of rocks; I jumped up onto them. There I could look down at the tree. I couldn't see the road from this location.

I could see a bunch of cars parked under the branches on this side of the tree. Also there was a small fire burning with kids sitting around it. I could smell the alcohol from where I was perched. I could hear voices and laughing coming from the tree. Kids were all over the place; some were making out. Some of the kids were in small groups, drinking and laughing. It was close to midnight, so the party looked like it was winding down.

I could see why kids came here to party. The tree provided cover, but the real appeal was the view. I could see why they called this Mile High Rd. I was overlooking a valley; below was a city of lights, and, above, was a city of stars. The mountains on the other side of the valley were like dark giants standing over the city.

The wind blew my hair into my face; I flipped it out of my eyes. A sliver of a quarter of a moon hung in the sky. It was like day to me, and, if I wasn't so hungry, I could sit here for hours enjoying the view, as the wind blew through my hair.

"pl... don't I... stop..." voices came through the air.

They were coming from the right of me. The wind was blowing from the left. When the wind died down, I could almost understand what was being said. The voice sounded like a female, and in distress; the second voice I heard sounded like a man.

"It's... come... love..."; I couldn't make it out, but it sounded like pleading, so I moved toward the sound; these two had moved far from the rest of the party. I ran through the field toward the voices.

I moved quietly into the bushes; there was a dry wash with soft sand running between the bushes. I could now see what was happening, and could hear what was being said. The girl was really drunk, and she had already lost her shirt. She was lying on her back in the sand, and there was a boy on top of her.

He was trying to tell her how much he loved her, at the same time trying to pull her pants off. She was saying no, but was too drunk to stop what he was doing. I smiled; dinner has been served.

I was standing in some dark shadows next to a bush. Then I said in a soft voice. "I want you. Come to me."

The girl was too drunk to even notice that I had spoken, but I got the boy's attention. He spun his head around toward where he heard me speak and then said with a booming voice. "Who's there?"

I was wearing a sexy red dress; time to put it to work. I stepped out of the shadows until the boy could see me. Then I said in my sexiest voice, "it doesn't matter who I am; the only thing that matters is what I want, and I want you."

The girl that lay upon the ground was just about pasted out; I was pretty sure she didn't understand what was going on. I wouldn't have to worry about dealing with her; she wouldn't remember a thing.

The boy looked a little confused, and then asked. "What do you want me for? Do I know you?"

I gracefully moved closer to the boy and then said. "Don't you think you would remember me if you knew me? And I want you for your body; look at her; she's no good. Come to me, and I will show you a good time."

"Shit, you don't have to ask twice baby."

As the boy said this, he jumped up holding his pants up with one hand. He closed the distance between us, and then he eyed me up and down, checking me out. This boy was much bigger now that he stood up; he towered over me.

Then the stupid jock opened his mouth. "You're one fine chick. Take off your clothes; let's see what you got."

Wow the sweet talk was nice, but also it was boring me. "On your knees." I commanded.

"Why should I?"

I smiled, and started to rub his chest. "I will give you everything you want; on your knees." I commanded again.

He looked at me confused, but then his small horny brain figured if he listened then he would get laid faster. So he gave me a big goofy smile, dropped to his knees saying. "Okay baby. Now I am on my knees; how about you get on your elbows." Then he laughed at his stupid joke.

I flashed behind him. So I am sure, for him, it was like I disappeared. On his knees his head came to my chest; I grabbed his throat with my right hand. Then I pulled his head back with my left, so now he was staring up at my face. My teeth were out and I said in a happy voice. "Did I say I was going to give you everything you wanted? I meant everything that you deserve."

He tried to reach up and grab me, but I was too strong. He started to spit out. "What the f...?"

I lifted him off the ground with the hand that was holding onto his throat. I used my left hand to grab his arm, then, pulling his back tightly to my chest, I bit into his neck, and started to feed.

He struggled, pulling me all over the place. He had so much weight on me I couldn't hold him in one spot, but I was so much stronger, he couldn't get me loose from his back. Also, by pulling him backwards, he couldn't get enough leverage to lift me up. It only took a few minutes before he started to slow down; the blood loss was making him weak.

I could taste the alcohol in his blood. I continued to drink, and I could feel his life slipping away. I stopped; I don't know if I can kill him for this. He was still conscious, but I don't think for long. I spun him around so that he was facing me. I could see the fear in his eyes; I knew any minute he would pass out.

I was holding him up by his shirt; he wasn't strong enough to stand. Then I said in the meanest voice I could make. "I am a demon from hell. You get one more chance at life, and, if you ever take advantage of a girl again, I will rise from hell, and drag you back down with me. DO YOU UNDERSTAND SHIT FOR BRAINS?"

"Yes... I will never... I swear to... God, please."

As he spoke, his eyes rolled to the back of his head, and he passed out. Well I don't know if that will work, but I hope he remembers enough never to do this to a girl again. I dropped him to the ground; his friends will find him soon enough.

I went over to the girl who had passed out while I had been feeding. I picked up her arm and fed from her as well; that's what she gets for being a dumb bitch, with no self esteem. Of course, if she keeps this up, next time it won't be a vampire feeding. She will get raped and probably not even remember it.

I licked her wound closed. Then I stood up to leave; the world spun and I fell back onto my knees. I laughed out loud; I was drunk.

I wobbled back onto my feet. Well this was not the first time I have been drunk. Living with my father, I took a lot of liberties that I shouldn't have. This is the first time I have been drunk without drinking anything.

I stumbled through the bushes and up a hill. I saw a nice large boulder up ahead; that would be a good place to lie down, I thought. The boulder was further up the hill, and the world kept spinning as I tried not to trip.

I looked up at the boulder and concentrated on getting there. I felt like I was flying through the sky. The boulder was getting closer and appeared to be below me; the rest of the world was too out of focus to see anything but a blur.

Then it was like memory loss; I was lying on my back looking up at the stars. I was lying on a rock; I couldn't tell you how I got here or if this were the same place I wanted to go. I couldn't stand to be drunk; I had hated it in life, and I hated it in death. I can't stand not having control.

I guess I should have figured this could happen by drinking someone else's blood. They don't call it blood alcohol level for no reason.

My mind was clearing; I was sobering up. I sat up with only a little head spin, but I could focus on the world again. Below me I could still see the glow of the fire under the oak tree, and not too far from that I could make out the area where I had fed on my victims.

I looked up into the sky; the moon had not moved too far; it couldn't have been more than an hour since I fed on those kids. If I healed at a thousand times the rate of normal, then it only makes sense that I would sober up really fast. That's a good thing; I don't have time to spend the rest of the night running around this mountainside drunk and lost. I still needed to find my own kind.

As I looked over at the Mile High Rd, I could see it runs up through a valley. How many houses could be up there? And how will I be able to tell which one is the vampires' house? Also, I should try to find a place to hide and sleep before the sun comes up just in case I don't find these vampires; I can't just sleep in any old place. For now I will wait until I finish sobering up; it shouldn't take much longer. So I just sat on the rock and enjoyed the view.

After sobering up, I felt great. I was full, and the view and the quiet had put me in a good mood. I started to head through bushes, small cactus, and sparse trees toward the road. I headed in a direction that cut away from where the oak tree was, and headed up toward the canyon where I saw the lights of homes.

I came out into a clearing with high grass; I was crossing to the other side when I saw something out of the corner of my eye. I whipped my head toward the movement, but I couldn't see anything. In fact, the only movement or noise I heard was the wind blowing through the trees.

Something else moved in front of me.

I spun my head to the front, but, once again, nothing.

Something is wrong, I just felt it in my gut, and it was getting darker. That's when I noticed a baby crib sitting in the middle of the field.

I was sure that wasn't there before; I had a bad feeling about this. I started to head toward the crib; in my mind I couldn't stop thinking; this is a stupid idea.

I walked close enough to look down into the crib. And there lay a little baby, sleeping soundly. Then, as if I had made some kind of noise, the baby's eyes opened and it turned its head toward me.

It started making a little cooing noise, and then it reached forward with its little arms like it wanted me to pick it up. I looked around me in every direction, and I couldn't see anyone around.

Who would have left their child in a field all by itself? I couldn't help myself; I reached down and picked up the small baby. I held it in my arms, and I started to speak in my baby talking voice. "Oh little baby. Who left you out here? Do you know? You're so cute."

The baby just looked up at me. Then it began to fuss a little bit. "It will be ok. Don't you cry, little boy. Or are you a girl? I wonder where your mom is."

The baby started to get more upset, so I rocked it in my arms, and then I began to sing; I loved to sing, and I have held other babies in the past. This had worked to calm other babies, but I also knew, if it was hungry, my singing would not be enough.

The baby started to cry, followed by screaming, and I tried to soothe the child. Then the little thing started to freak out on me.

The baby started to kick, and throw its body about; I was having trouble not dropping the child. Then it bit me; the little monster bit me so hard that it drew blood from my arm. "Ouch... you little shit, knock it off."

The baby screamed in my face and flailed around even more. I was having a hard time not dropping the child, when it started to try to bite me again.

Something's not right, and now I was fighting the baby as it ripped at my clothes.

Its hands looked like little claws. Not only did it have teeth, they looked sharp.

The baby reached up and bit me in the left tit. Ok, enough of this shit; I ripped the baby off and shook it really hard. "What the hell is this?" I screamed at the little monster in my hands.

The baby stopped moving. It looked dead as I held the body in my outstretched hands. It was limp, and its head just hung to one side.

Oh my, what have I done?

"WHAT THE HELL HAVE YOU DONE TO MY BABY?" a woman came from nowhere. She ripped the child from my hands. She was in an old fashioned dress; she had a bonnet on her head. She reminded me of some old western movie from what she was wearing. She held her baby in her arms crying.

"Sorry... I didn't mean to..." before I could finish that sentence, she reached up and slapped me hard, so hard I had to take a step back.

The lady had a look of rage and hatred as she spit at me. "How could you? It was just a baby. What kind of monster are you?"

With that, she reached up and slapped me again. This time blood came down my face from where she hit me. Before I could come to grips with what had just happened, she hit me on the other side of the face, and again blood came down the side of my face.

I felt my cheek, and there were four gashes; it was like she used her fingers like claws. That's when it hit me; this is not real. I jumped forward and attacked the lady, but, instead of slamming right into her, I flew straight through her. She was gone; so was the crib and baby.

I was standing out in the field again all alone. That did not feel like a ghost, but it must have been. Then I heard a little giggle.

The giggle sounded like a little girl. I spun around until I spotted where it came from. In the direction that I was originally heading stood a little girl. She was wearing a black dress that was very old, or at least it was an old design. She had white as snow hair that spiked up in every direction. She was holding what appeared to be a toy doll.

I looked a little harder, and I could see her eyes; her eyes were blue, and huge, then she smiled. When she did, I could make out her fangs. I thought the second I laid eyes on her she could be a vampire, but now I knew. The smile and look she was giving me sent chills up my spine.

I found my kind, and I don't think she is friendly.

Chapter 8
Dads & Dolls

I caught movement out of the corner of my eye.

Something was moving through the grass; I was surrounded.

Whatever was moving through the grass was closing in on me from all directions. I looked up at where the strange girl was; now she was gone. Now I could hear sounds, like clicking and drooling. Whatever it was now was close enough for me to look over the grass to see what it was.

I had to hold in a shriek of terror; they were giant spiders; they were the size of small dogs. They were almost knee high and coming in from all directions. They were so gross, black with short hair and lots of black eyes across the top of their bodies.

Now I could see one of their nasty mouths; it was like a lot of little black hairy fingers moving really fast.

The first one jumped into the air and landed on my back. I tossed it off and screamed all at the same time. At the same time one of them bit me in the ankle. It hurt like hell; I kicked at the spider, but failed to make contact.

A spider tried to jump on me again, but this time I was ready and moved only to get cut open by another spider's leg as it leaped out of the grass at me. It cut me right above the knee; lucky for me I heal fast.

I hate bugs; I have always hated bugs. They were my worst nightmare brought to life; not only was I outnumbered, but these spiders were faster than me. I flashed from one spot to another only to find more spiders.

I tried to attack them swinging at them, but to no avail. Every time I tried to hit one, another one would bite me or claw me. I was getting cut to ribbons, and the spiders just kept coming. The cuts hurt, but it was the blood loss that was becoming the problem. I could feel them stealing my life away one drop at a time.

I could not keep doing this forever; and now there were even more spiders. I don't know why I didn't think about this until now, but I needed to use my second sight. Then I would be able to see behind me and deal with multiple enemies faster. I started to use my high pitch whistle, but it wasn't working.

I couldn't seem to see the spiders with my second sight, and if I didn't do something soon I was in deep shit. The spiders were tearing me to pieces; they were attacking me faster, and I couldn't even hit them.

I was trying to use my second sight again when I noticed something; it was a girl. None of the spiders were showing up in my second sight, but there was a little girl. I closed my eyes and whistled, this time letting my second sight become my only sight. All the spiders were gone and the only thing in this field was me and a girl holding a doll.

Damn, I am slow; vampires can screw with your mind. And, if that's true, that explains the old lady. The girl flashed up to me really fast, bent down and slashed my leg, then flashed away. I opened my eyes and could see all the spiders that were trying to get me. And now I understood what she was doing; every time I blocked an attack, or attacked a spider, she would flash up to me and slash me; only I would see a spider do the attack.

No wonder I couldn't hit these spiders; they didn't even exist. I closed my eyes and pretended I didn't notice her working her way behind me. This time I would be ready when she flashed to cut me.

As soon as she flashed in close behind me, she went to slash me with her free arm. She was still holding a doll in the other.

I spun around at the same time moving my leg so her slash fell short of its target. I jumped at her, only to swing at empty air. She had sidestepped me; I swung at her again, but she moved and twisted herself away from every swing I threw at her.

She flashed away, but I flashed right next to her and kept trying to rip and claw her little face off. She was fast; not only that but she would block me with her one arm. Then she would kick me, or throw me off balance. I found myself on my knees more than a few times; it didn't take long before I wasn't attacking her.

She was attacking me again, and she was winning. With one arm and never letting loose of her doll, she moved like a ninja, kicking, punching, and clawing me to pieces.

I had thought the two men in the cabin had known how to fight. Well I was wrong. I had never even been in a fight in my life, and, in death it had been nothing but one. I thought I had understood how to fight now, and now I realize that I knew nothing. I couldn't help but think of the statement, couldn't see the forest because of the trees. Well now I was seeing stars.

She moved so fast and surefooted, that, every time I thought I understood what she might do, she hit or clawed me again. I struck at her; she moved out of the way, grabbed my extended arm, and then pulled me forward. I fell onto one knee before I caught my balance, and could get up; she hit me across the face with her fist. She hit me with such force, that I found myself on my hands and knees.

I was spitting teeth out onto the ground; then she landed on my back; she reached around my neck and tore my throat out. I fell to the ground in pain and was dizzy; I could feel my life spilling out of my neck onto the ground. The blood formed a puddle around my still body.

My neck healed itself and stopped bleeding, but I had been cut so many times I had lost a lot of blood. I felt weak and unable to stand. I had really hoped to kill the men who had done this to me, and I really am going to miss David and Carrie. I should have kissed David.

"Oh dolly she is tougher than she looks. I think I broke her." The little girl said in very sweet voice. "I know she needs a doctor."

And this girl needs one too, but not in a study of medicine but psychiatry. The girl then flipped me onto my back. She looked down at me as if trying to decide on what to do. Then she said with a little smile looking down at her old twisted looking doll. "I think she needs surgery. It's the only way to save her."

With that she grabbed one of her dolly legs, and pulled. Out came a knife; it was about six inches long. The handle was the doll's leg; the blade was curved and wicked looking. She looked down at me with an evil smile, and a look of mischief.

I finally found my voice. "What do you want?"

She put the edge of her knife to her lips, and said, "Shhh." Then, in one quick movement, she tore away what was left of my dress.

She put the tip of the knife on the bottom of my rib cage, and then began to cut. She slowly pulled the knife down my stomach; then the crazy little girl began to sing.

Hey, like a surgeon,
Cuttin' for the very first time
Like a surgeon
Organ transplants are on my mind

She laughed at her own joke, and then said. "Get it? You know, instead of like a virgin."

My stomach was already beginning to heal. I hate being toyed with, but I didn't want to piss her off yet. I had to see if I could get out of this mess. The best way would probably be to just play along with her? So I said as nicely as I could manage. "Sorry I don't get the reference."

I could feel myself again; some of my strength had returned. If I was careful, maybe I could escape this crazy girl, but, just as I was thinking that, she said to me. "You heal fast; regaining your strength already; well you're more than what meets the eye. Like a transformer."

"A what?" I asked.

She pointed her knife at my face and said. "You're a strange little girl. What do we do with this one?"

Who was she asking? I wondered. Then a man's voice said. "I am not sure Alice. Does she have a name?"

"Do you have a name, girl?" Alice parroted.

"Melabeth." I squeaked.

"What is your birth name?" the strange man asked. I still could not see him without moving; and I didn't dare with Alice holding a long knife to my face.

"It's Melabeth, none of your business." I answered calmly.

Alice drove the knife into my chest. I gasped in pain, as she giggled. She left the knife in my chest; the pain stopped soon after being stabbed.

The knife being stuck in me didn't really bother me after the initial stab. Alice must have known this, because right about the time the pain stopped; she grabbed the baby's leg handle, and roughly yanked the knife out. I had to hold back a scream. That hurt worse than going in.

Alice said in a mean voice, "Answer the questions bitch. And answer them truthfully. If you don't we will know. What is your birth name?"

"Melabeth the vampire." I answered.

Alice smiled a wicked smile. "She's strong and tough; I should just kill her."

The man stepped closer, so now I could see him over Alice's shoulder. He was tall, and thin. His arms and legs looked to be stretched; even his neck was longer than most. He had dark brown hair that fell around his face; it was shoulder length. Brown eyes with an older looking face, I would guess him around thirty. He sported a goatee and over all he was good looking, but not in the traditional way. There was kindness in his eyes.

He looked down at me and said in a kind voice. "My name is Ezra White; this is my daughter Alice White. My birth name was Ezra Bovine. Alice's name has always been the same; we wish to ask you questions. I will require honest answers; if I get them you may leave."

"When, and in what condition?" I asked.

He laughed along with Alice. Alice said, "You get to leave in pieces."

Ezra bent down with his long knees, so now he was resting his elbows on his knees. Alice was still sitting next to me on the ground. He still towered above us; he was much taller than I had thought he was.

He looked down at me and said. "As long as you're honest, you are my guest. And when, or if I give leave to you, you will leave in the same manner you came."

"So you'll get me a new dress?" I smarted off.

Alice turned her head toward Ezra, "let me kill her?" Alice asked Ezra.

"Yes I will get you a new dress," Ezra answered me while staring down at me. He didn't really acknowledge Alice's request for my death. Then he asked me, "Your birth name?"

Well I don't believe this man will let me keep living unless I start talking, so against my better judgment, I said. "Melanie Elizabeth Dare, but the name is dead to me."

His face lightened up a little, but Alice frowned. I guess Alice was hoping I would keep resisting, so she could torture me. Then Ezra asked me. "What are you doing here?"

"Looking for my own kind."

"And what kind is that? I wonder?" Alice said with a look of disgust.

"Please Alice." Ezra said with softness in his voice. Then with a more serious tone he said to me. "You mean other vampires? And, if so, why?"

"Yes vampires," I said, not sure what to say, or how to say it. "Well… I need help. I don't know how to be a vampire."

Alice burst into laughter; between bursts of laughing she spit out, "she is so full… of sh… it." Ezra gave her a disapproving look, but, as soon as she stopped laughing so hard, she added. "Oh come on; just let me rip her head off. Pppplease," she begged.

"Alice that is enough." A strange woman said. The voice came from above me, for I was still lying on my back. If I were to lift my head to see who this was I would have to take my eyes off of Ezra and Alice. I didn't think it wise to stop paying attention to Alice.

The voice sounded very authoritative as she spoke. "Go play your games elsewhere. Let me and Ezra deal with this girl. She speaks the truth so far Ezra; find out why she needs to know how to be a vampire."

Alice stuck her tongue out at me. "After you're done answering questions for mom and dad, you and I have some unfinished business." She said this while pointing the tip of her knife at me. Then she stood up and moved around to the back of Ezra.

Ezra reached down and grabbed my neck. He lifted me up off the ground; he was now standing, and so was I. Then he released my neck as the new vampire moved around to the side of Ezra. Ezra, standing in front of me, I could now tell he stood almost seven feet tall.

Then Ezra put his arm around the new woman and said. "This is my wife, Charlotte White. Dear, this is Melabeth. Now Melabeth, if you would like to live, please explain why you are here to me and my wife. A little warning; my wife will know if you lie."

I looked over at his wife; she was a beautiful woman. She looked to be in her early twenties. She looked short standing next to Ezra, but she was about my height. She was white, really white, even for a vampire. She had a round face but was really thin. She had big blonde curls that hung around her head; her hair hung just a little bit past her shoulders, but must be a lot longer if it were straight. She had a Chicago accent when she spoke. "Go ahead child; what is your business with the White clan?"

Well I told them my story. As I told them the story, Alice made remarks; I was a little liar that needed to be spanked. Charlotte would say things to Alice like, "I know if she is lying, Alice. So far what she says, she believes. And that is what the truth is, our own personal take on things around us. Now be quiet and let her finish."

I wouldn't go on talking, only to be interrupted by Alice, and then Ezra or Charlotte would settle her down again. Alice scared me; she was out of her mind. Or she was a child, a child with a lot of power.

At the same time, the looks they gave each other as I told my story were somehow off. They didn't believe what I was saying, or what I was saying was incorrect somehow. I ignored this and finally I finished. "And after I sobered up, that's when I went for a walk, and that's when I ran into Alice."

"She is lying. Lying, lying, lying." Alice whinnied as she stomped her one foot on the ground.

"Saying it more than once does not make it true, Alice," Charlotte calmly said.

"You watched me fight her, didn't you? Explain that." Alice said in a much more serious tone.

Ezra spoke with a very knowing certainty, "This may be easily explained Alice. She has false memories, which could explain why Charlotte cannot see the lie. As Charlotte said just moments ago, truth is what we believe it to be. I believe the blood will tell; you can't hide age in the blood."

Alice looked at him. "Yes, test her blood. It still doesn't explain why Charlotte can't see the lie. You can't wipe vampire memories. The memories are in the blood, and if you could, I would know how, and I don't know how. Therefore it is not possible."

"So what you're saying is that it is me and me alone who she can trick?" Charlotte said with a smirk on her face. "I don't think she fooled me. Once Ezra determines the blood, I don't believe any kind of torture will result in a different story."

"You haven't seen all my tortures then. I will get different results; not saying they will be any closer to the truth, but they will be different." Alice said with a grin, and then all three of them laughed at Alice's joke.

I didn't find it so funny; it was my torture they were referring to. Also I'm not even sure why they didn't believe me, or what part of my life story was a lie. Why is it, that, since I died, it always felt like I was jumping out of the frying pan and into the fire.

"Give me your wrist," Ezra ordered me.

I thought about resisting, but that would get me beat up, and they would take what they wanted. There were three of them, not that they needed three. I couldn't even fight their little daughter, let alone Ezra. He looked like he could fight, and I have lost a lot of blood. And I was hungry again; damn, I had just eaten. My body had repaired the damages, but I felt weak and tired, so I handed Ezra my wrist without a word.

Ezra bit my wrist; at first it hurt, but then the feeling started to change. It felt good, really good; no I mean really good. Oh it felt, Oh my... then he stopped and pulled his mouth away. I felt a wave of dizziness as I stumbled. Ezra grabbed me and kept me from falling onto the ground.

"She has very little blood left, and she's weak," Ezra announced, and then said. "I am amazed; her blood agrees with her story. She could only be a few days old, a week at most."

"How can she be so strong then?" Alice about yelled.

"Let's take her back to the house, Ezra," Charlotte suggested.

"Yes, we need to find out more about this one," Ezra said with a little too much curiosity in his voice for my liking.

"Well I don't know if I can stay," I said.

Alice laughed. Then she looked at me with what appeared to be hate. "You gave me enough problems for tonight little one." Then she stared into my eyes with her bright blue eyes. "Sleep."

It was the middle of the night, and I was not going to go to sleep with these three vampires in control of my body. Then Alice, still staring in my eyes; "sleep... sleep." I am not going to...

I woke to darkness. What now? I stood up and looked around, but couldn't see anything but darkness. I looked at my hands, and I could see them as if I were standing outside. I was wearing a dress that I had never seen before. Why could I see myself like it was day, but the floor was as dark as night?

I wasn't hungry and that's when it hit me; this was a dream. There was something not real about this. Well, just when I was thinking, what a strange empty dream, a door appeared in front of me. It was arched at the top and just stood all by itself in the darkness. It was made out of wood, really old wood. Well why not? So I walked up to the door and opened it.

Inside the door was a room or maybe a library, there were books and scrolls everywhere. The books were all very old. The room wasn't set up like a library the book shelves ran in all directions. There were stacks of books on the floor piled up against the walls. Tables with books in all matter of disarray, it looked as if no one ever tried to put anything back where it belonged.

I stepped into the room, and of course, the door disappeared behind me. It was replaced by a bookshelf full of old books. In the middle of the large room was a giant square fireplace; it had huge stone work all around it.

Then I looked up; wow, my imagination was working overtime. There was no roof; instead it was the night sky; no moon but all the stars. In fact more stars then I ever remember seeing. It was breath taking.

As I walked deeper into the room, I came to realize that the room was much larger than I had originally thought. It was not square; the walls had openings that went into large round shaped rooms. And there were passageways that lead into smaller rooms. I didn't see any other doors, just doorways.

Up ahead on the far side of the room from where I came in, there was a large arch opening. It was kind of funny looking, since the arch, had no roof on either side of it. On the other side of the arch was another room.

This one was different; there were two large stone owls guarding the entrance. Inside this room it was a lot cleaner, or maybe a better word would be more organized. Books were put away on the shelves, and the ones out were neatly stacked. Also there were nick knacks all over the place. They were strange and had no rhyme or reason. There were strange looking glass bottles, toys, and I even spotted a small gong. At the far end of this room was another fire place; only this one was against the wall with a giant mantle. On the mantle stood a giant owl with a clock built into its chest.

In front of the fireplace there were two seats; both facing the fireplace. They had really tall backs, so you couldn't see if anyone was sitting there. In-between the seats' there was a coffee table with one large mug sitting on it; the mug had steam coming out the top.

An arm reached out from the seat on the left and grabbed the mug, then took the drink behind the seat where I could not see. Then the hand returned the mug; time to find out who is in my dream.

I entered the room and worked my way around the outside of it. There were a lot of benches and worktables placed in the middle of the room. I finally was at the wall with the fireplace; as I approached the chairs, I could see one of them was empty.

In the other chair, Nicks sat with a large book on his lap. His head was looking down at the pages. I cleared my throat to get his attention; he snapped his head up in surprise at the noise I had made. Then his eyes met mine; our eyes stayed locked on one another, for what felt like eternity.

He stood up letting his book hit the ground.

"What an unexpected surprise. One would think it was my birthday. Come to me." Nicks said this at the same time he was already heading over to where I stood.

Something felt off about this dream; like it wasn't a dream, just dreamlike. I was so happy to see Nicks, so I let that thought go and I walked quickly to meet him halfway. We embraced in a hug.

I said almost weeping. "Finally; I was wondering when you might show up. Please be more than a dream."

Nicks pulled his head away from my shoulder so he could now look me in the eyes, but he was still holding onto me tightly. Then he said with a kind smile. "This is much more than some dream dear. This is what we call a mind connection. You have found me; you're in my head. I am so glad you did; we have much to talk about."

"Yes, yes we do. I have a hundred questions or more."

He laughed; it was wonderful to hear him. "In that case, we better take a seat, not even in my mind can I stand through a hundred questions."

He moved me over to the empty chair. He twisted the chair so it was facing toward the other chair. After taking my seat, he adjusted his chair so now we were face to face with the coffee table between us.

Like magic, he reached into his pocket and pulled out a large mug like the one that was already on the table. It was the same shape and size; only the mug that was already there, a green mug, and this one was a dull red. He set it down so it was close to me.

Then he said. "In my mind the world is how I like it; and I like hot, strong, coffee. Drink, you will find it wonderful."

So I did drink, and I did find it wonderful. "Thank you. It is really good coffee; in fact I didn't really know I liked coffee. So a lot of things have happened, and I may be in trouble as we speak. I need to know how to be a vampire or what I can and cannot do. Can you tell me?"

Nicks picked up his coffee and set back into his chair. Then he said, "It's nothing to be a father, but I wish to be your dad. Or maybe it's the other way around. Never mind, that's unimportant. What is important is that I understand what's been happening with you. So first, if you don't mind, I need to ask the questions."

"Ok, shoot, what do you need to know?" I answered. I didn't mind answering his questions first; maybe it would give him the best information to help me.

"So how long have you been out of the grave?"

"Four nights, maybe five; I have kind of lost track; it's been… eventful." I couldn't believe it has only been a few nights; it feels as if it's been forever.

"Wait, what year did I bury you? Was it in 1975?" Nicks asked surprised.

"Yes."

"You have been in the ground for fifteen years. Wow I didn't see that coming." Nicks sat back in his chair and had a look of someone in deep thought.

"What?" I said surprised. "You didn't understand how long it would take me to change into a vampire?"

Nicks didn't answer me for minute, and then said. "Vampire; Yes you're a vampire. We need to set rules to this conversation, things I must understand, before anyone else. I am unable to come to you physically. And I cannot answer all of your questions, and this is why. Information is power, and I cannot risk someone finding out... details about you. Don't get upset; I trust you could keep a secret, but some vampires can steal what's in your mind. They can trick you; hell you might even think you are talking to me."

"Alice made me see things that are not there."

"Oh, don't tell me; you have met Alice the White?"

"Yes, in fact that's who has me captured right now." I said a little worried. The look Nicks gave when he said her name was not a good one.

"She is a child. Please understand she cannot know too much of our business. If you don't know, then no one can steal what you don't have. Have you told anyone else how long you were in the ground?"

"Yes, the Whites, David and Carrie, I didn't know that was a bad thing." I said, with worry; I hope I didn't make yet another mess for me.

Still all the mystery was making me feel curiosity, like a cat. I would like to know why I am different and different how?

Nicks let out a huff of air, and then started talking again. "What's done is done. Tell me what I have missed for the last four or five days."

I poured out the story I had just told the Whites. I had started the story from the point when Nicks had buried me. It surprised me when he wanted to know what had killed me. I quickly found out that Nicks had not known what had happen to me prior to changing me. When I finished telling the story, Nicks got mad.

Nicks eyes had turned a bright red; it was like something had lit a fire behind his eyes. "DAMN... if I would have known... I would have HUNTED DOWN those no good... ripped their dicks right off." After Nicks said this, he set quietly for a minute to calm down.

What really amazed me was even through this dream I could feel his power. Nicks was strong, and there was something different about him that I couldn't even explain to myself. Then he looked up at me with softness in his eyes. They still had some red in them, but it was passion I felt, not anger.

He said to me, "I am sorry for you. And I know those words do nothing for you, but I will do something for you. I can help you find your peace, find your revenge. Still there are things you must know and do before you can have your peace. For starters I know some of these men you speak of. And they are not just men; they are monsters as well. I do not know where the bikers are, or your father, but the film director Devon I know where he might still be. Know this; he is a member of a powerful member of a group that calls themselves The Order. They act as if they are the supernatural police; nothing is further from the truth. They are just a group of people wielding power over others."

I couldn't believe he was going to tell me how to find Devon. "Where is he?"

Nicks smiled. "First you must promise me something."

"Anything" I said without even thinking about it.

Nicks chuckled at me. "You must not run off and just kill this man. You must do it in secret, undercover like ninja. You cannot get caught, and before you can even start, you will need to prepare. You will first learn as much as you can from the White's on how to be a vampire. Second, you will observe your target for no less than six months before killing him."

"What?" My mouth fell open and hit the floor. I am so slow, I had already agreed to this.

Nicks smiled, or was he smirking, hard to tell. Then he repressed a laugh and said. "I have reasons. I am afraid you will awaken soon; I must tell you things before you do. It might be a few days before we are able to link up again."

I didn't like the sound of that. "Why?" I asked a little winey.

"Don't worry about why, not right now. More importantly you must understand a little bit more about vampires. Do you remember all the information I told you about turning?"

"It's like a drug. And after a while it kills you and you might rise from the grave to become a vampire. I know you put more detail in there, but I think I remember most of it."

Nicks continued. "Good, but you need to understand more. Vampire's blood has amazing healing for the living, but it's kind of fake. It will not cure cancer or other sickness. In fact it only makes people with those kinds of diseases just think they are better. It will stop healing you as soon as it leaves the system, and, if the user keeps taking it, they will die. If someone dies with blood in their system, they could turn; some things keep people from turning our age, too old or too young, sickness, cancer or Aids; it's a cruel curse that only changes the healthy and strong. I have never seen a child turned that had not gone through puberty; and I have never witnessed a person over sixty. It is important that you understand that not all people can simply be changed. The blood becomes the life, not just the blood you drink, but your own blood. If you blew a vampires head off, it would grow back, amazing as that is, he or she would remember everything."

"How can that be?" I asked in astonishment.

"Well the memory is in the blood. The blood just uses your body for things it cannot do by itself. The blood cannot think, so it animates the brain. It cannot see, so it uses your eyes, and if something in your body is destroyed, the blood reanimates it back. That's why vampires never change. The moment they die, their blood takes over; it only remembers what they looked like when they were changed. Understand, the blood ages; everything ages. Even the mountains are getting older and someday will be no more. Vampires can live for thousands of years, but not forever. Now that you understand that you are the blood, understand that is the one true way to kill vampires. Destroy the blood, destroy the vampire. Obviously the blood changes; it becomes flammable. Your blood will burn like oil; fire is the vampire's true destroyer. Two things will set your blood a-flame. One is fire of course; the second one is the sun. For some reason or another if UV light hits a vampire blood, it will combusts."

"I have been outside; and I didn't catch on fire. Why is that?" I asked.

Nicks snickered. "Your blood combusts, not your skin, you're fine as long as you don't get cut or shot."

Now that creature in the alley made more sense. "The man in the alley said all he had to do was claw me and I would die. I thought he had magical claws."

Nicks burst into laughter. "No, no he was most likely a shifter or werewolf. They must have thought you would run away. That's what most vampires would do if confronted in broad daylight. What was I saying? Well the important part is that you understand the blood, and this is why. Without life energy we die, so the only other way to kill us is to starve us to death. Most all vampires would be weak as a human in 90 days. They would be dead in 120. That's why you must be careful with whom you tell your story to; they will want to know how you went fifteen years without food."

"How did I?" I asked with curiosity.

"You need to take the next six months while you are hunting Devon and learn how to use your power. The Whites will teach you. You are strong but inexperienced."

"You didn't answer my question" I said angrily.

Nicks lifted his one eye brow, "Didn't I?"

Ok I get it, no answer means no. "Why do I need to take six months to learn? I am strong, and I have fought before."

"You got lucky." Nicks quickly answered. "You will need more than luck to survive this world. And I wish to see you live a long life. Have you already forgotten about your battle with Alice?"

"Ok," I said in a grumpy voice.

Nicks said in a much softer voice. "Let me tell you a story. Once there were four men who were good friends. Three of them were brothers and very close. The man that was not a brother, his name was Tim; he was caught sleeping with one of the brother's wives, all three brothers came to Tim, to beat him up. One brother was stronger than Tim; the other brother was faster; the last brother was both faster and stronger. Who won the fight?"

I felt like I was missing something. "Well if I had to guess from the information you gave me. The brothers won, but then why tell that story? So my guess is Tim won the fight."

Nicks then said, "What question would you ask? To find out who won for sure."

"Did Tim have a weapon?"

"Good question, but no, you are right in your assumption that Tim won. Let me tell you why. One brother was a teacher. The second brother was a brick mason, and the last brother was a lawyer."

I smiled; I think I know where he is going with this story. "What's Tim do for a living?"

"Tim, well Tim was a Ranger, for the Army. He had fought on two continents. He not only won the fight; he left the brothers in a pile."

"Why the story? I am not sure what that has to do with me killing Devon." I said.

Nicks took another drink of his coffee, which reminded me to do the same. Then he said. "Devon is no mere man. He is one of the local leaders of The Order. He is much more then what he looks like. You need to train with the Whites; you have the power; now you must learn how to use it. You will find him at Beaumont High school. There is where he pretends to be a teacher. And now I expect he chose the position for other reasons than the summers off; six months, Melabeth, don't let me down."

I moaned and in a very winey voice I said. "Six months; that's forever."

Nicks did that one eye brow lift again, and then said. "Will a stake in the heart kill you?"

"I think so." I said very unsure.

"You have so much to learn before you face your enemies." Nicks then put his hands together, and stood up. He then walked over to me, bent down so our faces were at the same height.

The look on his face was full of love and compassion. His face had love for me, and it made my heart hurt; I felt like I should make him proud. "Yes father; I will try to do as you ask."

Nicks smiled. "Know this; you are my daughter. I love and miss you; I will not be whole until we stand together. It's time for you to go."

"Already, I'm not ready." I cried.

"Just for now." Nicks said with a knowing face.

"Bye... I love you." I barely said when the room went dark. My eyes opened, and I was awake.

I awoke lying in a bed. It was a four post bed with a canopy over the top. The sheets were pink silk, with purple trim. The room was dark for it was still night outside. There were two windows next to the head of the bed, but both windows had heavy curtains drawn tight. The curtains matched the bed.

The room was full of dolls; there were shelves and book cabinets on every wall. The dolls were in all shape and sizes; some looked really old. I sat up in the bed; I felt strong again. It must have been pitch black in this room because it seemed dark in the room.

The door to the room opened. I was blinded when the room filled with light from the hallway. Then Alice flipped the light on; it took a second for my eyes to refocus.

She gave me a strange look as she stared at me. The creepy little girl was still holding onto her doll, and she was still wearing an old black dress. Her hair was no longer white, but black. She also had a very large plastic cup in her other hand. Then a scent hit my nose and I knew that she was holding a cup of blood.

Alice put on a giant smile, and, instead of looking welcoming, she looked insane. Then she said. "I see that you're awake sister. You're so strong. You have recovered already. Good news; father said it's ok for you to stay. So now we are sisters; Ezra is our father and Charlotte is our mother. I will even share my dollies. Are you thirsty?"

"Yes I am." I simply answered.

Alice's face turned mischievous, and then she said. "Can you smell it?"

"Yes, I can smell the blood."

With the same look on her face Alice said. "What if I say you can't have any? What do you say to that?"

With a monotone voice, I said. "I would say that I was going to stay hungry."

With a screech of delight, Alice burst out. "Only four days old. Such control; where is the madness? Father's right; we should keep you; you are so neat. We are going to have so much fun... aren't you excited?"

With the same flat voice I said. "Ecstatic."

Alice giggled, and then said. "You wait and see. This is going to be fun."

"Alice." Ezra said as he stepped into the room.

"Yes father."

"Enough for now. I must discuses the ground rules with Melabeth now that she is a new family member."

Alice turned and did a curtsy; then she flashed out of the room very quickly. I couldn't even hear her leave she moved so quick and quietly. And then I realized that the little bitch took the blood with her.

Ezra crossed his arms behind him holding his hands; he began a slow pace as he spoke. "Melabeth, welcome to the family. It is your choice to stay. I will give you that."

He was honestly giving me a choice to leave. And in some ways that sounded like a good idea to leave; Alice scared me, and this room with all these dolls gave me the creeps. Still Nicks said I must stay with the Whites and train.

So, I said. "I have nowhere else to go. I don't know how to be a vampire; I need your help."

Ezra eyed me then added. "If you stay... you are not a prisoner. You can leave whenever you choose, but while you stay there are rules. If you can follow the rules, I am sure we will all become family. And in the end you will not want to leave."

"Thank you. Thank you for making me feel, welcomed." Alice scared me, but Ezra made me comfortable.

Ezra smiled, then in a very serious voice he said. "You are strong, not just physically, but mentally as well. You have heart, the heart of a lion. I seldom see the willingness to die in battle; you never ran, even when all was lost. If you're half as smart as I think you might be, then you will make a magnificent vampire. You need guidance and direction; that is what family is for."

"I will try to make you proud."

It was like he was my father; another dad, that I was trying to make happy. So now I have three fathers. One I must learn from, Ezra. One I wish to be with, Nicks, and one father I need to kill. I was looking around at all the Dolls in the room as I thought about my fathers. Dads and Dolls, looked like I have plenty of both.

"I am sure you will." Ezra said beaming at me. "In fact you already have made me proud. The fact you haven't lost control even after Alice took your blood. And you have suffered a great deal of blood loss. In fact you should be a lot weaker than you look. Then again nothing seems to add up with you."

I was a little shocked; what did he mean by that. "Is there something wrong with me?"

"No, no nothing like that." Ezra held his hand up with one finger while he stopped pacing. He was deep in thought, and then he began to speak. "You are ignorant."

"Did you just call me stupid?" I said defensively.

"No, ignorance can be fixed by knowledge, but stupid is forever. You have much to learn, so try to keep hold of your emotions and listen to what I am saying." He said this calmly. Then he sat next to me on the bed. "In our family there's five of us; you make us six. You have already met Alice and my wife Charlotte. You have not met our son, Michael. And also there is our newest member, Lea; our daughter as well. I will give you a short family history, so you may understand why you are so different."

"Ok, I would like that."

"First you will follow me to the kitchen. You need to eat, and I don't think Alice is bringing you anything back."

Just saying it reminded me about how hungry I was. "Right behind you." With that I followed Ezra out of the room and down the hallway.

We stepped into the kitchen. It was a large kitchen with an island in the middle. Of course a house full of vampires has a large kitchen. What did make sense was the size of the refrigerator; it was a side by side, basically two refrigerators.

One door was open with a man leaning bending inside the refrigerator. I could see there were bags of blood stacked in side. Even as hungry as I was I still noticed this guy's butt, if I wasn't close to starving, I don't think I could be thinking of anything else.

The man stood up with a bag of blood in one hand; as he turned around, Ezra said. "This is my son, Michael; Michael this is Melabeth."

The man that stood before me was a Greek god, or at least he looked like one. He stood six foot; he wasn't as tall as Ezra; he had long blonde hair that hung to his shoulders. His hair was a mess, but stilled looked good. He was very well built, and the tight shirt he wore showed his chest off nicely. He was wearing jeans and shirt that said Star Wars on it. I have to watch those movies. His face was strong, and, if I had to guess, he was turned in his early twenties.

I was trying not to spaz out; all I got out of my mouth was. "Hi."

With an angry face, Michael about yelled out. "So this is her. I am NOT taking care of her Ezra."

"You will not have to." Ezra pleaded.

"I would like to go to school. A four day old in the house, she is a BABY. And you have a four year old too. How will you manage both?" Michael said with a lot of hand jesters. The way he was swing around that bag of blood, I was sure it would rip open and blood would go everywhere. Then he tossed the bag onto the island.

Ezra said in a very stern voice. "This is a conversation for another time."

"Yep, I got to go and feed the four year old anyway." Michael said as he stormed out of the room.

"Ignore him." Ezra said laying a calming hand on mine.

Michael flashed back into the kitchen. "Yes, ignore me. Everyone else does; my opinion doesn't matter." And, with that, he picked up the bag of blood that he had forgotten on the island; then he flashed back out.

I was more than a little taken back. I was sad that the sexy man already hated me. Then I remembered David, and I felt like I betrayed him. I didn't do anything; why can't I look? I am chalking up, all these crazy emotions up to lack of food.

I said to Ezra, "food then. I mean food please."

Ezra smiled, and then said. "Your control; it is amazing. Let's get you some food. Charlotte, join us."

I looked up to see where his wife was when she flashed into the room. I would love to know how he knew she was there, or could she hear us from somewhere else in the house. Charlotte gave me a small hug then with a tight smile she said. "Michael will come around; don't worry dear. So what do you think about Michael? He is a real hunk isn't he sweetheart."

While Charlotte played matchmaker, Ezra heated up blood for all of us. We sat around a kitchen island drinking blood out of glass goblets. We talked and joked; all in all it wasn't too bad of an evening. Ezra promised information tomorrow night. He said we all had enough for one night. I couldn't really argue with that, because, after the blood kicked in, I was tired.

So, off to bed I went; of course I got the bedroom with all the creepy dolls. It took a little time to fall off to sleep; my last thoughts were about David and Carrie. I was hoping they were faring alright.

Ok I also may have thought or two of Michael.

Chapter 9
Vampires 101

I awoke to the light of the sun peering through a few small cracks in the window drapes. The clock next to my bed said it was 1:45 PM. I had gone to bed around 6 AM.

I had slept about eight hours; I wasn't tired anymore as I lay upon the bed thinking. There was a cute skirt with a nice top laid out for me. The top was light pink, and the skirt was faded blue jean. There was a white bra and white panties. Long black stockings set on the bed, and on the floor were my tall black boots. Someone had cleaned them up, and they looked close to new.

Across the hallway there was a bathroom, and there I drew a nice hot bath. After the bathing, brushing of the hair and dressing, I was ready. It was now 3 PM. I was in no hurry; it was nice to take things easy for once.

I was just now realizing that I had no real idea of my surroundings. I had awoken last night to find myself in a room with Alice. Then, after a short walk down a hallway, I was lead into a kitchen by Ezra. After hanging out with him and Charlotte for a few hours, I had just come from down the same hallway to sleep. Ezra had pointed out the bathroom.

Now I found myself heading down the same hallway, but, instead of going into the kitchen, I headed down an adjoining hallway. This led to a giant set of doors that went outside. They had large glass windows in the doors. I could see that on the other side was an in ground pool.

It was surrounded by a wooden gate. This was a huge house; if I whistled, my second sight would bounce around the hallways. I could see there were doors everywhere; I could even see stairs that went up to a second story.

I kept walking around when I came to a big open room. It was full of all kinds of plants and furniture. It had a grand piano in the corner; there were books on shelves, also different style couches and chairs. As I took the room in, I could see all kinds of different instruments hanging all over the place; even an electric guitar with an amp lying next to it. So I guess this is the music room.

I entered the room and was looking around. At the same time I heard someone coming into the room from another direction. At first I was thinking it was one of the Whites, but then I realized, as they he got closer, that none of the Whites make that much noise walking. Also this person was dragging something.

It didn't take long before I could hear breathing, and then their heartbeats; a heavyset black woman entered the room. I could smell her sweat now; she was dragging a vacuum cleaner behind her. Also she was wearing a baby blue dress with a white apron in front. It was obvious she was the cleaning lady. She was setting up the vacuum and unwinding the cord; she still had not noticed me in the room.

Then I heard another set of feet coming from the same direction. Someone was coming to join her. A skinny black girl came in behind her; she was much younger than the first cleaning lady. I was guessing, but I would bet that the heavyset lady was the skinny girl's mother. They shared so many of the same features, and the age difference was about right.

The young girl spotted me first; she let out a loud gasp that nearly scared me from the sudden noise. She quickly put her hand up to her mouth as her eyes opened in surprise. The older lady was now staring at me, eyes wide; I could hear both their hearts speed up.

I could smell the fear.

I could feel my teeth elongate in my mouth as my hunger twisted my stomach.

Their fear made me want to feed on them; I could feel my claws fully extended. I also knew that my eyes were wide open and unblinking as I stared at them like they were meat. They could see my teeth because I had my mouth partly open.

I didn't know what to do; I was afraid to talk; it would only scare them more.

The oldest lady calmed herself a little bit. She dropped the cord in her hand and took two steps so that she was standing between me and the skinny girl. Then she said very quietly, but still plenty loud enough for me to hear. "Tangy, go… walk away slowly. Go now girl, I got this."

Well these girls knew who they worked for, and what I was. Tangy shakily responded to the older woman's request. "Momma… I don't think I should leave…"

"Shh… go now. Everything is ok," the older lady said with a very calm voice, but she never took her eyes off of me.

I had time in this moment to get control of myself. I pulled my teeth back up and retracted my claws. It was the sudden fear that I wasn't ready for.

Then I said. "I am sorry for scaring you. My name is Melabeth. I will let you two alone so you can finish your cleaning in peace."

I turned and started to walk away; I figured this would be best.

I heard the older lady say. "Thank you Melabeth for showing some control around here. That will be a nice treat, not to have worry about getting eaten by another young one. By the way my name is Betty and this is my daughter Tangy. You take care now."

It was kind of funny to have people talking to you after you have left the room. I had traveled down the hallway pretty far but could still hear her speaking. She must understand better than me how well vampires could hear.

Then I heard something further down a hallway that I had not traveled down yet. It took me a moment, but then I knew what it was. It was TV; I haven't seen a TV in forever, so I headed toward the sound.

I came into a room that I would have to describe as comfortable. It had lots of woodwork and it was all stained to a dark finish. And there were dark couches, loveseats and other padded chairs. They were all against the walls and most of them were pointing at the biggest TV that I have ever seen.

On the screen was a show that I had never seen before. Well I bet all my shows have been off air for a while. Directly in front of the TV, was a long black couch. In the middle of the couch was the back of what I knew to be Michael's head.

I started to move toward the couch when Michael turned his head around; then he said. "Oh, it's you. Up already? I would have thought you would be a later sleeper." He turned his head back to the TV show.

"Why is that?" I asked, wondering what makes some vampires sleep longer than others. That is if that's what he meant.

Michael just shrugged his shoulders. "Your age." It looked like he was done talking when he suddenly turned his head and stared at me with accusing eyes. "Have YOU hurt any of the help?"

"No… I haven't; what makes you say that?"

Michael stared at me for a minute; then he said. "You're young. I forgot today the cleaning ladies are here. Lea's still asleep; she doesn't get up until after 5. I guess I am lucky you didn't run into the help. I didn't realize you awoke this early." He turned his head back to the TV.

This kind of hurt my pride, and I didn't like being treated like a child. "I did meet Betty and Tangy. I have traveled across this country on a bus full of humans, and, guess what? I didn't kill any of them. I took what I needed; I don't kill, unless I have to."

Michael didn't look at me, and then he said. "Whatever, I am sure all humans are safe with you. Now quiet down, I am trying to watch Knight Rider."

I walked over and sat down next to Michael. I haven't seen this show before; I wondered if it was any good. I was having real mixed emotions about grumpy Michael. On one hand, he is a real ass, on the other hand he has a really nice ass. Then again I was missing David, and Carrie.

I hadn't sat down for a minute when Michael said. "Don't you have someone else to go bother?"

"No. Shh… I have never seen this show before; don't ruin it for me with all your blah blah." I said very calmly.

Michael laughed. Then we sat there for an hour watching a stupid show about a talking car, and I thought they reached the bottom of the imaginary barrel with Mr. Ed.

After that, I had had enough TV, so I excused myself; Michael just grunted. I found my way back to the kitchen and made me a cup of Oh positive. I also scored a pair of sunglasses that were left on the kitchen counter. That was all I needed to take a walk. I went out the back door that I had spotted earlier. I went out the wooden gate that surrounded the pool, and then I found the most amazing garden.

I found my way into a corner of the garden. There was a wall of vines, and an arch doorway that lead into the prettiest little area I had ever seen. Two walls were made out of vines; the other two walls were stone walls. The walls had round green stones, and they held back the higher ground.

Trees grew out at the top of the walls and hung over the little area making a natural sun block. There were a couple of stone benches. Next to one of the benches, water came out of the wall, and fell off making a small waterfall that rushed down into a little pond sitting in the middle of this area.

There were flowers of all types; I don't know my plants, but it doesn't matter; all of them were pretty. I sat down on one of the stone benches. There I sat and thought; six months, what had I agreed to?

I heard, and then smelled before I saw both Ezra and Charlotte come under the arch of vines; they joined me in this little hideaway. Charlotte was wearing a nice looking outfit; she had slacks on and it made her look smart, ready for work. The gray material made her blue eyes shine. Ezra was in a blue shirt with jeans with a pair of sunglasses on. He looked as if he was ready for some gardening, while his wife left for work.

Charlotte spoke first. "Good morning. Oh there are my sunglasses; I was looking for them."

She was talking about the ones I was wearing. I had found them on the kitchen counter. "Sorry… I would have put them back." I said; then I handed the sunglasses over to Charlotte.

Now it was so bright I had to squint my eyes. I was in the shade, and I still couldn't stand the brightness.

"It's fine." Charlotte responded with a smile as she put on her glasses. "I have to run to the bank, and take care of some business. When I come back, you, Alice and I are going shopping. You need clothes and, why we're out, I will pick up a few more sets of sunglasses. You can never have too many sunglasses around here." She lowered her sunglasses and gave me a wink. Then she gave Ezra a big hug and kiss; Ezra told her to drive safely, then Charlotte left. Ezra sat down on the stone bench next to mine.

We sat quietly for a little while until Ezra broke the silence. "It's a lot to take in; most of us are Ren for almost a year. We have had time around vampires to learn what we need to know. You're different; you have been dropped into this world without a roadmap. Last night you told me what you understood about the blood. Your master told you some of what you will need to know. He told you, if you chopped a vampire's head off, he would grow another one; but did he tell you that the head could grow a new body?"

"No."

"Well it sounds like he didn't have much time with you. See, if you did get your head chopped off, it would take days to grow another one. If your body was destroyed, and I had your head, it would take months to grow a new body. Also you would need a lot of blood. See, if you get your head chopped off, you better hope one of your friends finds a part of you because it will take time and a lot of human blood to fix you."

"Could there be two of me? If someone chops my head off, would my body grow a head, while my head grows a new body?" I asked.

Ezra laughed, and then said. "Everyone asks that. The answer is no; a long time ago I got my head removed in a fight, and there is only one of me. This is how it works. Your blood animates the body, but it is your soul that animates the blood. You cannot split the spirit, and the spirit cannot exist without the blood, and don't forget the blood cannot exist without energy; that we steal from humans. Your spirit will chase the blood; it will go to the largest quantity. That is until there is no more blood. So your master is right; there are only two ways to really destroy us for good, burn the blood or starve it. Of course if you get your head cut off and no one picks you up before the sunrises… poof, you're ashes. And if you get your head chopped off underground, and no one comes to get you, your body will slowly die, for your blood cannot animate a head without a body or a body without a head; without an intact spine you have no motor control."

I thought about what he said. "That does make more sense. When he first told me, I didn't understand. What about wooden stakes?"

Ezra rubbed his hands together, and then he said, "Time for the basics; we can call it Vampire 101 if you like. Wooden stakes are one of the oldest ways of killing us, but it only works if you do it right. See, you will find that most of the ways you hear about what will kill vampires is information that is either wrong or incomplete. Records were never reliable back in the day. Also vampire hunters trained each other, so a lot of it was by word of mouth. Of course the problem with this is, that vampire hunters are often killed before they have a chance to train someone, or if he has an apprentice, the apprentice is killed with him. So a lot of information was lost in the past, and some information was told to one person after another until the end result was incorrect information."

"That reminds me of something I read once. It was about repeating a rumor. They had a group of people sit in a circle. Someone whispered a secret in the ear next to them. Then that person whispered that same secret to the next person, on and on until it made it back around the circle to the person who first told it. Then you could hear how much the story had changed."

Ezra leaned back against the rock wall, and then he said. "Yes that is what happens. Of course this has been in our favor. See, a stake to the heart will never kill you. In fact it has most likely saved more vampires in the last 100 years. That kind of wound will only awaken you from your sleep; we are all heavy sleepers."

"I thought you said it works?" I asked

"I said it works if you do it right," Ezra responded then went on to say. "The original way to kill a vampire with a wooden stake was first to soak the stake in oil. Then you find a sleeping vampire. One man holds a torch while the other man has a stake, and a mallet. Now you need to understand that you don't really have to hit the heart, but it does help to hammer in between the ribs. That way it sticks in better. Right after you hammer it in, the vampire awakes, and sits up. That's when the second man steps in and lights the stake. The fire goes right into the blood, and we burn up from the inside out."

"Wow; why not just cover us in oil and light us on fire?" I asked.

"You could, but then you have a pissed off a vampire on fire, and it takes a few minutes, maybe seconds, to burn through the skin and ignites the blood. In that time the vampire will rip apart anything it can get its hands on. Many a hunter has died doing just that. And if there is a water source, it can jump into, therefore the vampire can save itself before it's too late. A hunter figured out the stake method. It was sometime during the Dark Ages; now everyone believes if you stick a piece of wood in our chest, we will die. It's kind of funny when you think about it. Why would a shotgun blowing out a heart not work, but a giant splinter would?"

I chuckled, and then I said. "It comes back to fire; that makes sense. What about mirrors? I can see myself."

Ezra shook his head back and forth. "Some legends are just stupid, and that one is one of the worst. I do not know for sure, but I think I know how the legend was started."

"By a mirror salesman?" I chimed in.

Ezra laughed. "I hadn't thought of that, maybe. Mine was based on bad spirits. Some might call them demons. Some evil spirits have been known to take blood from the living, stealing the same life energy that we need. Spirits never have an image in a mirror no matter how well you can see them. I believe that through time, some people have mistaken spirits for vampires. Of course, we are much different than spirits; we have physical bodies. Even if we didn't show up in mirrors, our clothes would."

I had never thought about it until Ezra said that, but Carrie had no image in the mirror. Of course, she really didn't need one. She looked the way she looked; she couldn't change clothes or change her hair style. She was always the same. "I have met a spirit; that makes sense to me. So let me guess, the garlic thing is not real."

A little smile crossed Ezra face. "Well don't jump to conclusions. Garlic works. It won't kill us, and, in fact, it wouldn't even bother us, but it will help safeguard humans from vampires."

"How?"

"Well, we cannot smell it. And, if something or someone is covered in it, we can't track it. Our smell is almost as keen as a dog's, so it is of great advantage to be covered in garlic while hunting or hiding from vampires. That is how it protects. Of course someone read somewhere that it protects against vampires, so they think that somehow it hurts us."

That made me think about, when I had read *Dracula*. Then I said. "That makes sense, because, in *Dracula*, Van Helsing hung it up in Lucy's room. She was a lady of a large house, and I am sure whatever room they put Lucy in, was then called Lucy's room. He was trying to hide the scent from Dracula."

Ezra stared at me for a second, and then said. "You do know that story never happened."

"Really, damn; I liked that book." Then I stuck my bottom lip out.

Ezra smiled. "If it makes you feel any better, I really liked that book too."

"I have already experienced, about being invited in." I said. Then came the next part; this is the part I asked him about the cross. I was really scared to find out, to think that God may hate me, or that I was now a devil against God, dammed even, but I had to ask. "So do crosses burn us?"

"The right ones, yes; that's not the question you're asking." Ezra paused, and then said, "We are not soulless creatures from the abyss of hell. Is there a hell? I don't know; what I do know is that people have used God's name to do great harm and good through the centuries. So you know the difference between a cleric and a wizard?"

"I don't even know what they have in common." I answered.

"A wizard's power comes from him. A cleric will tell you his power comes from God. Let me tell you a story; in New Mexico there was group of vampires that were worshiped. They were worshiped as children of God. Their believers in that church believed that the power that vampires had, had been gifts from God. When the vampires changed someone into a vampire, they had to die; now you know that not all will rise again. The ones that did not rise were not worthy. The ones who did were blessed by God, for each one that died, one must have gone to heaven to stand before Jesus and be judged. And only the righteous, could come back as vampires to rid the world of evil."

This almost made me laugh. "That's not what I've heard about vampires; I always heard that vampires are from the devil."

Ezra looked at me very seriously. "Is the devil telling you what to do?"

"Well, no; but that is what all the books that I have read said."

Ezra laughed, and then in a serious voice said. "And those books, did they say that a stake in the heart would kill you, and if you stepped outside you would burst into flames."

I said. "Yes, you're right." They weren't very accurate.

Ezra looked at me thoughtfully. "You're young, so you don't remember that most of these writings you have read are new. Most of them are based on *Dracula*, and a lot of the stories have been written in Christian countries. The older writings about vampires, say all kinds of different ways of destroying us. It has always been to our benefit that there is misinformation. If you believe in God, then you must believe in forgiveness, and you will find yourself asking for it; for, in our life, it is hard not to take others."

That is kind of what I was worried about. Then I added, "No need to ask for forgiveness yet. I have some killing to do; then I will ask."

Ezra had a worried look then said. "I will support you where, and when I can. You started your story when you awoke from the grave; I know the men who put you there did terrible things. If you ever need to talk… well you know."

"Thank you; thank you for your kindness."

Ezra looked as if he was trying not to cry, then he spit out. "Where was I, crosses, yes that is it. So my point is that evil or goodness is not the domain of man, and evil is not the domain of vampires, but, on one hand, we, as a race, have earned our evil reputation. The reasons are many; absolute power, the long lives and the fact we are always taking. We are killers."

I thought about what he was saying. "I can see it; I can see how a long life would get you disconnected from the world. I already felt that way.

Everyone I knew, my parents, friends and family, dead. I don't understand this generation; then again I never understood my own generation… So is it a form of magic that makes some crosses hurt us?"

"Yes. Think about it; if God wanted to help you, do you think you would need a cross. And why would he help someone who doesn't believe in him just because he had a cross? Of course the funniest thing to me is the thought of a man coming before Jesus, and Jesus saying; welcome to heaven. Too bad you couldn't keep hold of your cross. Then that vampire wouldn't have eaten you, so come on in, butterfingers."

I started laughing with Ezra. It was good to laugh, and it reminds me of how much I was missing David. David had brought a smile to my face when I needed it the most. "So I think that covers most legends."

"What about silver?" Ezra asked.

"Wait, is that not for werewolves, or is that for vampires too?" I couldn't remember.

"It's for all kinds of evil supernatural creatures, and it doesn't work for anything. You don't need silver to kill werewolves, and the only thing it does to vampires is make them look nice."

"So where do you suppose the silver legend came from?" I wondered.

"That one is easy. Back in the Dark Ages, the hunters figured out that it was best to hunt the supernatural as godly men. They came as priests and monks, and every creature they hunted was from the devil. If they used magic, they were not supernatural creatures themselves but using the power of God. The drawback is, that during the Dark Ages there was a plague; so this also led to an economic downturn, and the priests found it hard to get paid, or, as they would have called it, donations. The people believed that the priest should be willing to serve for free, do it in the service of God and God's people. So, back in the day money was gold, or silver. The only ones who had gold were the lords of the land, and they weren't worried about how many villagers were eaten by the vampires. So some smart priest came up with the fact that silver kills the devil's children, and, after you killed them with the silver, the silver turned to lead. The part of silver turning to lead was lost with the invention of the gun. The priest would melt down the town's silver, and then they would cast them into bullets. And of course they never actually used them. That's where the legend of silver came from." Ezra said very excited; obviously he loved his history.

All this history had me wondering, so I asked. "How old are you?"

Ezra took a moment as if he had to think about it. Then he said. "I was born in 1812; that same year my father died in the War of 1812. He fought in protection of the city I grew up in, Washington D.C. It was 1847 when I was turned; I was thirty-five years old. You will find that most vampires give their age from the time they were turned, in vampire years, I am 143 years old, and you're five days old."

I giggled, and then in a babyish voice, I said. "Feed me, feed me."

Ezra laughed. Then he said. "After your shopping trip with the girls, I would like to start your training, just some basic stuff tonight."

"What will I be learning?" I wondered.

"How to fight, how to be a vampire; you will be my star pupil. Don't worry; I think you will like it."

I smiled. "Oh, I wasn't worried; that is exactly what I want to do."

Ezra smiled a smile that told me that was exactly what he wanted to hear. Then he told me. "It's going to be a little while before the girls are ready. Do you have any more questions?"

I thought about it for a minute, and then said, "Yes, yes I do. What about our powers, like mind control, or flying, or how about our flashing."

"Flashing?" Ezra asked.

"That's what I call it when I move so fast it feels as if I teleported." I answered.

"That's a great name, flashing, I like it; we refer to it as spirit walking, but I like your name for it better. Funny thing is that it takes most vampires five to ten years to have enough power to do it. Lea still cannot spirit... flash."

It felt to me that they were really surprised about my powers. Ezra was saying that I was doing things that I should not be doing for another five to ten years. I felt like there was something wrong with me; it also reminded me about what Nicks told me. He was worried that the Whites would find out too much about me. What it all means is still a mystery to me, and I don't like not knowing. Still it is probably best that I play down my powers if I can.

Ezra went on. "Well from talking to you last night, I realize that you have an understanding about most of our powers, but you have had no experience with using your mind powers. What experience do you have if any, with your hypnosis?"

I thought about that for a second. So far I was unable to do anything as far as I could tell. So I told Ezra. "I don't think I have been able to do it. Is that what Alice did to me?"

Ezra looked thoughtfully then said. "Yes, the best way I can explain this to you is that all vampires have the same powers, but, like instruments, some are really good at playing them and some are not. Also there are different kinds of abilities in using your hypnosis. First is defense, the ability to block other vampires' mind games. Second is mind control; Alice is a master of this; the girl can make you see or not see anything she wants.

She still has great ability with her other mind powers, but she is world class at mind control. Third is reading, the ability to know what another is thinking or feeling; my wife Charlotte is a master of this one. That is why you can't lie to her. It is useful in a fight too, because you know what your opponent is about to do a second before they do it. I personally am partial to the first one, defense of my own mind; because I am an expert in hand to hand combat. Even though I try, Alice can always trick me with her mind games, and there is no blocking my wife. Of course this is probably because she knows me so well. With other vampires, it is not such a problem."

"So can Alice or any of you change someone's memories?" I have always wondered if I could do that. It would be a nice power to have; if I ever said something dumb I could just make people forget it.

"No." Ezra answered shaking his head back and forth. "Changing a memory would be like trying to change a painting. The only thing you would have is a mess when you were done. The trick to changing a memory is changing it at the moment it is happening. Alice made you see spiders in that field, along with some other crazy things. If you didn't know the truth, if you didn't know that Alice made you see those things, you would believe that you fought spiders or you had the craziest dream ever. Don't worry; you will get a chance to figure all this out. Alice will work with you on all the mind stuff. I will teach you how to fight. Charlotte will work with you on flying, so you will have lots of instruction."

"So you're saying we can fly! Do we turn into bats?" I said almost jumping out of my seat in excitement.

A strange look came over Ezra's face. It took me a moment to place it; then I knew that look, confused. Ezra said. "Yes... normally it takes vampires fifty to hundred years to have enough power to fly. I only said that because Alice said you already knew how to fly, because, when she first spotted you, you where flying."

"What?" I said a little caught off guard. "I don't know how to fly, and if I did, I think I would remember that."

Ezra looked thoughtful, and then said, "Yes, of course you would. We shall talk with Alice soon enough. We will figure this out; I am sure I just misunderstood her."

What he said didn't match his body language. Maybe it was my reading power, but I was sure he believed Alice and not me. Then I said. "At least I don't have to worry about being shot."

Ezra was starting to stand when I said that. He sat back down, and then said. "I said silver doesn't hurt us. I never said we had nothing to fear from guns. I used to believe back in the day that guns would never be a problem to our kind. I was a fool; during World War One or as we used to call it, The Rise of Man, they developed lots of new weapons. Some of these weapons work well against vampires: flamethrowers, explosives and tracer bullets. Tracer bullets are built with a small pyrotechnic charge in their base. Ignited by the burning powder, the pyrotechnic composition burns very brightly, making the projectile visible to the naked eye. This enables the shooter to follow the bullet trajectory in order to make aiming corrections. These bullets, if shot into vampires, can also cause our blood to ignite; if you see strikes of light flying by as someone shoots at you, they are vampire hunters."

"And don't get shot. They burn like hell." Michael said, as he stood next to the arch of vines.

Ezra said, "Good afternoon Michael," Then he turned to me. "Michael speaks from experience; he took a couple of those rounds to the chest a few years back. Luckily I was able to pull him to safety and pull out the bullets. Then I had to put him out; scared the hell out of me."

Michael said with kind of a sad smile. "And then Ezra went nuts; as soon as he realized I wasn't going to die, he spirit walked, right out to those hunters, and ripped them limb to limb; we haven't had a problem with their kind since."

Ezra let out a small laugh, and then said with a voice of passion. "What can I say? No one messes with my boy."

He stood up and threw an arm around Michael and pulled him into the little area. There Michael and Ezra took a seat together. I had no doubt of their love; they were family. It made my heart ache. I wanted that, but it felt out of reach, out of reach until I have had my revenge.

Michael looked at me, not a mean look this time, but a hollow one. "Lea would like to meet you." He said flatly.

"Ok".

Ezra stood up. "I will let you three get to know each other. I have some work to attend to; Melabeth, come to the basement after your shopping trip with the ladies. And, Melabeth, we do not turn into animals, but we can control them and see what they see. Michael is really good at that; maybe someday he will show you how." He turned to Michael and with a head bob said, "Michael."

And Michael responded. "Father," and, with that, Ezra left, then Michael said to me at the same time throwing me a pair of sunglasses, "Charlotte said you would need those; so come, on, follow me. Lea can't take much of the sun." With that, he headed toward the house.

I can't say I was excited to meet anymore vampires. I have had my fill of new persons. We went into the house the same way I came out, and, when we passed by the pool, I asked, "Maybe we could go swimming tonight?"

"Maybe," Michael answered indifferently.

He didn't turn around or even change the speed he was traveling; I was getting real tired of his attitude, and I had just met the guy. The only thing he had going for him was the view.

We entered the room with the oversized TV. There sat a girl with strawberry blonde hair; it was pulled up into a ponytail with a few strands hanging loose in the front. Her hair was wavy and ran almost halfway down her back. She was very beautiful, and, when I entered into the room, she looked me up and down and then stood up to greet me.

She held out her hand and said with a sweet voice. "Hi, I am Lea. You must be Melabeth."

I took her hand and we shook; she squeezed hard, but not hard enough to hurt me. In fact, from the surprised look on her face, I think she meant to.

Michael said in his usual grumpy manner. "Well, she is four days old, so I think YOU can handle her, Lea, until Charlotte gets back. I have some stuff to do, so you ladies have fun."

Lea had a look of what I could only describe as troubled, she blurted out. "I have to watch her… I can do it. Don't worry, Michael."

Mike nodded, turned and started to leave; on his way out, he said. "Don't worry, Lea, I will stay within yelling distance." With that remark, Lea visibly calmed down.

I was starting to get the idea that Alice, Ezra and Charlotte had told these two very little about me. Both of them acted as if I was a newborn that needed a babysitter at all times. I couldn't tell if they were playing a practical joke on these two or if they were hiding my power from them.

Nicks warned me about Alice. The fact that Alice thinks I can fly, even though Ezra said that takes fifty to one hundred years to have that much power, I need to really pay attention to what's going on.

"So, little sister what do you think of Michael?" Lea asked, but there were threats behind that smile.

"I am trying not to; he is so rude and grumpy." I answered honestly. I will leave out the part where I think he is so sexy.

"Good." Lea responded, and I could see her calm down now that she didn't think I had a thing for her man.

Then again I don't know if he was her man; I didn't get that vibe when he left. So I asked. "So you and Mike, are you, like… you know, a thing."

Her face became sad, when she said, "No, he sees himself as my older brother, but he is not related by blood or anything. Then again, no one in this madhouse is. You'll get used to it, the game of house, that is. And he is not Mike; it's Michael."

I ignored the name correction, and then asked her a question. "The game of house?"

"We live like most vampires in the wild. We aren't mommy, and daddy, sons and daughters. The oldest and the strongest rules the coven, and the weakest, that's you, is last to have a say in anything." Lea said the part about me being the weakest very proudly.

She was probably sick of being in last place, but, if it works how she said it does, she's going to be sick all over again, but I had no reason to show her that I was stronger than her.

I had to ask her, "What did you mean by, in the wild?"

Lea let out a dry laugh, "Wow, you are a dumb bitch."

I was stunned and speechless. She walked over, picked up her glass and drank; I could smell the blood in it. Then she looked over at me and sneered, "What? You thought I would be like, hey, sister, let's go shopping and be best friends or whatever. I know your slutty kind; you need to know how shit works around here."

It took a second for me to pick my jaw off of the floor, as she went on saying, "Another thing; let's get some rules about Michael, right now."

I didn't let her finish that statement.

I didn't even really think about it; I was standing there listening to her verbally assault me. Then I had flashed the distance between us.

I punched her across the side of the head. She fell down like a sack of potatoes, but I caught the cup of blood before one drop hit the floor.

I stepped back as she was now trying to get back up, but she was having trouble. I washed back all the blood in the cup and set it down on a table. Lea was just managing to get back on her feet and find her balance.

Then she said in a shaky voice, "You're about to learn a hard lesson."

The fight was short; it was like fighting a child. I was so much stronger, so much faster.

Breaking her arms and ribs was easy. In a matter of seconds, she was laying on the floor weeping. That's when Michael came, flashing into the room.

He looked down at his sister, then up at me. I was wondering what he would say, I guess nothing because he just attacked me. I barely dodged to one side; he was bigger and, with those large muscular arms, I was guessing a lot stronger too.

My early dodge didn't last. We were in close quarters, and there was nowhere to run. The only thing I could do to slow him down was run behind a couch; then he just threw the couch to the wall.

He was not like fighting Alice with all her speed and skill; he reminded me of the men in the cabin, trying to throw all his weight and power in straight line attacks; it didn't take me long to figure out that I was a lot faster.

I punched and clawed him without a problem. At one point he grabbed my arm and twisted it around. Instead of fighting it, I threw my body into a flip; as I landed on my feet, I pulled him towards me. Then I punched him in the nose has hard as I could; that made him lose his grip on me.

He swung at me, but I had blinded him when I hit his nose. So I simply ducked under his swing; then landed a hard kick to his knee. He buckled and fell to the ground; before he could recover I was on his back.

I grabbed his one arm and locked it into mine, I took my free hand and dug my claws into his neck.

With all the authority I could manage, I said. "I will rip your throat out if you don't stop. I don't want to hurt you."

I was amazed now that I was holding his arm that he didn't feel a lot stronger than me. Larger, yes, and, like the men in the cabin, the extra weight was tricky to deal with in a tight fighting area.

Of course this had me wondering just how old and strong Alice was; she looked like a little girl, but she was so much stronger than Michael.

Before Michael could say anything, a laugh broke the silence in the room. It was the laugh of a child. "Oh good; you have all met. Mom didn't think you would get along, but here you are playing in the living room together."

I looked up to see Alice smiling away at me.

Michael said in a very angry voice. "You could stop touching me now… Melabeth."

Did he take me for a fool? "How do I know you will stop?"

Michael's voice changed; he said in an almost confused tone, "Alice is here. Don't you think, this over now?"

Alice let out a small giggle. She passed by me and helped Lea off of the floor. Lea was still crying and I could see she was badly hurt.

Alice pouted, "Good job, Melabeth. I wanted all the girls to go shopping and now Lea is too broken to go."

This family is so weird, I thought, as I let go of Michael. Michael had cuts all over his body; he looked bruised up. I was just now realizing he never even got a hit in, and, for the first time ever, my dress was fine.

I looked over at Alice and said, "She will heal in a few hours; we will still have time."

Michael looked at me as if he had never seen me before, and then said, "It will take her days to heal from all those broken bones. Do you think if I broke your arm like that you would be ok in an hour?"

I held out my arm. "Twenty minutes, tops."

Michael shook his head back and forth and looked over at Alice and said in an angry voice. "What is this game? Why did you tell us she was newborn?"

Alice's voice changed; she suddenly sounded as if she had finally grown up. "Enough, Michael."

Michael's whole body stiffened. "Sorry... I didn't mean to yell at you. The thing is, that Lea wouldn't have picked a fight, if she would have understood... that's all."

Alice, in that same voice said. "Take Lea and care for her. I will explain later, but know this Michael; I didn't lie." Then, like a switch, her child voice came back on. "Isn't Melabeth fun? I will take care of Melabeth. Come along sister."

And without waiting for me to answer, she headed out of the room. Something told me that Lea's remark about this not being a family, was really talking about Alice. I had thought she was a child, because she acted like one, but she was no child.

In fact, as I followed her, through the house. I was getting a bad feeling that maybe Ezra was not in charge, that this really was Alice's coven. I remember Ezra telling me the first time we met that his real name was Ezra Bovine, and not White. When he introduced Alice, he said she had always been a White, and this is the house of Whites; great, I now have a crazy child as my new master.

We entered into a little study area, and there Alice took a seat on a small couch, and then patted the seat next to her. I sat down, and asked, "So you're the master of this house?"

Alice's face exploded into a smile; in fact, in this moment, she looked loveable. Then she said. "You're smart; most take longer to figure it out. They always think Ezra's in charge, and I turned Ezra myself. Ezra turned Charlotte and Michael, and I turned Lea, kind of a mistake on my part. How old do you think I am?"

"I don't know?"

"That's not a guess. You're not even trying." She demanded like a child.

"Two hundred," I guessed.

"You're half right." She smiled in glee.

I was more than a little taken aback. In fact I wasn't even sure if I even believed her. "So you're saying that you are 400 years old."

She looked at me funny. "Over, actually; I was turned in 1587. And you know what is even more amazing than that?"

"No" I said hoping this wasn't another guessing game.

"Well that settles it; nothing is more amazing. You don't even believe me." Alice said.

"How do you know I don't believe you?" I asked.

Alice turned her head like an owl, and then said. "You have great power, with no knowledge. Yet your mind powers don't match. In fact, I dare say you don't have any. I left myself open to you; I didn't block you at all. You should know if I am lying, and the blank look on your face says you have no idea what I am talking about."

"Maybe I am too young for mind powers."

"No," Alice said quickly, then added, "You're too young to fly. You're too young to spirit walk, but you should have some signs of mind powers. Even Lea can control minds of lesser animals, like bats and rats. And, then again, I still do not know how you fought me in the field. How did you see through my spiders?"

Doesn't she know that her mind tricks don't affect the second sight? Wait, maybe I should not tell her about that power. So I lied and said, "I am not sure."

A slow wicked smile spread across Alice's face. "Do you think you can lie… to me?"

I just looked her back in the eye. I wasn't about to let her bully me. "No, no, I don't. I am just not ready to talk to you about that. Soon, I promise; tell me why you think I can fly?"

Alice smiled. "Nicely played, still you didn't answer me, and showed no fear. Then even tried a subject change." She let out a laugh. "Fine, we will play Melabeth's game, but know this; you will tell me later, and dolly never forgets."

"Where is your doll?"

"Sleeping silly, and to answer your question, the reason I said you could fly is because I saw you do it. After you fed on those drunken teens, you flew, not far, and then landed on a boulder. There you lay for at least an hour."

I kind of remember that now. "You saw all that?"

"No, I entered your mind and you showed me." Alice said with that wicked grin.

"Really!"

"Really, don't worry too much about what you show me. You are… difficult to read." As Alice said this, there was a look in her eyes. I knew this look. It was the look of someone who had a mystery in front of them, and they had to solve it.

Alice went on. "Go shopping with Charlotte. I need to talk with Michael and Lea."

"Ok." Is all I could say, I wasn't doing a good job of hiding my power. I hoped Nicks would not be mad at me.

"She is back and ready to go," Alice stated.

"Who?"

Alice looked at me as if I were slow. "Charlotte, time to shop until you drop."

"How do you know that?" I wondered.

Alice pointed to her head, and then said. "Don't worry, I'll teach you."

"Great, I will go join Charlotte." I got up and started heading out of the room.

Then Alice said, "Melabeth... one more thing. I love my family; control yourself, Lea is as close to me, as if she were my own child. Ok maybe not that close, but I do protect my family."

"Ok, I will."

As I left, I couldn't help but think, Alice may have been a crazy child, but there was more. She loved her family, so just maybe, she is not all bad.

And, just maybe, they will help me find my way.

Chapter 10
A Happy Thought

Charlotte had been waiting for me.

On the way to the mall, she had a few small complaints about having to travel further. I soon found out her favorite mall was the Inland Mall, the same mall I killed those Order Members at, and it was obviously not a good idea for me to pop in any time soon.

Charlotte had this huge black, Chevrolet Blazer K5; it had oversized tires, with oversize steel bumpers front and back. It had big round spotlights on the top, and on the front bumper. Charlotte told me she had a great love of cars.

When I asked her why, she said, "I was turned in 1928, at the age of twenty. Ezra and I met at a speakeasy where I liked to dance as a flapper. Let's just say I can remember my first car ride. Cars were all the rage in the twenties."

We didn't talk much on the ride to the mall, and, when we started shopping, we never stopped talking about clothes. Come to find out me and Charlotte had a lot in common when it came to dressing up.

We both liked dresses, and we both liked older styles. Of course I could barely pass for eighteen, and she didn't even look twenty. She had a fake ID that said she was twenty five; she told me she needed to get a new one soon. I asked her how I could get one, but she dodged the question by pointing at a dress.

"Oh, my, look at this, you would look like you were on fire in this. Let's try it on you; come on slow poke." And off to the dressing rooms we went.

We shopped at a dizzying rate, and, before I knew it, we had more boxes than we could carry. We had to make more than a couple of trips to the Blazer.

At one point, Charlotte wanted to go to a bar to get a drink, and do a little hunting. I got into the Blazer, and we were on the way to the bar, when Charlotte said, "I need you to show some control. I know you can do it; NO killing."

I felt so grateful toward Charlotte and the Whites for all they had done for me in such a short period of time. So, I said. "I will control myself, and if I haven't said thank you for all these clothes, thank you for everything."

"You have already thanked me ten times; that's nine times more than you needed, " Charlotte said with a big smile.

She never turned her head from the road. Then it went quiet. Without the clothes, me and Charlotte didn't have a lot to say. I thought Carrie's constant talking was a bother, but now I can see its usefulness. If Carrie was in this car, there would be no awkward silence; then again, there would be no silence at all.

After a little while longer, Charlotte said, "I hope you know that I am going to be jealous of you."

Caught off guard, I asked, "Why?"

A strange smile crossed her face, "because my husband can't stop talking about you. Alice too, but I really don't care what she goes on about."

I was almost speechless but not completely. I wanted her to know how I felt, and fast. Speaking quickly, "Charlotte, I have no interest in your husband."

"Are you sure?" Charlotte asked calmly. She wasn't upset as she spoke.

"YES." She wasn't upset, but I didn't like being second guessed.

Charlotte laughed. "You are a spirited one, but you should be careful to remember, that I am not Lea, and I was just teasing you, for the most part."

I calmed down a little. "What do you mean... for the most part?"

Charlotte let out a deep breath before she continued. "I love my time with Ezra it is most important to me. When I say you have an interest in my husband, I didn't say sexual. You wish to learn how to fight, and my husband wishes to teach you. So you see I am jealous because he will want to spend so much of his time with you. Don't worry; I wouldn't hate you, but some days I may not like you."

I wasn't sure what to think of that. I didn't want to steal her husband away. "I will not train with him if you like."

Charlotte laughed and then took a quick look at me before returning her eyes back to the road. "I love you. You didn't even lie when you made that offer, but don't worry about it. You need to learn how to fight, and I will help. You have blood and sand in your future... Do you like to dance?"

I don't know what made me smile bigger, the fact she said she loved me or that she sounded as if she wanted to go dancing. I was going to ignore the ominous bloody future. I was sure the blood and sand was a reference to fighting in pits.

Trying to hold back my eagerness, I said, "I love to dance and sing. I haven't been dancing in a long time."

"Have you been dancing as a vampire?" Charlotte asked.

"Well, not at a club or anything. In the woods... not really."

Charlotte made a turn, and then pointed at a sign in front of a building. "Well then you'll love our hunting grounds tonight. This is a great dance club, and we will grab a bite while we're there. Stay close to me; this is an adult club; if anyone who works there asks your age; I will do the talking. When they ask for your ID, just raise your empty hand in front of their face; I will do the rest."

"What will they see?"

"An ID, silly girl; I can make them see things. Now I am no Alice, but then again these are just humans. It will take a strong mind to defy me. Let's go." With that, Charlotte parked the Blazer and hopped out. I jumped out and followed her into the club.

It was fun dancing with Charlotte. After a few songs, Charlotte found another partner. She passed him off to me; then she went and found another man. The man she left me to dance with was drunk, but I could also tell that she had messed with his mind.

He had no problem letting me take him into a dark corner of the dance club, and there I fed. I stopped before he passed out but barely. I helped him to an empty booth and then just left him there. Not long after I walked away, he passed out; not one person noticed or cared.

Charlotte did the same thing to another man; then she found two guys that were cruising for a good time. She brought them over to me and introduced them. Then we let them buy us drinks. We laughed at their jokes and over all pretended to like them. After some time Charlotte told the guys she would like to get out of here. Of course the guys thought this was a great idea probably because they thought they were going to get lucky.

Both these men were older, around their early forties. Once we had them out in the parking lot, where no one could see, we had our way with them. We both fed until the men passed out. We did put them into a car so that they wouldn't get cold. They would wake up there in the morning, and then they both will try to remember what had happened the night before, and what doesn't make sense they will blame on the booze.

My mind was still recalling all the new songs that I had heard at the club. When I looked over at the clock inside the truck, it wasn't even that late. We had left the club around midnight. I still had a long night ahead of me; I was excited about learning from Ezra. I really hope that does not hurt my relationship with Charlotte, because I was really enjoying her company.

It was a strange thought, that I might have more friends now in death, than I did in life. I was feeling a little drunk from the blood I had taken in. I laid my head against the window and watched the world go by. After a few minutes, Charlotte turned off of the main road and started heading down a dirt road.

I had to ask, "Where are we going?"

Charlotte laughed, and then said. "Running… after a big meal I like to run."

I picked my head off the window and started looking around. I could already feel that I was mostly sober now. I answered by saying. "That's sounds like fun."

After ten minutes or so, Charlotte found a place to park under a few trees. There weren't very many trees; this was high desert. There were bushes of all shapes and sizes, but every once in a while there would be a couple of oak or pine trees bundled up together.

We got out of the vehicle and started to run; I left my shoes in the truck. I loved the feel of the ground against my bare feet. The sharp rocks and plants didn't hurt for more than a second, if at all. The wind in my hair felt wonderful as the scenery flew by. It was amazing how fast me and Charlotte could run.

I was not sure but I would bet that I was running close to sixty miles per hour. In the open parts we would flash over great distances; we moved so fast it felt as if I were watching someone change a channel.

The best part about running is that it wasn't like working out. I wasn't sweating, and my breathing wasn't labored; in fact I didn't even need to breathe. I took in air as we ran, just to bring in the smells that brought the world alive. I didn't know all the different senses I was taking in, but each were wonderful in their own way.

Of course the best part of this was my sight. It may not have been day, but who cared when you could see the world as I did. The world was full of color and shadows, and not even the mice escaped my sharp eyes.

We worked our way up the side of the hill and toward the ridge. At this point we were jumping from boulder to boulder. The plants gave way to huge rocks, as we reached the crest of the hill. From here you could see everything; below was the valley floor with a river of lights. The crest of the hill ran upwards towards the mountains. I followed Charlotte as she jumped, ran and climbed up the rocks. She finally came to rest at the top of a large rock. This rock stood above everything except the distant mountains.

I jumped up to the top, and joined her; the view was breathtaking. On top of the rock the wind whipped my hair around as I surveyed the land. I spoke first, by saying. "This is the best part of being a vampire."

Charlotte responded flatly with. "Maybe." Her mind was elsewhere, so we stood in silence for awhile.

After an undetermined amount of time, Charlotte spoke. "Let me tell you about Michael."

I wondered why she wanted to tell me about him, but I didn't ask; instead I just said. "Ok."

Still staring off into space, Charlotte asked me. "So, what do you think of Michael?"

"He seems pretty cool." I answered before I thought about it. I was never one to bad mouth someone especially to their mother.

A small laugh escaped Charlotte's mouth. She turned and looked at me, then said. "That is the first time you have lied to me."

"What I meant to say, is he's an asshole." A sad looked crossed Charlotte's face; I regretted my remark as fast as it flew out of my mouth. "Well that wasn't a nice way to put it. I just met him, and I am sure once I get to know him… I am sure he is not an asshole all of the time."

Charlotte went to the edge of the boulder; there on the other side of the rock was a steep cliff. Charlotte sat down with her legs hanging off; she motioned to me to come and sit next to her.

"No, don't make excuses for feeling the way you do, and, if I were honest, he is an asshole. He is also my son that I love deeply."

I sat down next to her. There was sadness in this conversation that I didn't understand. I said. "Just because I said he was an asshole, I didn't mean that I don't like him."

Charlotte, looking at me, smiled. "I know; in fact I think you do like him. Don't forget I can tell what you are feeling."

"Wait…" I tried to interject.

"Don't get upset." Charlotte interrupted me. "Let me tell you about my son, and then you will understand."

I was not sure what she was trying to say, but I guess one needs a history lesson to understand. I said. "Fire away, I'm all ears."

Charlotte launched into her story. "It all started in 1969. Someone broke into our home during the day. When Ezra went up to investigate, he believed it was vampire hunters. When he went around the corner where he knew someone was standing, he attacked. We are strong, and Ezra is really strong. He hit the boy so hard, it shattered his skull. It only took Ezra a second to realize what a mistake he had made, for the boy he hit was Michael; Michael was homeless, and he was only nineteen. He had just broken in to find some food. Poor kid, not only did he pick a house full of vampires, but it was also empty of food. When I came to see what had happened, I was amazed by Michael's beauty, he lay on his back in front of an open fridge door. Even though he was lying on his back bleeding out of his head, he still was handsome. Also understand that I had now lived for forty years with Ezra and Alice. Alice likes to play the child, but she is not a child. In fact, she has always taken care of me. I had been longing to have a child, the one thing I couldn't have. So when I saw Michael lying on the floor dying, I asked, no I begged Ezra to save him. Ezra didn't want to do it, but, as you well know, I won that fight. Ezra fed Michael his blood; it took so much to save him that there was no chance that he was not fully addicted. He had two choices; go without our blood and die, or turn. So, to cut to the chase, he spent almost six months as a Ren. Then he finished the transformation and joined the family. Even though he didn't take to all the hand to hand combat that Ezra was always trying to teach him, we found that he had other talents; his ability to control animals is second to none. He was happy and brought great joy to our house. We had all forgotten what it was like to be young; these were good times."

"So he was happy once?" I asked.

That sad face washed over her again. Then she went on. "Yes... yes he was happy once. He was also in love once. He met a beautiful girl named Robin in 1976; the only problem with her was the fact that she was human. We all loved her, and she even got along with Alice. It wasn't long before she was ready to join our family. She was head over heels in love with Michael, so, naturally, she wished to join him forever. Alice enjoyed playing with her so much; she decided to change her herself. See you may or may not know this, but the older you are, the better the chance that the person will make the transition from human to vampire. Robin was a Ren for about a year. In 1977 when her time came for her to die, she was ready. We prepared her body and buried her; she never awoke... and it devastated Michael."

"I had no idea." Still he was being a jerk. It's been over ten years ago.

"There's more to it than just the death of his lover." It was annoying that she could read me like that.

Charlotte went on. "After ten years passed by, we were all really worried about Michael; he never really recovered, and he spent all his time with his animals, so Alice did something foolish. Without consulting anyone; she went out and found a girl that looked a lot like Robin, and, within a month, she turned her. I am sure that you know that girl was Lea; this happened in 1987. Lea has only been a vampire for four years. Alice brought her home, and, of course, Michael saw right through her little hook up. To make matters worse, there are some issues with Lea. Ezra's not interested in vampires unless they want to train to fight. He doesn't deal with young vampire issues. Alice has a habit of torturing someone for punishment. Of course, all the things Alice does to people are in their head; Lea did not deal well with Alice's mental punishments. She had terrible nightmares, so we had to keep Lea separated from Alice, and I don't get along with the girl; I can't stand it when someone lies to me, and that's all the girl knows how to do, not large lies, but little ones."

"What kind of lies?" I wondered.

"Lies about anything and everything. Does my dress look good? The girl will tell you it does, even though it doesn't. That's not a good way of describing it; she wishes to be accepted and will say what she believes you want to hear. She has been better but only a little. I can always tell when someone is lying, and she knows this. So it drives me batty that she is not straight with me. Do you know what I mean?"

"Yes I do. I can't understand why you let it bother you. You know she was just looking for your approval."

Charlotte answered me with a grin. "Are you looking for my approval?"

I thought about that for a second; then I answered honestly, "Can't say that I am."

"And that is why you and I are going to get along." Charlotte stated while pointing at both of us. Then she went back to her story. "I don't hate Lea; I just don't get along with her, so it is hard for me to help her through being a young vampire. Michael, on the other hand, ended up feeling sorry for her. It was probably because how the rest of the family was treating Lea, the fact that she did not want to become a vampire, and Michael had no choice either. He ended up being a true brother to her, and soon they were as close as any siblings. Of course there is one thing still out of place; Michael had been looking forward to going to school, and then Lea is dropped in his lap. He now feels he can't leave until she is strong enough to take care of herself. He doesn't believe we will help her; he is wrong… we would. Still it keeps him in the house, and I am in no hurry to see him leave."

"What school does he want to go to?" I asked.

"A school for vampires… there are requirements to go; one of them is that you have to be strong enough to pass the entrance test. Most of our kind who decide to go there wait no less than fifteen to twenty years. That way they know they are strong enough to attend."

A school of vampires, or maybe a house of horrors, it really made me think of how much of this world I didn't even understand. "Where is this school?"

"In the City of the Dead, I will give you the real quick version; my husband is the storyteller. There is one city we own completely, no wizards, or hunters. It is our city, and no one would dare face our kind there. Every place outside of our cities is referred to as the wild. It is wild because there are no laws; it's kill or be killed."

"No laws?"

Charlotte smiled. "Man laws maybe, but no laws we follow. As I was saying, Michael wanted to go to this school. When he found out about you, he thought he was going to have to take care of you too. He is being cruel so he doesn't get attached to you. He will feel free to leave when Lea is strong enough. Once he figures out you don't need him, I am sure he will come around. I also noticed when he was looking at you that he was a little turned on. Now that he has witnessed your strength, I believe he will be nicer. The next step is to get you guys some alone time."

I was speechless; the whole reason she wanted to tell me her stupid son's life story, is so she could hook us up. "What the hell are you talking about? I don't want to date him."

Charlotte's face had a look of shock, like I just told her I was a man. "Well you would be the first. I feel your desire when you look at him."

"I… have… things, things I have to do." I stood up. "Look, just take me home."

Charlotte stood up next to me. "I got it, a great idea. Let's say you wanted to go swimming, and we didn't get you a bathing suit. We bought you one, but he doesn't need to know everything; anyway you could go skinny dipping in the pool. I will arrange it with Michael…"

"Stop, no more. I just want to go back and train with Ezra. I don't want to play matchmaker with you." She was starting to affect my calm. She wanted Michael to walk in on me while I was nude.

Charlotte gave me a strange face, and then said, "You'd rather get punched by my husband, than banged by my son. What… some kind of virgin?"

I couldn't tell if I was mad, or what. Was I a virgin? It was taking effort on my part to stop the tears. "One more word, just one more, and I will…"

I never finished that sentence; damn she was fast. She had tossed me off the cliff faster than I saw it coming.

I fell; when I hit the rocks below, the world went black. I woke up in pain; I could feel my body healing itself. I had broken more than a few bones on that landing.

As I laid there looking up, I could see Charlotte standing at the top of the cliff. Then she did something that made me forget how pissed off I was. She stepped off the cliff and floated down. The wind whipped around her dress as she softly moved towards the earth; she was FLYING. She landed next to me without a sound.

Before I could really speak, Charlotte said. "I am so sorry. The virgin remark; damn I didn't know. I didn't see the truth until I threw you off the cliff. If it makes you feel any better, in my mind you are still a virgin; what those men did, well, it didn't take that away from you."

I was now healed enough to sit up. "Well to tell you the truth; no, that doesn't make me feel better. In fact I don't give a rat's ass what you think. You know what would make me feel better? Let me tell you; first, stay out of my head, and, if you can't, pretend that you don't know shit about me. Second, teach me how to fly."

"Maybe to the first request, and a big yes to the flying. Do you forgive me?" Charlotte said with kindness in her voice.

"For throwing me off a cliff?"

Charlotte laughed out loud. "No, for hurting your feelings. Throwing you off the cliff; that was your first flying lesson little bird."

*   *   *

I was getting back into the truck; my mood had been soured. For at least two hours I had been practicing how to fly. More like, falling down, flying not so much. My outfit was ripped beyond repair.

Charlotte had explained that flying was like spirit walking, and she said, "Our spirit cannot be measured by science. No one can explain the bond between mother and child. That spirit is the power you will use to pull your body skyward."

I managed pulling my body, but it was not skyward. Instead, I flashed, only I was looking upwards. I flew right into a bush full of stickers. I was still pulling them out of me; all the little cuts healed fast. Now I had dried blood all over me, and, of course, I fell onto the ground at least a thousand times. I looked homeless again.

"Wait." Charlotte yelled at me as I was getting into the truck. "Let me throw a towel down; you're filthy."

Soon we were bouncing back down the road when Charlotte said. "Don't worry little bird; we'll try again and soon. Maybe we can find a taller cliff."

"What, afraid I didn't hit terminal velocity before I hit the ground?" I snapped back at her.

Charlotte laughed. "Motivation dear, motivation."

When we hit the paved road and started heading home, I asked. "Can you swing me by my friend's house? I would like to check up on David."

I wish I would have been smart enough to have asked for his phone number.

Charlotte huffed, "David, is he that Necromancer kid?"

"Yes," I nodded.

Charlotte made a face, as if something smelled bad, and then said. "I don't really care for Necromancers."

I said with a huff. "You don't have to talk to him; you don't even need to meet him. Just wait in the car."

"Don't you think you've kept Ezra waiting long enough?" Charlotte said nicely, but there was more to it. She really didn't want me to go, and, to tell the truth, I didn't give a shit why.

"So are you going to take me, or what?" I demanded.

Charlotte sat still, staring straight ahead at the road. After a little bit, she finally said. "You have twenty minutes, and I am waiting in the car, and, if anything happens, it's on you little bird."

"Thank you," and I meant it.

"Whatever," Charlotte grumbled.

Twenty minutes later we pulled up to David's street. Charlotte parked four houses away and then announced this was close enough for her. It was close to 2am; I hoped that David was still awake. If not, Carrie would be; I had so much I wanted to share with her, and I only had twenty minutes.

I will have to get David's number so I can call him. It didn't take me long to walk up to his house; everything was quiet. I could hear the wind rustling through the trees; dogs were barking in the distance. I looked around using both my eyes and my second sight. Then I snuck up to the side of David's house and to his window. I tapped on his glass quietly.

"You're back," I jumped and spun around baring my teeth; a hissing sound slipped out of my mouth. Carrie stood behind me with the biggest smile that would fit on her face. She jumped over and gave me a huge hug. "Scared ya. Where have you been; I have been worried sick. Did you find vampires? Are they nice? What took you so long?"

I couldn't help but smile. "I missed you too and have a lot to tell you and David. I don't have much time. One of the vampires, Charlotte, is waiting for me."

Carrie looked concerned. "They aren't holdin ya hostage?"

"No, they have been nice, but a little on the crazy side. Still there is more going on than I can explain in a short time, and I know where one of the guys who did this to me is."

Carrie looked at me shocked, "Let's go kill him."

Carrie was eager for me to have my revenge, but something came to me at this very moment. I had never understood why Nicks made me promise to wait six months to kill this man, and he told me I had to hunt him first, find out information. Then, as Carrie got excited about just killing him, it came to me why we couldn't.

I said to Carrie, "We can't just kill him."

Carrie looked at me like I was crazy, "Why?"

"Well, because we need info. For example, what does he know about the others that I am hunting? Does he know where they are? And where is the film of my death? Who paid to have such a terrible film made? How many copies of this film are there? I want my revenge; I want it so bad I can taste it, but I must be careful or I will miss some of it."

Carrie's eyes softened, and then she said, "Tell me how I can help?"

I was glad I had friends, for I was going to need their help. "I have an idea. I will need you and David's help; I don't have time work out all the details; I would just like to talk to David real quick, and we will work this out later."

Carrie nodded her head. "Sounds good; let me go in and wake him."

Then I noticed something. "Hold up girl. You have a different outfit on. How did you do that?"

Carrie laughed. "I wondered if you were going to notice. I have learned some new powers with David. I can change clothes; well, it's not changing. I just look at an outfit, and… bam, I am wearing it. I also found out I can be naked; that's nice for baths."

"You take baths?" I was amazed.

Carrie giggled. "Girls gotta wash; well, not really, but I like to none the same. We got so much catchin up to do girl. You better talk with David; he would hang me high if I didn't wake him. He has been pining after you, all worried. If I didn't know better, I think he's sweet on you." She said this with a wink.

Then she walked thru the wall of the house into David's room. It was hard to get used to a ghost… solid one minute, walking through walls the next.

It only took a minute when the curtain was drawn back. David slid the window up; he was standing there without a shirt wearing a pair of sweats. His hair was a mess, and there was a big smile plastered on his face.

"Made me wait long enough. Get in here," he ordered me with a smile, and a laugh.

It was the first time I could remember that I enjoyed being ordered around. I jumped through the window with inhuman speed, and I wrapped my arms around him. I could feel his heart pounding, and he smelled just as I remembered. "Missed you." I whispered in his ear.

"Ditto" David whispered back.

"I don't have a lot of time; one of the vampires I met is waiting for me. I was hoping I could get a phone number. That way we can talk; I have so much to tell you and Carrie."

David smiled, and then his smile faded; he said. "I was hoping you could stay awhile; I have a lot to tell you as well. Also I will give you two numbers."

He went over to his desk and grabbed a pen and paper. He wrote two phone numbers down; as he was doing this, he said, "The second number is to a man named Alex. He is a detective, and he is the one investigating the killings at the mall. He happens to be a friend of my stepdad."

Oh my gosh, I forgot all about that. "So how much trouble are we in?"

David looked at me kind of funny. "Not that much, but I thought you knew that. According to Alex, The Order is terrified of Alice. So this Alice called and told them that one of her children had a little accident. She told them she was sorry, and it wouldn't happen again; I was told by Alex after a small talk that he wanted to talk to you. I don't think anyone is going to do anything about what happened, but we better be careful, because I am sure they are watching us."

"I didn't know that Alice called anyone. She never told me; I guess it is a good thing." I said with uncertainty.

David said with a smile. "Well, lucky me; not being in trouble means I can start school."

That made me think, "Where… are you going to school?"

"Beaumont High, it's right down the road. I will be going with my stepsister; at least I will know somebody."

A plan was forming in my head, so I said to David, "look, I don't have time to explain all the details, but one of my killers is a teacher at that school."

David's face was shocked. "No way, you never really told me what happened to you. You just said that you had to get revenge against the men that killed you."

I could see the deep concern in his eyes. "I will call you later, and I will tell you everything, but for now you need to do one thing for me. See, before I can kill this man, I need info. I also need to see if he knows where a certain film is."

"Film?"

I didn't have time or the heart to explain what was in this film. "Look you have more time with Carrie. I don't know if I can tell you; ask Carrie to tell you the story."

"Or ask me yourself." Carrie said from across the room.

I laughed. "Sorry Carrie; you've been so quiet, I thought you left."

Carrie stuck out her tongue. "Just trying to give you guys a moment, but I can't leave that far away from David, even if I wanted to." Sadness washed across her face. "Don't worry, I will tell your story."

"Thank you Carrie," I looked back at David. "There is a teacher named Devon Wright. I don't know what he teaches; try to get him for a teacher if you can."

"I will." David simply replied, "Without even knowing what happened to you, you have my help."

As he said those last words, we were staring deeply into each other's eyes. The rest of the world melted away; the only ones in this room were me and David. David reached up and pulled me into his arms.

We then embraced each other; if I would have had a heart, it would have been beating against my rib cage. I could feel David's heart, and it was accelerating; I pulled my head up and we were face to face.

"Maybe I should take a walk." Carrie announced, and, just like that, David and I both jumped.

Damn her, that Carrie. She could have taken a walk quietly. David stood up, and he was nervous and a little embarrassed.

Carrie was nowhere in sight. I wasn't going to leave without kissing him. I was almost killed, on the hour every hour. The next time I die, I will not have this one regret.

I stepped over and pulled David to me.

David started to say something, but I put my finger over his lips and shushed him. We moved our heads together; as I closed my eyes, our lips came together.

At first it was slow as I took in his warm, wet lips. Then the pace quickened, and, at the same time, our arms grasped each other tighter.

His hands rubbed around my back and down my sides. After a little bit we opened our mouths and let each others' tongues explore the inside of our mouths. The taste and sensation of this was incredible; I didn't think it could be more blissful; I was wrong.

The excitement made my teeth slide out, and it only took a second for David's tongue to find one of my sharp teeth. His tongue slid across one of my fangs; then the blood filled my mouth.

David jerked but didn't pull back. Instead he grunted in pleasure. It only took a second for my saliva to heal the cut on his tongue. I bit his tongue with one of my fangs, so the blood started again.

Now our bodies were moving as one. One of his hands slipped up and cupped my breast. I moaned in pleasure. And then… I heard a horn honk twice quickly.

I could hear the impatience in the horn; I knew it was Charlotte. I pulled my mouth away and then stepped away from our embrace. David's eyes and body were full of passion.

I said. "I got…to go. I would like to stay."

David said with a voice that sounded out of breath. "Yea… I know. Call me."

Then he stared at me for a minute; I was wondering what he was thinking and was about to ask him when he said, "Did I go too far?"

I smiled, moved forward and gave him a big hug. I kissed him passionately but only for a minute. "I wish we had more time. Don't worry, you didn't go too far; it was just right."

With that I flashed over to his window and then hopped through it. I gave David a wink and said. "See you later, lover boy."

As I was moving away, David said. "Call me, tomorrow between 9 and 10... bye."

As I moved toward the front of the yard, Carrie reappeared before me. "Melabeth and David sitting in a tree..."

A small laugh slipped my lips. "Bye, Carrie, take care of David; I will be back soon."

"Don't forget me, and be safe," Carrie said as I walked away. I turned from the yard to the sidewalk and headed toward Charlotte's truck.

I was happy, truly happy.

Some part of my mind was still having trouble with the kiss. I kept trying to compare it to those men who forced their lips upon me. I shook my head and pushed that thought out of my mind. This was so much different; there was no guilt, just joy.

I had some good laughs with David and Carrie, but this was the first time since I clawed out of the ground that I felt happy. In fact, I don't think I can remember the last time I felt so euphoric. I had spent so much time living around drug heads and no one of my own age; I can't remember being this happy.

There was a great freedom in my life, yet it felt as if the rage I had would eat me alive. My rage will end with the death of my wrongdoers; hope filled my heart that maybe after I killed these men, there will be something more to my life.

My head was replaying the kiss over and over again when I reached the truck. As soon as I opened the door, Charlotte turned over the truck. The Blazer had oversized tires and a lift kit. I was not that tall; I had to jump to get in.

I looked up at the seat and thought about moving up to it. It was the thought, or maybe my frame of mind, but before I acted on what I was thinking, my body rose into the air, and, in one fluent motion, I slid into my seat.

I just flew!

Not very high, two feet, but still, I needed to start somewhere. This was turning out to be a great night. I realized there was a huge grin stuck on my face, and Charlotte was not happy.

Charlotte looked at me with disgust, "I guess Peter Pan was right. All it takes is one little happy thought... and a little bit of David dust."

"Sorry, I don't get it. Why are you so upset? I thought you wanted me to learn how to fly?"

Charlotte let out a dry laugh as she threw the truck into gear and sped down the street. "Flying, good; kissing Necro boy, bad. I could feel your hormones four houses away. Why do you think I honked? And to think, you could be kissing Michael. I think that throwing you off that cliff was a bad idea; I didn't realize that it would do permanent damage."

"Ha, ha, what bothers you about David, the fact he is a Necromancer? Or the fact that he is not Michael?" I challenged.

With anger Charlotte said. "BOTH."

It was a quiet ride home. We parked in front of the house when Charlotte finally spoke again. "I am not mad at you. Well I am not mad at you anymore. I like you, and I am kind of teasing you about Michael. You have some issues you will need to resolve before you can be with anyone. I just worry about you getting involved with a Necromancer. Their magic can hold power over us, and they are not known for their goodness."

I looked at her for a minute and tried to take in what she was saying. "Thank you for caring, and you are not teasing about Michael, nice try, and, for your information, vampires aren't known for our goodness either."

A smile spread across Charlotte's face. "Let me help you with your clothes, and, just for your information, Michael likes smart girls. Just thought a smart girl like you would like to know. We better hurry and unload the clothes. Ezra's going to be in a mood; we have kept him waiting."

With that, she flew out of the truck, opened the back and started to unload. Charlotte was not going to give up so easily. Even so, I still found myself liking her. I am not even sure why; she's kind of manipulative and mean.

The woman could see into me with her power; she knew how broken I was, and still she loved me; she loved me enough that she wished her son for me. No matter how crazy she acted toward me, few had given me so much, for so little, and let me not forget about the clothes.

"Lazy ass… help." Charlotte interrupted my thoughts holding up bags in her hand.

There was a smile on her face. Of course she knew what I was thinking. I jumped out of the truck and grabbed some bags.

After putting the bags in my room, Alice came in, along with Lea. Lea was still limping and in pain. One arm was in a sling.

Alice started off by saying. "You must model for us. I would like to see everything that you purchased."

"Maybe later; I need to get with Ezra; he's been waiting for me." Then, looking over at Lea who was leaning in the doorway with a less than happy look, I said. "Sorry for earlier. I had no right to attack you; will you forgive me?"

Lea looked at me for a second before answering. "Whatever, no big deal. I just hope that Michael can forgive you. I would hate to see him pay you back."

Both Charlotte and Alice burst into laughter. Lea looked back and forth at both of them. "What's so funny about that?"

Alice, between giggles, said. "Oh, I am sure Melabeth will be losing sleep over that."

Charlotte chimed in. "Michael grabbing her and rolling around on the ground with her."

Alice spoke the next part, "Pushing all his weight down upon her."

Charlotte finished it, "The suffering, maybe Melabeth should go into hiding?"

Lea's face went from shock to anger. As she stormed down the hall still limping, she yelled back. "Michael thinks she is an ugly whore."

Alice and Charlotte burst into laughter. I was taken aback about how mean they were to Lea. "Why are you ganging up on her? You know her feelings for Michael."

Alice, still smiling, said, "Because it is fun. I will make her see you kissing Michael later."

There was a mischievous look on Alice's face.

Charlotte stopped laughing. "You're probably right, Melabeth; I will talk to her. Alice, please don't do that."

With that, Charlotte left the room to chase after Lea. Alice was staring at me.

"What?" I asked.

"That girl hates you." Alice said. "Why are you worried if we hurt her feelings?"

"I don't know?" I said with a shrug.

Alice shook her head, "You have a funny mind. On one hand you would have killed her earlier, yet here you are coming to her rescue. I would still like to see all your outfits, so try them on."

"I am supposed to go meet up with Ezra." I said as nice as possible.

"Fine" Alice said; she stomped her feet and yelled. "I don't want to be your friend anymore."

"I will try them on tomorrow, as soon as you get up." I quickly promised.

With a face hung low and a quiet voice, Alice said. "Ok then... promise?"

"Promise."

It only took me a minute after that crazy exchange with Alice to find the danger room. The danger room was the basement of the house; if I remember correctly, Ezra named it after some comic book. I hadn't read it, so I had no idea what it was about, but Ezra had assured me that he had a large collection for me to read.

As I went down the stairs into the basement, it opened into a large room. The walls of the room were completely covered in weapons; I guess that is why he calls this the danger room. There were swords, bows, axes, guns of all kinds and just about anything else you could think of. The floor was a flat white; the walls and ceiling were of red brick. The ceiling stood about twenty feet high so this area felt huge.

Sitting Indian style in the middle of the room was Ezra. He was wearing sweats and a T-shirt. I was wearing a blue workout outfit that me and Charlotte had picked up.

Ezra spoke first. "Most of the night is gone. Why have you kept me waiting?"

"Sorry, it will not happen again," I replied.

I offered no excuse. I don't think he really wanted one.

"Good, let's begin," Ezra said as he rose to his feet.

And then, with great speed and grace, he came at me.

Chapter 11
Dwarf and the Basilisk

I awoke in Nicks' library.

The stars of the roof came into focus, I awoke in one of the tall chairs in front of Nicks' fireplace. The fire crackled, and I could feel its warmth. Nicks was sitting quietly with a manuscript in his hands looking at me. When I looked over at him, he smiled.

"Hello, long time no see."

Nicks laid a cup of coffee next to me, "It's been a month since I last saw you. I cannot wait until you fill me in."

"I can't believe it has been so long. I have been waiting for you in my dreams; I was getting worried."

"Sorry… things have come up." Nicks stated, with a far off look on his face.

"Things… things that keep you from entering my dreams? Tell me." I demanded.

Nicks' face hardened, "No, I cannot. I do hope you will not be mad at me, but it is for your own protection. Instead, a story of *The Dwarf and the Basilisk* will have to suffice."

"What is: *The Dwarf and the Basilisk?*"

Nicks smiled, then handed me the manuscript that he had on his lap. "It is a short story that I have written. I hope you like it."

It bothered me that he wouldn't tell me where he had been, or what was happening with him. I guess I will try and be understanding. And I do not wish to be mad at him; I didn't want to spoil our moment. Plus, there is so much I would like to share with him and so many questions to ask; it has been a month now living with the Whites, and things have been crazy busy.

I haven't been able to see David again. Our schedules are black and white. The only time I get to speak with him is on the phone. And that doesn't happen every night. David's family only has one line at his house; and his sister throws a fit, if he is on for more than an hour. The only time I can talk to him is between 8 and 9 pm. Sometimes I can't call him, and sometimes he can't call me.

I have only snuck out to see him once, and that didn't even work out. At the last minute he couldn't get out of the house. He was still hiding the fact he had anything to do with me from his family; they didn't understand. At least that night wasn't a total bust, because Carrie's range was further now. At least I got to hang out with her that night. She can't stand David's family except for Lizzie. It was funny to listen to her complain.

On another note Carrie let something slip about that necklace David was wearing. She believed it was giving David power. It worried me a little.

Of course I would have rather been kissing David then hanging out with Carrie. I have been having dreams, dreams of the last time I kissed him and sometimes nightmares, nightmares of kissing David, then losing control and killing him.

I hope I have enough control not to hurt David or kill him.

I had been quiet for too long. "What are you thinking?" Nicks asked.

"David… I miss him. It's been hard to find time to hang out with him." I answered.

"Why?"

"Well… if I could sum it up in two words, the White's and the Abbott's." I said.

Nicks laughed, and then asked. "They wouldn't let you see him?"

"Yes and no; the Whites don't say I can't see him, and then again they do everything in their power to throw a monkey wrench in my plans to see him. Of course the Abbott's, David's family would flip if they knew he was still talking with me." I could hear the bitterness in my voice when I said this.

Nicks looked at me thoughtfully. "The Whites don't like him because he's a Necromancer. Well, I think it is to be expected. They are vampires, and vampires have always disliked the Necromancers and not without reason. Let's face it, you'll find it hard to find acceptance outside of vampires."

"I know, but David's different." I kind of had the feeling that Nicks agreed with the Whites about Necromancers.

Nicks gave me a tight smile and said. "I am sure that he is. Now what have the Whites done to keep you busy? I would like to hear all about it."

Well that sounds like a subject change to me, but I was happy to tell him. I didn't feel up to fighting with him, about David. "Every night I have been training with Ezra. He says being a vampire makes training how to fight easier. Strength and speed come natural, so we don't have to work at those things. Also we don't get tired like humans. We run low on energy, but, until that happens, we can run at full speed. If we run low on energy, we can replace it quickly if we can find someone to feed on. Of course you probably already know all this."

Nicks nodded his head, "I do, but I still like to hear what you have learned. Go on… please."

"The only thing I need to learn is how to move my body, what moves counter other moves, and how to use different weapons. Our ability to heal has made our training realistic, and painful, but it only hurts for a minute. Getting beaten up every night is still nothing to look forward to."

"I bet."

I went on, "Ezra is amazed with how fast I am learning hand to hand combat. I am really quick with the weapons; guns, knives and swords. I really enjoy firearms. Next month Ezra wants me to learn how to use the bow and arrow. I still need more practice with knife throwing and darts. This brings up one of the questions I have. Ezra keeps talking about how much power and speed I already have. They already know how strong I am; do I need to hold back? How much should I be hiding from them?"

Of course I would like to know why I am hiding this from them or why I am different. I know he would not answer those questions.

Nicks thought a moment, and then said. "It sounds to me that you are not hiding much anyway. I'd rather the Whites not know too much about you, but it may be too late for that."

Defensively I added, "I am holding back… a little anyways. Also, I haven't told or shown them about my second sight. I am not sure how much longer I can hide that either."

"Second sight?" Nicks said with curiosity.

Doesn't he know? I explained to him about my ability to see sound, and told him about how I have used it. Nicks seemed excited about this power.

I finished telling him about how I used it to see through Alice's visions, he said, "You might have to tell them sooner or later. I would rather they did not know more than they have to, but you need their help for now, and I can't see you hiding this forever, but hide it as long as you can."

"I will; how much training do I need to kill Devon anyhow?" I asked.

Nicks thought for a second, and then said. "I am not sure; he is a sorcerer. I have been unable to find out what his specialty is. Whatever it might be, I believe him to be a powerful foe."

"Specialty… what is that?"

"I am sure that Ezra will explain it if you ask. We do not have a lot of time, what else have you been doing with your time?" Nicks asked.

I thought about it for a second, and then said. "Well I have kind of a schedule now. I get up around two or three in the afternoon. David's at school, and on the weekends, his dad keeps him busy training. I can't see David, so I have been hanging out with Michael. Later in the evening Lea joins us, and sometimes Alice too. It has been a lot of fun hanging with them, but it has been educational as well."

"In what way?" Nicks asked as he took a sip of his coffee.

I took a drink of my coffee and then said, "Well, my time with Michael and Lea has been a good time for me to catch up. They have been showing me a ton of must see movies. We got to the movie theater at least twice a week. It's a lot of fun, and some of the movies are so wild. Some of the special effects are real. Also I love Star Wars; that's my favorite. When Alice hangs out with me, she is always challenging me to use my mind powers. We play games. Her favorite game is tea time; we sit and have tea with all her stuffed animals. She will make all her animals and dollies come to life. They start to move, talk and even dance. I have had the craziest tea parties with her and she makes me feel like I am in wonderland. Of course she does all this to teach me how to use my power, so Alice's says."

"And does this help you learn?" Nicks asked.

"No." I answered, hoping he was not disappointed in me. "See, Alice believes me to be the first mental mute. She has never met or even heard of a vampire with fewer abilities in the use of mind powers. Of course I think she is extra mean to me, because I have not shared the reason I can see through her mind tricks. I am trying Nicks… I will do better. I will work hard on the mind powers."

Nicks gave me a big smile and then with a reassuring face, he said. "Do not worry about it. You may not have mind powers, but believe me when I say you are very special, and Alice knows this."

His words made me feel better. I hate not having mind powers; it makes me feel different. Then again, everything about me seemed a little bit different. Everyone thinks it would be great to be a one of a kind, but what I have found is that means I am all alone.

"Thank you. I don't feel like I fit in with anyone, not even with vampires."

Nicks gave me a serious look. "I know this, but fitting in doesn't make anyone love or care about you. I will be proud of you, no matter what, and I will love you no matter what you are or become. You will never be alone."

That remark brought a smile to my face, and one small tear to my eye. I wiped it away and went on talking. "Well I flew once, but I have not been able to do it since. I have tried and Charlotte has been working with me. She wants to throw me off higher cliffs, but that just hurts. I know I can fly, but I have been unable to control it. I guess I have flown twice. The first time I was really drunk, so Charlotte's new theory is that I need to get drunk; then she is going to throw me off a cliff."

At this Nicks laughed. "She has a different approach to teaching than I am accustomed to."

"You can say that again."

"Learning to fly will help you. Have you figured out any kind of plan to deal with Devon?" Nicks asked.

"Not so much; I have been so busy learning all this new stuff."

Nicks said, with a thoughtful look. "Good, I don't want you rushing into battle with Devon. I want to check in with you soon and come up with a plan; I would like to hear it before you do it. What is going on with The Order?"

It's been a month since I talked with Alex, David had me call him. I guess I better tell Nicks; I hope this does not complicate my task of killing Devon. I said, "Well apparently there is this detective named Alex McDonald. He is good friends with Tony Abbott; that's David's stepdad. David's stepdad works for The Order, and he hires his friend Alex to help solve cases for The Order. Well both of them have decided to cover up the mall killings; not for me of course. David being a Necromancer would not get a fair shake from The Order, and, even if The Order wanted to pin it on me; they are afraid of Alice and her family. In short, they are giving me a second chance. If anything like this happens again, The Order is going to put a price on my head, and you know something is going to happen again when I catch up with Devon. He is a high ranking Order member."

Nicks said. "I know he is. This is one reason that you must plan your revenge carefully. It would be best if you killed him, without bringing too much attention to yourself. If you plan well, you should be able to kill him in such a way that it will take them forever to solve the case… if ever."

I said. "Yes, I now understand why you had me wait to kill him. I need to get information from him first. I don't need the whole Order chasing after me while I am trying to hunt down the rest of the biker gang."

Nicks smiled with pride in his eyes. "You are showing wisdom, listening to others rather than your feelings. Only when your emotions are under control… is when you will make wise choices. I must leave soon, so read my story before you go."

I opened the manuscript and started to read. The story was funny and entertaining. I finished reading and handed back the manuscript to Nicks.

Nicks asked. "Well, what did you think?"

"I loved it, but I am not sure of the life lesson at the end. The Dwarf's greed is what saved him at the end? Or was it that greed devours everything?"

Nicks laughed. "Sometimes it's up to the reader what the story means. In the end, it is what it means to you that makes it enjoyable or important. From my point of view, I was trying to make you laugh."

"Well then it was a hit, and later I would like to read more of your writings."

Nicks smiled and said, "Most of all my writings are poems, but I would be glad to share them with you at another time; for now we are out of time. I am glad you liked my story. I love you, be careful... next time we meet I will want to know your plan."

I got up, went over to Nicks and gave him a big hug. "I love you too... try not to worry."

The world went black.

My eyes opened; I was lying on my back on my bed. I looked over at the clock; it was only 11 am. The breaking of our mental contact had awoken me early, but I still felt tired.

I closed my eyes and let sleep take me once more.

Chapter 12
Swimming Lessons

I got up around two.

I got dressed then headed downstairs to get some food. I was warming some blood up in the microwave when Michael came into the kitchen. He was wearing black, faded sweat pants; and nothing else. I had seen him without a shirt before, but not up close.

When I went to go to training with Ezra, Lea and Michael went swimming. On my way to the basement door, I would pass by the rear door that went to the pool. Through the glass I had seen Michael in a swimming suit; and that was a sight. Up close was another thing all together.

I had to peel my eyes off his chest to say, "Morning."

A big smile spread across his face. "Morning, sunshine, you're up early. Sleep well?"

" Fine... You?"

"Like the dead," Michael joked.

Now that he was over the fact I was here, Michael was easier to get along with. He was still quiet and sometimes he lost his temper with me, but he has had his reasons. I couldn't help but be difficult; it was in my blood.

"Nothing clean?" I said this, and then made myself busy by getting my blood out of the microwave.

A moment of silence passed before he said. "Why? Does this bother you?"

"No... not at all. Why should it?" I tried to act indifferent.

Michael let a little smile slip across his face that made him look... so sexy. "I don't know. You seemed a little bothered by it... that's all."

"Not at all," I replied curtly.

Michael laughed. If I would have had a pulse, my face would be red. Then I heard another person giggling from a few rooms away. It was Charlotte eavesdropping. She loved this.

I changed the subject. "Why is everyone up so early?"

Michael shrugged his shoulders. "Don't know. Want to go swimming?"

"Sure." I had a bathing suit that I got when me and Charlotte went shopping.

I had been too busy to go swimming. One reason is that everyone around here swam at night, and that's when I was training with Ezra. I grabbed my cup of blood, and then said. "I'll go get my suit on, meet you at the pool."

"Okay, take your time. I need to get some breakfast, then I will be out." With that, Michael went into the fridge and retrieved some blood.

I left with cup in hand, and headed toward my room. I got to my room and went in; there on my bed were both Charlotte and Alice, great… what were they up to?

Alice smiled and said. "Hi, sister, how are we doing on this fine morning?"

"What are you two up to?"

Both Charlotte and Alice said in stereo. "Nothing."

"Well could you two do nothing somewhere else?"

Alice stuck her tongue out at me. Charlotte said. "She has no manners; I think she must have been raised by werewolves."

Alice giggled at this remark.

"I need to get dressed," I stated.

"We'll help," Charlotte said, and then looked over at Alice. "I'll put up her hair. Can you get her a bathing suit?"

Alice hopped off my bed and headed toward my closet, "Love to."

This wasn't the first time these two had dressed me up. At first I felt kind of strange being naked in front of them, but I got over it quickly. There was one time I was a little taken aback by Alice. I had been changing, and she was staring at my naked body; she was staring in a way that made me feel a little uncomfortable.

Later Charlotte explained why she did that. Alice was turned too young and was just starting her change into womanhood. I had seen her naked so I understood what Charlotte was talking about. I guess sometimes Alice would stop and stare at women.

Still I knew that arguing about them helping me would take more time than just allowing them to help me. Alice came out of my closet with my blue swimsuit. I was glad they weren't trying to dress me in some string bikini. I had bought a really nice blue one piece suit; I was not going to wear one of those modern swimsuits.

Alice helped me get dressed while Charlotte put my hair into a ponytail. Charlotte left two long strands of loose hair in the front. Then she banded my ponytail every six inches. I looked into the mirror; I was wearing a very nice one piece blue swimsuit. It covered me well; it did not show too much skin. I liked it; I put on a white robe.

"Thank you for your help." I said to both Charlotte and Alice.

Alice smiled. "Have fun."

Charlotte simply said. "No problem."

I left my room and headed toward the pool. Something felt wrong, but for the life of me I couldn't figure out what. Whatever it was it probably wasn't that important. I walked out the double doors to the outside.

I froze in my tracks; there was a giant black tent over the pool. It wasn't a cheap looking tent. On one half there were huge poles placed about every ten feet apart to hold up the base of the tent. The other half of the tent was attached to the roof of the house. Michael had beaten me into the pool and he was already swimming around. He popped his head out and threw his arms up onto the side of the pool.

Michael smiled. "What you think? Alice and Charlotte said that Ezra was keeping you too busy to go swimming and that you really wanted to go, but I figured that you couldn't handle the direct sun in a bathing suit. I had this put up; now we can swim anytime."

I think I could have handled the direct sunlight, but the fact that Michael did this for me. Wow, how nice. "Thank you. I don't even know what to say."

"Say nothing, come swim... and enjoy."

I dropped my bathrobe and then tossed it onto a chair. When I turned back toward Michael, he had a look on his face that I have never seen before.

He looked surprised and hungry all at the same time. Then he said with a quiet voice. "Wow... you're... hot. I mean pretty... beautiful. You look good."

I was stunned at his response; I have never thought of myself as beautiful. Now I don't think I am ugly, but he made me sound stunning.

Then I looked down; I was wearing a red string bikini.

I may as well have been naked. I have seen more fabric in a hanky than the outfit I was wearing. I was stunned.

While I was still having my out of body experience, Michael said. "I like you in red; it looks good on you. I haven't made you feel uncomfortable have I?"

"No."

"Then come on in," Michael said with a grin.

It all came together... those evil hags; that's why they wanted to help me. Alice played one of her mind tricks on me. She made me believe I was wearing my blue bathing suit. They had told Michael how much I wanted to go swimming with him; heck they even made sure they were awake for this.

As much as I wanted to be mad about all this, I did want to go swimming. I would get those two back later. I guess there is no reason to be embarrassed about my outfit any longer. Michael already has had an eye full. So, with that thought; I took two steps and jumped into the air. I flew up about ten feet and then dove into the middle of the pool.

The water felt great as it wrapped itself around my body. It was a completely different experience swimming now that I was dead. For starters, I didn't have to breathe, and as I spun in circles, it didn't hurt when water went up my nose. It helped that I was so strong; when I kicked, I flew through the water. I almost smacked my head against the wall of the pool because I was moving so fast. I could see why Michael and Lea loved to swim so much. Charlotte had told me that all of them liked to go out to the ocean at night to swim. That would be fun, and I can't wait until we all go.

Under the water Michael joined me as we swam around each other. He made a noise under the water. I think he was saying something, but I was unable to make it out.

The sound messed with my second sight. I was confused, and then smacked my head against the bottom of the pool.

It really didn't hurt, but it did cause me to swim up and take my head out of the water. Michael popped out right next to me. "What were you saying?"

Michael had a concerned look on his face. He reached up and touched my head where I hit bottom. "I said, this is fun, but who cares what I said. What happened? Why did you hit your head?"

I let him feel my head where I had hit the bottom of the pool. The bruise, if there was one, would have healed by now, and he knew I wasn't hurt. Still I didn't mind him touching me.

I should, the voices in my head said; I told the voices to shut up.

"I am alright. I just got turned around that's all."

"I have never seen a vampire get turned around." He said this with a smile.

I couldn't tell him that he just showed me the weakness in my second sight. I had read somewhere that sound travels faster in water. It would make all the shapes in my head the wrong size, even the wrong shape; it was very confusing. I would have to be careful not to let those images take over while I was underwater.

"Are you sure you're alright?" Michael's smile had fallen from his face.

I had been in thought too long. I was about to tell him that everything was alright but then thought better of it. "No; everything is not alright."

"Well what is it?"

"It's not you. Are you sure you want to hear about my problems?"

Michael swam over to the shallow end of the pool. There he sat down on an underwater seat that was built into the side of the pool. He motioned for me to join him. "I am all ears."

The next few hours I bent poor Michael's ear off. I told him almost everything and explained to him about how dealing with Devon was stressing me. I didn't tell him about my second sight, or Nicks. I just made him think that all my information about Devon was coming from David.

Then I said to Michael," I also found out that Devon was a sorcerer, and I don't even know what that means."

Michael had been quiet, nodding his head at the right times and saying "go on" or "I understand".

Michael said. "I can help you if you would like me to?"

"I don't know if I want to drag you into all of this."

Michael responded. "Yes, yes you do. I am older than I look, and if you like, I will start by helping you with a plan."

I smiled at him, "Okay."

"First you need to know what a sorcerer is. Should I tell you now?"

"Yes, if you don't mind?" I wouldn't mind getting a lesson from Michael.

Michael pretended to clear his throat. "Tonight's lessons are going to be about the following: we will be discussing what it is to be a magic user." I laughed and Michael said with fake authority. "Please no interruptions during today's lesson."

"Sorry professor," I teased back.

"Sorcerers are kin to Witches, Wizards and Warlocks. I don't believe you have much experience with any of them, so here we go: Witches and Warlocks are the same thing, different sex. Some of us refer to them as the W's; they cast spells, make potions and magical items. When they study long enough and have enough magic, they can go to a school for magic. There are lots of schools; most are very small. Most magic schools only have a dozen students. Studying at a magic school can take decades, and, when they're finished, they get the title of Wizard. That's also why you don't meet young Wizards. It is a rank of achievement, not something that you are. Wizard goes for both girls and boys."

"So do all W's become Wizards?" I asked.

"No, because some will never have the power or the intelligence, but they all are magic users. Magic users in general use spells potions and magic items. Don't ask me how this works; I have no idea. What's the difference between a magic user and sorcerers? The best way I can explain this is: magic users have to have spells ready or potions on them. Their magic items have limits, and they can't carry one for every occasion, but a prepared magic user can do about anything. This is why you never want to face a Wizard if he knows you're coming. Sorcerers are lazy wizards; instead of spending decades learning tons of spells and potions... and it takes long periods of time to make magic items... the sorcerer learns just a few spells and then becomes really powerful with just the spells he knows. The plus side of this is that a sorcerer can be super powerful in a short period of time. The downside of this is that, if any other wizard knows of the sorcerer's powers, he can bring spells to counter them. So, what I have come to understand about sorcerers is, that most become masters of the elements, earth, wind, water and fire. Of course, your Devon could have mastered any specialty; it would be an advantage if we could figure out what that is."

This made me wonder about David. "How does a Necromancer fit in?"

Michael said. "Once again I am no expert on the matter, but this is what I have come to know. Necromancers, unlike sorcerers, are born into this world, but not all Necromancers come from families of magic users. See, most magic users never become powerful enough to become wizards, and it is a choice to practice sorcery. In fact, I was told that some sorcerers get bored after awhile. Then they go back to school and become wizards. Necromancy is not a choice; and it comes with great power, and I have even heard of these terrible magic items made for Necromancers. They trap spirits; then the Necromancer can wear these items and use the power of someone's soul. So you see all their powers are based on death, and that's why no one trusts them."

"Or they're just all afraid of ghosts," I said with venom.

Michael smiled. "I'm not afraid of no ghost; look, I am just telling you about what I have heard and read. Personally I have no real experience in dealing with magic users of any kind. Alice and Ezra know a lot more about them than I do, and they don't trust your friend, but I will give him a chance, and, yes, it is because they are all afraid of ghosts, and Necromancers."

"Why… why will you give him a chance?" I questioned his motive.

Michael stared right into my eyes. "I will give him a chance… because I trust you, and if you say he is okay, that's good enough for me."

Well that was good of Michael. Now we were staring into each other's eyes. He was so good looking, and now there was a lot more to him than before.

He moved closer.

My mind was moving a million miles per hour. What about David? David who? Is he going to kiss me?

We were so close now. Michael moved his head to the side.

I was sure he was moving in for the kiss. I closed my eyes.

Was I going to let him kiss me?

"WHAT ARE YOU DOING?" Lea said as if she had caught us about to start a forest fire.

Michael pulled back and said. "Talking... you're up. Are you going to join us swimming?"

"Doesn't look like there's much swimming happening," Lea muttered under her breath.

Then she said, a little too loud and a little too sweet, "I would love to join you."

And, with that, she jumped into the pool, and swam over and sat right between us. This is going to be a hoot. About the same time that Lea had made herself comfortable, the hags, Alice and Charlotte came out to join us.

Alice looked at Lea with daggers. Charlotte was smiling at me. Damn, I can't stand her power; she knew that I wanted him to kiss me.

Then I suddenly felt all ashamed; I almost cheated on David. In a way I did. I cheated on him in my mind; if it weren't for Lea I would have kissed him. Well, it's not like me and David, are steady or anything. I don't even know if he thinks I am his girlfriend.

In fact he could be dating someone else... he could be in a pool right this moment with another girl. That made me so mad. I am going to kick David's ass if he is with another girl. Great... now I am mad at David for something that I almost did.

Charlotte broke into my self-loathing by saying. "Lea... did you want go shopping with me and Alice?"

"No thank you, Charlotte. I would like to stay in tonight." Lea responded with an angry look.

Alice just said what everyone was thinking. "Let's just force her to go. So Melabeth and Michael can have more time alone. I think they were about to kiss."

"No..." me and Michael both said at the same time.

Then we both started to state our reasons that we weren't about to kiss; at the same time, we both stopped talking when we realized the other was trying to speak. We looked at each other and started laughing.

Then Michael said. "Enough of the dating game. I have a plan to help Melabeth with her Devon problem."

"What's a Devon problem?" Lea asked.

Michael said. "I will fill you in later. The first part of my plan is that Melabeth needs to go and see David tonight. Charlotte, could you let Ezra know that Melabeth will be taking the night off?"

Alice looked at him, and threw her arms up in the air. "Go see David. That is the stupidest plan I have ever heard."

Charlotte added, "It's the ravings of a madman."

Lea said in the happiest voice I have ever heard come out of her mouth. "This is a great plan, and I fully support it."

Michael was laughing, "You all need to get hobbies, other than worrying about my love life. There is more to this plan than Melabeth hanging out with David. I need to get together with Ezra and get some fake ids, one for Melabeth and one for me."

Alice said. "Now that sounds like a better plan. You both get id's, and I will plan a trip for you two. What were you thinking... Europe? Oh I know... Hawaii?"

Charlotte chimed right in. "They wouldn't need many clothes in Hawaii. Good choice Alice." She high fived Alice.

Michael went on like they hadn't spoken. "Melabeth, you need to plan with David. You and me are about to go to school. It's been so long since I have been to high school; this might even be fun."

"What about me?" Lea whined.

Charlotte answered like a mother scolding her. "You can't take the sunlight. You can't get out of bed before five in the afternoon. And you can't even control yourself; God forbid some kid has a nosebleed in class."

Michael looked at Lea and quickly took her by her shoulders, then looked into her eyes. "Do not let those two upset you." It was a little late for that; tears slid down Lea's face. Michael quickly added. "I will be going as her older brother."

Alice stomped her foot. "She cries, and now you have to be Melabeth's brother at school. Don't you think that will bring unwanted attention on you two?"

Michael looked at Alice with what the hell are you talking about face. "We look alike. We are both white with blonde hair, and we both live at the same house, and it would be easier and safer if we traveled back and forth to school together. How would that bring unwanted attention to us?"

Alice threw her hands up into the air, and said, "Because Michael... it will be scandalous when a sister and a brother are making out all day, every day."

Lea got out of the pool. "That's it... I am leaving."

Michael pleaded. "They're just teasing. Don't let them run you off."

Lea was already leaving when she turned around and looked at Michael. "I can handle teasing. Let me ask you a question. Have you been kissing Melabeth this whole time? Have you been rubbing her breasts while you talk? I know you haven't, but that's what I have been seeing. I have had all I can take of Alice's teasing."

With that she flashed to the door and ran into the house.

Charlotte let out a breath. "Well, Alice you have done it this time. You better come inside with me. We need to have a talk."

Alice gave her a strange look. "Why? What do we need to…? Oh, we need to leave them alone. Ok, Charlotte, let's go."

With that, Alice and Charlotte started to walk back to the house.

Michael said in a nasty tone. "You're not funny Alice, Charlotte. You two need to stop screwing with Lea."

Both Alice and Charlotte went into the house, laughing.

I looked over at Michael. "We live in a madhouse. Poor Lea, should we… go check on her?"

"I will. You get ready. In a little bit you and me will go see David."

"Oh… we are both going?"

Michael smiled at me, but the smile didn't touch his eyes. "Don't worry, I plan on dropping you off. I need to go to town. We will need some school supplies and a few odds and ends, and, if I don't take you out of here, Alice and Charlotte will do their best to stop you."

I laughed. "And their best is pretty damn good."

With that, we both got out of the pool. I went over and picked up a towel so I could dry off. When I turned around, I caught Michael staring at me, only he was staring at my ass or he would have noticed that I had turned my head, and now I was looking at him. When his eyes met my eyes, he quickly turned away.

He let out a laugh, and then simply said. "Busted."

I stared at his ass for a minute; I had to do it; it was only fair. Then I said, in a teasing voice, "Don't let it happen again."

"Never, it's a couple of hours before dark. We will leave then. Do you mind if I invite Lea?" Michael asked.

I did, but I shouldn't have. I was off to see David. I felt conflicted, but I answered the only way I could. "No, I don't mind. It will be fun, plus she needs a break from Alice and Charlotte."

"Ok, I will meet you at your room when we're ready."

And with that, Michael wrapped his towel around his waist. Then he dropped his wet bathing suit on the ground. Using his foot, he flung the shorts onto the back of a chair. He went through the door and headed down the hall toward his room, and the whole time all I could think was. Fall towel, fall.

I went back to my room and dressed. Half an hour later I started to brush my hair. I had finished putting on my makeup and was thinking about putting my hair into a braid. There was a knock at my door.

I knew it was Alice. "Come in Alice."

Alice glided through the door; shutting it behind her. She came up behind me and took my brush from my hand. She started to gently brush my long hair.

"I was thinking about braiding it."

"That would be pretty; I'll help." With that Alice started to work through my hair.

After a few minutes of working with my hair, Alice said. "I had a chance to talk a little bit more with Michael. He explained his plan to me. It should work, but both of you better be really careful."

"Thank you Alice, for everything."

A mirror sat upon my makeup dresser. It was one of the four pieces of furniture in my room. There was a bed, dresser, night stand and a makeup desk with chair. The room itself was rather large and painted a light green. Lots of dark wood trim ran along the base boards and ceiling.

I could see Alice in the mirror; after I had thanked her, she smiled as she continued with my hair.

She had braided halfway down my hair when she spoke. "Charlotte is hopeful about you and Michael. She feels your desire for him, but lots of women desire Michael. She doesn't think about that, or chooses to ignore it. There is a difference between love and desire. Do you have feelings for Michael?"

I thought about it for a minute. "It's hard not to desire Michael; you're right about that. When I first met him, I desired him, but I did not like him. He was such an ass to me, but the more I have got to know him... well he's not so bad. Then there is David... he is beautiful too, not as good looking as Michael but he's still good looking, and I have had so little time with him. Yet I have these deep feelings for him, and I don't even know why? So I guess, to answer your question, I don't know, but I don't think I am in love with Michael... but I am not sure if I am in love with David either."

Alice was quiet for a moment before she answered. "I really don't care who you choose. I don't even care if you take both of them for lovers. Let me tell you what I care about."

I was a little taken aback by her attitude and the comment about taking two lovers. All I could say is. "Okay."

"Through the mirror Alice stared into my eyes. "Don't let David control you. I don't believe you understand the power of a Necromancer. I don't believe he understands his own power, and don't fall in love with Michael. I do believe, if you did, he might fall in love with you back."

"And what's wrong with that?" I asked defensively.

"Your future is uncertain, but the two things I see happening will never fit into Michael's life. One, you die in your search for revenge.

Michael is weak when it comes to the heart, and I don't believe he will survive another heartbreak, and two, you spend your time destroying all your enemies. This might take years of battle. Michael does not have the heart of a warrior. What would you have him do as you ran around hunting your enemies? Sit at home maybe?"

Alice was right. Of course it brought one fact to my mind. I can't go kissing on David, or Michael. Both of them deserve more. I sat quietly as Alice finished my hair.

She stood back and admired her work. "You're breathtaking."

"You're right… about Michael, and David."

Alice walked around me so that she was now standing in front of me. "Take David as a lover. It's alright to break a few hearts but not Michael's. He can't handle it."

"You only say that because you don't care for David."

At that, a smile spread across Alice's face. Then her face became really serious. "Michael is coming to get you. Do not tell Charlotte about what I said about Michael. I would have to kill you. Her heart is set on you two being together."

With that, she headed toward my door and opened it. Michael had just reached the door; his arm was in midair about to knock.

Alice giggled. "She's all yours. Have fun tonight." With that, she slid past Michael. Then she skipped down the hallway singing, "Melabeth and Michael sitting in a tree…"

*   *   *

Michael had an 89 GMC Jimmy. It was two tones, blue and silver. I sat in the back seat, Michael and Lea sat up front. It wasn't a long ride and most of it was listening to Michael talk about the plan. It was a simple one. Michael figured, with David's help, we would fit right into the Goth crowd.

I guess Goths were loners and most of the time came from broken homes, a perfect subject for someone to victimize; it also helped that, with all the Goth makeup, no one would notice us being vampires. I think Michael was worried about Devon himself.

Devon would know what vampires looked like, and we don't know how many other teachers may be in The Order. So, we would try to learn as much about Devon as we could by getting close to him first. Then we would lure him to a place and time of our choosing.

They dropped me off in front of David's house. Lea had to jump out to let me out of the truck; it was a two door.

Then Michael said. "Take your time; we'll be a few hours."

Then Lea added. "We will honk twice when we come back. If you don't come out in fifteen, we'll figure you know your own way back. So don't feel rushed." She said this with a wink; she jumped back into the Jimmy, and they drove away.

I turned around and looked at David's house. It was only about eight, and the sky was still full of light as the sun had just fallen behind the horizon. That meant everyone was still awake. I had no idea how I was going to get David's attention. I had tried to call earlier, but all I got was a busy signal. His oldest sister lived on the phone.

I had been staring at David's house for at least ten minutes without moving.

"Can I help you?" I was so deep in thought about the plan I didn't even notice a girl walk up behind me.

I turned around, and there stood a girl about my age. She was shorter than me and looked to be thin. It was hard to tell with her clothes two sizes too big. She wore all black, and nuns showed more skin. Her hoodie was so big that the sleeves came over her hands. Her fingers were the only thing sticking out; her nails were painted black, and her hair was dyed jet black; it hung around her face at shoulder length. Her hair looked like she had never combed it. Her face was painted white with black lipstick and eyeliner to match. She wore silver necklaces with all kinds of different pennants. One of them was a giant pentagram.

She looked at me with wide eyes and froze. If I hadn't known why she was acting this way, I would have thought there was a bear behind me. I think that this is the Goth look that Michael had told me about. So, this might be David's sister. She knows what I am, and she is afraid.

The only thing I could think to do was to give her a reassuring smile. I did my best to look friendly. This just caused her to take a step back. Great, now she looks scared and about to run.

I came to a realization; living at the Whites, I had become relaxed. Holding my fangs up and putting my claws away, is like standing with a straight posture; it was easy to do if I put a little thought into it. Around the Whites, we all walked around with our fangs out.

Smiling, with your fangs out, looks like a threat, or I am hungry.

I pulled my teeth up and put my claws away. I held up my hands like I was at gunpoint. "Sorry... I didn't mean to scare you. I..." wasn't sure I should tell her I was looking for her brother. "My name's Melabeth."

I could see her trying to keep calm. She crossed her arms over her chest. "David's mentioned you. What do you want?"

It sounded rude, but I knew she was afraid. So I said as softly and nicely as I could. "To talk, to talk to David, or Carrie."

"Who's Carrie?"

Carrie still had not shown herself. Who would have thought she could keep to herself so long. It wasn't dark yet, so Carrie wasn't going to be around for a little while. I decided not to answer her question.

"So, is David at home?"

"Maybe... so who's Carrie?"

This girl had a one track mind. "A mutual friend, but I came to see David. Is he around?"

"What if I don't tell you?"

What I was thinking was. "Then I will eat you." But what I said was. "I guess I will be stuck out here waiting for him."

"I've never met one of your kind... vampire before. He told me about you; you killed those men in the alley."

I wasn't sure what to say, I simply said. "Yes."

I noticed her eyes flickering to the right, toward her house. I realized that she had to pass by me. Then she needed to travel about thirty yards to get to her front door. She would never make it, not if I wanted to stop her.

"Well, it has been nice talking to you. I better get inside... I will check if David's there."

I couldn't blame her for wanting to get to safety, but I needed to talk to David without her warning the family I was here. If David's mom and stepdad knew I was out here, it would all turn to drama. "Wait, you haven't told me your name."

"Tabatha Doyle, but everyone calls me Lizzie... so I will go check up on David."

She started to walk around me; I sidestepped into her path, blocking her. "What's the hurry?"

She looked as if she was about to cry. With a shaky voice, Lizzie said, "Please let me go."

I felt like a bully. "Look I don't want to hurt you. I really need to see David for all kinds of reasons. If I let you back into that house, you'll tell your parents. Then they will want to chase me off; kind of hard to have a moment with David then. I am not going to hurt you."

She was quiet for a second then said. "You keep saying that you're not going to hurt me. Then how do you plan on stopping me from going into my house?"

I laughed, and then said. "My plan was to bully you with my size until David showed up. Now, before you rag on my plan, I haven't had much time to think one up."

Lizzie smiled. "Well you're not that big. I will tell you what. David and I have become pretty close this last month. He's told me a lot about you; can't say I believe him about everything, but I know he wants to see you too. If you will trust me to go into my house, just to get David and not warn the rest of the house, then I will trust you not to hurt him."

"Deal." Then I stuck my hand out for her to shake on it.

Lizzie stared down at my hand like I was holding out a cup of water that could be poison. "You offer your hand to a witch?"

I wasn't even sure what that meant. "Yes… I do." Then she laughed. It took me a moment, but she was laughing at me. I said with a little hurt in my voice. "Hey, what's so funny?"

"You don't even know why you shouldn't shake hands with a Witch." She said this through fits of laughter.

"Yes I… what does it mean?"

She stopped laughing, and then said. "I am sure David can tell you. I'll go get him."

And, with that, she stepped around me and headed toward the house. I didn't try to stop her. What choice did I have? I couldn't stand out here holding her hostage in the middle of the street, hoping that David would come out of the house first. I had no idea what this Lizzie would do.

Chapter 13
Teleporting

It was fifteen or twenty minutes later before David came out of the house.

I was starting to get worried that Lizzie wasn't going to tell David I was out here. Then I started worrying that she had told David's parents, and I could be attacked at any minute. Soon as I saw David come out, all that stress melted away. Then I got a better look at David.

I hadn't seen David in a month and boy had he changed. He was wearing all black like his sister, and, like his sister, it looked as if he received all his clothes from a giant. Unlike his sister, he didn't have on a hoodie so I could see his bare arms. He had black fingernail polish on, with silver bracelets piled on each wrist. The only visible jewelry around his neck was the necklace I had given him. His hair had been dyed jet black, and the closer he got to me, the more I could see his face.

He was wearing makeup, black eye liner and some powder that made his face whiter than it already was. At least he wasn't wearing any lipstick. He stopped in front of me, and held his hands out to his side.

Then he said. "So what do you think?"

I put my hand to my chin; I needed to check that my mouth hadn't fallen wide open. "Well... hold on give me a minute."

David laughed nervously, "That bad?"

"No... I didn't say that, but it is a lot to take in. A lot of change... yeah, that's it, change. You know the more I look at you... I think I like it."

David shook his head back and forth. "I told Lizzie you wouldn't like it. All her friends dress like this and what can I say her friends are kind of my friends now."

I smiled, and then gave him a big hug. "I think you're cute no matter what. And, to tell you the truth, this look is just more shocking than anything. I better get used to it."

We were face to face, and David looked really happy. "If you don't like it..."

I put my finger to his lips. "Shhhh... don't change for me."

"So I should change for other people?"

He was right, so I said. "Didn't think about it like that. So are you willing to change your look for me?"

"Yes. I'll change right now if you like."

I pushed a strand of loose hair from his face. "You didn't ask me what I wanted you to change into."

David laughed, and then said. "You're right; what would you like my new look to be?"

"I command you to become… a Goth."

David laughed again. "Done… no really what would you like?"

"No really, Goth. I will be dressing like a Goth queen myself. Long story, maybe we should take a walk, before your parents come out, and I will explain on the way."

David gave me a funny look. Then he said real serious. "Sorry but Warlocks such as myself… never walk."

"What?"

David pulled me closer; he was squeezing me hard. Of course it felt great and, if it wouldn't have been such a mystery as to why he didn't want to walk, my mind would be in other places right about now if we weren't standing out in the middle of the street.

Then David said. "Hold on, and no matter what… don't let go."

With that, David closed his eyes and started to chant. "We are standing outside in the daylight, on the sidewalk, David."

"Oh shit… we need to go somewhere else." David let go of me and grabbed my hand, and, in a hurry, he half dragged me down the sidewalk. "Thank you. It's bad to do magic where humans can see you."

That's what I was thinking. The other thing I was thinking was what in the hell was he trying to do? It didn't take long for David to find the entrance to an alley. We went down a little ways. We stepped in between two dumpsters. No one could see us unless they came right up to the side of the dumpster.

"How romantic, David."

"Alright smart ass… hold on."

He embraced me again, and then started to say strange words; I didn't know the meaning of them; they must be in a different language.

David chanted away, and, at first, I thought all he was doing was making me sleepy. Then it felt as if he were vibrating next to me. The vibrating wasn't a good feeling, and it was a little uncomfortable. Then the world started to spin; the sky and everything around me looked like some kind of oil painting that was being washed away. All the colors melted together and spun around and around.

"David, what are you doing? You're making me sick."

I was really thinking about pushing David away. I don't think I am up for his half ass spell, but, before I had made my move, the world fell away; it was like someone or something vacuumed up all the swirling colors. The vacuum left nothing but blackness.

Then the ground disappeared, and we were falling through nothing. We weren't even falling fast. The air was wrong; everything was wrong. It felt like we may be falling sideways.

I squeezed David in fear.

The next few seconds were disorientating. First there was a cracking sound quickly followed by a loud popping sound. Then the world came back together much quicker than it had fallen apart.

It took me another second to realize I was standing on grass. Then I came to realize I was in a cemetery that I had never been to. The last thing I came to realize was David was struggling in my arms.

I let him go. He fell to the ground and was gasping for air, holding on to his side.

"Something go wrong with the spell? Are you all right?" I asked.

Of course he wasn't going to answer; he could hardly breathe. He put one finger up telling me to give him a minute. I sat him gently next to a cemetery stone. Then I waited.

It took him a minute to gather himself. "That was so dumb... of me." David took a few more deep breaths. "I should have warned you... I thought it would be kind of fun to surprise you. That was the first time you teleported, and I knew you would be surprised."

"Yes, I was surprised. What went wrong with the spell? Why are you having a hard time breathing?" I noticed how he was holding his side. "Did you hurt your ribs?"

"Broke one... I think." David gave me a weak smile. "My fault... didn't think that through. Must have surprised you a little bit more then I should have."

Then it hit me. I broke his rib or ribs; I was the reason he was suffocating. When I got scared, I squeezed him harder. "Oh my God; I am so sorry."

"Once again, my fault."

"How bad do you think you're hurt? Should we take you to the hospital or something?" I felt so terrible.

I felt like I just killed a litter of kittens. "I am a terrible friend... and a monster. How could I do this to you?"

David started to laugh but then grabbed his side in pain. "Stop it, really. I was saving this for an emergency. My sister Lizzie is really good at potions. She gave me a healing potion." With that he pulled out a small vial made of some kind of wood.

He pulled the cork top off; then he drank it back really quickly. "That should do it. In about an hour I should be all healed up."

"An hour, why so long?"

David started laugh again, then stopped because of all the pain. "How long do you think it would take me to heal from broken ribs without magic?"

I knew that kind of thing took months to heal. "Okay, I know... I just can't stop feeling bad until you're better."

David gave me a dirty look. "Stop it... you're making me laugh. That hurts... so stop feeling bad now. Not all of us can blow off some broken ribs and then heal in ten minutes."

I didn't want to make him laugh, and, since everything I said he was finding funny for some damn reason, I decided not to say anything. Instead, I sat next to him on his good side; I put my arm around him and slid him close to me.

There we half sat and lay in silence, and it was so nice to feel him next to me. It brought me great peace, but it couldn't last forever. Alice's words were still in my head, David and Michael deserve better. I have to let him go if I care about this boy. How can I drag him into my hell? Then say I love him.

After about twenty minutes passed, the potion showed signs of working. David stretched a few times and said that he was feeling better. Then, before I knew what happened... I was staring into his eyes.

His soft lips somehow found their way over to mine. I was going to have to stop this.

Next, I knew we were making out. I found my brain and pulled away. "Whoa cowboy; let's take a break." With that, I pulled away and stood up. I helped David get to his feet. "Let's go for a walk. We have a lot to talk about."

"And if you're done kissing, I like to talk too." Carrie said.

She was standing on the other side of the gravestone we had been sitting against. She had on yet another outfit that I had never seen before, and on her face was a super large cheesy smile.

I was embarrassed. "How long have you been there?"

"Sun went down like twenty minutes ago. Always a treat to repair to some place there is no TV, but wait... look at what's on. It looks like one of those emergency shows; look how that boy is trying his hardest to give that girl mouth to mouth." With that, she came over and gave me a big hug. "I was really hopin' you two weren't going to do that all night. I was tryin' to give ya'll some space, but now that you're up for air. What's been happenin' girl?"

"I missed you two. First thing first; I would like to know a little bit more about this teleporting." I asked because, let's face it, it is the coolest damn thing. Carrie laughed. "Now sweetie you know I do the askin'. So, David, go on boy and answer the lady."

David let out a small laugh. "Well you want to learn about teleporting do you? The first thing is you never take a scared vampire with you."

After quickly explaining to Carrie, and boy did Carrie get a kick out of me breaking David's ribs, David explained teleporting to us. Carrie asked more questions than I did, but, in the end, I think I understood it. It was pretty obvious that Carrie still didn't get it. It was a great spell, but it didn't allow you to just go anywhere.

I thought about what David said, and tried to put the information together in my head. Magic users can create what they call a master stone; David wore his around one of the bracelets he was wearing. Then they could enchant other stones that they called key stones. Magic users magically attached the different key stones to the master stone. David showed me where his sister Kelly had buried one a long time ago. He explained that he dug that stone up and attached his master stone to this key stone.

He and Lizzie plus some of her friends like to hang out here. The cemetery itself is set far out of town; it was easier to teleport than to drive or walk.

It took a week to make one master stone, and attaching the key stone to the master stone was a long affair as well. David said it took him ten hours on his first try. Making a key stone was hard work as well, and it could take days to make one key stone. That is why magic users hid their key stones. Someone could steal a key stone and deactivate it or they could use it for themselves.

David had been working on teleporting for most of the month. His master stone was attached to three key stones, one at the cemetery, one in his bedroom, and one that he handed to me; he had set a little stone into a silver bracelet, and I loved it.

He could only teleport four times in one day. He told me this part with pride, because it showed he had strong magic. Of course, if he used his magic up on other spells, he couldn't teleport as much, or at all. The more powerful the magic user, the more powerful the magic item. David told me that his master stone couldn't handle more than three locations.

Once he got stronger, he could try to make a more powerful master stone, and you can't carry more than one master stone on a single magic user. This magic stuff was confusing. Also the further you traveled the more power it took to teleport. I think I understood it, but then again I can't teleport anyway.

I realized a small problem with this teleporting. "So, if I understand this right, when you go to teleport us back, we will not reappear in the alley. Instead, we will be in your bedroom."

"Yes…" David paused as he caught on to what I was saying. "My mom's home along with my sisters; I will have to sneak you past them."

"Don't worry about it. I love running. I will make it back on my own."

I really did love running and I wanted to try my hand at flying again. I would like to try when Charlotte wasn't around trying to throw me off cliffs.

We hung out for a few more hours catching up on all kinds of things. Well, a little bit more than catching up; there was a lot I hadn't known about David, like the fact that he loved baseball; he loved everything about it. He loved to watch it, play it and collect baseball cards. He admitted that he wasn't very good at baseball, but I quickly pointed out that now he could just scare the shit out of the other team.

I also explained Michael's plan for us going undercover at the school. David was quick to offer his help; I knew he would.

"I need to get home; I have to be in by eleven." David said this as he looked at his watch.

It was ten after eleven now. "You're already late."

David smiled. "Yep, I don't want my mom to worry or think that I am up to anything. If I come in on time she will think I was doing something that I wasn't supposed to."

"That seems kind of backwards to me, but what do I know. My parents didn't even send me to school let alone give out a curfew." I had been putting off this last part. I need to somehow be friends with David without all the kissing. I couldn't be with him for his own good. "Carrie, do you think you could go hang with some of the other ghosts?"

Carrie looked around. "What ghosts…? Oh, I get it. You want to have a quickie. Don't you worry none; I'll cover my ears; I am going for a walk… ya'll have fun."

Carrie walked away, and she put her hands over her ears. Then she disappeared laughing. I turned to find David taking me into his arms.

"Do you think she is really gone?" David asked.

I was being held by David looking into his eyes. This will be harder than I had hoped. "No, she's probably eavesdropping… we need to talk."

David's smile dropped. "What's up?"

"Everything, where do I begin? You are already late getting home, so I will make this short. We can be friends but not together." David started to talk, but I hushed him, and went on. "Let me say this before you interrupt me. I am no good for you; I am a vampire with no future. On top of that, I am headed down a dangerous path of revenge, and, if I am lucky, I will survive. There is a good chance I'll get myself killed… I can't do that to you… I can't."

Before I could finish what I was saying. David's lips were pressed against mine. There was passion, love but, above all, there was need.

I felt like I would fall if he was not holding me up. I realized after a minute we were still kissing, and I wasn't fighting it.

So much for convincing him that we just needed to be friends.

David stopped and pulled away, then looked at me and said. "I know that I might not be able to follow you. I know that we may have no future, but I don't care. I will pay for this relationship, but later; for now, let's be together in any way that we can. You need me as much as I need you."

"I don't know… let's just take it slow."

Wow, I just did not say that. What happened to breaking it off?

David smiled. "I couldn't agree more. I need you to do one more thing with me."

"Sure, what is it?"

"Hold on tight." And, with that, David started to chant.

I don't like teleporting, I thought, as the world started spinning. This time I closed my eyes and tried not to squeeze too hard. When I opened my eyes, we were standing in a living room, not just any living room, but David's living room and we were not alone.

As I turned around, David said. "Mom, Kelly I want you to meet someone."

What on earth was he doing? Only bad things could come from me meeting his mom. I had never seen his mother or Kelly before now. Lizzie walked into the living room; her face was full of worry and shock.

Kelly, the oldest of the sisters, didn't look anything like Lizzie. She wasn't dressed as a Goth, and she dressed more like girls I had seen at the mall. She had short strawberry blonde hair.

David's mom had really curly hair that was brown with gray coming in. She was short and a little overweight. If I were to see her in different circumstances, I would say that she looked trustworthy. She had a real grandma look with a kind face, only the kind face had a look of surprise, and that look of surprise was melting away into a look of rage.

Before anyone could lift their chin off the floor, David went on speaking. "Mom, this is Melabeth. Don't get mad, but I wanted you to meet her."

"You brought this into my home?" David's mom stood up from the couch as she said this. She straightened her shirt. "Can't say I have ever met one of your kinds before, but it would have been nice to have a little warning."

Lizzie said really dryly. "Warning? Are you saying if David would have warned you, that you would have let her come over? And, if so, wouldn't warning you only allow you to plan something that might hurt her?"

David's mother looked harshly at Lizzie. "I'll take it you knew about this visit… to your room." David's mom pointed down the hall.

Lizzie did a little curtsey. "It was nice meeting you Melabeth. Goodnight mother." And, with that, she headed toward her room.

All this time Kelly had never moved, not even blinked. David's mom, Mab, looked over at Kelly and said. "Follow your sister." It took a minute before Kelly responded.

Kelly got up and went down the hall toward the same room. I heard the door shut, and now it was just me, David and Mab. Carrie reappeared behind Mab, waved at me, and then disappeared again. Well, that makes it the four of us, but Carrie was smart enough to stay out of sight.

Mab was staring at me with hate in her eyes. Mab said coldly. "So you're Melabeth?"

David quickly added. "Be nice, mom."

"What, that wasn't nice enough for you?" Mab said, shifting her hateful looks over at David. "You teleport her, right into my living room, a vampire. And now… now I am not nice enough for YOU?"

I just loved the fact that David put me in the middle. I had to say something. "It's fine, David. Sorry for popping in on you, Mab; it's probably best that I was going."

David said. "No, wait; I want my mom to meet you for a minute. She needs to know that she is wrong about you, that you are not evil or bad; I want her…"

David's mom interrupted. "You want to force this down my throat. Well since you need me to talk to your dead girlfriend, let's talk."

"Yes, let's do that." I said, and, before she or he could say anything, I quickly added. "Let us say what's on our minds. First we both care for the same person. Second we don't care for each other, and, third we both believe that I should be out of his life."

"What?" David said loudly.

Mab's face went from rage to shock; it took her a moment to regain her voice. David started to argue about my last statement when his mother hushed him.

Mab looked at me strangely when she said. "David…leave; I wish to have a minute with Melabeth."

David started to say. "No, I think I should…"

I interrupted him. "David listen to your mother; you wanted us to talk, so, let us."

Mab added before David could talk back. "You said she wouldn't hurt me. Are you afraid to leave me alone with her?"

David let out a huff of air, and then said with emotional exertion. "She wouldn't hurt you. Fine for you to talk, but I disagree with both of you about her being in my life."

David stomped down the hall, back into the same room that his sisters were in. The door slammed, and now it was just me, Mab and Carrie eavesdropping.

Mab took a moment before she spoke. "So, if you truly feel that you shouldn't be around my son, why are you still hanging around with him?"

I said, without thinking. "I need his help."

Mab asked. "Help with what? What are you leading my son into?"

"I can't really talk about that."

"I see, so, you plan on using my son, involving him in something dangerous, and, most likely, illegal. David is always trying to tell me that Tony is wrong about your kind, that you care about other people, but he is young and easily fooled by a pretty face. You care for nothing but yourself, and, whatever your agenda is, sacrificing David is a price you'll gladly pay."

Mab said all this and never looked away. She stared at me and for a second I was afraid she could see my soul. The worst part was she could be right. My revenge was my number one priority. I was willing to put David into harm's way to meet my goals.

Then again, there was a little bit more to it than that. I wanted to send David away, and I didn't want to see David get hurt. His help wasn't the reason that I was willing to put him in harm's way, but it was the way I felt about him. I need him, and that need is why I refused to send him away.

I said, "David means a great deal to me, and I owe you no other explanation."

And no explanation would have satisfied Mab anyway. Mab was quiet for a second, and then she turned her back to me as she went over to a bookshelf crammed with all kinds of stuff: books, scrolls and more items than I could make out.

As she walked over to the shelf, she said, "Many magic users believe that Necromancers are all evil. I don't believe that; on that same note, most people believe that vampires are evil. David does not believe that, and that is the problem."

"I don't think I understand what you're saying." She still had her back turned to me.

She was looking for something on the shelf when she said. "Let me put it to you another way. In David's mind if he can prove that you're not evil, then he will know that they could be wrong about him. The problem with this is to prove you are not evil, he has to trust you. Let's just say…" she took a book off of the book shelf. "That this is not going to happen. Tee loo loo tee."

With the last set of words I could hear all the doors lock.

I said. "I think I should be going now."

The witch turned around to face me. There was a look on her face, a wicked look. She was hiding something behind the book in her hands.

I took a step away from the witch and toward the door.

She laughed a villainous laugh. "I don't think it would be wise for me to let you leave. How will I sleep at night, knowing that my son is running around at night, with a vampire who is using her mind powers to control my son."

I started to say. "Well, you see... I don't really have the mind power thing."

Mab screamed. "LIAR...I will not have you destroy my son."

With that I could hear David pounding on his door. He was trying to get out of his room but he couldn't. I could not make out what he was screaming. He was not in harm's way, I was.

It was time to leave.

I went to the front door and tried to open it. I pulled, and then I pulled harder. I punched the door, and then pulled it as hard as I could. I could not open this door; it must be some kind of magic.

I could hear Mab laughing behind me. What should I do? I cannot hurt David's mother!

I turned to face the witch. "Don't do this Mab... I don't want to hurt you."

Mab dropped the book and revealed what she had been hiding. She had in her hand a medium size wooden cross. It was made of dark wood, and, at first, I didn't understand why she had it.

My eyes began to hurt from looking at it. It had only been a few seconds and already I had to divert my eyes.

Mab said, "I have been waiting for you and a chance to purge the evil out of David's life."

She was starting to piss me off, but I was having a different feeling come over me: heat, I felt heat like I was standing next to a huge bonfire.

I moved away from the heat until I ran into the wall of the house. The heat was getting stronger. I tried to use my second sight but I couldn't concentrate enough because of all the heat.

I tried to get away from the fire. I slid down the wall trying to get away from the fire.

I ran into a couch, and then shoved it out of my way. I was now screaming in pain; I threw whatever I touched away from me.

I crawled up the walls... I couldn't see.

My skin was burning; all I could feel was pain. "Please stop, please it HURTS... STOP PLEASE. AAAHHH."

I could feel the tears falling. I had enough sense to know that I was now huddled into the corner of two walls.

I tucked myself into the smallest ball that I could, but it did not help. The fire was all around me, and I could not open my eyes.

I couldn't hear anything but my screams. I was in too much pain to even worry about what was coming next.

The pain started to lessen. The only reason I didn't believe the witch had killed me, is because, if I had died, I think the pain would have left faster. It took a few more seconds before I had stopped screaming and was able to concentrate on what was going on around me.

At first I was confused by all the noise I was hearing. It took me a few more seconds to sort out all the different sounds, and make sense of it all. First there was noise coming from a distance that sounded like someone screaming with a gag on. I realized it was David and his sisters.

Then the louder and more confusing noise was coming from Mab.

I looked up and could not believe what I was seeing. Carrie was attacking Mab, and it was like nothing I had ever imagined.

The cross that Mab had held in her hand was now lying on the floor. I guess it had no power unless she was holding it.

Carrie was hitting and pulling Mab's hair. Mab was trying to fight back, but she was unable to get a hold of Carrie. Carrie went from solid to mist and back again over and over. Every time Mab attacked her, her fist would just fly through Carrie harmlessly.

At the same time Carrie would pull her hair and punch or slap Mab in the face. Carrie fought like a girl, but it was enough to take Mab's attention off of me. So all I had to do was figure out how to get out of this magical madhouse.

I had destroyed the living room while she had chased me around with that awful cross. I picked up an overturned lamp and smashed the front window, only, instead of the window breaking, the lamp exploded.

Great, even the windows were magically sealed. Carrie was still attacking Mab, and now she had her on her knees. Carrie was on her back choking her.

I was not sure what I should do. Then I heard the door slam open from down the hall. David, Kelly and Lizzie came out into the living room.

Their faces were in shock as they surveyed the scene playing out in the living room.

I was about to ask David for help, but, before I could, David yelled out, "Carrie let my mother go."

Carrie was still choking her, and Mab was starting to look a little green. David yelled out again, but this time his voice sounded different. It sounded deeper, with more authority behind it when he yelled. "Carrie…leave…now."

Carrie was suddenly pulled up into the air. All was quiet except for the sound of Mab trying to catch her breath. David ran over to his mother followed by his sister Kelly.

David and Kelly both started shouting. "Mom… you ok? Breathe, are you all right Mom?"

Mab was now staring at me with hate in her eyes, like, somehow this was my fault, like I had made Carrie attack her. I saw her slide her hand over to the cross that was lying on the floor. David like his sister was too busy consoling her to notice what she was about to pick up. I had to think fast, before she could use that cross on me again.

I yelled over at David. "Stop her David… the cross." I said this as I pointed at the cross.

David looked down at what I was pointing at. He came to a realization, "Mom, don't…"

Before David could finish, his sister Kelly cast some sort of spell on him. David went as stiff as a board and fell to the ground. With that, Mab grabbed the cross, and rose to her feet, and I could start to feel my eyes burn.

I didn't have much time; if I didn't attack, I would be in horrible pain again. David would never forgive me for what I was about to do.

A cloud of smoke burst into the living room. I couldn't see my hand in front of my face.

No matter, I could still use my second sight to see Mab, but, before I could flash forward to attack her, I saw another person lunging toward me. I turned to face this new attacker.

With my second sight I could see someone heading right for me, and, to make matters worse, I was starting to feel the burning on my skin from the cross. I was ready for the attacker.

This person ran at me with their hands outstretched in front of them. I grabbed both of her wrists and twisted.

"AAAA…THAT HURTS MELABETH." It was Lizzie.

I let her go; it was getting harder to concentrate, and my body started to feel like it was on fire again. I yelled at Lizzie. "Get away from me."

With my second sight I could see Mab waving the cross around herself. This is probably why it was taking longer for the cross to affect me. Before she could see me, I would flash over and kill her.

Lizzie threw her arms around me. "Don't hurt my mom. Let me get us out of here. I threw the smoke bomb, and we only have a few seconds, so hold on."

With that, Lizzie started to chant. I knew with this chant she was about to teleport us out of here. The smoke was starting to clear, and my skin was starting to burn worse. I screamed, "Hurry it up Lizzie."

The world was just starting to melt away when the smoke vanished into Kelly's hand. Now Mab was looking right at me. Mab yelled out in anger, "NO LIZZIE…"

I saw Mab move toward us, in one hand with a cross, and one hand with a ball of fire, but it was too late; we were already falling.

When we landed, it took me a second to get my bearings. Between all the spinning from teleporting and my skin still feeling like someone torched me; I was confused and had lost all my bearings.

Lizzie had stepped away from me and was staring at me as my world came back into focus. I was outside standing next to a brick wall. I looked around, and I was standing inside yet another cemetery.

It was different from the one me and David had just left. This one was small, and, unlike the first cemetery, it was surrounded by houses and was not in the middle of nowhere.

I said with anger, "What is it with you guys and cemeteries?" I calmed myself, and then said with a softer voice, "Sorry, I don't mean to be rude. Thank you for saving me."

"I wasn't saving you; I was worried about my mom, and this cemetery is mostly empty day and night, easier to teleport into without being seen or run over by a car." Lizzie said all this very matter of fact.

"Well, thank you anyhow. David would have never forgiven me if I would have hurt or killed his mother."

Lizzie eyed me funny, and then said. "I think David is right about you; you do have a heart, but he was an idiot to bring you home to mom. My dad says you're evil, but I will take my chances. So, what's the plan?"

She was a strange girl. "No plan, just going home." I was a little turned around. "Which way is home?"

Lizzie laughed; it was a quiet laugh, and she hid her mouth when she smiled. "I will walk you home." With that, she started to walk across the grass.

I flashed up next to her and fell into step with her. "Lead the way."

We walked and talked. I came to find out that Lizzie and David had become real close since he moved here. David had shared almost everything with her. It was upsetting that he had told her so much, but, then again, I was pissed off at David in general. I shared my plan with Lizzie; I figured there was no harm; David will tell her anyway. Plus, I would be going to school with her and David.

Lizzie said, "I'll help."

"Why?"

"My father says you're evil; my brother disagrees. I don't know what to think, but, if I understand you, you're not out for justice. It sounds as if your life goal is to kill the men who wronged you. I will not support a vigilante."

I stopped walking and looked at her. "What about justice? Is there any for me? Screw you; you don't know what you're talking about. This is justice, and I will see those men dead. I don't need your help."

Lizzie looked at me and calmly said. "I said I would help. You don't need to get your panties in a wad. I just don't agree with the way you're doing it, and you need to understand my part...I will help you because my brother is involved, and I think I can help you bring these men to real justice."

"Whatever, you are either on my side, or you're not." I said trying to hold back my anger.

Lizzie turned and started to walk again. It forced me to start walking with her. "You're not dumb, Melabeth, and I very much doubt you see this world in black and white; good and bad. You cannot have me and my brother involved with the killing of this man. You do know this... don't you?"

I felt like a child being scolded. "Yes."

Lizzie spoke with purpose, "Then understand that David and I will help you. We can help you blend in at school. We can help you gather evidence or information, but when the time comes to killing, it's all on you sweetheart. I will help in any way that doesn't involve me and my brother in murder."

I stopped walking again; after a few more steps, Lizzie stopped. She turned and faced me.

Then I said, "Thank you... sorry, I guess. I do appreciate your help, and I don't want you or your brother to be involved in the killing of Devon. Sorry I lost my temper."

Lizzie smiled, then turned and started walking again. Once again I flashed up next to her. Lizzie said. "You're not mad at me; you're mad at David, my no good brother; I still can't believe he put my mother in danger like that. Don't get me wrong, you don't seem like you are out of control or anything, but my mom attacking you was a given. If you would have defended yourself... well let's just not even think of that."

I added, "If I hurt or killed your mom, not only would David hate me, but my plans to get revenge would be ruined. I would have members of The Order trying to kill me because of David's stupid stunt."

"Yes, my mother's death would really screw up your plans for murder; we can't have that." Lizzie said this with no real emotion.

"I didn't mean like that... I am just glad no one got hurt."

Lizzie and I walked along talking. She was not a super pretty girl, but she was not ugly. She hid her face when she laughed, but what I noticed the most was that she was smart. So many ways she reminded me of David; I liked her at once. We both agreed that David needed to suffer for what he had done.

Of course Lizzie was under the belief that David was suffering right this second. She figured minutes after we teleported that her mom was on the phone with her dad. Her dad would teleport home, so right about now there was a search for both of us. She also told me that she had taken me to her secret teleporting area and that no one else knew about it.

He had a good head start on them. The problem was that her secret teleporting area was about ten miles away from the Whites' house.

I stated my idea, "We need to hitch a ride, before someone sees us. If any of The Order members catch me with you... well I think you know the saying, when the shit hits the fan."

"Hitchhiking is dangerous," Lizzie said. I turned and looked at her. She had a little smirk on her face, "That's what I have heard."

I laughed, "That's funny; I heard that it was dangerous to pick up hitchhikers."

Lizzie responded, "I think you are right... at least tonight."

Of course that brought back memories of being picked up by those brothers. It didn't take long for me and Lizzie to catch a ride. Two girls walking at night time, who wouldn't stop? The lady who stopped to pick us up gave us a ride all the way to the Whites' house. It only cost us a lecture about how it is too dangerous for young girls to be hitching. We thanked the nice lady, and she drove away.

"Well it was nice of you to see me all the way home, but you should probably teleport home now." I wasn't even sure why she came all the way here with me.

"Not going to invite me in?" Lizzie said with a straight face.

"Not a good idea."

"Well I would like to meet your family." Lizzie said, still just staring at me.

What on earth did she want? "Have a nice night Lizzie." And with that I started to walk up the driveway toward the Whites' house.

I could hear and see Lizzie with my second sight. She followed me up the driveway just a few feet behind me. I turned and faced her. "What do you want?"

"To meet your family." Lizzie simply said.

"I need more reasons than that. My quote unquote family, are dangerous. So give me one good reason." I crossed my arms over my chest as I said this.

She let out a breath, as if the mere fact that she had to explain herself was exhausting. Then Lizzie said. "Look, I have always wanted to meet vampires before. There are not a lot of you guys around, so I thought this would be a rare experience, to meet vampires who might not eat me. Plus, when I get home, I am in for hours of lectures followed by a grounding. I probably will be stuck in the house for a month. My mom is going to be pissed that I teleported you out of there."

"Well that's not good enough. Goodnight, Lizzie." I turned and started walking toward the house again, and again I could hear Lizzie fall in step behind me. "Come on." I said as I turned to face her again.

She hid her face; which meant she was smiling. Then she looked at me and said, "You owe me big time." She crossed her hands over her chest like I had done and stared me down.

"Ok, your funeral." Me and Lizzie walked up to the Whites' house.

When we got up to the door our timing was perfect. Michael and Lea pulled up in the truck. Lea looked a little upset, so I asked her as she hopped out of the truck. "What's wrong? Did everything go alright?"

Lea gripped, "Fine… until we got home." She went to the rear of the Jimmy and started unloading bags.

I looked over at Michael, "What's her problem?"

A small smirk crossed Michael's face. "Lea is pretty good at feeling emotions, nowhere as good as Charlotte. Soon as we pulled up she could feel the anger off of you. She's guessing things didn't go so well with David."

"That's not the half of it," I said.

Lizzie cleared her throat, "Hi, I am Lizzie."

I quickly introduced her, "Oh yeah… Michael, Lea, this is Lizzie. Lizzie is David's sister." Michael started to speak, but I interrupted him. "Before you ask, let me help you two unload. It's a long story."

Lizzie walked to the back of the Jimmy and said. "I will help too." And she grabbed a bag.

Michael lifted one eyebrow, and then said. "You know this is a bad idea."

I laughed. "I warned her."

Well the whole thing turned out alright. It helped that Alice was out. She had left with Ezra; Charlotte didn't bother to tell us where. Charlotte could care less about Lizzie and went off to do God knows what.

That left Lizzie, Michael, Lea and I. We all had a good laugh of the retelling of what had happened at David's house. Lea thought it would be a good idea that I forgive David; she was relentless.

I told Lea, fat chance.

Lizzie was a lot of help. She threw half of what Michael and Lea had bought away. She helped me and Michael set up Goth outfits. She pulled old clothes of Lea and Michael's out. Lizzie said we couldn't come to school in all new clothes. She mixed and matched our outfits until she had made us a sizable pile of clothes. With enough different outfits we could pass for Goths, and we had at least nine days before we would be wearing something over again.

Michael and I dyed our hair jet black. Then Lizzie did all the makeup. She also showed us how to do it ourselves. It wasn't too hard, a lot of white followed by some black lipstick and eyeliner. When I looked into the mirror, I was horrified. I was staring at myself in a full length mirror. I looked like some girl from the eighteen hundreds; that someone had just dug up.

Then I said, "Well, Devon will never know it's me. Hell, I don't know it's me."

Everyone laughed at my reaction. It was early in the morning when Lizzie called her dad. I could hear him screaming across the room. Lizzie hung up on him, and then she said. "Well it has been fun. See you two at school Monday, that's if my father doesn't kill me."

She cast her teleporting spell, and off she went. I didn't know what I thought about Lizzie. She was really hard to read. I could never tell what she was thinking. She was smart; that was clear enough. I didn't know what she thought of me, but I felt like she was studying me like I was some kind of plant. I liked her; we would get along just fine.

I needed to go to bed. It was going to be impossible to change my hours, but I needed to get used to sleeping at night. It was three in the morning, and I was wide awake. Tomorrow was Sunday, and then we go to school Monday morning. Not a lot of time to switch the hours around. Michael warned me that we would be tired at school, but we must not fall asleep. If someone tried to wake us, they would probably call 911 because we were dead.

When we sleep, we don't breathe; hell, we don't move. In fact, I remember seeing Ezra and Charlotte in bed. I had walked in to ask some question, and there they both lay on their bed face up. They didn't bother getting under the sheets or even getting out of their day clothes. I realized right then how weird it must have been for David the first time I slept in front of him on the bus. It was like staring at two corpses. If I hadn't known better, I would have thought I was at a wake.

I just lay down on my bed, when Ezra came in my room. He never knocked; then again he never needed too. I always knew when one of them was about to come into my room. I was still staring at the ceiling when he sat down on the edge of my bed.

Ezra said with a soft voice. "Nervous about school?"

"Yes" I said simply.

"You will be fine. Here is your ID. Your name is Melabeth Alice White."

I took the ID out of his hand. I looked at the photo; the girl looked like me, but it wasn't me. "Let me guess who thought up my middle name." Ezra laughed. "Who is this girl?"

Ezra looked at me then at the ID. Then he said. "No idea, she looks like you. Just in case, it is always a good idea to use someone else's face on your ID."

"No one will question this?" I asked.

"If you ever looked at most people's drivers' licenses, you wouldn't be asking me that. Plus you're not taking out a loan, and if you're wearing all the makeup you are right now, trust me, your own mother wouldn't know who you are."

I looked over at Ezra's kind face. He had soft eyes when he looked at me. "Thank you." Then waving my hand in front of my face, I said. "Do you like?"

Ezra shook his head in a no pattern. "Goodnight Melabeth."

He left, I guess Goth wasn't his thing.

Chapter 14
The First Day

Monday came without a warning.

It was four thirty in the morning. Michael and I were supposed to leave for school at seven. I only had two and half hours to go. I was almost ready, Goth gear was all on and makeup applied. I just needed to paint my nails black. Gee, I wonder if it would match with the rest of my outfit.

I felt like a checker board.

The fact that I didn't sleep at night and my nerves were a mess, I didn't get a wink last night. I don't think it will matter. I would be too nervous to sleep at school; in fact, I am two hours away from going and already thinking about chickening out. Maybe I should just let bygones be bygones. Get a grip, Melabeth. I can do this.

I could hear two vampires heading toward my room. They always made a little noise so that you knew they were about to come in. Otherwise, you could not hear any of the vampires moving around in the house. My guess was Michael and Lea were about to come in.

The door opened, and in came Michael and Charlotte; I guessed wrong.

Charlotte smiled at both of us, and then said. "My children are off to school. I feel like I should make you lunch in a brown bag or something. I hope both of you enjoy your first day. Also remember I am proud of both of you."

Michael laughed. "You do know we are just going so we can kill someone?"

Charlotte gave him an over the top frown. "I can still be proud. I just will have to skip the bumper sticker. *My kid is an honor killer.* You two watch yourselves, and I mean it. You both will be outside during the day and putting yourself in danger if anyone figures out who you are. I will be worrying every day."

I said, "Charlotte I promise not to do anything dumb during the day. We are just there to get info, not to start a fight. The fight will be later in a place and time of my choosing."

Charlotte then said. "Still, I think that you are both old enough that we have a little talk. Now that you both are in high school I think if you... you know; you should have protection."

I said, "What?"

Michael burst out with laughter and followed with. "What are you talking about? It can't be sex; we don't catch diseases. And we can't get, or become pregnant."

I looked at Michael as I felt... loss. I knew I couldn't get pregnant, but something about hearing it out loud bothered me.

Charlotte was giggling, and then she pulled two small hand guns out from behind her back. "I am alluding to using this protection." Then she tossed a handgun to me and Michael.

We all laughed, and Michael said, "I wondered where you were going with that."

After that, we sat around and talked. We were soon joined by Ezra and Alice. I knew, with them in the room, Lea would not make an appearance. Ezra and Alice gave us gifts.

Alice gave a box to Michael, and Ezra handed me a small box, then said. "These will take away from the beauty of your eyes, but I doubt it will affect you as much as the outfit you are wearing."

"More like a costume, Ezra." I huffed at him, and then I took the box from him and opened it. Inside there were two contact lenses.

Alice explained, "Your eyes will not be the right color, and it will mess with your vision, but you will look more human. In the past we wouldn't normally worry about hiding our eyes, but Devon will know what you are in a second if he noticed your eyes. So have a nice day and make lots of new friends. Of course, when I say new friends, I mean, snack pals."

The conversation took my mind off of the time. We all talked about the day to come. The next thing I knew, Michael said. "Well it's that time... ready Melabeth."

"Ready as I'll get." Everyone said their goodbyes, and Michael and I went out to his Jimmy to leave for school.

Michael and I were in the truck heading to school when Michael asked, "Are you ok? You know this will be no big deal."

"I don't know that. I don't know shit; I have never been to school in my life."

Michael stared at me funny, and then turned his eyes back to the road. "Don't worry, you'll be fine. Less resourceful kids go to school every day. Trust me when I say it's not hard, just painful. It is kind of like a mind torture."

I laughed. "Well, you took my worry away. Then you replaced it with a whole new one."

"Is that all you're worried about?" Michael asked.

"Well no, there is David. I want to see him, but I also would like to eat his face off."

Michael burst out laughing. "Well, hold off on that second emotion until we are off school grounds. Remember, no biting and no eating faces off while we are at school."

That brought a smile to my face. "Yes, sir."

The car ride felt as if it had only taken a few seconds. The next thing I knew Michael was fighting for a parking space. If I had a heart, I would be having a heart attack right about now. I had never been so nervous in all my life. Yet I have always wondered what it would be like to go to school.

I remembered living back in California with my father. I had just turned fourteen, and was still taking care of him. Life there was always crazy; you never knew when a drug head was going to do something stupid. My dad was really worried about me being spotted by the cops during the day. He knew if I were seen around town during school hours, I could be picked up by the police. So, I was on lock down at the house during school hours. All I could do was clean, read and watch TV, also try my hardest to stay away from the drug heads hanging around the house.

I remember asking my father, "Dad, why can't I go to school?" Of course, this was a question I had asked him more than once.

My dad answered. "I have told you Mel, I would have to sign you up. Then they would take you away from me. Your grandparents told them lies about me. Do you want to end up in an orphanage? Well, do you? Because that's what's going to happen to you... if you don't learn to listen."

With tears in my eyes, I replied. "Yes daddy... sorry." Then I went to my room and cried.

I watched through my window as all the children my age left and came back from school. Someday I thought, someday I will go to school. Of course, when I was thinking that, I was imagining I would be alive.

I stepped out of the Jimmy. I had to already put my sunglass on; the sky was so bright. I followed Michael as he led the way. He told me first thing we had to do is check in at the office and get our schedules.

My time in the sun had been limited. I remember being outside in Colorado in February, while there was cloud cover and the snow still lay on the ground. It was now March in southern California. The sun was out, and it wasn't even eight in the morning. I could already feel its rays.

As we walked from the student parking lot, we had to cross a wide open area. There were no trees and we moved at a human pace. The students moving along with us were slowing our pace. More than once we had to move around groups of students congregating.

The sounds of all the students talking sounded like a factory of noise to my ears. They spoke loudly and with the same words over and over again. Words like, dude, word, what's up, and then all the sounds were mixed up with a soundtrack of swearing and laughter. By the time we reached the office door, I thought I may be getting a headache.

Once in the door, things were not much better. Everyone was talking. Kids and administrators were moving around and making noise everywhere I looked. Then there was someone talking over the intercom. Only with my hearing, it felt as if a thousand bees where trapped inside my head. I rubbed my temples and tried to focus.

Michael put his arm around me, and then he said quietly, so that no one else but me could hear him. "You will get used to it. Give it a second, it is hard because our senses are so much better than humans, and you have been living at the Whites for a month. If you think about it, the mice are loud at home."

He was right; it was always quiet. Vampires make no sound when we move; the only time we do, is just to let the other vampires in the house know we are coming. Even when we spoke it was in a whisper. No reason to speak loudly when everyone could hear you in the next room.

"Next... can I help you two?" I realized about the same time as Michael, that the lady was speaking to us. She had her brown hair up in a bun and wore really thick glasses. She spoke to us with contempt as if her punishment in life were to sit at this job and deal with us. "Earth to whoever you two are. Do you need something?"

Michael spoke up. He spoke with a charm that I had never heard him use. "Yes ma'am; we need to get our schedules. This is me and my sister's first day."

It took me a second to realize that Michael had thrown in some of his mind power. The woman's look of torture melted away. It was as if she was ten years younger.

She looked at Michael with... well the way grown women should not be looking at a student. "And what did you say your name is?" She may as well have asked him out.

"I didn't; my name is Michael White, and this is my sister, Melabeth."

She smiled at him; she couldn't peel her eyes off him, not even to take notice of me. "Oh, let me look that up for you. It will only take a sec; would you be a dear and just sit over there?" She pointed at some seats against the wall. Then she added. "My name is Mrs. Corke, but you can call me Jess."

As we headed toward the seats she had pointed out, I caught the eyes of another student. She was looking at Mrs. Corke, then Michael, and then back again. She had a look of astonishment on her face.

I whispered over to Michael. "Knock it off. We are supposed to blend in, not make the adults want to hook up with us."

Michael sat down and laughed a little bit, then said. "Sorry, couldn't help myself. When I meet a woman that unhappy in life…well, I just want to make her smile."

"Do it again, and I will do something to wipe the smile off your face."

Michael looked over at me. He was trying his best to keep a straight face. "Yes, ma'am…just don't eat my face off."

"Shut up." I said as I hid my smile from him by turning my head.

We had been talking so quiet no one would have heard us. I also noticed that it helped me deal with all the noise. I guess I can filter out sound or at least manage it. If I keep practicing, maybe I will not go crazy before the day's out.

A girl handed me and Michael a schedule. Michael had thought it best if we were twins. Therefore, we were both the same age and had all the same classes, except that someone in the administrative office must have felt different. All of our classes were different.

Michael went up to Mrs. Corke and started up a dialog, but, as much as Mrs. Corke would have loved to help Michael out, she couldn't change the schedules. Michael came back in a huff. I told Michael don't worry about it, but, before I could say much more, a girl walked up next to me and said, "Melabeth?"

"Yes."

"Hi, my name is Jessica. I will give the grand tour and take you to your first class." She started to walk away turned back toward me and said. "Come on."

"What about my brother?" I spoke up and pointed at Michael who was now engaged in a conversion with some boy.

Jessica smiled, "Jason will take good care of your brother. So, come on girl; I promise I will not lead you into the lion's den, Girl Scout's honor."

I followed Jessica out of the administrative office. I told myself, do not panic; not everything always goes as planned. You must learn to adapt your plan to the circumstances. At least that is what Ezra was always telling me.

As I followed behind Jessica, I took a look at my new schedule.
First period, English from 8 to 8:55 with Mrs. Trexlor, Room 133.
Second period, Science from 9:00 to 9:55 with Mr. Carter, Room 136.
Brunch 9:55 to 10:15
Third period, Social Studies, 10:15 to 11:10 with Mr. Boyd, Room 204.
Fourth period, Art 11:15 to 12:10 with Mrs. Zacky, Room 220.
Lunch 12:10 to 1:05

Fifth period, Physical Education 1:10 to 2:05 with Mrs. Miller, Room P2.

Sixth period, Math 2:10 to 3:45 with Mr. Wright, Room 523.

It looked as if I would be in for a treat by the end of the day. Devon Wright, Room 666 would be my Sixth period Math teacher. I hadn't even really thought about it until this very second.

I hadn't realized why I had been so nervous. I kept thinking it was because I have never been to school before. Seeing his name on this little white slip…well I knew that I would have to face him sooner or later. Just how do I look at a man who filmed me…dying and more? How can I remain calm?

I put the little white piece of paper into my pocket, took a deep breath and then tried to concentrate on Jessica's voice. Jessica asked to see my schedule; I handed her my little white paper.

She looked at it for a minute, and then said, "We have five minutes between classes. It looks like all your classes are close together so you will have plenty of time to get to class. All your classes that are in the one hundreds, are in Building One. The building we are standing next to, is Building Two. That's Building Three over there, but you don't have any classes there. Oh, and Building Five isn't really a building."

"Let me guess it's a basement." I said dryly.

Jessica giggled. "No, silly, we don't have a basement. Building Five isn't a building; it's a group of trailers on the other side of the auditorium. Wow, you're lucky because I have to about run between third and fourth, or I will be late. After lunch, you just go to the girls' locker room which is right next to the auditorium. After P.E. you can walk right over to the trailers. I have never had Mr. Wright, but I've heard he is a real creep."

"So have I,"I chimed in.

It wasn't long before I heard a bell. After a few minutes, all the kids started to disappear. Then, by the second bell it was just me and Jessica. She was showing me where they served lunch. She pointed out all kinds of things; I was only half listening. I think she showed me which locker was mine. After that, she led me to my first class of the day.

We stopped in front of Room 133. Jessica said with a smile. "Here you are. This is Mrs. Trexlor's class. I have her in fifth period. She a real bitch…have fun." And then, she left me.

I looked at the ugly blue door with the numbers 133, painted in black. I was frozen; I couldn't open the door. I took a deep breath; the air smelled bad. It smelled like dirty socks. I couldn't stand out here forever. I mustered up the courage and opened the door and stepped inside.

The teacher was talking. She stopped what she was saying, and then looked at me like I had just interrupted her. I guess in a way I had.

Then she said in a stern monotone voice. "Can I help you?"

"New… I have my schedule. They told me to hand this to you." I held out the little white paper.

"Oh, you must be Melabeth White. I have already received the paper work of your transfer into this class. Do you have a book?"

I had nothing in my hands so the question was ridiculous. "No."

"No ma'am is how you will address me in this class."

"No ma'am, I do not have a book."

"You may sign a book out from me; grab one from that shelf."

I felt all the eyes of the class on me as I grabbed a book.

Then, Mrs. Trexlor said. "Sit here." She pointed at a desk in the front row.

Great, I didn't want to sit up front. I sat down in the seat she picked out for me. Mrs. Trexlor's eyes never left me.

Then she asked. "Do you have a pen, paper or a pencil?"

"No," then I quickly added. "No ma'am, I do not."

She gave me a tight smile, and went to her desk, fished out a pencil and some paper. She handed them to me.

I took them with a, "Thank you." She then went back to wherever she had left off with the class.

At the end of the class, Mrs. Trexlor asked me to stay. So, when the rest of the class piled out after the bell. I had to walk up and talk to the teacher. Then I got a speech about how I needed to be prepared for class. I left feeling like me and my parents were a bunch of losers for not preparing myself for high school. I think that's what she was aiming at.

During the tour, Jessica had pointed out my locker. I had the combo and the locker number from a slip given to me at the office. I couldn't even remember what building my locker was in. There were lockers attached to every wall. I didn't care to look for it right now, so I decided to carry my book to the next class.

Of course that was easy. My next class was Room 136, only two doors down. When I went in, there were still plenty of students who hadn't come in. A lot of the students were hanging outside the classroom door, waiting until the last second to come inside. Then I heard a familiar voice.

"Melabeth, sit next to me." In the Science class room, instead of individual seats there were benches. Each bench sat two. In the furthest bench sat Lizzie. She was waving her hand at me and pointing at the seat next to her. This was starting off a lot better than the first class.

I checked in with the teacher. Mr. Carder was a nice man, young and handsome to boot. He retrieved a book for me, and even smiled when I told him I was going to sit next to Lizzie.

As I walked back to where Lizzie sat, I could hear Mr. Carder say under his breath, "It's about time someone sat next to that girl."

I didn't get a chance to talk to Lizzie, because, as soon as I sat down, the final bell rang. Mr. Carder was a great teacher. He was funny, and loved what he was doing and I couldn't help but learn. Mrs. Trexlor should have to sit in his class and learn how to teach. She was sooooooo boring, and I think that I was now dumber for sitting in her class.

After second period was brunch. How clever, a break between breakfast and lunch, brunch. Soon as the bell rang Lizzie said. "Brunch time, so how's it going so far?"

I answered her like I was high. "It's the best, and the sun…it's all so wonderful."

Lizzie added, "Those contacts make you look silly. Still at least you don't look like a vampire. I just knew you would find school wonderful. Now you know the wonder of being human. So what's your next class?"

"Mr. Boyd, Social Studies, are you in that class?" I was crossing my fingers.

"Nope, but David is," Lizzie added with a grin. I stuck my tongue out at her. Lizzie went on. "If it makes you feel any better, we're both grounded for two months."

"I don't feel better that you're grounded. I might be mad at David, but that doesn't mean that I don't want to see him."

Lizzie looked at me. "Yes, yes it does. I wonder how mad you really are?"

She picked up the rest of her stuff and shoved it into her bag, then tossed her bag over her shoulder and headed for the door.

I could never tell what Lizzie was thinking or feeling; she was so hard to read. I followed Lizzie, now carrying two books and a binder of paper thanks to Mrs. Trexlor. Soon, as we stepped free of the room, David was standing there waiting.

Our eyes met, and I could see the pain in his face. The sad puppy dog face made me want to forgive him right away, but, if I did that, then he would know he could get away with his shit in the future.

David about tripped over himself to take my books for me. "Melabeth, let me get those for you. Let me say, I am so, so, sorry. I really screwed up. I would have called you, but my stepdad put a spell on the phone. When I touched it, I got electrocuted."

I laughed at that, and, from David's wounded look, he didn't find it funny. "Well I guess I owe your stepdad a thank you letter."

Lizzie jumped in, "Now that's cold, so cold. If you keep that up, David will need a jacket."

I said, "I don't know about a jacket but a handkerchief for the tears may be a good idea."

David just shook his head back and forth, "Will you ever forgive me? What can I do?"

"You could start by groveling." Me and Lizzie said in stereo.

Lizzie hid her mouth, and then David said, "I really need to separate you two. I will make this up to you, you'll see."

Lizzie started walking, turned to me and said, "Come on. I'll show you where all the Goths hang out. We all go to the same place for brunch and lunch."

It didn't take me long to see half a dozen kids sitting and standing around a bench. The bench was under a tree and had lots of shade. It also stood away from anything else; the rest of the student body was hanging out under a giant awning. There were rows of picnic benches set up there; you ate year round outside. You only went inside to get the food.

I wasn't going to have to do that. Michael had said that lots of kids don't eat lunch, so it wouldn't make us stand out. I wondered where the Goths hung out when it was raining. Lucky it didn't rain much in California.

When we got closer, I could see Michael was already there. He was talking to some of the other Goths. Michael even looked good as a Goth; you couldn't even hide his sexiness under make up. I could already see some of the Goth girls eyeing him.

Michael looked up at me as we approached; he smiled at me, and then said. "He still has a face?"

"Thanks to you," I retorted.

David looked puzzled, and then asked. "What's that supposed to mean?"

Michael answered for me. "Well, Melabeth said something about eating your face off."

I chimed in, "But Michael said I couldn't, well not at school."

There were chuckles and laughs. Michael and I both knew that the others would take it as joking. The other Goths introduced themselves to me. By the time I made it around the group, I had forgotten most of their names. Michael introduced himself to David; I had forgotten that they had not met yet.

Most of the Goths told me their nicknames, not their real names, like the girl who introduced herself as October. Somehow I didn't think her parents named her that. A boy made a remark along the lines of, "Melabeth? Now that's a cool Goth name." I guess it kind of is; it's not my real name; I made it up too.

We didn't have much time to hang out; it was only a fifteen minute break. The first bell rang, which meant we had five minutes to make it to class. I did find out that the Goths hung out under this tree rain or shine. The Goth's hangout was right next to Building Two. In fact, I could see Room 204, and that was where my next class was. So, I didn't have to hurry. Almost everyone had to get going to keep from being late. It was just me and David.

David was leaning against the side of the tree. I could see the stress in him, and I could feel his worry. Maybe it was because he was a Necromancer, or maybe it was because I was a vampire. No matter the reason, I wasn't mad enough at David to see him suffer. I walked up next to him and gently rubbed his arm. He looked over at me with hope in his eyes.

So much for being tough on him. "I forgive you; in fact, I am not even sure I was ever that mad about it."

"Really?"

I went on. "Since those bikers kidnapped me... well let's just say it's been one thing after another. I have been in countless fights, and that was the first fight where no one died. Well, second, if you count the one I had with Lea and Michael. Wait, make it the third...I forgot about the fight with Alice. No one died; I just lost."

David smiled. "I think I understand what you're saying. It's been rough for you."

"Yeah, it's been rough, but you have always been there for me, and, even though what you did was stupid, it was also amazing. You tried to bring a vampire into your life. I do believe that normal people wouldn't even think of bringing me home to mom."

David looked as if I had taken a hundred pound weight off of his back. Then he said. "Thank you, you will not regret it, I promise. We better hurry before we're late."

Even though we were only twenty feet from the door, we just got inside when the final bell rang. David hurried to his seat while I headed toward the front of the classroom to the teacher's desk.

Now that I was looking at Mr. Boyd, I was taken aback by him. I would have to describe him in two parts, first his head; he was balding with some brown hair around the sides. He looked to be in his early forties. He wore large glasses and sported a very large mustache. In a word, his head and face reminded me of a middle aged nerd. Then there was his body; the man stood at least six two. He was huge; his muscles looked as if they were going to rip out of his shirt. He reminded me of that actor that Michael likes, Arnold Swarchhammer or something like that.

He looked at me with a big smile. He had a friendly face. "The new girl, Melabeth right?"

"Yes, sir."

"Well, it's good they have manners in Transylvania. Go ahead and take a seat next to the other vampire." And with that he pointed at David.

David yelled out, "It's Goths."

Some other boy said, "Goths suck."

That was followed by, "I bet she does."

Mr. Boyd said with great authority, "Quiet...I will have no disrespecting women in my class. Tim, why don't you come and see me after class."

"Yes sir."

Mr. Boyd gave me a wink as I sat next to David in the back of the class. The class was fun, Mr. Boyd was funny, and I loved the way he taught history. The next 55 minutes flew by. The bell rang, and I was off to Art class. No one had Art with me, like first period I would be on my own.

David had to go in a different direction to get to his class. We said our goodbyes; it wasn't far to my class so I walked slowly taking in all the activity around me. I had never witnessed this in my life. These kids were rude and mean; they swore every other word. I was called a freak at least four times before I reached my class. It didn't bother me that they called me names, because I was looking at them all like they were fish in a bowl.

I walked into my Art class. The teacher was an Egyptian woman, who could hardly speak English. I had to have her repeat herself three or four times. The class was ridiculous. The teacher gave us an art assignment, and then most of the kids fell into conversations with each other. Only a few kids did anything. I found myself sitting in the back while no one gave me any attention. I guess this Goth outfit sent a signal out; leave me alone; I don't want anything to do with you.

I worked a little on the art project, but it didn't really interest me much. It was nice to just sit quietly and think. Listening to all the kids' gossip made the time pass quickly. Before I knew it, the bell rang, and I was off to lunch.

I met up with the rest of the Goths under the tree. Michael and David hadn't gotten there yet. Lizzie walked up about the same time I did. She was walking and talking with the girl who introduced herself as October. A few seconds later I could see Michael and David heading our way.

David, Michael, Lizzie and I kind of formed our own little circle. There we started to do a little bit of planning. We didn't get much accomplished because one of the Goth boys, who called himself Bran, came up and wanted to join in on our conversation. Michael and I were new, so everyone wanted to know more about us. October didn't join in with the rest of them, but I noticed that she eyed me. I don't know if she knew anything, but I do believe that she noticed something is different about me.

Lunch was over quickly. It probably had to do with the fact that I was dreading sixth period with Mr. Wright. It's a funny thing; when you dread the future, it comes fast. If you are waiting for something you want, it takes its sweet time.

October was in P.E. with me. Lizzie asked her to take me with her. October nodded her head but didn't really say anything. I didn't feel like talking, so we both walked in silence toward the girls' locker room.

Mrs. Miller was a middle aged woman with curly blonde hair. She probably colored it because it didn't match her features. She was tall for a woman, but not over six feet. She looked taller than she was when I approached her. It was her build that made her look so tall. This was the second bodybuilder I had for a teacher. Huge muscles looked a lot better on men, or at least that's what I think.

Mrs. Miller looked me up and down. It was a look of disapproval; at first, I thought it was because of the Goth outfit. Then she said. "You're a scrawny little thing." Then she gave me a hard slap on my back. "Don't worry; I'll whip you into shape. Go get changed."

Michael hadn't bothered to give me paper and pen, but he did pick me up the required P.E outfit. He had given it to me at lunch; he was wearing a long black jacket. The shorts and shirts had been shoved into the side pockets.

David was still trying to make up for his mistake, so he had taken the four books I had required and delivered them to my locker. Of course that meant that I still had no idea where my locker was, and now I didn't know where my books were.

I went inside the locker room with October to change. The girls gave us dirty looks. I could tell by October's face this was the worst part of her day. Michael hadn't bothered to get me a lock; I noticed that the other girls were locking up their stuff. Oh well, I thought, if anyone steals any of my stuff, I will hunt them down and kill them.

I stripped down to my undergarments. I looked over at October; she was staring at me. If she would have been looking higher than my neck, she would have noticed I was now looking back. I really looked at her for the first time. Outside it had been hard to look at anything because of how bright it was, but in this locker room the lighting was poor or great for me.

October had straight black hair that hung below her shoulders except for her bangs. She was shorter than me and skinnier. She, like me, was standing in her undergarments. Before she had been wearing so much clothing, I hadn't realized just how small she was. If she weighed over eighty pounds I would have been surprised.

Her eyes finally met mine; I could see her embarrassment. She quickly looked away and started to get her P.E. clothes on. Our P.E. clothes consisted of blue shorts and a white T-shirt. I had worn black sneakers so I didn't need different shoes, but October did. She had been wearing really high boots and had a pair of white gym shoes to replace the boots.

October finally spoke. "Sorry, for staring. You're really pretty, but you probably know that."

I didn't know what to think; she had caught me off guard. "Thank you… you're pretty too."

Why did I just say that? Wait, is that why she was staring at me at lunch time? I thought it was because she knew there was something supernatural about me. It never even occurred to me that she could be staring at me because… well, I didn't see that coming.

October was now beaming at me. Telling her that she was pretty had most likely sent all the wrong messages. Oh well, she will figure it out sooner or later. Plus, she seemed nice enough, and I could still be misreading the situation.

"Look at the Goth Lesbian having a moment." A fat Mexican girl was standing next to me. She was glaring at me. October shrank in the presence of this girl. "I am talking to you, fag." She pushed on my chest with her pointer finger.

October touched my arm, "Don't worry about her; let's just go."

"Go, you stupid Dyke. Before I beat the…"

She never finished; I had my right hand around her throat. I wasn't squeezing hard for me, but it was hard enough she couldn't breathe.

She reached up to pull my arm off, but she couldn't make me move an inch. Then I shoved her back, releasing her from my grip. I had shoved her a little harder than I wanted to. She smacked up against some lockers that were across from mine.

I said with as much venom as I could, "Just say anything… go ahead, say something."

The girl was taken back, she just stared at me with fear in her eyes. Her friends started talking shit for her, but the girl wasn't going to let her friend push her into a fight she would lose.

She straightened herself up, and then said. "You're lucky I can't get into any more trouble, right now."

With that she led her friends outside where they could talk crap from a distance. October touched my shoulder and said, "I have never seen anyone run off Carmen before. She picks on everyone, well everyone but the cheerleaders."

"Why not the cheerleaders?"

"Because they are mutants and run this school, that's why. Well to be technical Veronica runs this school. The rest of the cheerleaders are just her robots. They do and say whatever Veronica does or says."

I laughed, as me and October headed for the door. P.E. should be an easy enough class for me. Let's face it, I might not be well educated, but I had the physical element in my pocket.

*   *   *

I couldn't believe I was sitting in the nurse's office with October about holding me up.

As soon as we got outside, we walked down to the field. Then Mrs. Miller told us all to run a mile, four easy laps around the football field. The best part was there were lots of guys practicing football. So, as we started running around I could check some of the cute guys out.

After ten minutes of running, I wasn't checking out anyone. The sun was killing me, and I didn't sweat so I felt like my blood was boiling. It felt like the sun's rays were heating me from the inside out. My stupid P.E. outfit gave me no skin cover. It didn't take fifteen minutes before the world started to spin.

I found myself lying on the ground looking up at October. I could hear her saying. "Melabeth, you ok, what's wrong?"

I could hear her, but it took me a minute before I could answer her.

So, here I was, sitting in the nurse's office; so much for being the queen of P.E. In fact, I am going to need a doctor's note that says. *"Melabeth is a big wimp, and, for this reason, please put her inside with air conditioning. Signed, Dr. White."*

I explained to the nurse that I felt fine now; that I hadn't been drinking water and the sun had just gotten to me. She ordered me to drink a huge glass of water before leaving. The water did actually make me feel better.

When I got back to the girls' locker room, the girls were all heading in. Mrs. Miller gestured for October to go change.

Then she said, "Let's talk, Melabeth."

"Yes, ma'am."

"At the end of the week, the class will be inside the auditorium playing volleyball. In honor of you being new, and passing out on the first day, I have decided to go ahead and move up the time. So, we will be inside tomorrow playing volleyball. Even an albino like you can handle that."

"Thank you." That was great news. I had been worrying about what I was going to do about tomorrow, but now it worked itself out.

I was about to turn to go into the locker room, but Mrs. Miller said. "Before you run off, what happened in the locker room between you and Carman?"

"Well…nothing really," I lied.

Mrs. Miller reached over and squeezed my biceps. "Tougher then you look, you better go get ready for your next class."

She gave me a strange smile, almost as if I did something to make her really proud. Almost beating up another student was her idea of a good job. Well, the way I get into fights, I was sure to keep her proud for the rest of the year!

I got dressed and walked out of the locker room with October. October said. "My next class is in Building Three, so maybe I will see you after school, and, if not, I will see you tomorrow."

The way she looked at me made me feel uncomfortable, but that feeling was being drowned out by fear. I said to October as I started walking toward the trailers, "Yeah, I'll see you later."

As I walked toward the trailers, my feet became like bricks. Every step was labor; and I found it hard to take a breath. Of course, I didn't need to breathe; I knew how ridiculous I was being. I was afraid; I was about to enter my nightmare. His face was the one I saw when I closed my eyes.

It had been fifteen years ago for him, but, for me, it had all happened a month ago. I walked up to the trailer with number 523 on the door. There was a wooden ramp leading up to the door. Kids where already heading up the ramp going inside.

God help me, please find me the strength. I must face the devil and pretend that I don't know him. I don't pray much; ok, not at all, but I will take whatever help there is.

I swallowed, took a deep breath, and calmed myself. Then I realized a boy was talking to me. "Are you lost?" A boy was standing next to me. He was thin but tall with short hair and glasses.

"No, just a little nervous," I said

"New? I remember my first day here. My name is Steve."

Two boys passed behind us, then pushed Steve. One of the boys said. "Steve… his name is Poindexter, the homosexual nerd boy." Both the boys laughed as if the joke was funny. They both kept walking and then headed up the ramp into the classroom.

I looked at Steve who was feeling the emotions of embarrassment and anger. "They're jerks; don't worry about it. Let's go before we're late."

Steve gathered himself, and then said, "Throwbacks of evolution. Let's hurry; Mr. Wright is quick to hand out a slip for being late."

Steve made me forget about how afraid I was. I found myself following Steve into the classroom. I was numb; I couldn't tell how I felt. Then I saw him, sitting behind his desk talking to a girl student. He had a big smile, and, if I didn't know who he really was, I would have thought he had a nice and inviting face.

He looked almost exactly how I remembered him. The years had been kind, but I am not the years.

I was shaking with fear... I could have screamed.

Run away.

I closed my eyes and tried to pull myself together. The bell rang.

I jumped and yelled at the same time. The bell had scared the shit out of me, but now everyone was looking at me.

"The bell scares me every time." Mr. Wright said with a smile. The kids laughed, and the girl he had been speaking with hurried back to her seat. "Quiet, class." The class went silent. "Come over here young lady."

He was speaking to me. I moved, but it felt as if my whole body weighed tons, and every step was agonizing. I held out my white piece of paper; he took it out of my hand.

Then Mr. Wright said. "Melabeth White, nice to have you. You may have a seat over there, and, right at this moment, I am fresh out of books, but I am sure that Steve will share with you."

I headed over to the seat he had pointed to. It was in the back row and right next to Steve, and, on the other side of me, was the wall. I sat down, and Mr. Wright began to speak.

Mr. Wright gave instructions for the first half hour. In that time, my fear melted away and was slowly replaced with anger. Then the anger was replaced by rage.

It took all my willpower not to get up and rip his head off. The entire time he gave instructions I had flashbacks, flashbacks of him giving instructions to the bikers, telling them how and what to do to me.

Then he handed out a quiz; at least for the next half hour I could look at something other than him, and I wouldn't have to hear the sound of his voice.

After writing my name on my paper, the next five minutes became very frustrating. I was in Algebra I. I would have understood Greek faster than this. I didn't understand anything I was looking at. I knew how to add and subtract and some of my multiplication. For the next half hour I stared at my test.

My anger drained away and was replaced by a new feeling; I felt like a dumb ass.

Mr. Wright broke up my pity party. "Times up, pass your test forward. Tonight Pages 335 and 336."

The class moaned at the sound of homework. I passed my blank test forward. Then the bell rang, I couldn't get out of the classroom fast enough.

I hurried out to the student parking lot. When I got to Michael's Jimmy, Michael was already there. David and Lizzie had also beaten me.

"How was class?" Michael asked.

I let out a breath. "And all those years I thought I was missing out, because my parents didn't send me to school."

We all had about twenty minutes to sit around and talk. Lizzie was still trying to figure out how to bring Devon to justice, when we got a hold of the evidence. Me and the boys knew there wasn't going to be any justice. Revenge would be the justice of the day.

David and Lizzie had to go. Their mother would be here soon to pick them up. Her work hours made her run about a half an hour after school let out. I didn't feel comfortable enough to kiss David in front of Michael. I am not sure what that says about me. I am sure David took it as I was still mad at him.

As soon as me and Michael got home, we both went to bed. I fell right to sleep. I woke up about nine, and then I had to relive my whole day with Alice, Charlotte and Ezra. They wanted to know every little thing that happened.

Michael came down after I was already done telling them about my whole day. Lea even joined us when Michael was forced to tell everyone about his day. I guess being a vampire could get pretty boring, because Alice never missed a word.

The next four days were repeats of the first day. The good news was that Nicks had come and visited me in my dreams twice. The bad news was he made me tell the story again. I wasn't only sick of going to school; I was sick of telling people about my time going to school.

I finally understood what they meant by T.G.I.F. I had been really looking forward to the weekend and to getting a break from school. The bad news was that David was grounded, and I wouldn't be able to see him until Monday. So, here I was on Friday night waiting for school on Monday. What a mess.

I had only been home for a few hours. I was lying in bed thinking about sixth period with Mr. Wright. It was on my fifth day at the end of the class that Mr. Wright asked me to stay, I almost said no.

"Melabeth, the reason I asked you to stay…well, it's your grades. You haven't done any of your homework, and you didn't even try on the two quizzes I have handed out. You may not know this because you're new, but quizzes make up fifty percent of your grade."

I could hardly listen to him speak, and I couldn't keep eye contact with him. So I looked at the floor when I answered him. "I don't know how to do anything that we are working on. I don't get it."

Mr. Wright gave me a reassuring smile. "You should have said something. I offer tutoring after class. Would your parents let you stay late?"

Our cover story was that me and Michael's parents had died in a car accident, and we were now living with our grandmother. I said, "I live with my grandmother, and she really doesn't even understand what's going on. So, whenever... it doesn't matter."

There was a look on Mr. Wright's face... a dark look. He thought for a second, and then he said. "You need a lot of work to catch up. Why don't you come by my house Wednesday night?"

He went over to his desk and wrote his address down for me. Then he handed it to me and said. "Let's say around six, ok."

"Thanks, see you Monday."

I left, and went to met up with Michael, David and Lizzie at the truck. They couldn't believe the bastard had already made a move. Lizzie said she had an idea, and the next thing I knew Lizzie and Michael were plotting away. I would spend the rest of this weekend getting ready.

It's time we gathered some evidence.

Chapter 15
Plan A

Over the weekend I took it easy.

I went swimming with Michael and Lea a few times. I also got some practice in with Ezra. He took no prisoners during our practices; he hadn't liked me missing all this training time, so he was trying his hardest to catch me up. I think I really surprised him in our sessions.

We had stopped to heal; Ezra looked over at me and said, "You truly take to this like a fish in water. You can't teach talent. You're slower and weaker than me, but you always manage to put up a good fight. It seems like you can see in all directions; I can never sneak an attack on you."

"Thank you," I said; Ezra looked at me; he was standing perfectly still. "What is it?" I asked.

"Tell me, do you feel stronger and faster, than you did a month ago?"

"Yes, I believe so."

Ezra then said. "Yes, you are stronger and faster than you were a month ago."

He turned and started to put up some of the weapons we had been training with. He had meant more than what he had said.

So I asked him. "Why, is there something wrong with that?"

"No," he replied.

I put the last weapon away, and Ezra was heading toward the staircase. "Is there something different with me? Do other vampires become stronger and faster in such a short period of time?"

Ezra paused; he didn't answer me for a few seconds, and I was almost thinking that he might not answer me at all. "No, they don't; it is curious."

He walked up the stairs without a backward glance. Great, I just love being different and curious; I was now glad that I was having a planning meeting with Michael. I needed the distraction from thinking about what had just transpired between me and Ezra.

I went into the living room to find Michael; Michael was sitting there with Alice. "Hey, what are you two up to?"

Alice smiled at me, but Michael just stared straight ahead as if he didn't hear me or see me. "What is wrong with Michael, Alice?"

"Nothing, dear, I am just using my power on him. I can make you see and hear what I want; most people can't see around that, and, when I say most people, I mean you. I wonder why that is?"

Alice has never stopped asking me how I see around her power. I didn't answer her; instead I just change the subject. "So what are you making him see?"

A wicked smile crossed Alice's face. "Not sure if I should tell you; it might upset you. Probably better that you don't know. Michael asked me to show him, and I thought to myself that I probably shouldn't, but he was so persuasive. How could I say no?"

I knew she was up to no good, that, whatever she was saying was probably just teasing me, but she is really good at that, so I took the bait. "Alright Alice what is it? What is he seeing?"

"Before you get mad, just remember that he is a boy, and boys like girls, and it's perfectly natural to want to see them naked."

"You are NOT showing him me… are you?"

Alice put her hands up like I was pointing a gun at her. "Look, don't blame me; I am just doing a good friend a favor. I tried to warn him, but he wouldn't listen."

"Stop showing him; stop it before I rip his eyes out."

Alice laughed. "He's seeing this through his mind; ripping his eyes out wouldn't help you." I gave her a look of anger. "Ok… ok, I am stopping, but he is going to be disappointed; I was just getting to the good part."

Michael's look changed as his own mind returned; he looked at me, and said. "HI Melabeth, you're here, great we can go over the plan now."

I tried my hardest to hold back my anger in my voice, but I wasn't very good at holding back. "Did you ask Alice to show you…you're such a pig!"

Michael had a look of surprise; I couldn't tell if it was surprise because Alice lied to me, or surprised, because he had been caught.

Michael quickly answered. "Yes, I asked Alice to show me. She warned me about it, but I wanted to know."

"How dare you?"

"Wait… what did Alice say that I was watching? I asked to see some of her past… that's all." Michael said this as he gave Alice a dirty look.

Alice still had a smirk on her face; she looked at him and then me. "Well, technically I didn't tell her what you were looking at. I might have… made it sound as if you had requested Melabeth in a show of sorts." Then Alice burst into laughter.

"What she's saying is, she made it sound… that you asked to watch me naked… did you?"

Michael shook his head no; at the same time he said. "I wouldn't do that, Alice. Can you stop it? Isn't there enough drama around here?"

Alice stopped laughing and looked at us as if we just falsely accused her of a crime. "Joke… just a joke. You two need to relax. If you both are going to act like this, I am going to my room to play with my dolls." Alice stomped up the staircase as if we had been mean to her.

Michael motioned for me to sit, "Sorry about that; she is always doing shit like that."

"I know, I don't know why I let her suck me in. I knew better."

Michael smiled at me as I sat next to him. "You are stressed, and what we have to talk about is not going to help that."

"You're right, so what's the plan, boss?"

"Lizzie, has worked out the plan, and it's a two part plan. Before you interrupt me, Lizzie and David's part will be less dangerous than yours. Lizzie thinks that, once you have the evidence, that she will be able to get The Order to serve justice. Of course, we know better, and so does David; for this reason, Lizzie should have as little do with this as possible."

"And David too, I want both of them to have very little to do with this. I would prefer nothing at all, but, if we need their help, and there is no way around it, so be it."

Michael looked at me for a minute, then said, "I really like these kids, Lizzie and David, but they are just children; I guess you are as well. The plan that Lizzie worked out will work, but I think you should do this on your own. I am not sure how, and it will probably take you longer to get Devon, but in the end it will be better."

The thought of having to sit through more classes with Devon was unbearable. "I would like to hear Lizzie's plan. If you think it will work, we will keep their involvement to a minimum."

Michael shifted his body around in the couch. Then he let out a breath, "I thought you would say that; I just hope you don't come to regret it. Lizzie and David are bound and determined to help you, so here it is. Like I said, this is a two part plan; the first part of the plan is called Plan A; that's your part."

Michael pulled out a calendar and flipped it open, grabbed a pen, then he started to explain, Plan A. "Ok, Tuesday, is March the 6th. You will ride over to Devon's house with him after school. He will believe that no one knows you are with him. Once you're at his place, you will wait a few minutes, and then excuse yourself to go to the bathroom. Once you're in the bathroom, you will take that teleporting stone that David gave you, and hide it somewhere. Now Lizzie told me it is better to be hidden in a low place, because they normally teleport above it. Once you have done this, you will flip the light switch off and on twice; I will already be there watching the house with Ezra. Flipping it on and off will let us know that you are done, and it wasn't Devon using the bathroom."

"It will still be daylight."

Michael smiled, "good point, Plan A, part two. Wave your hand out the window when you have finished."

I laughed, "We're doomed."

"Shh… and listen. After you wave your hand, I will come to the door and inform Devon that our grandmother is sick. You will act all worried, and we will rush away. That's all for Plan A…easy."

"Don't you think he will be wondering how you knew where I was?"

Michael shrugged his shoulders, "No plan is perfect, Melabeth. He will probably be thinking that you lied to him and cannot be trusted, and, for that reason, you may never get a second chance. We need to do this right the first time."

"Ok, that part sounds easy enough, so I am guessing that me and David will have to teleport back later and get the evidence."

"Close, but no; we have another plan."

I said, "Let me guess, Plan B."

Michael smiled. "That's a good name for it. I was going to call it mission break and enter, but I like your name better."

I laughed. "Seriously, what's next?"

"Ok, I have Mr. Wright in fifth period and you in sixth period. So starting at lunch time, we can keep eyes on him for almost three hours. David will teleport to his house, and only David."

I started to argue, but Michael put his finger up to my lips and then continued talking. "David, will go alone; everyone will have a part in this plan for this to work. It will also be bad if he thinks you had anything to do with it. If you miss class the day after being in his house, well that may send up red flags. So far he knows nothing of David, and we need to keep it that way. David will find what evidence he can. Our job will be to watch Devon; he only works three minutes from his house."

"How will we warn David in time?"

"That's were Lizzie comes in. She has study hall fifth period. She always sits next to the window; if Devon tries to leave, I will leave class as well. Soon as I head up toward the office, Lizzie will see me. She will go to the girls' room and then teleport to Devon's house to warn David. In sixth period it will even be easier. Her class is right across from Devon's, but there are no windows in those mobile units. If he leaves, you need to rush over to Lizzie's class and tell the teacher that Lizzie has a family emergency, and you know what will happen from there."

"How will we know that David makes it back safely, and we don't need to rescue him?"

Michael said, "We figured that out too. David will teleport back to his house. From there he will call the front office and have you paged; when you hear the page, you don't have to call anyone. It will just let us know that he has made it home safely. Then later that night, you will meet up with David at some cemetery…Lizzie acted as if you would know it. There you will find out what evidence he found, if any."

"This doesn't sound so bad, and Lizzie will hardly be involved. In fact, if it goes according to plan, she will sit the whole thing out."

Michael gave me a look, and then said. "I don't like it; and you have my help, but after this, I don't want Lizzie, or David involved."

"Agreed."

Michael had a real serious face. "You have to cut all ties with them. These are their lives we're talking about. They are children; you can't put them in anymore harm's way, do you hear me?"

"Yes, I hear you. And Michael…"

"Yes, Melabeth."

"Thank you, for everything." I got up and left. I went up to my room.

The last thing he said had upset me as much as the first thing he had said. Of course, he didn't know about the first, and he was right about the second.

First thing he had done to me was he had opened the calendar up, and pointed out that I would be with Devon on March 6th. Melanie had a birthday coming up, a sweet sixteen birthday. It appeared that I would be celebrating it by flirting and hanging out with one of Melanie's murderers. I will never be sixteen anyway. Plus Melanie is dead, and Melabeth doesn't need a birthday.

The second thing he did to upset me is that he was right about David and Lizzie. Lizzie, in one short week, had become a friend. I couldn't really define it, but she was someone that I could see hanging out with a lot. It helped to talk with her at school; I didn't get to see Carrie, and I needed a girlfriend.

Michael had been right; I should not let them help me with this. Their magic would help me get this done faster than me or Michael could do on our own. How would I say bye to David? This is going to be a crappy week.

Stressed about going over to Dr. Evil's house, stressed about David going to his house, feeling sorry for myself on my birthday, saying goodbye to David the next night. I was about to cry, when Charlotte burst through the door.

She flashed up to me and wrapped her arms around me. She didn't say anything as I cried into her shoulder.

After a little time went by, and I stopped crying, Charlotte said, "Let's go flying."

She pulled me out of my room by my hand. Being thrown off of cliffs would get my mind off my other problems. Living on Mile High Rd., we didn't have to go far to find an overlook.

We were sitting on top of a boulder that outcropped from the edge of a cliff. There you could see the whole valley of lights below. Me and Charlotte both sat Indian style leaning our backs against the cliff. Charlotte had been mostly quiet; she had left me to my thoughts.

Then she said, "I have been talking to Ezra, and Alice, and they agree that I have been approaching the flying thing wrong with you. We all know you are strong enough, and the fear of falling normally will get most vampires flying. Apparently, you are not afraid of falling or hitting that head of yours. Let us try something new."

"Okay, ready when you are," I said, but I didn't really mean it.

"Ezra is better at the technical stuff than me; I will try my best. When we spirit walk, or flash as you like to call it, we are not running; in fact, we are not moving at all. If you film a vampire doing this, study the frames; you would see us standing still, but we look out of focus. Ezra believes that we break our molecules apart, and that's how we move so fast. You see, spirit walking is a better description of what we are doing."

"I have never really thought about it, but when I do flash it's just a blur, and then I am somewhere else, but now that I think about it, you're right. I don't run; it's not like my legs suddenly move at the speed of light."

Charlotte nodded in agreement. She went on by saying. "Ok, now to understand flying; maybe we should stop calling it flying. I can't really fly, I float. I can control how much gravity is pulling on me. I can make my body as light as a feather and then jump up into the sky. I guess if you happen to see a vampire do this, it would look as if he flew away, but the vampire could only control how fast he is falling. If I make myself heavy, I fall faster; making myself weightless, I float, but, unless I bring a fan or wings, I cannot change my direction. The only way to make a direction change is when you kick off of the ground, but, once you are already heading in that direction, you can't change it. It has always felt like a giant jump to me."

"That sounds like it could be opposite of what we do when we flash, almost like we slow our molecules or something like that, and somehow earth can no longer pull us down."

"Ezra says stuff like that; I don't really understand it. I just know I can do it."

Charlotte gave a small push with her hands. Still sitting Indian style, she floated just a few feet above the rocks. Then she continued speaking, "I don't even know how I do it; I know I can fly, so I do. All you can do is try."

The whole try to float, fly, hover, worked well, if my goal had been getting my mind off of all my worries. If my goal would have been flying, then it didn't work at all.

I tried my hardest to think back to the night when I had kissed David; I thought back to that night often anyway. I couldn't remember what I had been thinking when I had made myself weightless and floated into the truck. I do remember feeling as if I weighed nothing, not that some force had shoved me into the air.

The walk back with Charlotte was good; we had some laughs, and, by the time we got back to the house, my heart was lighter. I think that's what Charlotte was trying to do; I don't believe that she was worried about my flying lessons. Charlotte brought up strange emotions in me; she made me feel better like I had a mother. She made me miss my mother.

*   *   *

Sunday, Monday, and now it was Tuesday, on my way to Mr. Wright's class.

Happy Birthday to me; I still hadn't told anyone it was my birthday. I don't really know if it is anymore; I don't know if Melanie is dead, and all there is now is Melabeth.

Yesterday should have been my birthday, for that's when I got a birthday gift. After school me and David met at the truck as we do every day after school, but yesterday had been different.

Lizzie had something she had to do in the library, and Michael had to stay after class. It was funny because he had to write, 'I will not pass notes in class', one hundred times on the chalkboard. I didn't even know they actually did that; I had thought that was something from the TV. That's the problem with getting all your information from a box.

David and I had some alone time inside Michael's truck. It was the first time I had ever made out with a boy. I have to say, it has made this whole day fly by. I have been so busy reliving the memory that I haven't had time to dread my time with the Devil, I mean Devon; no I mean the Devil.

So, here I was walking to his class; the whole day passed away, while I day dreamed. Not even the memory of me and David was strong enough to stop the dread now, now that I stood outside of my math classroom door. The hour in the class will be easy. Deep breath, I can do this, and, with that, I went to class.

The hour passed faster than it ever had before; even his speaking didn't bother me as much, not when I knew that I was about to ride in a car with him, alone. All the other students leaped out of the chairs when the bell rang...last classes of the day...the kids were fast to get out. It only took a minute before it was just me and Devon; he was still sitting at his desk with his head in some papers.

He finished writing and then looked up at me. "You ready to go?"

NO, I thought, but I said, "Yes, sir."

I grabbed my book bag and followed Devon to the door. He opened the door for me; after I passed through; he shut off the lights and locked the door. As we headed toward the teacher parking lot, Devon said. "I think this will be good for you; you have to pass my class. If you don't, you will have to repeat the same grade next year; with a little bit of my tutoring, you will be passing my class in no time."

I understood what he was trying to plant in my head. For a little bit of something gross, he would pass me. He didn't think I could make up my grade, and he was probably right. I had no idea how to do any of this math, and I had a strong F to prove it. Yep, this is going to be my worst nightmare, all over again. I took a deep breath to calm my nerves; I don't think that really helped.

It was only about a three minute ride to Devon's house. We didn't really talk, but I noticed he checked me out a lot as he drove. He had looked me over before we had gotten into the car; at first it made me nervous. I thought that maybe he was remembering me, but then I realized he was just checking me out, and then it just made me sick. He obviously had plans for tonight, and I already knew what they were.

His house was nothing special; it was a ranch style home, but, then again, that's the only kind of house I saw in this town. He opened the door and went into his house; I started to follow when I felt something push me back.

Oh, crap, he has protection. Of course he does; how on earth could we have not thought about that. I would put money that every member of The Order has spells protecting their homes. I had to think fast; I had to get him to invite me in, but he wouldn't want to do that.

I took two steps away from the door, then I half turned as if I were thinking about leaving, I had to play this right. "I don't know; I don't know if I should go in." I said this very quietly but still loud enough for Devon to hear me. I tried to sound nervous.

Devon had stopped walking and was looking at me. "Don't stand at the door; it's rude, and we have work to do."

That wasn't an invite; I bet he never invites out of habit. I hope that the thought of getting lucky outweighed his good habits. "Well, Mr. Wright... I just don't know if I should. I mean, do you think it will be ok if I come inside?"

I could see the impatience in his eyes; he then said. "It's fine."

Oh, come on, what do I have to do, to get an invite? "You're right; I shouldn't come in…thank you for your honesty. I will see you tomorrow then?" I hoped I could confuse him enough to invite me.

A look of confusion came over his face, so far so good. "No, that's not what I said… I said you can come in."

I hoped that worked. "Oh, I misunderstood you." I slowly headed toward the door, I hoped he thought it was because I was nervous, but I didn't want to be thrown back by the wall.

His invite had worked; I walked right in. Wow, that was a close call. Let's just hope nothing else goes wrong with Plan A, now part 3. The best part is that, when I walked by Devon, he didn't even realize that he had invited me in. Devon closed the door behind me; with my hearing, I could hear the lock click.

We sat on the coach. He had a math book, paper and a pen sitting on a coffee table. "Let us talk about how we can get that grade from an F, to a B, or maybe even an A; it's all up to you."

"Whatever it takes," I said, but I was thinking, over my dead body. He wasn't going to waste any time, neither would I, "Can you excuse me for just one second? I need to use the restroom."

Devon smiled, and said, "Of course you can; it's right down the hall. I should have asked before we sat down."

I got up and walked down the hall he had pointed at. I went into the restroom, shut and locked the door. Plan A is stupid; there was a little window toward the top of the wall, above the bathtub. It was one of those windows that you couldn't open, or see out of.

So now for Plan A, part 4, I hope we have thought out Plan B better than this. I hid the stone between the floor and the wood trim. I wedged it in there pretty good; there was no way you could see it, and you would have to pry it out. There was no way the vacuum cleaner could suck it out; boy, I hope that's good enough. Now I needed to get out of here.

I started to gag myself, making the sound of throwing up. After about two or three minutes of this, Devon came to the door. He knocked lightly then said, "Is everything ok in there?"

I didn't answer him; instead I made a loud throwing up noise. After heaving a few more times, I said. "Sorry, I guess I am sick."

I flushed the toilet, and then went back to heaving; after a minute or more of doing this, I flushed the toilet again. I came out of the bathroom with my hand over my mouth.

"I think I need to go home."

Devon looked disappointed, but it's not like he wanted to fool around with a girl that was puking.

Devon said with disappointment, "We should do this another time. Let me grab a trash can and some trash bags for the car, and we will go. We can do this when you feel better."

He said this as he headed into the kitchen; he came back carrying a small white trash can, and some trash bags. We had just pulled out of Devon's driveway, when the next problem arose.

"Where do you live?" asked Devon.

I couldn't take him to the White's house without time to think about it; I just pointed, and Devon started to drive. We were now headed toward the residential area of Beaumont. I had no choice; I would have to pick out a random house and then hope no one was home.

"That's my house; just drop me off here."

"Ok, will you be alright?"

"Yes…" then I put my hand over my mouth as if I was about to puke all over his car. I jumped out and then yelled back. "Thanks for the ride."

I headed toward this house using my second sight; I was watching for Devon's car to pull away, but it didn't. If I hadn't of known what a creep he was, this would have been nice of him. He was waiting to make sure I made it inside the house ok. I decided on change of plan.. Plan A, part… I can't even remember.

Crossing the lawn toward the side of the house, there was a wooden gate. Like a lot of houses in this area, the backyard was surrounded by a wooden fence. I reached up and grabbed the latch; finally, a bit of luck; it wasn't locked. I went in, half turned around and waved bye at Devon's car, then shut the gate. Devon would just think that I used the back door.

As I looked through the crack of the slats in the gate, Devon finally pulled away. Then I heard the sound of growling. Oh great, I turned around only to see three giant Rottweiler's growling at me.

I was standing in front of the gate, but the gate swung inward, and, when I tried to move forward, the dogs' growls intensified. One of the dogs snapped at me; I guess I was about to be in my first dogfight.

As I got ready to fight, the dogs suddenly stopped growling. Then the dogs started barking; they started to bark what sounded like a song. They were barking Beethoven's Fifth; they were barking and howling Beethoven.

I opened the gate to find Michael with the biggest grin. "Hurry up, before these dogs attract any more attention."

As Michael and I hurried down these people's front yard, I could see Ezra sitting in the passenger seat of Michael's Jimmy. "I knew that you could control animals, but that was amazing."

We both jumped into the truck; Michael tossed the truck in gear, and we were off. "I can show you how to do it if you like. Some vampires are better than others."

Ezra said, "Animal control is difficult for most to learn, and few ever get as good as Michael. Don't let him tell you how easy it is, or how in one lesson he will have you making dogs sing. Did you accomplish your mission?"

"Yes, I put the stone in a safe place, but this Plan A was not planned very well."

Michael laughed, and so did Ezra; then Ezra said. "You handled it well. You will learn that there is no such thing as a perfect plan. You did well; you made it work, and you figured out what you needed to do and made it happen. I was extremely proud about how you tricked him to invite you in."

"I just hope that our plan for David isn't so… haphazard."

Michael said in a very reassuring voice. "David's part is the easiest part; he doesn't have to deal with anyone. The only thing that could cause irreversible damage is if Devon found out about David's involvement, and that is why we cannot let Devon go home until David is safely away."

Ezra added. "Things still could go bad, Melabeth. If things go bad, Alice and I have set up for departure. We can't have The Order coming after us in force. We will be ready to leave at a moment's notice."

I couldn't believe that they all were willing to do this for me. "Thanks, I don't know what to say. Sorry, I didn't mean to drag you all into this, and I hope it doesn't come to you leaving your home." Michael and Ezra laughed. "What's so funny?"

Michael answered. "Vampires don't have homes; we have pit stops, places where we lay our heads. We are always ready to leave at a moment's notice. We are hated, feared and hunted, and most of all…" both Michael and Ezra said at the same time. "We are family."

It felt like a hundred pounds were taken off my shoulders; now that I had done Plan A, I could relax. I had stressed so much about my time with Devon. The stress came back by the time the truck pulled into the driveway. Now I was full of worries for David; there was a part of me that said, let's just call off David's part. I could figure out another way to collect my movie from Devon.

I pushed that thought to the back of my head; I knew he could do this. When he finished his mission, I would be one step closer to getting my revenge. I was also one step closer to saying goodbye to David. I was getting ready for bed; tomorrow would be a big day.

I lay on the bed, and a knock came on the door. "Come in."

Ezra stepped inside and then shut the door behind him. He came over and took a seat at the end of my bed. "You are different than most vampires, so young, but so strong. I, we, forget that you are new to this life. Most vampires that are as strong as you, remember what it was like a hundred years ago. There were no special contacts that blocked the light and made your eyes look normal. In fact there were no sunglasses, so even if you wished to risk going out in the day, you would be blind."

I said, "You treat me well, I am not complaining. In fact, sometimes I wonder why you have taken me in."

Ezra smiled. "Why have we taken you in? If you could see yourself through my eyes, you wouldn't ask me that. What I was trying to say is that you still don't understand the vampire lifestyle. For example, the sun just went down, so, it is morning. This is the beginning of the day, first thing in the morning. The day does not end until the sun rises, and this is the daytime, and that's when we would celebrate a birthday."

Before I could say anything, the door of my room flew open. Alice, Charlotte, Michael and Lea flashed into my room. Charlotte was holding a cake with sixteen candles on it; Alice and Lea both had arms full of presents. Then they all started singing Happy Birthday; as they sang, Michael lit the candles.

Charlotte put the cake in front of me, and, as the song came to the end, Alice yelled out, "Make a wish."

I didn't know what to wish for, so I simply gave thanks instead. Then I blew out the candles; Charlotte took the cake away. Alice said. "I want a piece of cake."

Charlotte laughed, then said; "how about cake in a bottle?" With that, she pulled out a big bottle of wine.

Ezra brought out some glasses, while Charlotte poured. Ezra said right before he sipped the wine, "This is a real treat, blood wine; it's hard to find. Wine is one of the only ways to preserve the blood, for vampires that is." After he took a sip, he added, "ah, delicious, time for presents."

The wine tasted wonderful; I could drink myself stupid on this stuff.

Alice and Charlotte had bought me a lot of clothes. I loved them; Alice had even bought me more clothes that went with my new look. I had mixed emotions about always dressing in black.

Charlotte bought me a leather jumpsuit; she told me that it was more comfortable than it looked. Ezra added that it was really good for combat, and that is why Charlotte had gotten it for me.

Ezra had bought me a beautiful set of knives. He told me they were made out of a new metal, titanium, light and strong. The handles had a good feel; the blades were only sharp on one side with a slight curve. They were both six inches long, including the handle, and they would be easy to hide.

Michael had bought me a pair of sunglasses. They were special, he said. Tougher than most, and also darker; they fit me perfectly. They were tight enough that they would not come off easily. I gave Michael a big hug that got me a dirty look from Lea. Charlotte and Alice both hooped and hollered at my hug with Michael. Ezra shook his head back and forth in disgust with the whole thing.

I pulled back from my hug; Michael gently kissed me on my forehead, and then said, "Happy Birthday, but you're still not even one, in vampire years."

Lea handed me a small box. Inside was a necklace with a half of a heart charm attached to a chain. She had the other half. She showed me that, when you put the two necklaces together, they said Best Friends Forever. "Thank you, Lea... and I don't half heartily say that," everyone laughed.

I really hoped she didn't expect me to wear this. Best friends, I wasn't even sure we were friends at all. I didn't say anything; I didn't want to give Alice and Charlotte anymore ammo to tease Lea with, but, from the smirk on Charlotte face, it told me that she knew exactly how I felt.

I would have loved to drink the night away, but thank goodness I wasn't the only one who had to get up for school.

Michael was on his third glass of wine, when he announced. "Alright, I am sure Melabeth is grateful, but I... and, when I say I, I mean we, we have school tomorrow. So goodnight all, and happy birthday again...see ya in the morning."

He left, with Lea in tow.

Lea yelled back, "See you tomorrow Melabeth."

She was really trying to be my friend, even if I was a threat to her love, Michael. In the future I would have to remember to be nice. Charlotte and Ezra excused themselves, and then left my room hand in hand. I lay back on my bed. Alice finished her glass of wine, and then she lay next to me. It was kind of strange as we both lay in silence.

"Goodnight birthday girl," Alice whispered, as she closed her eyes.

I cleared my throat, "This is my bed."

Alice giggled, and then turned her head to look at me. "No one should be alone on their birthday. I am not Charlotte; I don't know what you are feeling, but I am sure of how I would feel after a day like you have had. Plus, I have wanted to have a sleep over. We could build a fort if you like."

"No fort, I am tired...'night Alice." I closed my eyes and turned onto my side. I felt Alice put a blanket over me.

She was right; I was glad she was here with me.

When the alarm awoke me, I was alone in bed. When I thought about it, the only ones sleeping at night were me and Michael. Alice was sweet, even if she hid behind crazy.

*   *   *

The first two classes flew by, and, before I knew it, I was headed to brunch with Lizzie in tow. I couldn't wait to see David; I was already worried about him, and he hadn't even left today. As soon as I saw David, I ran up and gave him a hug.

He whispered in my ear. "Easy there, you're forgetting how strong you are." I laughed and loosened my grip, but I didn't let go of him. "It's going to be fine, Melabeth; I can feel your worry across the whole school. I can do this; we can do this."

I nodded my head. Lizzie stuck her head really close and said, "P.D.A. you two."

I ignored her. She and Michael started talking; I was getting a little uneasy about that relationship. I hadn't said anything to David about it, and it wouldn't have worried me if it were just Lizzie, but Michael smiled more and stared just a little bit too long. Michael glanced my way; I gave him a dirty look. He just winked at me and went back to talking to Lizzie.

I had enough to worry about, and now I had one more thing. Brunch was only fifteen minutes, but it felt like two, and then it was like I had traveled into the future. It was lunch time.

I didn't have much time to talk to David; he needed to go. The plan was that he would walk off campus; there were some orange groves in a field across the street from the high school. There he could teleport without anyone seeing him.

I gave him a big hug, but I made sure I didn't squeeze too hard. "Be safe, and hurry back. If you don't find it, don't worry about it. You are important. I don't want you getting into any trouble."

David smiled at me. "You worry too much; I will be back before you can say, 'You love me'."

He kissed me. Then he started walking; he looked back over his shoulder and gave me one more smile, then he rounded a corner and was gone. I said to myself. "Love you." If anything happened to him… I couldn't say it to his face, not when I knew I was going to leave him.

After that, time went from, so fast I couldn't stand it to so slow I couldn't take it. In fifth period, October was worried about me. In the last week, October had been getting steadily more aggressive. She touched me whenever possible, and she talked about me and her having a sleepover. If it wasn't for the fact that I was trying not to bring any more attention to myself… well let's just say October would understand how I felt. Still, as annoying as her unwanted advances were, there was still something I liked about her as a person. If that hadn't been true, I would have already put my foot down.

I was full of emotions, so I was glad to get away from October before I said something I would regret. I don't really do regret. Sixth period was a horror from the moment I walked into the room.

Devon asked me, "Do you feel better today?"

I put forth my best pretend smile, "yes sir."

Then I had to listen to him speak for forty-five minutes, and he gave us the next fifteen minutes to work on an assignment. It was only eight minutes before class let out. I was about to tear all my hair out when, over the loud speaker, they announced a phone call for Lizzie.

It was supposed to be for me originally, but, at the last minute, there was a change of plan by Michael; he didn't want me away from Devon until we knew for sure that David was ok. Michael figured if things turned violent, that I was best suited for it. I was stronger, faster and better trained. Of course the last part was only because Michael didn't care for fighting.

I couldn't get to Michael's truck fast enough. Lizzie was supposed to meet us and let us know how it went. I got there about the same time as Lizzie. Michael was still jogging over.

"Is he alright?"

"Yes, everything went perfectly," Lizzie said with a smile, and she didn't even cover her mouth.

"Tell me everything."

"Wait for Michael," Lizzie demanded.

Michael finished running up, "Yeah, wait for Michael."

"You could hear her speaking a hundred yards away," Then I turned to Lizzie, "So?"

Lizzie said, "Ok, now, it all went as planned; he teleported over and searched the house. He found that there was a secret basement. The most amazing part was that he said the house was full of spirits. He must have killed dozens of people there. He can't see or hear ghosts during the day, but he can sense their presence."

"I didn't know that," I said.

"He didn't either, until recently. David's still discovering his powers, but what I was saying was that the ghost helped him. He found all kinds of films, and he said he found your film, Melabeth."

I think the color drained out of my face, not that I had any color. Then Lizzie jumped forward and wrapped her arms around me.

She said with tears in her eyes. "My brother… well he had to find out what he was taking. I know… we will bring that man to justice, now that we have evidence. The Order will punish him, and all that were involved."

I pulled away from her hug. "I don't need the damn Order, or their justice, Lizzie. I didn't even need the evidence. He will pay... you're right about that; he will pay."

Lizzie looked at me as if I were being unreasonable. "But The Order... I don't want to upset you anymore. We still have time to talk about this. I need to go; my mom will be waiting for me. Don't worry about tonight; I will cover for David to get out. Meet him at the cemetery at eleven."

I was thankful for all Lizzie's help, even though she had no idea what she was talking about.

I gave her another hug, and then said, "Thank you, thank you for everything."

Lizzie gave me a strange look as she left. Then Michael said. "Well, she got that message."

"What message?"

"You just said goodbye, and she's not ready for that. Also we need to deal with her belief about The Order helping you."

I looked at Michael and said, "We need to say goodbye, both of us; you said this, and I don't care what she thinks about The Order; they will not help us."

Michael got into the truck; I jumped into the passenger seat. Michael said. "I will talk with her."

"I think you have a thing for her."

Michael said a little too quickly, "No, no I don't; what are you talking about?"

"Michael, she is too young for you, and, before you say anything about how impossible it is to find someone your own age... she's not even fifteen."

Michael was mad. "I like her, and I don't like her like that... she reminds me of my little sister. You don't need to be a bitch. I know we have to stop hanging out with them, but I will say goodbye the way I want to, and you are underestimating her when it comes to The Order. She cannot go to them about this."

Michael drove home like a maniac. I said I was sorry, but he wasn't talking to me. Ok, maybe I didn't have to accuse him of being a pedophile. With Michael mad, I decided to go alone to see David. Michael was supposed to go with me, but now I would have some alone time with David.

I put on a nice skirt, with a blouse and some good boots, then I went for a run. I would be there in an hour, I left earlier than I needed to. I would have some time to kill, but that was ok.

On the way there, I felt better than I had in a week; the stress of dealing with Devon melted away.

Chapter 16
The Cemetery

Finally, David showed up.

He looked sexy with his black hair and Goth getup. Carrie floated behind him, not even bothering to walk. Why not, she is in a cemetery and dead. David and I moved together to embrace. We kissed, and Carrie made the Yuk noise.

Then I said. "Good, you made it. So, what did you find?"

David smiled, and then flipped his book bag off his shoulder. "I got it... here it is."

He pulled out a round film can.

"Are you sure this is it; this is the movie of my death?" I asked, as I took the film can out of his hand.

David stopped smiling and cleared his throat. "I had to be sure; I knew you were watching Devon, and it would have all been for nothing, if I would have gotten the wrong one. Devon had them labeled by years. I am sorry for what happened to you."

"So you saw it?" I wasn't sure how I felt about that.

"Just the beginning, and, as soon as I knew it was you, I turned it off." Then David added quickly. "I had to watch other films looking for yours. They're all nasty, but a few of them had him in it. They clearly showed him committing the crimes."

David opened his bag wider so I could see in; there were about five more round film cans. I felt the anger boil up in me, not at David, but at Devon, the same man that I had to hang out with. Lizzie was always talking about finding the evidence; well, here it is.

"We don't need evidence. The only reason I want the film of my death, is so that I could destroy it. The only thing I can plan on doing with my film or other films is shoving them up Devon's dead ass. That way when they find the body, they will know why he had to die."

David's look was between fear and sadness. Then he said in a sad voice. "If you must... if you must kill him, then know I will help you."

I pulled David to me and embraced him. "No... not in this, my love; this time you and Carrie will stay home. I will not involve you in my revenge. I am afraid no matter what that The Order will come after me. I don't want them after you as well."

Carrie jumped in and said, "That's why we got the evidence. Lizzie said they will find him guilty. We don't want to be left out, while you are running from The Order. We're a team, and we should stick together."

I started to argue, but David interrupted me. "Until the end... we are with you Melabeth. Carrie and I will not leave you now. We will kill this man, and then we can prove your innocence."

I was truly touched. "No amount of evidence will keep The Order from coming after me. Don't you understand? Look in your bag; look at all those cans of film. He wasn't hiding this from all the members of The Order. Hell, those bikers are clearly in the film, and they are members of The Order. If you two follow me into this, evidence will not save you. We will have to fight our way through it. It might take years... just think about what I am saying."

"I have never been known for thinking; no reason to start." Carrie said.

David laughed, and then added. "I have thought about it, and, when I offered my help, it wasn't on any terms. I have your back no matter what."

I had to hold back the tears. "You guys... you're too much."

Before I could say another word, there was a loud popping noise.

All of our heads whipped toward the sound, and then David said. "Someone just teleported into the cemetery."

I could see the visitors before David and Carrie. It was Tony, Mab, Kelly and Lizzie. "It's your parents, and sisters."

"Great, what has Lizzie done? This will complicate things," David moaned.

Yes, it would, and all four of them walked up to me and David. I noticed that Carrie pulled the disappearing act as soon as I said someone arrived. I could have probably flashed away, but I have a feeling that Lizzie ratted us out. I am not going to leave David to take all the heat by himself.

You could feel and see the anger coming out of Tony, and Mab had that mother's face that said: how could you have done this to your own mother?

Tony didn't wait for us to speak. "I know what you two are up to. It is one thing to still be hanging out with this... this... vampire. She tried to kill your mother, and now you are planning on killing someone with her. Wait, not just someone... but a leading member in The Order. Why? I don't even care why. I don't even want to know why... this dead creature wants him dead for some past crime. The only thing I care about is that she is dragging my stepson into a life of crime. I don't give a shit about her cause."

Lizzie looked at me; she had been crying, "Sorry, you were right."

David started to say something back when his mother interrupted him in a fit of tears. "What were you thinking, dear? You could still be charged with a crime. Did you know it is a crime to even plan a murder? Let alone help her go through with it; is she using mind control on you? Have you been using the blocks I've taught you? It's one thing that you allowed this monster to talk you into this craziness, but it is another that you involved Lizzie."

Well, I could have told you this would have been all about me, and, really I didn't mind them blaming it all on me. In a way they were right; I may have not used mind control, but I was dragging David and Lizzie into a dangerous situation that could get them killed, or worse.

David looked at both of his parents right in the eyes, and then said, "I have evidence of what Devon has done." David held up the film can in front of Tony's face. "I found the film, the film of Devon murdering her."

Tony's voice softened, but just a little, "If you have evidence, let us bring it to The Order. If he is guilty of these crimes, then The Order will serve justice, not you, and not her. If you two help her in this, you will be murderers, and no one will care why, so let me help you, David. Let me help my daughter and stepson."

I couldn't help myself; I laughed. Now everyone was staring at me, with hatred; David, between anger and tears. Lizzie stared at me while she was still wiping at her smeared makeup.

"They raped me in that film, and then they choked me to death. There is no way that I can prove I was human in that film. All he has to say is that I was a vampire, and it was a fantasy film, and, of course, he paid me to do it. What do you think would happen then, Tony?"

Tony didn't take a second to answer. "Devon's version makes more sense than your story. How would anyone turn you… when you're already dead?"

I knew this is how he would feel, but it still sucked to hear it out loud. I pushed my emotion back. I must keep a clear head. David was now fighting with Tony, basically telling him that he was an ass and that there was no way that I was lying about this, and then it hit me like a ton of bricks.

Tony was not surprised by what I said. He even knew Devon's defense… how? I interrupted the fight by yelling out. "You have already talked to Devon? He knows that I am live, and he has already told you his lies. When did you talk with him?"

Mab spoke for him, waving her hands in the air as she spoke. "We need to protect David from you. There is no way we're going to allow you to drag him into a life of crime. You will not take my children from me."

Lizzie spoke out. "As soon as I told him about it, he called Devon. I am so sorry; you probably should get out of town before it's too late."

Before David or I could respond, Carrie reappeared in front of us. She scared the living shit out of David's family. She ignored them and started to speak at one hundred miles per hour. "They're here ya'll... we're surrounded, and they cast some spells around the graveyard. I don't know what they all do, but I couldn't go through them. They have a bunch of guys with guns, and you know what else. I saw Devon... we need to get out of Dodge... NOW."

"Too late," I said.

Now that I was paying attention to the surrounding area, I could make out movement in the tree line. The cemetery had a lot of tall gravestones, and large oak trees stood about every ten feet. This was a good thing, for they have guns, and we will need cover. The cemetery rests upon a hill, the crest was the center of the graveyard. I was unable to see the other half of the cemetery. My guess is that the spell they placed would keep the dead from leaving and anyone from teleporting.

Tony doesn't realize it yet, but he had signed his family's death warrant by telling Devon about this. I am positive that this spell has a roof, so there will be no flying out. So, the only question that remains is, will they wait for daylight, when I am the weakest, or will they attack now? My guess is they will attack soon, one young vampire and a few witches and warlocks; they will hit us hard and fast.

Tony looked over at David with pleading eyes. "Come on... let's get out of here, they're not here for us... you don't have to die for her."

David's eyes filled with anger, but, before he could let his stepdad have it, his mother said, "Take my hand and teleport with us. I will not watch my son die... not when I can save him."

Before David could answer his mother, an idea came to me; I need David's family to realize this attack isn't just for me.

"Go with them, David... and hurry," I said.

"I am staying..." David started to argue, but I pushed him into his mother's arms.

I yelled at them as I stepped away. "Go... go now, if you can."

David was about to pull away from his mother, but Tony was ready for this. He said some words and put his hand over David's mouth. David fell back into his mother's arms, unconscious.

I hadn't been ready for them to knock out David; I just wanted them to see that they couldn't teleport out of here. Then the whole family took each other's hands, all of them except David, and they began to chant.

Carrie stood behind me, "I can't believe you are letting them take David like that. I will have to follow. We want to help you; I can't stand to leave you all on your own. You could get hurt… or KILLED."

Carrie was now giving me a hug.

I looked at her. "If this is how it could be, this is the way I would have it. Sorry to say… you are not going anywhere. I need Tony to figure this out; he needs to understand that Devon isn't going to leave any witnesses. I need him to figure this out fast."

Kelly was the first to stop chanting and say. "Dad we are being blocked. We can't teleport; why are they blocking us?"

Tony gave her a reassuring smile. "They're just trying to make sure that Melabeth doesn't escape. All we have to do is walk out of the circle. Then we can teleport home. They will finish Melabeth without us."

Mab gave me a hateful look, and then said. "I would think twice before you try to stop us from leaving. You understand what I am saying?" She ended this by pointing her finger at me. She pulled that cross out from around her neck. "Don't make me use this."

Tony looked over at Mab, and said. "In this kind of spell, vampires can't leave, but it also renders your cross useless."

Well, the first good news I've heard tonight.

Lizzie spoke up. "She will let us leave, mom. She's not like that." Turning toward Tony, she asked. "Are you sure The Order will let us leave? I mean what about David?"

Of course this is why Tony had hoped to teleport out. He didn't want The Order to get a hold of David. They didn't like Necromancers, and he just broke into a leading Order member's house, and then stole property; if Tony realized just what kind of evidence David had on Devon, then he would know how much trouble his whole family was in.

Tony looked at each member of his family and said. "Wait, I will go and talk with them. Once I have assured David will not be held, I will come back, and then we will leave here together."

Mab looked over at me nervously. "Hurry, Tony." She didn't want to be left alone with me too long.

Kelly added. "Don't worry, dad. I got it."

Lizzie just huffed. "Yep she has it… since Melabeth isn't going to hurt us… if she wanted us dead, we would be. Damn, no one listens to me."

Mab yelled at Lizzie. "Watch your language."

Lizzie gave her a dirty look and said. "And that's what you're worried about?"

Tony talked fast but stern. "Stop, Lizzie; I will be right back; no one move."

Before walking away, he gave me one last warning glace. In that look, he promised me death and pain if I hurt his family. Of course, the sad thing was he was dead wrong. I was ready to die for them and probably would.

He walked away toward the edge of the graveyard. When he reached the edge, he put his arms up.

The sound of gunfire filled the air... I watched in horror as bullets riddled Tony's body.

Tony's body fell on the ground. He had been so sure they were on his side, that he hadn't even cast a self defense spell.

Mab let out a scream.

Chapter 17
Final Scene

I yelled. "Everyone take cover... now!!"

Kelly just screamed and started crying. Lizzie ran over to her sister and pulled her down to the ground. The sisters took cover behind one of the large gravestones. Mab ran over to her daughters, and then she dropped down with them, and pulled them into her arms. She was now weeping with Kelly; Lizzie looked to be in shock.

My teeth elongated, my claws came out, and I pulled the contacts from my eyes. All my emotion drained away; was it because I was a vampire, or was Ezra right, that some of us can become completely focused in battle. There would be time to worry later; there was only time to react for now.

I flashed over to David who was still lying on the ground unconscious. I pulled his body behind a large gravestone. I quickly grabbed another gravestone and dragged it over to David. I grabbed two more stones, and then I positioned them around David's body. He now lay upon the ground surround by gravestones. This would give him some protection from gunfire.

I was trying to think of what to do next; that's when my second sight showed me something.

Over the hill in the middle of the graveyard, someone had yelled an order. The noise made an image in my head. There was a group of gunmen heading up to the top of the hill. There were trees and gravestones up there. Once they were in position, they could shoot us dead.

I looked over at Carrie. "Watch over David, Carrie. I have to slow some of them down."

I could see Lizzie with tears in her eyes. "Kelly, mom... gets ready. They're coming for us. We need... we need to fight."

They started to cast spells; now they understood what must be done. I just hoped they could do it. I flashed over to another set of gravestones. As I moved from stone to tree, to stone again, gunfire erupted. I had to move fast, as streaks of light flew by.

They were using tracer ammo; if they hit me, the bullets could ignite my blood. I moved quicker; by the time I reached the crest of the hill, the gunfire died away.

Whoever was shooting at me must have lost their line of sight when I reached the highest point of the graveyard. I didn't have much time to think about it because, with my second sight, I could see four or five people working their way through the trees and gravestones.

They were heading right for me. I moved behind a stone so that I could surprise the first one. I could tell that they had rifles; I needed to keep them at close range.

The man walked right by me; he was moving like a soldier. He had an M16 assault rifle, and he appeared to be wearing some kind of body armor with a helmet. The man was in black, head to toe. Wearing black at night might work with humans, but I could see him like it was day.

He spoke into his microphone, "all clear, fall into positions." He said this quietly; he may as well have been yelling it with my hearing.

I flashed so that I was standing right behind him. Without a noise, I reached up and grabbed his head. With one strong, fast twist, his face was now looking at me. He grunted, but I gave it one more twist.

Snap… was the noise that came from his neck. His body went limp.

I was about to drop him, when my second sight caught movement from behind. I spun around using the body of the dead man as a shield.

Just in time, as a barrage of gun fire slammed into the dead man's body.

Soon as the gun stopped firing, I figured he was out of bullets. I snuck a look around the dead man's body, and the man in front of me was dropping his clip and reloading another mag.

I reached over the dead man and grabbed the handle of his rifle that had been hanging from his strap.

I fired… I was shooting without aiming; it was a good thing his rifle was loaded with tracer ammo. It helped me find the target; I put the stream of gunfire right into his face.

The man's head exploded, and his body fell to the ground dead; I guess he should have worn face armor. No time to celebrate; I moved forward.

I dove behind another tree as a fireball whizzed by my head.

I was now standing next to the body of the man that I just killed. He had an array of weapons on him. Two weapons caught my eye, his reloaded M16, and a large knife strapped to his boot.

Using my second sight, I could see two figures moving toward me. The man straight ahead of me was the one who threw the fireball at me, he must be a wizard. The second one was trying to flank me from my left.

I went for the weapons.

Knowing that I didn't have time to bend over and grab them, I tried something else. I did a cartwheel right over the dead man's body. I placed my left hand on the handle of the rifle and my right hand on the handle of the knife. In one fluent movement, I landed back on my feet with weapons in hand.

I didn't wait to even look around me; I flashed back behind the tree from where I just came out of.

As soon as I was safely behind cover, I watched as another fireball zipped by where I was just standing.

Then I could hear whoever threw that fireball let out a string of curses. She also yelled at the other man that I was now armed. Clearly the fireball shooter was a girl.

I flashed and moved behind some more gravestones. I could see, from my second sight, that the witch took cover when she saw me recover the gun. I took that moment to move; she didn't even see me leave. Her partner just finished moving into a position behind a large gravestone, and he had his rifle trained to the tree I was just hiding behind…too slow.

I quickly moved, and, without a sound, right behind him, I put my hand over his mouth, and then pulled back his head.

With one fast motion, I sliced his neck open.

With blood spilling out, I couldn't help myself. I bit into his neck and started to feed.

"Bitch!" I jerked my head up from the man's neck to see who had said that. I had been too busy feeding and had not realized the witch had moved, and now we were staring at each other.

The witch was not in military body armor like the men, and I couldn't see any kind of weapon on her... no knife, rifle or club; this made me more nervous than the heavily armed men. She was wearing all black: a shirt, skin tight jeans, and a leather trench coat that hung to her knees.

We stared at each other for a second more… then her lips began to move.

She was casting a spell.

I wasn't going to wait to see what it did. I whipped my M16 up to my shoulder.

At the same time, she lifted both her hands up; for a mere second, I thought she was surrendering.

I didn't wait to find out; I pulled the trigger.

The ground in front of the witch lifted into the air making a wall of dirt. My bullets slammed into the dirt.

The dirt fell back to the ground. The witch was still standing there. She should have used this moment to move. I opened fired again.

Her body fell apart. People don't fall apart because of bullets, and there was no blood.

Damn it, it was a spell; I used my second sight… too late.

The witch was standing to my right. I turned my head only to see her push her hand at me. A wave of air hit me like a tornado.

I flew up into the air and violently spun around in a circle. Both my rifle and my knife were flung out of my hands as I flew through the air. My head slammed into something hard.

The world got blurry. I couldn't see straight and was having a hard time moving. I couldn't seem to find my legs. I clawed at the ground trying to find my equilibrium.

With my head lying on the ground, I was looking down a row of gravestones. There lay the dead soldier. Standing next to him, checking his pulse, was the witch.

The look on her face let me know that he was dead. The witch stood up and looked over at me with eyes of hatred.

Need to get up... the witch grabbed the gravestone and started to chant.

Need to get up... the gravestone in her hands turned to liquid and started to wrap around her hands.

Need to get up... when the witch stood up, the gravestone was gone, and the witch looked like a stone statue.

The world spinning had slowed, and I now could feel my legs; as I got to my feet, the stone witch was three feet away and swung her hand back. I readied myself for the first blow... I thought I was ready.

I had put my arm up to block her. When her arm made contact with mine, my arm broke. Then she punched me in the ribs with her other hand.

I could hear and feel my ribs break; I lost my balance and fell to the ground.

I rolled out of the way as she tried to stomp my face. Then, with all my speed, I jumped up and sidestepped her.

She swung but missed me.

Then I kicked her with such force she lifted off the ground and slammed into a gravestone.

She pulled herself up... and she was unhurt.

The next three minutes were much of the same. She was stronger and could break my bones when she hit me, but I was fast as lightening and healed too quickly to worry about a few broken bones. As we battled back and forth, I was trying to figure out how I was going to end this.

The stone witch grabbed me and tossed me through the air. That act did not hurt me; I used my second sight as I flew through the air.

The fifth soldier that I had forgotten about had moved in to help the witch. When the stone witch threw me, the soldier threw a grenade. Their timing was good because I was going to hit the ground at the same time and spot as the grenade.

I didn't have much time to think about it, so all I could do was react.

I had been thrown backwards; I should not have been able to see the soldier, or the grenade that he had thrown.

The next thing I did, they could not have been prepared for. I spun around mid air and reached out with my foot. My timing had to be exact. I cupped the grenade with my toes as I was spinning.

Like a super ballerina, I landed on my other foot; I was still spinning and kicked the grenade right at the face of the stone witch.

I fell to the ground as the grenade blew up inches from the stone witch's face.

I stood up and flashed behind a tree before the soldier could even turn his head back to see what had happened. My timing had been perfect. The soldier turned and covered his face after he had thrown the grenade, so he never even knew what happened.

The witch was sitting on her ass, and the stone had broken off, and laying in pieces all around her. Blood was coming from her head as she moaned in confusion.

The soldier ran up to the witch. "You all right… what happened? How did you get hit?"

The witch was quick to recover; she squeaked out, "vampire…"

The soldier was a fool. I flashed up behind him, pulled his sidearm right out of his holster. Reaching under his arm, I stuck the gun in the witch's face.

I pulled the trigger.

Her head whipped back as her brains blew out of it. As she fell to the ground, I pointed the gun straight up.

My arm was still under the soldier's arm, so, when I lifted the gun straight up, it was pointing at the soldier's chin.

The soldier said. "No…"

I pulled the trigger.

I took the next few minutes gathering weapons from the dead soldier. I had two hand guns with extra clips, one M16 with a couple of magazines; I also slid one knife in my boot and another in my belt. I wish I would have brought Ezra's birthday gift with me.

I had worked my way right over the top of the hill. Now I was on the other side, and had no line of sight of David and the others. I started back to the peak of the hill; worry filled my head. I stopped and took two deep breaths. Ezra had drilled and drilled that worry, that emotion, would get me killed.

My worry made me want to run at full speed to check up on them, but I must step carefully. I have no idea how many enemies there are, or where they are. I let my emotions drain away for later.

I moved carefully toward the top of the hill, using my second sight the whole time. I kept whistling. I needed to keep alert. Good thing too; from my left, two more soldiers were coming. If I would have run up the hill, I would have run right in front of them. From the direction they were coming from, I believe they are the soldiers who were shooting at me when I was heading to the top.

I had all of the advantages; I knew where they were, and I knew where they were going. I changed my direction and moved to my left. I would let them pass right by. Then I would move up from behind and finish them quickly.

As I moved in this direction, the cemetery changed. It was newer, so the stones lay flat on the ground. This would make it harder. The only cover I had now was the trees, and they were fifty feet apart in some spots.

I flashed behind a tree and hid. The two men passed right by; I didn't have time to waste. I moved out from behind the tree and took aim. With their helmets and body armor, shooting them in the back might not work.

I yelled out; the soldiers spun around. I fired.

I was a good shot; the first solider I killed with a small burst right in the face.

I turned my gun on to the second, and I was fast. I fired again, and this time something went wrong. My aim was dead on, and, at this range, less than fifty yards, I couldn't miss.

If I hadn't been shooting tracer rounds, I would have no idea why I missed. The bullets spun around this solider as if he were behind some shield. I emptied my whole clip, and this gave him time to fire at me.

The bullets ripped through my shoulder and part of my neck. I fell back onto the ground with a screech of pain.

The bullets hurt, yes, but they also burned. I rolled behind the tree as another spray of bullets hit the ground where I just was. I pulled myself up and leaned against the tree.

Lucky... lucky is my middle name. The bullets didn't find bone, and he was also at close range using a high power rifle. The bullets passed right through my body, not having time to set my blood on fire. Ezra had told me this could happen but not to count on it.

It still hurt; it hurt a lot more than regular bullets. I could still feel where it burned me all the way through my body. It only took a few seconds for the pain and the bleeding to stop.

My rifle was out of reach, but, then again, it wouldn't do any good against this guy. He had some kind of spell protecting him against bullets. Where could I get that?

I tried to stick my head out, but, as I did, he almost blew it off. Great, he can shoot. The nearest cover was fifty yards, and, even if I flashed, I might not make it, if this guy is as quick as I think he is.

He wasn't moving in on me. I bet this spell doesn't help him in close range fighting like with a knife. The question is how do I get that close without him blowing my head off?

Whatever the answer, I needed to figure it out quick. He will have reinforcements soon, and I need to check on David.

Worrying about David right now may be a bad thing according to Ezra, but it motivated me. I looked up into the big oak I was hiding behind, and I knew what I must do. I climbed fast but quiet. I moved around the tree and onto a large branch.

Now if the soldier was to look up, he would see me, but he wasn't going to look up; he was using all his concentration on the base of the tree. He had to be ready because I could come out from either side of the tree.

I ran to the end of the branch. Then I jumped off and flew through the air. I spun around, and landed right behind the soldier.

He never saw me in the dark and I didn't make enough noise for him to hear me when I landed. I needed to make sure I was well feed before I could go into the next fight, so I checked my second sight and made sure there was no one coming.

I grabbed his face, pulled him back and fed.

He tasted good; there is something about magic user's blood. It has more kick to it than human blood. I was completely healed and feeling good. Grabbing his rifle, I headed back toward the original plan. I hope David and his family are ok.

I moved carefully to the crest of the hill. I came over the top and took cover behind a gravestone.

It took me a few seconds to process what I was seeing. There were no less than a dozen men with guns, plus four different people wearing trench coats. I couldn't make out their faces; I was too far away.

In front of the gravestones that protected David, I could see Carrie standing. Around her feet four men lay on the ground. The four trench coats were heading toward her while the gunmen moved around looking for more targets.

It's then that I noticed the other bodies. David's mom lay lifeless on the ground; only a few feet away I could make out the back of Kelly's head.

Then I saw her, Lizzie… her body was draped over a gravestone. A pool of blood was around the base of the stone.

She might be dead.

Things got a little blurry as my eyes began to water. I had to get a hold of my emotions; I could cry later. Lizzie is going to be fine; I tried lying to myself with no luck. I was trying to stay calm so that I could protect David and kill all these people.

"They had killed… they had killed Lizzie." As I whispered to myself, I could hear the pain in my own voice.

One of the wizards in the trench coat pushed his hands forward. Then a beam of light came out; it was so bright. It hit Carrie, and she let out a scream, but it was cut off as she dissipated into nothing.

Now there was nothing or no one between them and David, and does that mean they had destroyed Carrie?

How could I get there in time to save David?

My worst nightmare was unfolding as David stood up from in between the gravestones. He had just awakened from Tony's spell and he was a little confused as he looked at all the men with guns. Then he looked at his dead mother and sister Kelly. His eyes swept around until they fell on his little sister's body lying over the gravestone.

Then he just froze.

I was yelling in my mind, move, run, do something. I didn't want to watch him die.

The next thing I did brought shame to my heart as soon as I did it. I lowered my head below the gravestone and closed my eyes. I can't watch them kill him, and it did not matter for I would be joining him shortly. I hope I see him in the afterlife.

All I heard was the sound of gunfire.

I heard screaming… screaming as if someone was in great pain.

Then I realized it was me.

I forced myself to be quiet; so much for being emotionless; I can't avenge David… and David's family's death if I don't get it together. I don't expect to win tonight, but I will leave a pile of dead Order members before I die.

I started to lift my head…

Something hit me.

I opened my eyes and could see the stars.

I sat up quickly and looked around; all around me it was quiet. My M16 lay in the grass; all my other weapons were still attached to me.

What just happened?

Must have been some kind of spell; I was ready to come out from behind the gravestone and kick some ass. I picked up my rifle and got to my knees. I looked over at the gravestone where David was.

Everyone was starting to stand back up. David was still standing in the middle of the gravestones that I set up for him, and he was surrounded by ghosts. David was alive; my heart would have beaten faster if it could.

I looked a little closer. That's when I noticed David's eyes were glowing a bright green. I noticed that the ghosts were the ghosts of his family. Lizzie stood in front with her arms crossed.

I could see the other four wizards now standing in front of David. They started to cast some spells. The ground began to shake.

What now?

I aimed my rifle at the wizards; I was about to fire.

Then something grabbed my leg. I looked down, and there was a hand coming out of the ground. A half fleshed skeleton hand was wrapped around my ankle.

I jumped up and pulled my leg free; the only thing was the rotted hand was still wrapped around my ankle. I reached down and ripped it off…how gross!

I looked up and couldn't believe my eyes. There were corpses coming out of the ground; they were crawling out, and getting to their feet. I may be a dead vampire who lives on blood, but this is gross.

Half rotted bodies with bugs coming out of them; some of them were part, or whole skeletons. Their faces were twisted pictures of horror, and some of them were even moaning... moaning… really is that necessary?

I am totally freaked out. A vampire that's afraid of dead people; someone should write a book.

Then one of them grabbed me from behind… I screamed like a girl. With all my strength, I ripped his arms away, and then I turned around and faced the undead man.

Without even thinking about it, I used the butt of my rifle and slammed him in the face. I was so freaked out that I used all my strength. The head exploded on impact, and the body fell to the ground.

I stood there with this undead corpse juice all over me, rotted brain matter; I could even see some bugs coming out of the corpse slime that was on my arm.

Yuk… nasty… disgusting… gross.

The corpses were starting to circle me. This time I used the business end of my rifle, and I shot three of them down by blowing their heads off. Then I flashed through the hole I made. A lot of good it did me; I flashed right into another pile of dead.

They were everywhere.

It only took me a second to come to the realization, that, if I shot or hit them anywhere other than the head, it didn't hurt them. No time to think about David; plus I think he is the one who did this. I need to work my way toward the edge of the graveyard. There will be less undead there.

It only took a few seconds; after I started fighting the corpse, I heard the sound of gunfire mixed with screaming. Yep, David did this.

It only took me a few minutes to empty every bullet from my rifle. I wish these things knew that I was on David's side. They came at me in all directions, but I was strong enough to fight them off. I pulled out my handguns and continued to work my way to the edge of the graveyard.

I shot, kicked, and used my guns as hammers. It wasn't hard to kill them, but there were too many to kill. I ducked under their arms, and jumped over their shoulders; it was hard to move through the crowd of corpses.

I came across the body of two dead soldiers. One of them had a hatchet; he also had a string of grenades strapped around his chest. I had run out of pistol ammo, so I punched and kicked my way over to the dead soldiers' bodies. There were too many dead to flash, but I was still too quick for them to get a hold of me.

I grabbed a grenade and the hatchet; the guns weren't that effective anyway. You had to shoot the head right off their shoulders to get them to stop. The hatchet was much easier; I hacked my way through the sea of bodies.

I came up to a tree, where I climbed my way up. I needed to get my bearings. I stood upon a branch about twenty five feet up. What I saw was... scary... I don't know how to even think about it.

There were corpses of men and woman, bags of bones, and their clothes and flesh were in different stages of decay. I could see the edge of the cemetery. It was less than a hundred yards away; hardly any dead were there. They were all heading slowly toward David.

Quick supply check...still had two hunting knifes in my belt. One knife was tucked in front of my skirt and the other behind me. I hadn't dressed well for this. In my right hand I had a hatchet. I had tied the grenade into the bottom of my shirt; now my belly showed. After a closer look...it wasn't a grenade. It was a smoke bomb.

Time to go; the dead were starting to circle around the tree. They were looking up at me moaning and reaching. I needed to keep moving or else they might overwhelm me. I leaped away from the tree.

I landed on two different heads, and then jumped again before they could grab me. I landed away from the crowd of dead and headed for the edge of the graveyard.

I reached the edge of the graveyard only to run into a wall, not a wall I could see but a magic wall. I knew this spell; it keeps spirits from passing through. It is the same spell they put over houses to keep the dead out. I would need the living to invite me out.

Some of the dead were now heading toward me. I will have to figure this out on the move. I started by heading down the side of the graveyard. I knew I was moving in a large circle, but I am not sure what else I can do.

Five minutes later I was now coming around the hill and toward the front of the graveyard. I could now make out a couple of sedans and a van. I knew the van right away, it was Devon's van... there he was.

As I looked to my right, I could see Devon walking towards his van. His men were covering his retreat, but it was costing them their lives. One gunman after another fell into the wave of undead. I saw two guys with rifles take up position and start laying down cover fire. They were close to me, and they were going to make a path for Devon.

I flashed up to them, and, with my hatchet, I cut their rifles in half. Then I smiled at them and said. "Now you boys have a good time."

I flashed back to the edge of the graveyard. When I looked back, I could see the undead grabbing the two men; they pulled them back into a crowd of corpses.

All I heard after that were their screams.

Devon had broken free from the mass of dead. If one of them even got close to Devon, he would reach his hand up, and then squeeze his fist, and their head would explode. When he got a little bit closer, I could make out what he was doing.

Out of both hands were two shadows; it was night time so it was hard to see even with vampire eyes. The shadows coming out of his hands were in the shape of his hands, only they were as big as his body. When he reached out to grab one of the corpses, the shadow stretched out, and the hand became smaller the further out it went.

So he has a range with this spell, and he had not noticed me. He was too busy taking care of the dead that were trying to block his path. The last of the soldiers fell to their deaths behind Devon; he didn't even give them a backwards glance.

I would need to move fast; before he had a chance to use those shadow hands on me. I wish I still had a rifle. He moved clear of the undead and now was walking quickly toward the van. Before he spotted me or got past the wall and to his van, I flashed.

When I flashed, the world flew by; it always felt like teleporting to me. I looked at where I wanted to go. The next thing was a blur of colors, and then I was standing at the spot I was concentrating on. If something happened during my flash that caused me to stop, it made me feel disoriented.

That is what was happening now.

Devon was standing in front of me. His hand was straight out, and he was holding his hand closed. It looked as if he was holding an invisible cup because his hand was squeezing but it would not close all the way. I could make out the shadow hand; it had wrapped around my chest; that's when I realized that he was squeezing me.

It hurt as the shadow crushed down upon me. I tried to grab hold of the black fingers to pry them loose, but I couldn't get hold of the shadows. If I grabbed a finger, it would turn into nothing and then reform somewhere else.

Devon lifted his hand up, and, when he did this, I too was lifted into the air.

Devon looked up at me with a triumphant smile. "I thought I was going to have to hunt you down later, but look at this, you've come to me. I would have loved to know how or who revived you. No time, best just to destroy you." Devon pointed to his back. He had on David's backpack. "I got what I came for. After I destroy you, The Order will take care of David. He has proven to be a handful, too bad I didn't get to him before you... Oh well."

A happy thought, David's alive and well. Only if I could kill Devon before he kills me. I had to figure out how to get out of this hand. I have no leverage being held up in the air. My arms and legs dangled useless. All the strength in the world wouldn't help me if I didn't have something to push against.

Devon reached with his other hand. The shadow grabbed my head. Then he started to pull his hands apart, just like that giant I fought in the alley; he was trying to rip my head off.

I fought him with all my will and strength. It was working, and he was struggling and could not pull hard enough. He stopped and let go with the hand that was holding onto my head.

"How could you have become so strong in such a short time? I wish I had time to study you; Oh well I guess we will do this the old fashioned way."

He walked toward his van. I floated along in tow. That's when I noticed that we passed through where the wall should have been. Whatever magic user had made it must have died, I was no longer trapped in the cemetery. Then again, I was still trapped.

When we got to Devon's van, Devon used his free hand and opened the sliding door. Then his shadow traveled into the van. It came out with a can of gas.

I struggled harder.

A cruel smiled formed on Devon's face, one that I knew much too well.

We both noticed it at the same time. A small group of undead were heading right for him. The undead hands stretched out in front of them moaning.

Devon looked back up at me, and then said. "Just hold on for one second sweetheart."

I would have loved to say something smart ass back, but he was still holding on to me so tight, I couldn't breathe. Of course I wouldn't suffocate, but it sure did shut me up. Devon set down the gas can, and then he turned his attention to the approaching undead.

If I could do something, this was my moment. Not being able to breathe gave me an idea. Of course my plan hinged around me learning how to fly.

Devon's head was turned toward the undead that were approaching him. He was now using his free shadow hand to attack the first of them. The group of undead were not very many, so I didn't have much time.

I sucked in all the air I could; it hurt for it made his grip tighter. After a few seconds, I felt just a little less force. He was using his other hand to crush the corpse's heads. I could tell from the way he was sweating, that using all this power was weakening him.

I had been struggling the entire time, and he wasn't paying any attention to my movements. I was able to pull out the smoke grenade. I pulled the pin and let it drop. A cloud of white smoke poured out of the can. It rose through the air, and a few seconds later, I was engulfed by smoke.

I couldn't see Devon now, and I didn't have time to worry about what he was doing. I started the next part of my plan.

I concentrated… I relaxed… I did what Charlotte told me. I let go of my body, and I pushed upwards. I felt my body becoming lighter. I now knew how to fly, or float; I will celebrate later. I let all my air out, and, at the exact same time, I wiggled my whole body.

I slid free from the shadowy grip, and my dress came off as I used my foot to push on one of the shadows. I floated up into the night sky. I did manage to get a hold of both of my knives before my dress was pulled off. Now I was in my undergarments holding two military styles knifes. Not having time to take in the sights, I looked back down at where Devon was.

He had finished the last of the approaching dead; from up here, I could spot another group on their way, but we had a few minutes before they would arrive.

Devon was cursing as he spun in a circle looking for me. All he had in his hand was what was left of my dress. The smoke grenade had blinded him when I had wiggled out of his grip. He thought I fell to the ground, and he hadn't thought to look up.

He tossed the remains of my dress on the ground as his black shadowy hands flew through the smoke, searching frantically for me.

I had floated slowly over the top of Devon. I let myself fall, and I fell right in front of Devon; we were close enough to dance.

I moved fast... then I took three steps back so I could look him in the face.

Devon looked at me with surprise, then hatred. "Enough games, girl... now you die."

He put his hands out in front of him, and that is when he noticed what I had done.

There were no hands, just bloody stubs.

The blood was dripping off the knives, and the shadows had disappeared. I was sure that the magic was attached to his hands.

Devon's face went from hatred back to surprise. Then he fell on his ass; he was in shock and losing blood. The pain of what I had just done to him was starting to register.

The group of undead where almost upon us, and I had a new idea.

I flashed over to his van; it only took me a second to find what I was looking for. I ran back to where Devon was. I used my new trick; I pushed up into the air, not too high, just high enough that the undead couldn't reach me.

Then I put the camera on my shoulder, the one I had taken out of Devon's van.

Then as I floated above Devon, I said. "Devon, look at me." His eyes met mine, and I could see the fear in them, and it made me glad; I pointed the camera at him and said. "Final scene... action!"

The undead moved in a horseshoe shape around him, and then they ripped him apart.

He screamed; I smiled.

When they finished, there wasn't a lot left of him. I said into the camera, "here lies Devon Wright; in the end no one will miss him."

I turned off the camera; I felt I should be happy. I felt as if his death should bring some closure to the pain in my chest. It didn't make me happy, and his death wasn't worth Lizzie's life.

The undead stopped moaning, and then they stopped moving. All of the undead fell to the ground.

David! I dropped to the ground. I flashed across the graveyard, until I came to the spot I last saw David. I ran up to the circle of gravestones; David wasn't there. I looked around, and that's when I saw him.

He was sitting on the ground, and, in his lap, was the body of Lizzie. He was holding one hand on his necklace that I gave him. His other hand was on his dead sister's face. He was chanting in some language that I didn't understand. What was he doing?

He stopped chanting and then looked up at me. Tears filled his eyes, and then tears filled my eyes. I flashed over to him and took him into my arms. There we held each other.

"I am so sorry… this is all my fault. I should have never dragged you into this." I said this into his shoulder as I cried.

A dark chuckle came from David. "Don't do that. You cannot… blame yourself for another's evil. I wanted to help; I wanted to help because that was the right thing to do. My family lay dead… they're all dead, because no one believes in us. I am a Necromancer, and you are a vampire. We are bad; no one would back us to fight the true evil. Everyone, except my sister Lizzie, and she believed the lie, the lie of The Order."

I touched Lizzie's face, and then said. "We will take down this Order, a group of people who bring death to others… without evidence or trial. We can bring them death; we can bring them the same death they showed my dear Lizzie." I said this with blood filled tears, falling from my face to hers.

David gently slid the body of his sister onto the ground; he looked around, and then said. "Time to go; we will mourn later."

He was right; we had to get out of here. It would be hard to have to explain why all the dead are out of their graves to the local police. "We have to get the film first. Your bag is next to Devon's corpse, and I have to grab the film out of Devon's camera. I made a movie; you won't want to miss it."

David said. "Sounds good; can't wait to see your first film. While you do that, I will collect Lizzie's body; I wish to bring it with us."

When I got back, David and I gathered around Lizzie's body. He grabbed my hand, and together we left.

Chapter 18

Las Vegas

I was looking out the window of our hotel room.

The sun was almost below the horizon; soon it would be night. Please, I quietly prayed to God. I hoped that when the night came, so would Carrie. She never reappeared the night of the graveyard fight, but I was hopeful she might come back tonight.

Soon as the sun fell behind the mountains, Carrie reappeared. She was confused, looking right to left, before she realized where she was.

She looked at me and said. "I hate that... it's so confusing. Oh, my gosh, where's David? How did we get here? Did any of David's family live?"

I put my finger to my lips. "Shh... David's resting."I pointed to a bed in the room. David was under the covers, he had just fallen asleep. "Come, sit next to me, and I will catch you up."

"Ok, I was worried David was hurt, or dead." Carrie looked out the window as she sat next to me. "Is this Vegas? How did we get here? Are the Whites with us?"

I grabbed her lips and held them together. Once she got the idea, I let go. "I'll start from the beginning. After the battle, David had enough power to teleport one more time. We went to his house, and there we collected as much as we could shove in his mom's car. Then we drove to the Whites. Once I explained what happened, they packed us all up in different cars. We drove the rest of the night, until we got to Las Vegas."

Carrie asked. "Were they mad? And why Las Vegas?"

"Alice said this was the city of the dead. I don't know any more than that. I haven't really had time or felt like playing twenty questions; I will ask Ezra tonight, and, to answer your other question, yes and no. Alice, Ezra and Charlotte were not mad. In fact I couldn't tell them enough about the fight. They wanted to know all the details. Michael and Lea are a different story."

"Lizzie had the hots for him. Did you know that? I liked hanging with Lizzie at night... boy am I going to miss that girl. Is Michael mad because of what happened to her?"

I said, "Pretty much, he blames me for getting them involved. Lea's just as pissed because Charlotte told her how I felt about her birthday gift. I don't even care about her right now. Michael being mad at me kind of bothers me, but I don't know what to do about it."

Carrie gave me a hug, and then she said. "Don't worry about it; he'll forgive you, and, if he doesn't, it's because he's a stupid boy, and, most important, it's not your fault."

"If you say so," for not being my fault, I sure feel guilty.

Carrie looked over at the bed where David was, then asked. "How's David holding on?"

"I don't really know. He really hasn't said much, and I couldn't blame him, you know, if he blamed me."

A tear ran down my cheek; Carrie wiped it away.

"Look sweetie, I don't pretend to know how others feel, but I know David, and he will not blame all this on you. He knew what he got involved with; in fact, I bet he blames himself about Lizzie."

"You're wrong." David said this with a deep hurt voice. He was sitting up in bed; I hadn't even realized he had awakened. That shows how tired and out of it I was. David went on by saying, "I don't blame myself; I don't blame Melabeth… I blame The Order."

Carrie ran over, jumped through the air and gave David a big hug. "I am so sorry honey; I can't believe this has happened. Is there anything I can do for you?" David shook his head no. "What do we do now?"

David looked at her with hate in his eyes. Carrie couldn't help but shrink away.

The look wasn't for her, and then he said. "What do we DO?… what do we do?… I know… how about we hunt down all the bastards who raped Melabeth, and, while we're at it, why don't we hunt down and kill Order members. Let's burn The Order to the ground." David turned his eyes on me. "What do you say, Melabeth?"

"Yes, David; that sounds good to me."

As I looked into David's eyes, I saw: hate, hurt, pain, suffering, and, revenge. I now know that we now have the same heart.

And together we shall fill our hearts, with blood.